D0593764

China Silk

China Silk

Anne Worboys

St. Martin's Press
New York

Library of Congress Cataloging-in-Publication Data
Worboys, Anne.
    China Silk / Anne Worboys.
      p.   cm.
    ISBN 0-312-08156-1
    I. Title.
PR6073.0667C48   1992
823' .914—dc20   92-28380
                                              CIP

First published in Great Britain by Judy Piatkus (Publishers) Ltd.

First U.S. Edition: December 1992
10 9 8 7 6 5 4 3 2 1

Neither be cynical about love, for in the face of all aridity and disenchantment, it is as perennial as the grass

Found in old St Paul's church,
Baltimore, 1692

Author's Note

Though I have endeavoured to keep to an accurate background, for the purposes of the story I have had to amalgamate the two strikes of 1921 into one, and in Chapter 35 I have moved the Kun Yin temple, which is situated in Macau, into Hong Kong.

China Silk

Chapter 1

The Old Forest

Hellen thought afterwards their bizarre meeting was a portent. Portents are shadows, hints to the watchful. But she was barely twenty-one, and life was beckoning. One does not see the shadows when one's eyes are on the stars.

"If I had known what was to follow, I'd have turned and run."

She said the words to herself a dozen times in the year that followed, as though in the trite little phrase there was vindication, yet knowing she would have done the same again.

It was the last meet of the season. Hellen wore a veneer of sophistication that was meant to act as a shield against the superior airs of her fellow huntsmen. The usual crowd was there in the courtyard of Kemble Hall: men in bright coats; spruce horses in the peak of condition; elegant girls in jodhpurs; two or three older women in long habits, riding side-saddle.

Her glance rested on the rider of a very fresh roan. He had flaring eyebrows, and an expressive mouth. Hellen had a gut feeling of having known him before, and then the feeling went. He guided his fidgety mount away from the pack. The Master, stirrup cup half-way to his lips, eyed the pair doubtfully.

One of the riders close by muttered something and his companion replied, "I wouldn't worry. Oliver can handle anything."

Beyond the oaks and chestnuts a flock of wild geese rose from the lake and, honking noisily, flew in echelon across the lawns before lifting to clear the chimney pots. The roan had his excuse. He lashed out at the horses close by, rearing and bucking in an effort to unseat his rider. The whipper-in endeavoured to move the hounds out of the way. A huntsmen swore. Someone shrieked.

The Master shouted angrily, "Get him clear, man! Get him clear!" as though the roan's rider was not already doing his best. The sound of glasses smashing on the gravel was drowned by the squealing of horses, the clanking of bits, the thump of hooves. The butler and footman, dropping their silver trays, ran hell-for-leather to safety. A wounded hound, howling piteously, crept into the shelter of the high box hedge. Three riders lost control and careered across the barbered lawn to disappear behind a mountain of holly. The culprit broke free, the Master and his whipper-in glaring in his wake.

Lord Tynan, Jorrocks-like on his big-rumped hunter, pulled in beside the Master. "That's Clancy's horse," he said.

"A bit of a challenge, eh?" Sir Oswald Stratton Hyde spoke grimly. "I'll have a bit of Clancy when I see him. Young Marathon's either a fool or a show-of—or else too weak to say no."

There was nothing weak about the face of the man Hellen had glimpsed in the quiet moment before the roan reared. Young Marathon. Oliver. The name was unfamiliar.

Matthew Silver shouted that the hound in the hedge was badly hurt and someone had better give him a hand. Two men leapt to the ground, handed over their reins, and ran to his aid. The three runaways pranced back across the torn turf, haughty expressions hiding their riders' embarrassment.

Hellen smiled at them, but they ignored her. The goodwill of Farmer North's daughter meant nothing. Though Hellen had taken her share of tumbles, for those who went well were bound to lose their seat on occasion, she had never lost hounds, which was more than could be said for some of the uppish young women who ignored her. She had once overheard Prudence Bentley say, "It's quite amazing, my dear, whom one meets on the hunting field these days." Prudence lost hounds on a weekly basis. Hellen's brother Leo, working on the farm, would see her trailing disconsolately home through the lanes.

The North children had been educated at good schools and they kept good horses, but they were socially unacceptable because not only was Joe North a tenant farmer, working Lord Tynan's land, but his wife's money, that paid for the hunters and covered the school fees, came from trade: three department stores, and woollen mills in Yorkshire. At Christmas time His Lordship would stride, uninvited but confident of his welcome, up the path to the front door of Jolliffe's Farmhouse (the Jolliffes had been lost in antiquity, being of no more importance than either their predecessors or those who succeeded them), and drink a glass of Christmas sherry in Marnie North's pleasant drawing room.

"Don't know how the old place stands up," he would say affably, for here and there the walls had over the years drifted out of line, affording the building a lop-sided look. But Jolliffe's Farmhouse had stood since Domesday and would see them all out. Lord Tynan's grand home, Knight's Place, had been built seven centuries later.

The Norths went there collectively for weddings and twenty-first birthdays, behind some silver token of the tenants' esteem, for which the money was demanded by His Lordship's agent. "That'll be a quid from you, Joe. We're making it five bob for the cowhands, and ten for the grooms." Tenants were a part of the show. Having them lent a little something to a hundred and thirty-seven years of squiredom. But when the gentry held a party, they invited their own kind, choosing a date on which the local young people were bespoke.

"How very unfortunate that Jonathan's birthday coincides with the Young Farmers' Ball," Her Ladyship would say. They did not worry too much about offending those they had no need to please. The villagers knew they would in any case not have been invited.

The roan had been given his head. They all watched while he circled the lake, gradually losing pace. Suddenly he swerved to the right and, putting on an extra spurt of speed, dived beneath the low branches of a copper beech. The rider flattened himself in the saddle and emerged apparently unscathed. The runaway came pounding back towards the house, neck arched, tossing his head angrily as his rider fought the bit.

A murmur of admiration arose from the standing spectators, "He can certainly ride," but there were expressions of contempt from the hunting men, for it was one thing to lose hounds or take a tumble; quite another to lose control. The roan slowed, expelling the air in snorts from his powerful lungs, lifting his feet high, slapping them down with style. Rags of foam clung to his withers and floated away from his mouth.

"I'm sorry," apologised Marathon as he approached the Master, not looking sorry at all, looking exhilarated. Then he saw the expressions on the faces of the pompous men lined up to judge him, and the excitement in his face drained away. "I'm sorry," he said again, with dignity. "I'd have kept clear if I'd been warned he scared so easily."

The Master shifted in his saddle, frowned. "We had better get on. I'm afraid—"

Apprehension showed in Marathon's eyes. "He's got rid of his oats. That's all it was,—too many oats. I've got him under control."

There was a murmur of sympathy from the crowd, and black looks from those who were anxious not to have their day spoiled.

"I'll stay behind. I'll stay clear." Marathon sat straight in his saddle, daring Stratton Hyde to refuse him. Then the Master turned away.

3

At the first covert, while the riders waited, Marathon stood well back. The roan had apparently settled down. Then the hounds had the scent, the horn proclaimed "Gone away", and they were off. Hellen dug in her heels. Merry Astor sailed over the first hedge, landing easily on the soft turf of the other side, then leaped away with the thundering field, holding her own for a while against the big-rumped geldings with their long stride, and their burly, strong-armed riders. The hounds scrambled through the next fence and raced into the valley.

They had been riding for little more than an hour and the scent had twice been lost, when the hounds turned in the opposite direction and darted away at full pelt, the field following. Hellen knew a short cut that ran through a forest of rhododendrons. She gave the mare her head. Merry Astor dashed up the hill, and dived for the opening in the tall bushes. The track was steep and narrow, the foliage meeting at head height. Hellen was riding blind. Suddenly, behind her, she heard a rhythmic drumming of hooves. "Keep back!" she shouted. There was no room to pass.

A man's voice yelled, "Look out!" The roan crashed through, knocking aside the smaller mare. Merry Astor's forelegs buckled, and Hellen went over her nose. Though half stunned by the fall she swung back, automatically reaching for the loose reins, but the mare, as she staggered to her feet, swung away and dashed on down the track. Hellen looked round dazedly for her hat and crop, retrieved them, and set out at a shaky run in pursuit. Floundering light-headedly, losing and regaining her balance, she broke clear of the bushes. Before the ground tipped up and hit her in the face she saw the roan and its rider prancing out of the belt of trees ahead, with Merry Astor in tow. She came to a moment later with her head between her knees and Oliver Marathon crouched beside her.

"Take it easy," he said.

Hellen lifted her head. Pain danced in her temples. She ran a hand through her hair, then examined her fingers. There was no blood.

"I'm so sorry. I've never ridden this horse before. He's crazy. Under-exercised, Clancy said." Oliver snorted derisively. "I wouldn't mind betting he's never had the brute at a meet."

She turned to look at him. Blue eyes. Hyacinth blue. It was like looking into a blue blaze. "Please don't apologise," she said shakily. "I'm all right. Or will be in a moment." She closed her eyes again. When she opened them he was watching her intently.

"I'm Oliver Marathon," he said. "I'm staying with the Ashtons." He had the aristocratic look of the Ashtons' friends. "I seem to know you," he said. "Have we met in Hong Kong?" The blue eyes were wide set, and very intent.

4

"I'm Hellen North," she told him shakily. "Hellen with two Ls." Then she added, inexplicably aping the confident manner of the Prudences and Violets with whom she hunted but did not dance, "And I've never been out of England."

"Humph!" His blue gaze was disconcerting. She recognised with embarrassment that she had struck a jarring note. "Your colour's returning," he said at last. He swung back on his heels and in one movement, stood up. "This grass is damp. I don't want to be responsible for your catching cold, as well as getting a bump on the head. Would you like to sit under that tree? It should be dry close up against the trunk." He held out both hands. She grasped them and he pulled her to her feet. "I'll tie the horses up. What's your mare's name?"

"Merry Astor."

"Gee up, Merry Astor." He unbuckled the reins and tied them to a birch sapling. The roan he led a short distance away. Hellen crossed to the oak and settled herself on a bed of leaves that lay close to the bole. Oliver came and sat beside her, leaning back with the weight of his body on the flat of his hands, his eyes again on her face, grave, thoughtful, faintly puzzled.

Embarrassed, she turned away, filtering the dry leaves through her fingers. "Is this your first visit to Lake Willow?"

"No. Oh no. Since, as you say, you haven't been to Hong Kong, I must have met you here, for I'll swear I have met you. At the Ashton's? Or the Bentleys'? Or Knight's Place?" He said thoughtfully, "You're prettier than when we met before, if we met before. Maybe when we were both much younger. I haven't been here for years. My parents are mostly abroad. In the school holidays I used to be shunted around to friends and relations. Once in a while, I landed up at Kemble Hall. I enjoyed the cricket on the green. I got my first century here."

"That's where I've seen you, then," she said, yet knowing this odd sensation of warmth and familiarity could not have grown from a casual glance across the tea trestle in the cricket pavilion.

His eyes dwelt thoughtfully on her face. "I'm being awfully rude," he apologised. "I can't help staring. You're so pretty. Girls don't usually look pretty in riding clothes."

"I should be smart and haughty, I know." She smiled and her head hurt.

"I can't wait to see you in a dress," he said.

She flushed, knowing he never would see her in a dress. He would go back to the Ashtons and they would laugh because he had been taken in by her cultured accent, the fine leather of her boots, the

5

impeccably tailored jodhpurs that had been paid for with money that came unacceptably, he would think, from trade.

"What are you doing in Lake Willow?" she asked abruptly.

"I'm on leave."

"From the army?" He did not look like an army man.

"Army? Oh, no," he replied, amused.

"What do you do in Hong Kong, then?"

"Most things. I'm a general sort of runabout, temporarily elevated to King's Messenger." He grinned. "How about that?"

"Messenger?"

"King's Messenger." He waited, one eyebrow raised in surprise because she had not immediately understood. "There was an important something to be brought over, and as my parents were due for leave from the Malay States and I hadn't seen them for some time, my leave was put forward, and the package was entrusted to me. Now my parents have been held up. I shan't see them, after all."

Hellen picked up a piece of tree bark from the ground and broke it into small pieces. "Why didn't they use registered post for the important something?"

There was a small silence. "Yes, why not." Oliver agreed lightly, and she had an uncomfortable feeling of having again said the wrong thing.

He lifted her hand and kissed it, turned it over, stared at the palm, then put it carefully back on her knee.

She was immediately defensive. "Why did you do that?"

"Kiss your hand? I thought you might like it. Did you not?"

She felt the colour rise in her cheeks. She wondered if he already knew she would not know the kind of men who kissed hands.

"I was also reading your palm," he said.

"What do you see there?"

"That you will have a happy marriage. And that you will travel."

"How lovely." She saw he was teasing, now, and relaxed.

"Would you like to travel?" His eyes were quizzical.

"Very much. I would love to have met you in Hong Kong."

They smiled at each other.

"We'll be in Queer Street," he said, "if the hunt turns back this way—you with your sore head, and me looking guilty. Do you feel up to it?"

She nodded.

Oliver scrambled to his feet and held out a hand to pull her up. His look of concern was genuine. His sleeve smelt of horses and leather. She wished they could stay there all day. All year. All eternity. She had a ludicrous feeling that he was going to kiss her. She wanted, desperately, to kiss him.

6

"All right now?"

"Yes, I'm all right," she said, making herself sound brisk and sensible so that he would not guess her heart was racing and her legs were weak.

He kept his arm loosely round her shoulders as they went to the tethered horses. The contact was at once casual and protective. "I'll lead this brute for a while. Let me give you a leg up."

They set out at a swinging walk. The sky was now bluer, the fields greener, the hedgerows bursting with May buds Hellen had not noticed before. It was not yet May, but there they were, whitening. Within her, she felt the beginnings of a journey.

Oliver said, "He's all right. Maybe it's merely that he can't cope with crowds." She reined in. He vaulted into the saddle and they rode side-by-side, chatting. He was easy to talk to. He talked to her about his life in Hong Kong. He lived with some other young bachelors on The Peak, the highest point on the island. "It's cool up there," he said, "and we've got it to ourselves."

"You and the other bachelors?" she asked.

"Good lord, no." He laughed. "The English. The Chinese are down by the water. It's crowded there, and very hot. But they're accustomed to it." He added cheerfully, "We've got the fogs and the cold, and that's what we're accustomed to." He described the sampans in the harbour where the teeming poor lived in squalor, cheek-by-jowl. He talked about the races in Happy Valley. He told her about the boating, and the beaches. "Chinamen don't swim. Anyway, they couldn't if they wanted to," he added carelessly, "not on our beaches. They're not allowed."

Hellen had a comical vision of a Chinaman chasing Oliver off a Kent beach. She was curious to know why the natives weren't allowed on their own sands, but she was wary of asking questions, remembering the silence after she said, "Messenger?"

"It's all great fun. A little outpost of Empire. Very British."

"So you don't get homesick?"

"Homesick? Good lord, no. Anyway, I haven't got a home to be sick for."

"No one here?"

"A sister in Dorset, and grandparents in Scotland. I'll be visiting them shortly. You'd like my sister. She's a bit bossy, but all right. She has hunted here, so you might have met her. Marigold Wolfe? No?"

Hellen flushed. He put his head on one side and looked at her thoughtfully, wondering about the colour that came and went in her face. She blushed like a schoolgirl, and for no apparent reason. "Her husband's Campbell Wolfe, MP for Salmen East. D'you know him?"

7

She shook her head. "Well, she doesn't see much of the Ashtons. She and Sylvia are a bit too alike to get on."

They came up through Cox's Farm on to the high ridge near Downlands Cross, and paused to look out across the Weald. Here and there the sun, glittering on water, showed the river snaking its way down to Pooter's Dam. Automatically, they both drew rein. "What a view!" Oliver spoke softly. "You asked if I get homesick. When I look out on a view like this, I wonder what the hell I'm doing, making my life abroad. That's the nearest thing I know to homesickness.

"If we ever have another war, I'd come back and fight again for this." He gestured with his free hand towards the view. "Father rushed home, in 1914. He taught me that privileges have to be paid for. England has been good to the Marathons," Oliver said. He smiled at her. "I'm sure you feel the same way."

A picture flashed through Hellen's mind, so far removed from what Oliver was talking about that she nearly laughed out loud. It was of her grandfather standing with feet planted wide apart, knuckles on his hips, by the great stone fireplace in the hall of his ugly stone mansion in the West Riding, saying in his broad Yorkshire accent, "Built with the sweat of me own brow, and all mine. All mine. By God, where there's muck there's money, and thank heaven for it." It was the last year of the war. He had given ten thousand pounds to the Red Cross.

"A knighthood is little enough recognition for what I've done. It makes me blood boil t'think on't, that a man's hand-outs have t'be within sight and sound of those bastards down in Westminster. They'll not give him a handle for what he's done f'r his home town. I've as good as fought their war for them, me with me brass and me wool. Aye, I've got me handle, and by God, I've earned it."

Hellen smiled stiffly, looking across the great gulf that separated the county set from those at Jolliffe's Farm, thinking it was possibly those bastards in Westminster who doled out the good life to Oliver in his outpost of Empire.

"There's the village!" cried Oliver triumphantly, pointing with his crop. "There's the church tower. Is that the railway line? Yes, I believe it is. I came by steam train once with Howard Ashton. He was at Eton with me. We stopped at every station, all the way from Windsor to Willow Halt.

"There's Knight's Place. And there's—I think—the village pub? Yes. And Jolliffe's Farmhouse, part of Lord Tynan's estate. There's a jossing stone in the road outside where pack animals used to rest their packs. I once dropped my crop there and used it as a mounting block.

I believe the farmhouse is mentioned in the Domesday Book."

That was the moment to say, "It's where I live," but Hellen could not bear to watch his eyes turn cynical or tolerantly amused. "Since no one in the village has read the Domesday Book, it's pure hearsay," she said, her voice snapping.

"It's a nice little rumour," he replied mildly. "I'm only showing off. Proving how well I know the place. Let's move on, shall we? I must admit I'd never have found my way through here alone. I'd have been out on the road looking for signposts, and taking twice as long. Lucky you fell off." He grinned at her, and the tension drifted away.

They headed down the steep slope that would bring them on to the track by Kidd's Reservoir. The roan behaved impeccably. Oliver asked casually, "Are you coming to the Ashtons' dance?"

He was handing her the opportunity on a platter to say she had never been invited to his friends' houses; that as a tenant farmer's daughter she was not a member of county society.

He noted the bright colour in her cheeks and said, "I see I've jumped the gun. Sylvia probably hasn't asked anyone yet. But they're talking about having a dance. I've been told I can invite a partner to dinner beforehand. I'd like to invite you."

In her mind's eye, Hellen saw the expression on Lady Sylvia's face when Farmer North's daughter stepped over her threshold.

"What's so funny?" He looked at her intently.

She had to say something, so she said the first words that came into her mind: "I might have concussion."

Oliver blinked, as though baffled by her reply. "You haven't still got that headache, have you?"

"No."

"I shouldn't think you've got concussion at all. Just a little bump on the head. I'll warrant by tomorrow you'll be chirpy as a cricket. Right, that's settled. Clancy's got an old Rover he lets me borrow. I'll pick you up."

A baby rabbit sped across the lane in front of them, then a black cat, slinking on its belly, moving fast in pursuit. "That's luck!" said Oliver. "Proof you haven't got concussion. Let's go riding tomorrow. And the next day. And the next. On our own. We'll get to know each other properly." He reached across and put a hand over hers. "Would you like that?"

"To ride—"

"To get to know me better?" He looked directly into her eyes.

She thought she would die when she had to tell him who she was. "Yes. Yes, I'd like it," she managed.

They were approaching Courtauld's Farm with its gracious Queen

9

Anne house framed by massive oaks in spring leaf. Hellen waited for Oliver to refer to the owners as though they were her friends. Then she would tell him. She would say, "I don't know anybody of standing. Not socially." She would say it, this time. But suddenly two Irish wolf hounds loped across the intervening field to greet them, and the moment passed. Oliver began to tell her about the dogs his sister kept.

They came down into the village. "That's where I live." She pointed towards Jolliffe's Farmhouse with the sagging porch and the old, weather-stained, sun-gilded tiles.

His face was quite blank.

When she could endure the silence no longer, she said, "Thank you for bringing me home."

"Not at all." His voice was normal, pleasant, the same as before.

Of her own accord, Merry Astor turned and began walking towards the stables. Hellen was afraid to turn or say good-bye because there were tears in her eyes. She sat very stiffly in her seat, listening to the roan's departing footsteps. Departing? She swung round sharply in her saddle, and there he was, behind her. "Is that your father?" He gestured with his riding crop.

Joseph North had come out of the gate and was striding towards them. He wore his old tweed jacket, working trousers, and heavy farm boots. Oliver urged the roan forward until the two horses walked together, neck-and-neck.

"Hello." Joe North looked up curiously at his daughter, then at the stranger. "What brings you home?"

"I took a tumble. Father, I want you to meet Oliver Marathon. He kindly escorted me."

She waited, see-sawing between feelings of love and embarrassment. Let him not say it, just this once. And then her father said— how could it be otherwise today?—in his simple, kindly manner, "Pleased to meet you, young feller."

Her eyes were drawn painfully, irresistibly, to Oliver's face. He reached out and shook her father's hand. "I'm pleased to meet you, too," he said.

Chapter 2
Oliver

"Why not tell people you're pleased to meet them? Nobody ever tells you how they do."

They had all tried—Hellen, her brother Leo, and in the beginning, Marnie. It was useless. Joseph was his own man. He wanted no part of the petty nuances of polite society that governed other lives. Marnie, who loved Joe best, would quote a story, true or false, that Queen Victoria once drank tea out of a saucer in order to put a crofter's wife at ease. Hellen remembered that as Oliver replied.

At eighteen, fresh from her Swiss finishing school, Marnie Porchard had met young Joseph North when he came to Yorkshire on a visit. She had loved him immediately. For his good looks, that he had handed on to her children; for his kindness and his sense of fair play; for the fact that he was pleased to meet people.

With her ears attuned to Yorkshire accents, Marnie was innocently enchanted by the soft, Kentish intonation in Joe's speech. Brought up with the harsh realism of the industrial north among men who were set upon moving from clogs to fine leather in one generation, Marnie misread Joe's confidence and lack of thrust. It was some time before she discovered for herself that men who had left school at fourteen lacked ambition because there was nowhere for them to go.

"Why don't you come in and have a cuppa?" Joe asked Oliver now. "It's a bit early for tea, but I'm sure my wife will hustle things along." Cupping his hands to his mouth, he shouted, "Ben!"

The handyman emerged from the stables, cast Oliver a curious look and took the reins of both horses. "Lost the hunt, did you?" he asked Hellen sympathetically.

" 'Fraid so."

"Bad luck."

Joe opened the gate and Oliver motioned to Hellen to precede them. She went on ahead, carrying her hat in her hand, running her

11

fingers through her hair. The bruise on her head was very tender. There were stains from leaf mould on the sleeves of her jacket and one long grass stain on her jodhpurs. She was going to have to change. "What do you look like in a dress?" Oliver had asked. Well, he would see, though in the circles in which he moved good looks meant nothing unless backed by breeding. The county set were bred like horses. Sired by one of their own, out of one of their own.

The front door opened and Marnie came hurrying down the path. "What happened? Why are you home so early?" Hellen introduced Oliver and her mother said, very properly, "How do you do." Oliver explained all over again. Marnie caressed Hellen's cheek with her fingertips. "Thank goodness you're not hurt."

"I've invited Mr Marathon to tea, my dear."

"You're very welcome." She led the way, her head with its softly piled fair hair very erect, her back straight, her afternoon dress floating round her ankles. Oliver's puzzled eyes strayed to the homespun man at her side, then to Hellen, walking beside him with the dignity she had inherited from her mother.

Joseph removed his boots in the porch and showed their guest into the washroom. "The drawing room's at the end of the passage when you're ready."

"Who is he?" Marnie asked as they went on ahead.

"A friend of the Ashtons'."

Marnie saw the distilled excitement in her daughter's eyes, and sighed sharply.

"Don't look like that, Mother," Hellen said edgily. "He's very nice."

"I'm sure he is, darling." Samuel Porchard's daughter had been snubbed by the Kentish gentry long before Hellen was born. But there was no rule that said her own daughter should not join their hunt, so long as she had good horses and the right clothes. And of course it went without saying, a thick skin. Hellen had to hunt. It was all she had wanted of life, to date. Their cross was the knowledge that her skin was not so thick, but they were proud of the way she bore what she had to bear with dignity.

Hellen dived up the narrow wooden staircase that led to her room.

Oliver washed his hands, tossed some water over his face, and smoothed his untidy hair with his hands. No wonder the poor girl had met his comments with one fiery blush after another. What a bloody fool! And he had invited her to Sylvia's dance! He knew already what his hostess would say: "Forget it, dear," deeming such rudeness kinder than bringing Hellen to the manor where she would feel out of place. He contemplated saying, "She will not feel out of place if you make her welcome." No, better not.

He opened the door and walked down the passage. Several enlarged photographs in heavy frames hung on the walls. There was a bearded man—middle-aged? Old?—with the worn look that time brought to sons of the soil; a middle-aged, high-chested, severe-looking woman in black, indefinably resembling Helen.

The drawing room door was open. He had an impression of deep chairs neatly fitted with linen covers in a William Morris design; Regency, Edwardian and Victorian furniture, oddly compatible in the way of ill-assorted relatives gathered for a wedding or a funeral. There were little blocks of wood strategically placed beneath a Jacobean chest and a hardwood bookcase, combating the slope of the floor.

"Do sit down," said his hostess, indicating the sofa. "I hope you will excuse my husband. He doesn't want to change because he has to go out again."

"And you must excuse me." Oliver looked down ruefully at his breeches and boots. "I'm afraid I'm not dressed for the drawing room."

His hostess's smile, that did not quite reach her eyes, told him she was well aware that he had expected to have tea round a scrubbed table in the kitchen. He shifted uncomfortably.

Hellen came in. Oliver sat up straight, staring; trying not to stare, but staring none the less. She had changed into a soft pink dress with a boat-shaped neck and a skirt that swung across her lower calves, exposing the prettiest ankles he had ever seen. Out in the open her hair had been flattened by her hat, then ruffled by the wind. Now, neatly combed, there was a silky fringe, black as a boot against her pale forehead. The back of her head when she turned was shingled in the new style. Her neck, that had been hidden by the high stock, was long and slender. She had a glossy, sophisticated, young look. She was fresh as an apple orchard in spring.

"Do sit down," said Marnie again. He crossed the room and sat awkwardly, head lifted, his eyes returning obsessively to this chameleon of a girl. Tousled and tumbled she was lovely, but the delicate prettiness that emerged with the pink dress was, in a way, a shock. And those ankles! Such ankles!

She smiled at him and he smiled back.

A maid dressed in a white cap and apron wheeled in a trolley. Oliver's practised eye skimmed over the impressive silver. Sterling? Yes. There were plates of scones and a fruit cake, all neatly set out on finely embroidered doilys; a silver bowl of clotted cream; a pot of jam

13

in a silver stand. He noted the expensive china, the exquisitely embroidered, matching napkins. Hellen came and sat down beside him. He shifted a little, more as an acknowledgement of her presence than because the space was limited, and immediately forgot about his surroundings.

Out in the open air she had smelt of horses. Now she smelt of girl, and a faint perfume as of roses.

"Where do you come from, young man?"

"I've been in Hong Kong. My uncle's g—" Oliver swallowed. Hellen rose to pass the tea round. His eyes followed her. She was slim, straight, and round in the right places. "My uncle's got a—er—" Hellen held some cucumber sandwiches under his nose. He took one, stared at the cucumber between the bread, as though wondering what it was, then ended lamely, "a fairly good job out there."

"You've been holidaying with him?" asked Marnie pleasantly. "How nice."

"Holidaying? No, I'm working. I mean, I'm a cadet."

"Cadet?"

He looked uncertainly at the plain Kentish farmer sitting opposite in his socks. There was a small hole in one toe. "In the Colonial Service," he said. Hellen held out the fruit cake. He took a slice, placed it carefully on his plate, turned it over, poked it with his forefinger. Marnie watched him, her face still.

"Not in the government, then?" asked Joe.

"Yes. In the government. A—kind of civil servant."

"So what's your uncle got to do with your job?" Joe asked bluntly.

"Nothing. Nothing, really. Except I help him sometimes."

Marnie wondered if he lied, and if so, why.

Later, Hellen and Oliver walked back together towards the stables, side-by-side. Thinking she had nothing to lose, for certainly she would never see him again, Hellen lifted her head and asked, "Why were you so cagey about your uncle?"

He looked down at her, hesitated. He seemed to be making up his mind as to how he would answer.

"Is he a smuggler?" she asked, boldly.

"And me apprenticed to him? Can't I just see myself butting up the Pearl River in a disguised sampan, with a gun on each hip! Running the gamut of the water police! Not to mention acquiring pots of illicit gold. I'd like that," Oliver said. He opened the gate and stood aside to allow her to pass, then tucking an arm through hers, drew it close against his side. She caught her breath. The tobacco and horse smell of him was more pronounced now that she smelt of Ashes of Roses.

"Only you're not apprenticed to a smuggling uncle," she said as

14

they approached the stable door. She waited again. "You may as well tell me," she said. I'll not split on you. You've said you're a—what? General run-about? King's Messenger? Civil servant? Cadet? Assistant to your uncle who may be a smuggler. You haven't said he isn't."

"You might not want to come riding with me, if I tell you the truth."

She shot him a startled glance as they entered the stable.

"If I turn up tomorrow at two, will you be ready?"

She nodded, then waited for him to repeat the invitation to the Ashtons' dance. His warmth, and the undoubted admiration in his eyes, had given her the false impression it was still on. She felt the familiar sense of rejection that came from living with, without being part of, the county set. A ride together over the hills, where they would not be seen, was to be her lot now that he knew she was the daughter of one of Lord Tynan's tenant farmers.

She told no one about the invitation to ride, for she felt it had possibly been made only to smooth his exit, but she lay awake, dreaming her way through the night hours, the back of the hand that he had kissed warmly against her cheek. A marauding fox barked in the night, reminding her that she lived close to the farmyard. Close to the earth, her father would say.

She thumped the pillow with her fist, punishing it for her own naïveity in allowing herself to be so abysmally stupid as to fall in love with one of the Ashtons' friends. Of course he had only come in to tea out of curiosity: to see how the other half lives. Those who live close to the farmyard. . . . There was nothing of the farmyard about Oliver. Why did she have this feeling they had met before? Why did he? She drifted off to sleep, dreaming that in another place, at another time, they had been close.

AT a quarter to two the next day Hellen went to the stables. She hung her jacket on a saddle tree, then busied herself brushing down Persimmon, her chestnut mare, though she could tell from the feel of the mare's coat that she had already been groomed. The young sheep dog, Minnow, whose domain was the stables, sat watching her, head on one side.

Then she heard him. "Hel-len!"

She dropped the curry comb in the straw, tripped and floundered as she tried to pick it up, and was nearly knocked off her feet by Minnow, who, catching the flavour of her excitement, was diving and pouncing. "Here I am," she called, her voice unnaturally high, quite out of control. She snatched up the bridle and hastily slid the bit between the mare's teeth. "Persimmon, keep still!" She fumbled and fretted with the leather straps, extricating the mare's forelock, freeing her twitching ears. Persimmon hated having her ears bent over. She grabbed the saddle cloth, flung the saddle over the horse's back, buckled the girth and crupper, then with a quick snatch, retrieved her hacking jacket from the saddle tree.

There he was, silhouetted in the stable doorway, hatless, with his soft hair falling forward and his face in shadow. "Sorry," she apologised breathlessly, "I'm running a bit late. Or," with a rueful little smile, "maybe you're a bit early?"

"Always dead on time."

His mount shifted and in the light that caught his face she saw his expression was serious. Her shaky confidence weakened. Did he think, having crossed swords with the Ashtons on her behalf, having been good enough to keep his word, that she should at least be ready?

He must have seen the frail defiance in her manner, for he smiled reassuringly. "It's a sort of family motto," he said. "It comes of being born of a long line of servants of the Crown. Granny Marathon, who has delusions of grandeur, says punctuality is the politeness of kings. Father says—" he sat up straight in the saddle, looking stern "—'You be there on the dot. Or else.'" He smiled again, engagingly, and her heart thumped with excitement for he was still, or again, the lovely man who had helped her yesterday—knocked her off her horse and then helped her, she amended, trying to think prosaically, trying not to lose sight of the fact that he was merely an honourable man.

"How's the concussion?"

She led Persimmon to the mounting block. "I really wasn't hurt. I could have gone on, you know."

"Except for my selfishness. Ossie would have had me shot if I'd gone in again."

She noted his use of the Master's christian name.

He looked down at Minnow. "Hello, dog. What's her name?"

"Minnow," replied Hellen. "The stables are her especial responsibility. She lives here."

"Now who's this?" He turned his attention to Persimmon. "She's a nice mare. I'm quite a judge of horse flesh. I race in Hong Kong."

She settled into the saddle and adjusted the stirrups. "Do general run-abouts—dogsbodies—keep race horses in Hong Kong?"

"Just showing off," he replied modestly. "They actually belong to my uncle."

A frisson of laughter went through her, and suddenly they were close again, as they had been yesterday, before he discovered who she was. They took the track up over Jolliffe's Peak and into the ride on the edge of the oak woods. They gave the horses rein all the way up the long slope to the boundary fence where Lord Tynan's deer park

16

began. When they pulled up they were panting, but exhilarated. The horses fell into step together. Oliver leant over to pat his mount's shoulder. "Toby's a far cry from that roan brute."

"Why did Sir Clancy give him to you to ride?"

"Trying to prove something about the horse—or me, I suppose. Clancy's got Irish blood. I've Irish cousins, so I'm used to Irish tricks. They sent me over the border once with a load of poteen that they weren't brave enough to take themselves. I didn't get caught, and I sold the poteen, so I had the last laugh."

Hellen laughed merrily. The gallop had smoothed the uncertainties. She was anyone's equal with the wind in her hair and her mount pounding the turf.

"You're pretty good at standing on your own feet, aren't you?" Oliver asked.

She wished she had been a fly on the wall when Lady Sylvia said, "Riding with whom? The North girl!"

"Perhaps." A village girl with one of those feet on the hallowed ground of the gentry. They stopped at the five-barred gate leading into the parkland. Guy's Park. Lord Tynan's park. Oliver opened the gate and they rode through.

"Ready for another gallop?" he asked.

Persimmon, responding to the pressure of her knees, leapt forward, and they raced in a circle along the spine of the low ridge bordering the road. As they pounded past the great house Hellen was in the lead. She held it until, as they approached the lake, Oliver's gelding crept close with his long stride, and they finished together.

"Oh, what a manipulator you are." Leaning back and tugging at the reins, she laughed happily.

"Yes." He looked almost smug. "I'm good at that. Can I manipulate you into coming out with me for the whole day when I come back? I have to go to Dorset tomorrow to see my sister. Then I'm off to Scotland. But I'll be back in two or three weeks."

She nodded, carefully keeping the disappointment out of her face. She would probably never see him again.

Exactly a week later he rode into the stables. Ben was mucking out Merry Astor's stall and Hellen was checking a worn girth. She was wearing an old blouse with old jodhpurs and her hair was windblown, for she had recently taken Persimmon over the jumps in the paddock behind the house.

"I thought you were away for—" She couldn't go on. She went on gazing at him, soft and eager; big-eyed. He was so beautiful, sitting there in the saddle wearing a silk shirt that fell away at the neck, exposing a soft fuzz of brown hair on his chest. His sleeves were rolled up and his bare arms were brown, the hairs pale against the skin. He was lean. He was strong. He was handsome. She experienced again that curious sense of déjà vu. In another place, at another time, surely he had looked at her like this.

"I got bored with my sister," he said, "and Scotland was wet. Are you coming for that ride you promised?"

"Yes. Yes, of course." She swung round to Ben. He was watching them as he brushed Merry Astor, his weather-tanned face purposefully expressionless.

"I'll saddle her for you."

Hellen looked ruefully down at her clothes. "I'll have to change, but I'll be quick. As quick as I can." She fled out of the stable yard, across the drive, through the little white gate, leaving it to clang behind her, and up the path to the house. The front door was open. Her mother was crossing the hall.

"Don't you usually leave your dirty boots outside?" Marnie asked mildly.

"Sorry." Hellen rushed feverishly back, removed her boots and dropped them on the doorstep. "Oliver's turned up. We're going for a ride." She straightened. "Don't look like that, Mother," she added mischievously, "he's perfectly respectable," and sped upstairs.

Marnie stood looking after her, her face marked deeply with distress.

When Hellen came running back, spruce and sleek in a light jumper, wearing her new jodhpurs and shining black boots, Oliver was standing by the gate holding the reins of both horses. He gave her a leg up. As he swung himself into the saddle he said, "I came as soon as I could, but I only arrived this morning. I came down on the overnight train, and the Ashtons dawdled over lunch. I thought I'd never get away. But if you're free tomorrow we could go out for the whole day." Without waiting for agreement, he added, "I know a little pub in the forest where we can have a snack."

She was riding high on a dream, knowing the dream would disperse, but for the moment not caring. "I'd love it," she said.

The next day they rode all the way to Pike's Common, along the side of the hop fields and up over Stanton's Hill. They crossed the river and took a detour to The King's Well, a sixteenth-century pub that looked out over the valley. Oliver insisted on going into the public bar.

"It's more fun than the saloon." There were two local artisans amusing themselves with a ring on the end of a cord. A bull's head bucolically dominated the room from the wall opposite the bar. They were attempting to swing the ring on to a hook in its nose.

Oliver strolled across the room, hands in pockets, a friendly smile on his face. "You chaps aren't making much of a fist of it," he said. "What about letting us have a go?"

The men sheepishly backed away.

"Let's have a match," said Oliver, taking over, ignoring their diffidence. "You two against the two of us. The stakes are a pint of ale."

They played with great seriousness, and lost. Oliver was good-natured about losing. "That'll teach me," he said affably as he bought the drinks.

The men doffed their caps and shambled off. "Thanks, Guv."

Oliver grinned. "It'll be you paying next time, mark my words."

Hellen said, smiling as they rode off down the hill to the river track, "You've got the common touch."

He chuckled. "Oh, yes, very common."

She shot him a nervous glance, but he was looking out at the view, still smiling. The uncertainty went. They stopped at a vine-covered inn on the edge of Pike's Common. The landlord brought them a glass of cider and a slice of pie which they ate in their saddles with the reins hanging loose.

He came again the next day. As they rode back over the top of the ridge where they had paused that afternoon they met, Oliver guided his mount close and reaching across put a hand over hers where it lay on the pommel of the saddle. "Do you speak French, Hellen?"

Her first thought was that he wanted something translated. "Not very well," she admitted. "Schoolgirl stuff. Why?"

"Just a thought."

They came back to the farm, riding companionably side-by-side, talking only desultorily, and rode right into the stables. There was no one about. They slid out of their saddles. He put one hand in the small of her back and drew her towards him. His other arm went around her shoulders. His jacket was undone. Her breasts beneath the thin jersey met the warmth of his body. She felt the brush of his lips on her cheek. He kissed her on the lips, lightly, as though sampling the taste of them. "I love you, Miss Hellen North," he said.

"And I love you," she said huskily.

"That's why I came back." He held her at arm's length, looking down into her face. "Think about it." He picked up his reins, and leading his horse, went out of the stables and on his way. "Until tomorrow. Think about it, between now and tomorrow."

His abrupt departure left her trembling. Out of control. She watched him ride away with tears in her eyes, not yet wondering what he meant, exquisitely wounded, needing help. When she went up the

19

path to the house it was with the thought that she would wake up in the morning to discover it had never happened.

The next day was beautifully clear. They had lunch at the inn in the forest, tethering their horses outside. They sat on hard forms facing each other across one of the narrow oak tables, holding hands, looking into each other's eyes.

Afterwards, they rode along a path through the trees. The air was still, fresh from the young leaves, musty from the old. They tied their horses up and wandered among wood anemones, primroses, hollow tree stumps lined with velvet-soft fungus. There were bluebells, hazy as an early summer sky.

Oliver picked a wild violet. "Here's your bouquet. It's all you're allowed. Forest flowers are for the forest."

She kissed the violet, then threaded it in at the neck of her jumper. He watched her, smiling that very blue smile. They came eventually upon a shallow stream with a little water-fall and sat down side-by-side, hand-in-hand, listening to the forest sounds, and the sound of the water as it leapt over the rocks and fell chattering among the stones.

Oliver encircled her waist with his arm. "I told my sister and my grandparents I had to come back to you. They understood. They want to meet you. I'll take you—next week, if you can make it—to Dorset, to meet Marigold, and then Scotland." He heaved a great sigh, shaking his head as though in astonishment. "I never thought it would happen like this."

"Like—?"

"So suddenly. It's shaken me rigid."

Her fingers tightened over his.

"I lay awake all last night," he said, "coming to terms with what's happened."

"And I." She did not tell him she had had many troubled nights. Their problems were different.

He kissed her face, her neck, her hair. Suddenly a dog barked close at hand and the spell was broken. They swung round, she pink-faced, he disconcerted. They could hear the muted clop of a horse's hooves, but horse and rider were hidden behind the trees.

"We had better get back," said Oliver, glancing at his watch. "Crikey! How time goes on! There's the dance. You've got to be ready at seven."

Inside of her, Hellen jumped with shock. "It's tonight? You didn't say."

"Didn't I?" He held her hand in his. The fingers were hard, and very firm. "It is tonight. That's all right, isn't it?"

"Yes," she lied, distinctly unnerved. "Yes, that's fine."

20

"But of course, my dear fellow. Who have you asked?" Sir Clancy Ashton stood before one of the big Georgian windows in the library, a long, gangling man with a beaky nose, sandy hair and freckles. His wintry eyes were lashless in the light that streamed in from the setting sun. He smiled genially at his young guest.

"A girl called Hellen North whom I met at the hunt."

"Farmer North's daughter?" Ashton's brows rose. "From Jolliffe's Farm?"

"Yes," replied Oliver, speaking casually, rattling some coins in his pocket, treating his host to that friendly smile. "I was wondering if I could borrow the Rover to pick her up? You did say, if I decided to ask someone, I should bring her for dinner." He went to the silver box on the mantel, and helped himself to a cigarette.

Ashton's laugh was heavy, deliberate, quite without humour. "Well of course, my boy, if you've already asked her?" He set his head on one side, waiting for confirmation, daring it to come.

Oliver lit his cigarette, puffed the smoke out, tossed the spent match into the big stone fireplace. "I escorted her home that day. She took a toss. It was my fault." He added after a moment, breaking the uncomfortable silence, "I had tea with them."

"Oh, well!" Ashton's head came up. "You've done your duty—repaid your debt. No need to overdo things." He rocked back on his heels, puffing at his cigar, pushing his hands down into the pockets of his tweed plus-fours. "Spells her name with two Ls," he commented, his sneer half-hidden by a patronising smile. "Educated mother, too." He pulled at the flap of his left nostril.

"What d'you mean?"

"Two Ls. Hellen, with two Ls. Of course, the Father's uneducated. Can't be expected to know. But the mother . . ." Again, he pulled at the flap of his nostril. "Family's in trade, y'know."

"Perhaps it's Greek," said Oliver.

"What, m'boy?"

"Greek. The double L is Greek. There may be a Greek scholar in the family."

Ashton's mouth fell open.

Oliver's gaze hardened. "So you don't actually know her?"

"Humph!" said Ashton at last. "Seen her around. We don't actually—" He hesitated, sandy brows raised as he eyed his guest. "Seen her in church, of course. They all go to church."

Oliver noted the familiar "they", and knew it defined the village. The people one did not know socially. He waited. Clancy had made a fool of him with the roan. A gentleman did not chastise his host, but the knowledge that the Master of the Hunt was bound to do it for him gave him a certain edge. He said distinctly, "I asked her to come to the dance. Is that all right?"

Ashton cleared his throat, shambled across the room and grasped Oliver by his upper arms.

"You're a good chap," he said affectionately. "Pay your debts. Like your father. Hmm, now . . ." He released his grip, patted Oliver's arm, took a gold watch out of his pocket and stared at it. "Better tell Sylvia there's an extra guest," he said, sounding uncertain, as though the long dining table could not be extended to accommodate a dozen more, and the larders were not groaning with food.

"If it's inconvenient, I dare say the Norths would give me a bite," suggested Oliver innocently.

"Not at all, my boy." The colour rose dully in Ashton's pink-and-white face. Insolent young dog! God, he was so like his uncle! Made of steel. And clever. He'd watched Rowan rising in the Colonial Service, deftly stepping round people rather than over them. Clever buggers, the Marathons. Every one of them endowed with good looks and brains. Sharp as thieves until they got what they wanted, then butter wouldn't melt in their mouths.

"Humph!" he said. While Oliver waited, his host stared at the high plastered ceiling, the Wilton carpet and worn, comfortable chairs, the rows of leatherbound books that had been bought by the yard when the house was built and handed down, unread, from eldest son to eldest son. His eyes went back to his guest. The thought struck him, and it came as a shock, that Oliver had been oddly insistent about going riding alone during the last few days. He'd talk to Sylvia. She was pretty adept at showing people where they stood. Let the girl come, Sylvia'd manage her. And if she couldn't, he'd have no hesitation in cabling the young scoundrel's uncle and having him recalled.

22

Chapter 3

Lady Sylvia

Hellen stood before the cheval looking glass in her bedroom, a big, low-ceilinged, essentially country room with hand-hewn oak beams exposed on the walls and a queen post in the centre supporting the roof; supporting also, on one of its arches, her first saddle, made by the village saddler to fit a tiny shetland pony. Her ancient teddy bear, lop-eared and one-eyed, his shaggy coat worn with loving, hung head down over the tiny pommel.

Ribbons and rosettes from gymkhanas were glued to the beams. This oak was too hard for a nail or a tack. Its warm strength resisted everything but love. In lonely moments Hellen would put her arms round the queen post and feel the life that had been in the old tree. Outside, the farm was quiet. A barking dog behind the barn broke the country silence. She closed the window, shutting out the cold spring air. When the wind blew from the north east, always at the coldest time of the year, it shivered the curtains even when the windows were shut.

Her mother wanted to have the sashes straightened, but as her father pointed out with sturdy commonsense, Jolliffe's Farmhouse did not belong to them, and repairs were Lord Tynan's responsibility. Marnie's answer, that she could well afford it and the squire was not going to spend money on other people's comfort, cut no ice with Joe. Wrap up warm, that was the answer.

Hellen, terrified of letting Oliver down, eyed her reflection in the looking glass. Pale blue silk marocain, sleeveless, and very much à la mode with its rounded neck, dropped waist and hip sash. She took the pearls her grandfather had given to her for her eighteenth birthday and clasped them round her neck. They seldom saw the light of day in Kent. She wore them on holidays in Yorkshire where her wealthy manufacturing cousins led a lively social life.

Luckily, this dress had not come from the village dressmaker.

Hellen had had it made for the coming-of-age party of one of the cousins. Marnie North, having no social life in Kent, always patronised Miss Sedgwick, who was also patronised by the gentry. Marnie dressed solely for Yorkshire. She didn't go to village functions because she was not one of them. Not fish, fowl, nor good red herring, as you might say.

"You're beautiful. Beautiful, there's no doubt," said a teasing voice from the doorway. Hellen swung round, startled. "Where're you going?" Her brother Leo was leaning casually against the door frame, hands in pockets. He was still in his working clothes, old trousers and a hand knitted jumper covered in dirt stains and with threads pulled here and there. His feet were bare because Marnie insisted he leave his farm boots and socks in the kitchen.

Leo was short like his grandfather Porchard, but he had not inherited old Sam's fire. His hair was a tousled brown mop, his chin dark because he had not bothered to shave. Leo identified with the village lads who did not believe in shaving too often. Marnie had learned to live with the differences that were part of being a tenant farmer's wife, but she disliked her son's theory that hired help worked better with him if they were able to think of him as their equal.

"That boy forgets who he is," his grandmother would comment acidly when he brought the ways of the village into the house. "I notice his skin doesn't need a rest when he's taking a girl out."

The truth was that Leo did not know who he was. He had indeed attended public school, but Marnie had chosen a minor one, for she had not cared to apply in the top echelon with its attendant risk of a snub for her husband immediately he opened his mouth. But she had reckoned without heredity and example. Joe North, having attended the village school along with the parents of his ploughman, his cowhand and his handyman, identified naturally with his staff.

"I'm going to Kemble Manor for dinner."

Leo set his feet apart, thrust his head forward, pulled his forelock. "Cor, blimey, Hellen,' he said, mimicking the hop pickers who arrived from the East End of London each September.

She flushed. "I met a very nice man out hunting. He's staying at the Manor."

There was a moment's telling silence, then Leo said, "I thought everyone who hunted was "very nice". But you don't usually go to dinner with them."

"Do you think I'm all right?" she asked, lifting her head high, swirling in a half circle so that the petal points on her skirt danced round her knees, pretending his words had not struck her, in the circumstances, as particularly cruel.

"I don't know about those flashy silver shoes."

As though they were burning her feet, Hellen kicked off the silver shoes, ran to the wardrobe and took out a navy blue pair with a narrow strap across the instep. "I did wonder," she said as she slipped them on, breathless with shock at the possibility of appearing flashy.

"Why don't you wear one of those ribbon things round your forehead?" Leo asked kindly.

"I thought I wouldn't." She had seen a picture in *Country Life* of Prudence Bentley wearing a thin band of glitter across her forehead. It might have been paste; it might have been marquisette; but it might also have been diamonds. Hellen had an unnerving vision of girls with glittering foreheads staring at her ribbon bandeau, giggling, telling each other behind their hands that was no doubt what was being worn in the village hall.

The silver shoes had been purchased for a ball in York, where fashions were showy by southern standards. Yorkshiremen, especially those who had come to wealth in one generation, liked their womenfolk to over-dress a bit. Her grandfather referred to southern women's choice of clothes as "expensive dowdy". She looked down anxiously at her frock, hoping it was not too pretty.

"You look good," said Leo comfortingly. He changed his position, crossed his ankles, leaned more easily against the door post. "Who is this very nice chap? Do I get to meet him?"

"If you change your clothes." Leo turned away, walking slowly down the passage to his own room, kicking at the carpet, asking himself whether he was going to shave and tidy up, or whether he wouldn't bother to meet the fellow at all. It was highly unlikely he'd turn up again. Impulsively, protectively, he considered appearing in his working clothes, talking cockney, drive the joker away before he had a chance to hurt Hellen.

He stood inside his bedroom door, staring at the brass bedstead, not seeing it, wondering about his sister who was so lovely, and so brave, and so different from the rest of them. Although, perhaps, not so different from their mother, except that Hellen had more guts. Leo thought that one day, when Calum Finn inherited his grandfather's smallholding, he would ask Hellen to marry him.

Of course no one wanted to be an old maid, but Leo could not visualise his sister, dressed in shining black boots and well-cut riding clothes, setting out for the hunt from a cottage where chickens ran wild, and mongrel dogs lurked among the bushes in the untended garden. Calum was a cut above his family, but there was little hope of him escaping from his background. To see him on the cricket green in white flannels with a bat in his hand, you would never guess at his humble circumstances. The Norths weren't humble. He doubted if Calum's family could have produced a girl like Hellen.

Leo shrugged. Maybe she would end up marrying into trade, as Beth and Verity had done. His brothers-in-law were nobodies in the eyes of the kind of people Hellen was going to dine with tonight. Even Grandfather Porchard's title would mean nothing to the country set, being new.

Beth was well satisfied with her lot as Mrs Dudley Reid. Dudley's father had founded the one big departmental store in Harland. Marrying into southern trade was not very different, socially speaking, from marrying into tenant farming, except that there was money. She did not have to rely, as did Marnie and Hellen, on Grandfather Porchard for extras. Her husband had two racehorses and the family went to Ascot. Not, of course, in the Royal enclosure, so it didn't count.

Verity married into Longman's Tool Manufacturing and Farm Implements. Both girls were happy. But then, Leo reasoned, they had accepted what life dealt them as Joe North's daughters. Hellen, it had to be admitted, did not. Leo did not want her to live out her life, as their mother did, in no-man's-land. Feeling distinctly unhappy, he went into the bathroom and began to shave.

Oliver came, striding confidently up the path, devastating in black tie and wearing a superbly cut dinner jacket. Hellen caught her breath. He had been good-looking in a wind-blown way in his riding clothes, but this was another man from the one who had battled with Sir Clancy's roan. Another man, too, from the thoughtful one who had walked with her, sweetly sentimental among the primroses and the flickering leaf shadows of the forest.

She climbed into the borrowed car, an open tourer, rather old, with a dog on the back seat. "I thought you wouldn't mind if I brought one of the labradors. He jumped in while my back was turned. He's called Bosco." Oliver addressed the dog, "Shake hands, Bosco, if your right paw's clean."

Hellen turned. The dog was looking at her amiably, with lifted paw. She shook it, and laughed as she did so, thinking that even other people's dogs felt at home with Oliver.

"I like your brother," he said. "Looks a bit like you. Not as pretty, of course."

"You had better not let him hear you say that."

"How are you on the Tango?"

"Pretty good," she said, trying to look modest.

"Hurray! I'm pretty good, too." He switched on the engine. The noise was deafening. Hellen clapped her hands to her ears. The car leapt forward. "Sorry," Oliver shouted. "It's got funny habits."

They raged up the road, swept under the railway bridge that had been built for the little branch line, and swung noisily round into the High Street. Hellen pulled her mother's velvet cape round her. It was Marnie who had suggested it. "You'll be cool in the car," she said, meaning that Hellen's own evening cape was not in the same league, having been made by the village dressmaker for wearing to the village hall.

A group of locals were boisterously leaving The Cock. Everyone stared at cars for there were not many about, and all owned by the nobs, who expected to be stared at, anyway. Her eye caught that of Calum Finn. She tried to wave but her hand was entangled in the folds of the unfamiliar cape, and before she managed to extricate it, they had sailed past.

Lady Sylvia Ashton was an angular woman. One was aware of knees and elbows barely concealed beneath her clothes. Beaded crêpe-de-chine did not hide the fact that she was tough as an old boot. "How very nice to see you, Miss North," she said, managing to convey to the other guests by the judicious use of an element of mild astonishment, the fact that Miss North had never come this way before. "Such a surprise. We had no idea Oliver—" Tossing her head around in the horsy way she had, she accidentally caught Oliver's eye, and broke off. "Do take your cape to—oh!" She hesitated, re-sorting her strategy. "You won't know where to go." Her voice swept across the hall to a group of girls who were hurrying up the staircase. "Violet, dear, do be so good as to take Miss North's cape with you."

"I would rather like to comb my hair, if I may," said Hellen, managing to speak evenly, standing very straight so that no one would guess her hostess's rudeness had crushed her as flat as the floor. She even managed to meet those pale eyes levelly, though her own were glazed and near-sightless. "As you see, it's rather wind blown."

Lady Sylvia treated the hair to a surprised glance, as though curious that it should be considered by its owner to have any importance, while Hellen stood frozen, in her imagination hearing this gorgon send her to some servants' washroom.

The three young women, all members of the Old Forest Hunt, waited in silence on the stairs, their pretty faces quite expressionless. Then Lady Sylvia dismissed Hellen with a careless wave of the hand. "Show her the way, gels."

Violet Stratton-Hyde, hesitating half way up the stairs, said, "Hello, Oliver," and flapped her fan at him, smiling coyly over Hellen's head.

27

Hellen walked towards them. They turned their backs, all four of them, and went ahead, tossing their feather boas. They crossed the landing, still engrossed with each other, and entered a bedroom door, flinging off capes and cloaks, rushing to the looking glass, huddling together as they examined their perfectly marcelled hair. Hellen, her outrage carefully contained, slid out of her cape, laid it on the bed, and went with her comb to the long glass in the mahogany wardrobe on the other side of the room.

Oliver was waiting at the bottom of the stairs, smiling up at her. "You're quite the most beautiful girl here. Remember that." He spoke gravely, as one would deliver advice, then taking her arm, led her to the drawing room. She straightened her spine, lifted her chin and smiled back at him. His blue eyes spoke clearly in return: "Nothing can go wrong, because I am here."

And nothing did. They say side-by-side at dinner. Whenever his hand was free, Oliver held hers beneath the table. He skilfully drew her into the conversation. He was, she soon realised with gratitude and a certain measure of awe, a past master at subtly getting his own way. Both Sir Clancy and Lady Sylvia were civil, and the other guests took their cue from them. Hellen managed to relax a little but she did not enjoy the dinner. There was something vaguely unnerving about her hostess's abrupt volte-face.

The rest of the guests arrived after dinner in a hustle of happy laughter and shrill greetings. The band struck up in the distance and they made their way to the ballroom. There were lots of bandeaux, but not a diamond among them, and rustling strings of inexpensive beads as well as pearls. But Hellen was glad she had played safe. Moira Haversham unwittingly showed her how thin was the razor's edge on which she, as an outsider, balanced. Kicking up her long, thin feet in the tango, showing her silver shoes, she cried, "Don't you love them? So tarty! Such fun!" Hellen laughed with relief, and Moira gave her a cool stare.

She and Oliver danced together: the tango, with verve and dash; the waltz, thigh to thigh, cheek to cheek, with the strains of old Vienna wafting round them. Slow, slow, quick, quick, slow. She felt his heart beating; or was it hers? She thought they beat together.

The Excuse Me waltz came as a shock. Alan Courtauld, swinging her out of Oliver's arms, said, "I didn't know you knew Oliver."

She replied, quick-wittedly, "Why should you?" Then Oliver excused him and they were back together.

Magic crept over the ballroom. The chandeliers glittered and glowed, shedding their light like a benison. Thigh to thigh, heart to heart, there was only the maleness of tobacco scent and hard, silken lapels. Two hearts, beating. A closeness, a oneness Hellen had never known before. Girls who had ignored her watched furtively. There were tentative offers of friendliness.

As they came close to the French doors that led on to the terrace, Oliver swung her round precipitately and whirled her through, then sped her across the ragstone and into the moon-shade of a blossoming cherry. He held her at arm's length, looking into her face. His own glowed where it caught the moonlight filtering through the leaves. "Will you marry me?" he asked urgently. "Yes, you will. You must. I have to return to Hong Kong on the first of June. We've got six weeks."

Hadn't she known it was coming? Almost since the moment they met, the words had lurked just out of earshot. "I can't—" She had begun to say, "I can't take it in."

Misunderstanding, he stopped her: "You can, you know. Anybody can get married in six weeks. You could do it with your hands behind your back." He was suddenly very serious. "Don't say we don't know each other, darling. We've always known each other. Our meeting was a trick of fate. Very weird," he said softly, "but wonderful. I knew, almost the moment we met. Remember when I said you would travel, and go to Hong Kong? That first day, when you bumped your head? I nearly proposed then, but it was too soon. You wouldn't have taken me seriously." At that moment the clock on the stable tower struck midnight. "The witching hour," he said, and kissed her in that especially gentle way he had. "You're crying." He ran a finger across her cheek. "You're crying."

She leant against him. She did not know why she was crying. It was as though a terrible tension inside her had exploded into tears. He smoothed her hair, waiting for her to calm. "There are only two sailings a month," he said. "I'm booked to share a cabin with a friend—single cabins are always in short supply. I'll have to organise a reshuffle. Will your parents mind?" Then, answering his own question, "It doesn't matter. It's not their life."

They laughed, softly. His optimism was infectious.

"They may want to know something about you." She smiled up at him, her eyes still wet with tears. "I know little enough."

"Fair enough. If I can keep you, for instance? Tell them married chaps' salaries go up like fun. I'd be able to afford a house. We could live with my uncle for a while, until we find one. He's got plenty of room." Oliver laughed, as though at some private joke, and hugged her again. "I can't believe I've found you," he said emotionally. "I think I've been looking for you all my life. I think I know you so well."

She had the same feeling about him.

"It's only the mundane things we don't know, and who cares about them? Like, do you snore? Don't answer that." They laughed and laughed. It was as though the moonlit garden, the whole world, was full of happiness.

"Right," he said, "that's settled."

"Six weeks," she repeated, with awe.

"It's not unusual, for chaps like us. There's always someone coming back with a bride who's practically a stranger, because leave's so short. It's surprising how well these marriages work, though. Maybe it's the glamour of the east."

"Is it glamorous?"

"You'll love it." They walked in the scented garden until suddenly Oliver said, "You're cold. We must go back."

They slipped in by the French windows from which they had made their exit. The band was playing and people were dancing, but their arrival was noticed. A severe-looking Lady Sylvia, seated on a small gilt chair, treated Hellen to an unblinking glare. She smiled back, generous in the face of bad will. Nothing could spoil her evening, now. Nothing did, until, after the band had played the last waltz, she went to find her cape.

Her hostess followed her up the stairs. "I want to have a word with you in private," she said.

Warm with happiness and the confidence Oliver had inspired in her, Hellen replied, "If there's something you wish to say to me, Lady Sylvia, I'd prefer that you said it in front of Oliver."

Neither by gesture nor by word did her hostess indicate that she had heard. "Come in here." She ushered Hellen so swiftly, so effectively, into a small dressing room, closing the door behind them, that Hellen scarcely knew how it had happened.

"I wanted to tell you something that I suspect you don't know. It won't take a minute. It's about the Marathons. Oliver's uncle is the Governor of Hong Kong. Oliver is a government cadet." She saw the blank look on Hellen's face and explained, "He's one of a select band of young men destined for high places in the Colonial Service. So you'll understand that when he marries, he must be very careful to choose a suitable bride. One who speaks French fluently, for that is the Diplomatic language, and who has, of course, been presented at Court, for a governor is the king's representative. Oliver could very well be offered a governorship one day. His wife would need to know the social scene at home—I mean, she should be able to talk about Ascot and Cowes.

"His father is a British resident general in the Malay States," Lady Sylvia went on. "I have no doubt that he will be offered a governorship one day. His sister is married to a distinguished Member of Parliament. He comes from a very old family." Enunciating her words very carefully she added, "Marathons expect their sons to choose marriage partners with very great care. Oliver's grand-parents, the Earl and Countess of Stradlock, live in a castle in Scotland. It is possible, though not probable, for his father is the second son, that Oliver could even inherit."

She paused a moment to allow the weight of her words to sink in, then continued a little less harshly, as though the blank expression on Hellen's face drew some unlikely pity from her, "I tell you this now, so that you will not be hurt when Oliver comes to his senses, as he is bound to do. Young men can be carried away by a pretty face. It is, perhaps, one of the pitfalls of living in the colonies, where there are few single girls, that when they come home their judgement may be—shall we say—faulty.

"It was at his father's suggestion that he came to visit us, because there are some suitable gels of our acquaintance in the county. Tonight's entertainment was arranged in order that we should parade some of the more eligible before him. His family thought it was time he looked for a bride."

Not for a moment had she taken her eyes off Hellen's face. Now, seeming to like what she saw, she went on more kindly, "We can understand. You're an attractive young thing, and you have a good seat. But it is not enough, Miss North, for the wife of a future governor. Not nearly enough."

It was a terrible silence that followed. The walls of the room seemed to close in. Lady Sylvia said complacently, "Shall we go down now? I think you understand."

"So what?" shouted Oliver. "You'll probably never get to be a governor's wife, anyway. Doesn't it say in the Bible the yellow races will rule the world? By the time I get to the top, if I get to the top, it'll be about 1940 or thereabouts, and who knows what will have hap-pened to the British Empire by then. As to French . . . Hell! An intelligent girl like you could get schoolgirl French into working order in two shakes of a lamb's tail. And you can be presented at Court as my wife. There's nothing to that. I've got an aunt who's Thingummy of the Bedchamber. She can fix anything." He added in that way he had of making everything sound right, "Even if you had been pre-sented as a deb, you'd still have to curtsy again after your marriage."

The feeling of unreality was still with her. She had been in paradise, and a sledgehammer had split it asunder. The pieces were all around her. Now she was in a whirlwind of Oliver's making. She took refuge

31

in accusation. "You should have told me about your job."

"What? You have to shout. This engine noise is diabolical."

"You should have told me—about your job."

"I did tell you. I said I was a trainee."

"You didn't say you were going to be a governor one day. That I would have to be a governor's lady."

"Don't you listen, darling? We've just been into that. You probably won't. Hell, there are a million government cadets. Well, half a million. Certainly a dozen or so. Why should I be picked out, just because my uncle's made it?"

"Because you belong to a grand family. You should have told me . . . about . . ."

They came to a hill and he turned the engine off, coasting down. The silence was wonderful. "My family are more—" he shrugged deprecatingly "—well, more . . . than anyone I'm likely to marry. If I started swanking about my antecedents I'd never get a wife—or else the wrong one. I don't want to be married for my family," said Oliver.

She plunged on, suicidally, like a lemming rushing to the sea, "Do you know the Norths are a mixture of trade and—in a way, you might say—artisan?"

"Oh, I wouldn't say that. Not artisan. But it's a fascinating thought." He changed gears and the noise rushed in again. The car roared up another hill. They had long ago passed Jolliffe's Farmhouse.

"Where are we going?" she asked as they raced down another slope.

"You seem to have a lot to shout about. I thought we'd keep driving until you've got it out of your system. We might find a high spot and watch the sun come up."

They breasted the next rise, and the engine quietened in third gear. "Oliver," she said desperately, "stop and think."

"I can't stop here. Not in this narrow lane. What do you want me to think about?"

"What your father will say, for a start."

"He'll say it's high time there was another injection of good looks into the family. You should see my sainted sister. She's got the untidiest face in the Home Counties."

After a moment she asked in a small voice, "Did you know that tonight was a parade of suitable brides for you?"

"No, was it?" Oliver shouted with laughter. Then, kindly, "It wasn't wasted. I think they enjoyed themselves."

Chapter 4

The Pledge

"But you scarcely know him!" protested Marnie. "You can't marry a man you don't know." She had been replacing the spoon in the marmalade jar. In her distress she held it in mid-air, dripping stickily down the glass.

"I feel as though I've known him all my life. And he feels the same way."

Hellen's expression was so innocent as to break Marnie's heart. With her elbows on the breakfast table, her fingers threaded, chin resting on the backs of her hands, she smiled at them and her smile was gentle, for they would be hurt by her going away. She wanted them to understand it was something that had to happen.

How could one explain that Oliver's touching her was like the wash of the waves? That he had only to brush her hand with his to set a current in motion that swept her nearer to the gods? Up on Oak Ridge, as the sun rose, as they watched the stars fading, he had demolished the awful Lady Sylvia, proving beyond reasonable doubt that the outside world was merely a frame for their loving. That they could build their own universe.

"I love you."

"I love you."

What more did they need in the way of knowledge of each other? Their love, inexplicable, unbidden, magic and all-consuming, bound them together.

"It's not like you to take flights of fancy," Marnie said. Hellen was a level-headed girl. "You must give yourselves time to think." Yourselves, she thought, for she could see there was no getting through to Hellen, sitting there radiant as a bride already, deaf to advice. The young man must be spoken to. He was clearly an impossible romantic.

Besides, who would come to the wedding? Or, more pertinently,

33

who dared they ask? Would those who deigned to accept "for Oliver's sake" turn up under-dressed? "I shouldn't bother too much, my dear. Heaven knows what they will be wearing." Marnie knew she would be angry. Joe would be gentle with them, accepting with unassailable calm their bad manners, and their patronising smiles; Sir Samuel Porchard, stocky and pugnacious, would demand who know who in hell they thought they were, they who had sat on their backsides waiting for titles to drop into their idle laps, reiterating that he'd earned his, and asking rhetorically if any one of them could match the diamond necklace he had given the bride.

Calum Finn would have to be asked, because he was Hellen's oldest friend. Would he get quietly drunk? Or not so quietly, because once the knot was tied he had nothing to lose? (What else could you expect from someone with no breeding?)

Well, none of them had any breeding, and that was that.

Joe rose from the table, carefully folded his napkin, and put an arm round his wife's shoulders. He knew his Marnie, knew from the hunched look and the tightness round her mouth that her imagination was running away with her. "Why don't we go into the drawing room and talk about it? I dare say Lily 'as finished clearing up there by now."

Hellen went first, walking on air with her lovely black hair swinging. If anyone deserved to marry well, her father thought, she did. She'd learn over the years, on the way up, so to speak. Just as young Oliver had to learn. He didn't know everything, yet. Not by a long chalk. Joe told himself they'd learn together.

Lily had left the broom by the door, and a duster on a small oak table. Marnie picked them up and put them on the floor in the passageway. Hellen flung herself down on the sofa, her silk shirt open at the neck, her arms stretched along the back rest, booted and jodhpured legs set wide apart.

Joe selected a pipe from the rack and began to fill it from a tin on the mantelpiece. "Six weeks," he said.

"We shall have nearly five weeks of honeymoon on the boat," Hellen told them, her voice lilting.

"I'll fix us up with a cabin on the port side," Oliver had said. "Port out, starboard home. That's the way you do it, to avoid the sun. P.O.S.H."

They would be posh people. She experienced a silent trill of laughter. There were so many new things ahead. Oliver, her husband, would teach her everything she needed to know. They would sit out on deck, shaded from the sun, by—a verandah roof? An awning?—while the steamer puffed its way through the Mediterranean, into the Suez Canal and down the length of the Red Sea. It would be hot. Raging hot, Oliver said.

The open deck under a star-lit sky. Dancing in Oliver's arms. When the boat hit a wave, side-on, Oliver said, the dancers could be swept across the deck, could even land in a haphazard heap at the rail—laughing men in white dinner jackets (Oliver's had been made by a Chinese tailor in Hong Kong), laughing girls in dance dresses.

How many gowns would she need in order to look her best for Oliver, dancing every night for thirty-four nights? She thought of the silver shoes, and decided they would be just right—tarty, but fun—for dancing on deck. She laughed in the secret recesses of her mind.

Her parents were looking at her, anxiously, as though reading her dreams, and seeing them as flights of fancy that they could dispell, if only they knew how.

She turned towards her mother, with love and regret, then to Joe. "I hate to leave you. I shall miss you dreadfully."

Marnie cleared her throat. She said stiffly, "His grandfather is an earl."

"I'm not marrying his grandfather, Mother." Hellen smiled at them, indulgently. "Oliver wants to take me to Scotland next week to meet them. He says I'll love them. His grandfather wears a kilt. All the time—except when he's gardening, in case the wind blows and exposes his—"

Marnie gasped.

Hellen laughed happily. "Oliver's awfully honest. He uses—you might say—old Anglo Saxon words. Not trying to shock, just because he's down-to-earth." She was aware of having moved off their wave length. She tried to pull herself back, and failed. She was up in the air, drifting towards this new life.

Marnie fingered the soft material of her skirt, wondering if Oliver thought he was coming down to the Norths' level by sounding, as Hellen said, down-to-earth. "I wouldn't advise you to copy him," she said, stiffly.

"Oh no, Mother. Certainly not. I've been brought up as a lady, haven't I?" Hellen looked down at them from her rosy pink cloud, teasing them gently, smiling, letting them know that underneath she was still their daughter.

Joe put his pipe down on the ashtry. "We'd better talk about the wedding."

Real life came up and slapped Hellen in the face. She stared at a rose on the carpet, the small one that stood out by itself at the end of the little brown twig, beside the thin, green circle that ran round the centre. It was a good Wilton. Twenty-five years old and wearing well.

Nothing at Jolliffe's Farm was inherited. The furniture belonging to Joe's parents, being worthless, had been thrown out, lock, stock and barrel. Marnie had done a magnificent job, Sam Porchard said proudly, with the cheque book he had given her, though why she had to buy all that second hand stuff he couldn't imagine. He thought the Jacobean chest would look rather more at home in the barn.

Hellen's grey eyes were hazy now. "Oliver says it'll be all right."

Marnie leaned forward, her forehead creased. "What exactly, does he mean by "all right", dear?"

"He says—why shouldn't it be all right? A village wedding. I mean—I think he means—like when we went to Knights Place to the Tynan wedding—it was," she hesitated, "mixed."

Joe picked up his pipe again. Marnie saw a speck of dust on the arm of her chair and carefully removed it with her finger. They were all thinking the same thing, that at the wedding of Lord Tynan's heir the village guests were bidden. That it was not at all the same thing—let's face it—as the county being invited to Jolliffe's Farm.

Joe said, with an air of pouring oil on troubled waters, "Perhaps his sister would like to give the wedding? It would solve a lot of problems."

And Sir Samuel Porchard, none of them had any doubt, would be delighted to pick up the bill.

Ah Sam, the number one cook boy whose culinary skills could rise to a dinner for twenty-four at two and a half hours' notice, without calling into play anything more than a fearsome chopper and a pair of bamboo chopsticks, had excelled himself today. His Majesty's Plenipotentiary to the Crown Colony of Hong Kong scraped his blackwood chair away from the table and stood up, patting his buttoned waistcoat with satisfaction. He had, after much searching, found a cook from the north.

Peking food was the nearest to European, for the northerners used a good deal of wheat flour, their specialities being dumplings and noodles rather than rice. And Ah Sam understood when his employer insisted on soup as a first course. The governor was willing to go a long way towards pleasing his staff, but it was beyond even his capacity for goodwill to drink soup in the Chinese way, at the end of a meal.

Sir Rowan Matheson was an impressive man, above average in height and broad-shouldered. His very blue Marathon smile was disarmingly open, and so guileless that people, with due regard for his considerable achievements, regretfully concluded it owed its origins more to the bathroom mirror than to a gentle heart.

The table was littered with empty dishes from which he and his lady had been fed with buds of kidney beans, fried garoupa, pigeons' eggs, and the delectable Beggar's Chicken. Beggar's Chicken was young fowl stuffed with three kinds of herbs, wrapped in lotus leaves, then baked in sediment from the bottom of rice wine jars.

By Gad! as Sir Rowan was known to say, you had to watch the blighters, though. Poor old General Allerton, suffering lumbago, had been fed a cure of snake's gall bladder. Worse than that could come your way. Otter's penis! Weasel's liver! His number one and number two boys, picturesque in blue silk long-gowns, with floor-length pigtails, came into the room to clear away.

"I've recalled him, Lettice," the Governor said, "but that's as far as I am prepared to go. I will not communicate with the girl."

Behind Ah Sam's inscrutable features, his brain buzzed. They all knew Master Oliver had been sent back to his barbarian country to find a wife. And why? It was Lin Yan—Flower of Mercy—the Eurasian beauty, unacceptable to both the barbarians and the Chinese because of her mixed blood, who had caused it. And now what had happened? Out of the frying pan into the fire, as Lady Marathon would say. And for what? Ah Sam knew all the coolies employed in Lin Yan's household, and not one of them could swear that Master Oliver had ever stayed the night there. Now he had found a barbarian girl, and Master and Missie didn't like her! Ah-ee. There was no pleasing the great.

Lettice Marathon glanced up at the two boys, silently moving round the table, heads modestly lowered. She wished her husband wouldn't treat them as though they were deaf and dumb as well as self-effacing. She knew they dispensed colourfully embroidered gossip on Vice Regal affairs, not only in the servants' quarters, but down in the bazaars as well. She waited until they had exited, silent in their white-soled boots, then rose and crossed to the door. Brought up in streets, open shacks, and courtyarded compounds, coolies were incapable of coming to grips with doors.

"My dear," she pleaded, "you cannot let her come, and then send her home. That would be too dreadful."

The governor rose from the table. "It would be a salutary lesson for young Oliver," he replied unfeelingly. "He knows the rules. The Colonial Office doesn't allow a cadet to marry before he turns thirty."

"With special permission, dear."

"Who's going to give him special permission? Heh?"

"We're not entirely blameless," she protested. "We sent him home on a trumped-up excuse that has gone wrong. He was going to get permission if he found the right girl."

Sir Rowan shrugged. " 'The best laid plans of mice and men . . .' " He was fond of quoting Robbie Burns.

"It's not Oliver I'm worried about," Lettice went on. "The girl's position would be untenable. Imagine the gossip!" She saw he was considering. His head was lowered, one hand supporting his chin, eyes cast down. His thoughtful pose.

"A village girl, Sylvia says. I can see that could be awkward for her." Sir Rowan's tone was dry, but the blue eyes twinkled. "You've said yourself, Letty, that one should never underestimate a pretty girl, whoever she is. It looks as though Sylvia underestimated this one."

"You speak already as though she's an upstart."

He lifted his wife's hand. "Oliver's not a fool. He knows what's what." With the exceptional courtesy that was a mark of the Marathon men, he kissed the back of her fingers. "There now. Don't worry. You're looking very pretty today." She was wearing buttercup yellow. At their first meeting, at a friend's coming out ball,, she had worn yellow. He had said she looked like a buttercup. Later, he thought of her as a clotted cream woman.

"Wear any colour, so long as it's yellow," he would say when she asked his advice. Yellow meant lemon and gold, as well.

Weakened by his gallantry, as he knew she would be, yet she made a last effort. "I still think it's callous, to let the girl come. Couldn't you cable her to wait another month? Just until you can talk to Oliver?"

"No, my dear, I won't. I will not interfere with affairs of the heart. Not where Oliver is concerned. Think about it—he has nine ports of call. All she has to do is send him a cable saying she's not following, and if he's fallen for her hook, line and sinker, he could jump ship and catch the next steamer going in the opposite direction. I'm not going to do anything that might lead to his jeopardising his career."

"He wouldn't do that, Rowan."

"Wouldn't he? Maybe I know Oliver better than you do. Look at young Armitage." They were silent, each contemplating Denzil Armitage's tossing in his job at Lonewood and Southby, running off to England with Alan Burtenshaw's daughter, putting paid to a promising career. "I won't do it," he reiterated. "If she's unsuitable, I'll deal with her in my own way, on my own ground. Now," he glanced down at his watch, "I've got that Nip coming at three. I'm going to put my head down for half an hour."

He struck that typical attitude, long legs apart, staring down at his well-polished shoes while he hauled his mind back to the real issues of the afternoon, which included preparing himself for the air of resentment that would hang over Upper Albert Road for the rest of the day. All the way down the line from Chan Mei, the lacquered china doll who did his typing, to the chair coolies in their red liveries and white gaiters, after the visit of the Japanese Ambassador, the staff would sulk. Sir Rowan disliked atmospheres, and he was good at diffusing them, but it was beyond even his considerable powers to soften the ill-feeling between Japs and Chinamen.

Lettice crossed the room and stood looking out through the verandah arches, across the praya and the harbour shipping to the islands that lay like crouching green mice on the horizon. All morning fog had been silently drifting down from The Peak. By noon the sun should have taken over, but today was one of the bad days. She fluttered her silk fan, stirring the tendrils of fading golden hair that clung damply to her forehead. She hated the humidity. Her dress of fine cotton, so fresh and crisp a couple of hours ago, was now limp as an old rag. up against the stuccoed ceiling, the electric fans whirled uselessly. It was as though the air was too heavy to be moved.

She wished she could make her husband see the girl's point of view. Behind every successful man, it was said, stood a clever woman. Lettice was nobody's fool, and nor were the other Marathon wives, but none of them had managed to prove to their menfolk that that maxim was true.

There was a beetle clinging to the chintz curtains. Lady Marathon opened the window and flicked it outside. Three little birds that had come to perch on the slatted seats at the base of the umbrella tree, turned, beady-eyed. One of them swiftly dived on the unexpected offering. Feeling disturbed, she wandered into the hall. There were times when she loved being the first lady in the colony: when she had to walk past a guard of honour with the regimental band playing, wearing a silk gown and a pretty hat, her husband, heart-achingly handsome in gold epaulettes with his rainbow of ribbons and his jewelled orders; or standing proudly beside him while he received men in only slightly less glamorous uniforms, and their dainty little Chinese ladies.

But there were other times when she felt like a shadow or a cipher, part of the furniture as one might say, because a governor, bound to do what was right for the administration of the colony, had occasionally to ride rough-shod over special people. To Lettice Marathon, the individual person was the first priority. Oliver was like her in that. She hoped with all her heart this girl was suitable, for if Oliver had, as Rowan put it, fallen hook, line and sinker for her, and she was not. . . . With an automatic, nervous movement, she pushed the wisps of hair back from her forehead with her fan. Lettice loved Oliver, as dearly as she loved her own two sons who were at school in

England. She did not want to take her husband's side against him.

Looking for air, she went out through the hall and stood at the top of the steps of the mansion, looking towards the gate. Jock Lovell, one of her husband's aides, was paying off the half naked rickshaw coolie who had brought him home. Waiting to speak to him, she put on a practised smile. The effort served to lift her heart, just a little. In five weeks on board a steamer, dancing with glamorous girls, visiting exotic ports, a young man would have time to consider if he had perhaps been hasty.

It didn't solve the problem of the girl.

Hellen stared down at the cable in disbelief. "Report to the Colonial Office for immediate briefing," she read out loud. "And you've already been? And—what boat? Two days! You have to sail in two days!"

"You'll remember," said Oliver apologetically, "that I came over in the guise of a King's Messenger. I told you that. It sounds jokey, I know, but there's a glimmer of truth in it. I wasn't quite due for leave, and there was this job to be done. They send very important messages by hand. They gave this one to me so that I could meet my parents, who were due for leave. Now they can't get away. Riots have broken out in Perak, so my reason for being here has gone. I've reverted to temporary acting King's Messenger. I've already been to see the big white chief at the Colonial Office. He gave me the bag—"

"Bag?"

"That's what they call it. Diplomatic bag. You'll get to know all the ins and outs of the Colonial Service in time." Oliver put his arms round her. "Looking at it cock-eyed, which is the only way you can, it's not such a bad start, because you're seeing what an unimportant vassal you're marrying—the boss says jump and I jump—and also, perhaps, it's not such a bad thing to fall in at the deep end. It does let you know what you're in for. You won't be able to say you weren't warned."

She quickly blinked so he would not see that tears had sprung to her eyes. Oliver's kind of person would pride himself upon keeping a stiff upper lip. He was keeping a stiff upper lip now. "Who is 'the boss', Oliver?"

"Whitehall, Westminister, the King. They all tell you what to do." Oliver was sanguine about it. "And top echelon civil servants. It's them, really. They boss you round, and you boss the Chinks—or Injuns, or Malays, or whatever. And if things go wrong, like it has for my father, your leave goes for a Burton, because you've got to get out your big stick and teach the natives a lesson." He brought himself up

40

to his full height as though he was very much looking forward to waving a big stick among the natives.

"I see," said Hellen, seeing only that Oliver was going back to that far distant land without her. Crying inside.

He leaned against Merry Astor's stall, looking down at Hellen, suddenly grave. "Shall we go for a walk? I've got things to tell you, and to give you. Let's not ride today. There's so much to say, and so little time."

So little time! She hung up the bridle and halter rope, gave the perfectly clean saddle cloth a shake and stumbled over Ben's boots that he had dropped beside a sack of chaff in the tack room.

They left the stables and skirted the old house, wending their way through the Cox's orange pippins and greengages, crossing the orchard diagonally, coming to the river by the big bend, out of sight of the house. Spring vetch and milkwort were out on the banks. Because there had been little rain, the water was low. Wild balsam hung down towards the water. "I'm sorry you're not going to meet my grand-parents," said Oliver regretfully, "but Marigold's going to invite you down to Dorset for a weekend."

Marigold Wolfe, who was too like Lady Sylvia Ashton for the two women to be friends! Hellen tripped on a tussock, and gave a little gasp that she hoped Oliver would not recognise as raw fear.

"Careful, there." He took her arm, then slid his own round her waist, holding her tightly. She began to feel safe again. "By the way, I've got your steamer ticket in my pocket. When I left Whitehall, I went straight down to the P & O. Cabins are at such a premium. You're going to have to share. But I've fixed that, too. I was able to look at the passenger list, and get you in with a Mrs Ruth Washington. I believe she's a nice woman. A friend of my aunt. She'll be able to tell you anything you want to know. She's been in Hong Kong for donkey's years. Her husband was comprador of one of the big hongs."

"What?"

"A big cheese in an import/export company." Oliver grinned. "You'll pick up the jargon. When he died, she stayed on. You couldn't be in better hands."

"Oh, Oliver," she looked up at him, emotionally tearful now. "You're so kind."

"Kind?" He looked quizzical. "You're going to be my wife. It's usual to look after one's wife." He said fiercely. "If this boat only went next week instead of the day after tomorrow, I'd ask for permission, get a special licence, and we'd be married."

"Permission? You're over twenty-one."

41

"Under thirty, that's what counts. Anyway, it wouldn't be fair to you. Girls have to get their trousseau ready."

She had to stop herself from crying, "I don't care about the trousseau. Take me with you, please take me with you." But she knew no Marathon wife her salt would say anything like that.

"You'll bring your tennis racquet, won't you?"

"Y-yes."

He looked at her oddly. "You do play tennis?"

"Of course." She had played tennis at school, for a while, and then the school, under pressure from parents, had agreed that girls could bring their own ponies. Hellen had not thought again about tennis. If she had two lessons a week for six weeks—maybe three lessons a week—would she be proficient? She could do a little less riding for a while and have a lesson every day.

"Bridge?"

"I'm not very good at bridge." She avoided his eyes. "Do I have to play?"

"Everyone does. That's—" He had nearly said, "That's all women do in the colony, play tennis and bridge, and gossip, and talk about clothes," but he didn't want to risk putting her off. "Some women like bridge," he said, smiling encouragingly. "My aunt doesn't, actually. You'll find you've got a lot in common with her."

Could one learn to play bridge in six weeks? If everyone played, then her fellow passengers on the steamer would play. She would find someone in Harland to give her lessons, then she would have five weeks' practice en route.

She looked up at him. "Is it because your aunt is the Governor's wife that she doesn't have to play bridge?"

"She plays." Oliver's arm tightened round her waist. "Marathon wives have to do all sorts of dreadful things, whether they like it or not." He kissed her, long and slowly. "You're going to hate being married to me," he said, his voice full of warmth, and love, and laughter. Greedy for her, he pulled her down beside him in the long grass. The tobacco smell of his jacket, the rough tweed of his sleeve, his nearness, caught at her senses. She put her arms round his neck, kissing him with little soft kisses on his face and neck, her lips moving down to where the fuzz began on his chest.

"You know," he said, "this hiccup may be for the best. We'll be married in St John's Cathedral. That's across the road from Government House, and my uncle will give you away." Again that little glimmer of humour. "He's quite an important chap, you know."

She understood what he was saying. Being given away by the Governor would set the seal of approval on her; might even negate

42

the fact that she could not talk about Ascot and Cowes. But none of her family would be at her grand wedding. She saw herself standing quite alone, in a white dress, being given away by a stranger, in a world of strangers.

"If we ask him nicely, I've no doubt my uncle will put hislaunch at our disposal. We could go to one of the islands for our honeymoon. Maybe Cheung Chau. That's about ten miles from Hong Kong. We'll arrange for Queens Pier to be a-flutter with flags and pennants. The Chinese love weddings. They'll have fire crackers exploding all over the place. The noise is sheer hell, but it's their way of wishing happiness and long life, so you'll have to put up with it."

"Oh, Oliver, you make it sound so exciting."

"It is exciting. It's our wedding day I'm talking about. What could be more exciting than that?" His arms tightened round her. Already emotionally stirred, she made no move to stop him when he tentatively unbuttoned her blouse and put a hand inside. "I know a chap who has a bungalow on Cheung Chau. He might be persuaded to loan it to us." Oliver's voice was all at once husky. "Hellen, I love you so much." She felt his body go taut. His fingers began fumbling with the buttons at her waist. She pulled him against her, wanting to be closer. Suddenly he flung himself away, rolled over in the grass, and drawing up his long legs, put his arms round them, resting his forehead on his knees. "I'm sorry," he said hoarsely.

She came upright and moved over to him, on her knees. "Lucky I've got jodhpurs on," she said shakily. Tenderly, lovingly, she smoothed his hair. She put a hand beneath his chin, lifting his face, kissing his eyelids. "We've the whole of our lives before us."

"Yes," he said gravely, opening his eyes and lifting her hand to his lips. "It would be a pity to spoil it for a bit of—Well, a chap ought to be able to keep his emotions in check." He remembered his father saying, all those years ago, "If you don't respect a girl—and you know what I mean by respect, my boy, don't you?—then ask yourself seriously if you love her, because the two go together." He had believed it—up to a moment ago. Consciously, he brought his breathing under control.

Reaching into his pocket he drew out a small packet, tissue wrapped. "I have something for you. I went to the bank this morning, and took it out. It's not a ring. I'd like to get that in the East. All sorts of things come into Hong Kong because it's a free port. Burma rubies. Sapphires from Ceylon. And some of the Chinamen are magnificent craftsmen."

He turned back the last fold of paper and there was a red leather box with a gold clasp. He handed it to her. She slid a nail beneath the clasp, and lifted the lid. "Oh-h!" She was looking down at a gold link bracelet, every section of which was set with seed pearls that ran in a circular pattern with a cabochon sapphire in the centre. The clasp was a leopard's head, beautifully etched in enamel, and ringed with pearls.

"This is for me?" she breathed, scarcely able to believe her eyes. "Oh, Oliver."

"Oh, Oliver," he mimicked her gently, looking pleased at her delight in the gift. "It's an heirloom. My grandmother gave it to me when I was twenty-one, to keep for my bride. Since you're so beautiful that all the men on the boat will be after you, I want you to put it on your wrist every evening, before the moon rises, because moonlight in the middle of an ocean can do devastating things to people. When these chaps try to kiss you, what you do is lift your wrist up and show them the leopard's head, and say it's your fiancé's coat-of-arms, and the leopard has fangs."

"Oh, Oliver," she breathed again. He watched her absorbed delight as she fingered the smooth, glowing sapphires, ran a finger-tip along a row of pearls, studied the exquisite lines of the big cat. And then, nervously, she said, "It must be very valuable."

"It's insured. Anyway," he added confidently, "you won't lose it, will you?"

Chapter 5

Rape

Lady Sylvia entered by the little white gate and strode briskly up the path. Hellen spied her coming. A faint feeling of apprehension, uncrystallised, told her this was not a friendly call. The threat was in the confident set of that horsy head, and the way she placed her feet, flat, as though webbed. Hellen consciously lifted her own head as she went to answer the door. In the hall she met Lily, broom and dust pan in hand. Lily's morning uniform was a voluminous apron, with a duster round her hair and carelessly knotted on her forehead.

A mischievous thought darted into Hellen's mind. "Lady Sylvia Ashton is at the door, Lily. Would you mind letting her in?"

The maid looked astonished. One of the things she liked about working at Jolliffe's was that nobody stood on ceremony. The family answered its own front door.

"Bring her to the drawing room," Hellen added. It would be all over the village tomorrow that the Norths were giving themselves airs.

The bell clanged through the house. Lily scuttled down the passage to the kitchen with her broom and pan, undoing her apron as she went. Hellen went at a leisurely pace in search of her mother, finding her folding sheets in the sewing room. "Lady Sylvia's here."

Marnie put a hand to her head.

"Do you mind if I make a suggestion?"

"What, dear?"

"I'd rather like you to give her the impression that you have no objection to my marrying a man, as you put it to me, that I scarcely know."

"If I show myself to be pleased, dear, it will look to her as though we—er—"

"Have ideas above our station?" asked Hellen helpfully. "Just tell her I'm over twenty-one, then, and it's my affair. I've asked Lily to let her in. Do you think we've kept her waiting long enough?"

45

"Hellen!"

"I'm practising for Hong Kong where nobody answers their own front door."

Marnie put an arm round her daughter's waist, holding her affectionately close as they went towards the stairs. "I'm going to miss you, Hellen." They had been into everything the night before, Marnie and Joe hiding behind bright faces not only their disappointment at missing the wedding, their apprehension, too. But they understood that being given away by the Governor would give Hellen a head start. They said warmly it was her future that counted. Only that.

Lady Sylvia Ashton was standing at the window looking out on the lawn and flower beds, or perhaps at the duck pond and the barns that were so close to the house, bringing in the scents of hay and horses and, regrettably, a faint drift of animal dung. She turned as Hellen and her mother entered the room, stiffly rejected Marnie's invitation to sit down, and came right to the point.

"Oliver Marathon sailed for Hong Kong yesterday."

Marnie inclined her head.

"I understand from him that you intend to follow." She looked directly at Hellen, and when she did not respond, turned an enquiring eye, beady as a bird, on Marnie. Neither face changed expression. "Well," said Lady Sylvia with an impatient tap of one long foot, "aren't either of you going to answer?"

"I didn't realise you had asked a question," said Marnie mildly. "If you have something to say, Lady Sylvia, please say it."

The visitor straightened her spine. Her piercing blue eyes were fixed on Hellen, now. Hellen looked straight back at her, her own eyes wide, steady, and unblinking.

"I've come to tell you I've had a cable from Sir Rowan Marathon." She paused for a reaction. Hellen and Marnie remained apparently calm. Lady Sylvia pushed her hands into the pockets of her shapeless tweed skirt and extending her bony chin added, "He asks me to stop you."

There was only a fractional silence, then Marnie, advancing and holding out her hand, asked, "May I see the cable?"

Lady Sylvia seemed to grow taller. "Do you doubt my word, Mrs North?"

"I wouldn't dream of doubting your word," replied Marnie politely, withdrawing her hand.

"I have not brought it with me because there were other matters referred to, which are private. You must take my word for it."

"May I ask if he gave a reason?"

"The reason is obvious, Mrs North."

46

Marnie said baldly, "You must have told him Hellen would not make a suitable wife for Oliver."

"You are blunt, Mrs North."

"I am Yorkshire born, Lady Sylvia. Yorkshire people tend to be a little blunt." She repeated the question, "Did you tell Oliver's uncle that Hellen was unsuitable?"

Lady Sylvia looked flustered.

"I cannot imagine," said Marnie calmly, "why you should not expect me to ask."

The visitor thrust her hands even more deeply into her pockets, looked down at her sensible shoes, then glanced round the room as though trying to remember if she had put something down when she came in. "He wished to spare you," a quick glance at Hellen, "the public humiliation of having to return to England. I have talked to Oliver's sister at some length," she added ambiguously. "I think that's all I have to say. May I show myself out?"

Without a word, Marnie led the way. When she came back, Hellen was still standing in the same place.

"Oliver said his sister was going to invite me for a visit," she said in a quivering voice, her mind rocketting on to this smaller issue, by-passing the real tragedy because it was too immense, too horrific to contemplate.

"Darling." For a moment they clung together, then with a swift gesture, Hellen released herself.

"Perhaps we had better talk, dear," said Marnie, immensely distressed.

Abruptly, Hellen turned. "No, I don't think so." There was a kind of violence in her manner. "I don't want to talk." She shot through the door.

Calum Finn was passing Jolliffe's Farm, riding on the sledge behind his young shire horse, a giant of a creature who took his name from the white star in the middle of his forehead. Star pulled the plough, and the harrows, and the old creaking dray. This morning he was taking Calum to the railway halt to pick up a bag of grain that Williams and Sons, the seed merchants in Harland, were putting on the steam train for him. Calum enjoyed hurtling along on the sledge, muscles flexed. He liked the manly image it conveyed.

A Rolls-Royce, driven by a uniformed chauffeur, was moving out from the farm entrance. "Whoa there, sonny boy," shouted Calum, dragging at the reins, steering his horse on to the grass at the side of the road to allow the Rolls to pass. Star snatched at a clump of long grasses in the hedge, set his huge, fluffy feet apart, and set about emptying his bladder.

Calum leapt back. "Phew! You shocker!" The car turned into the road. Wearing an embarrassed grin, Calum about-faced and it was then he saw that the passenger in the back seat, eyes looking straight ahead, mouth like a stick, was Lady Sylvia Ashton. His pale brows shot up in surprise. After the car had gone on its way he stood rubbing his jaw, wondering what on earth Lady Sylvia was doing at Jolliffe's Farm; remembering how he had seen Hellen in Sir Clancy's old banger with that toff, and how he'd heard she had been riding with him, more than once, over in the direction of Knight's Place.

The Rolls turned at the T junction and disappeared. Calum stared at the farmhouse. A side door opened and Hellen, skirts flying, sped across the corner of the orchard. As though the hounds of hell were after her, he thought with quickened interest. "What'll we do, feller?" He stood with one hand on the horse's collar. He'd like to know what was going on. She was his girl, wasn't she? At least as far as she was anyone's. He turned the horse round and entered the farm drive. If Ben was in the stables, he'd not mind Star being tied up in the yard for a while.

Hellen wriggled through the wires of the fence that encircled the orchard, and kept on running until she came to the tree by the river where she and Oliver had sat among the long grasses. The grass stalks lay flat, as though a long, thing cow had spent the night there. She sat down and pulled her knees up under her chin, hugging them, and squeezed her eyes tightly closed, squeezing out the humiliation, which was beyond anything she had ever known. It shrank her to the size of a toy.

After a while she opened her eyes and put her hand, palm downwards, on the flattened hare's tail and sedge, as though she might feel a little of Oliver there. The grasses felt dry, and cold, and stiff. She thought of the valuable family heirloom Oliver had given her that was meant for his wife: that he had kept for his wife: that he had given to her, because she was to be his wife.

She tried to summon up his dear presence, and could not. They had dragged him away. There were no scents, neither of tobacco, nor muskiness of good tweed, nor man-smell of bare arms with the sleeves rolled up. There was nothing of Oliver left. Her eyes filled with tears.

"Hello."

She jerked upright. Calum Finn was walking through the long grass. She turned back to the river, not bothering to blink the tears away. He stood looking down at her, hands in the pockets of his working trousers, his face concerned. "What's the matter, Hellen?"

Distractedly, she ran a hand across her forehead and along the back of her head, wishing he would go away without having to be told. "Nothing."

He flung himself down beside her. "You don't look like nothing has happened." He bent his big, blond head, looking into her face. Something had happened, all right. A horse fly settled on his cheek, stinging. He slapped at it.

"I met the Ashton woman leaving your place. Thought I'd come and see if you were still in one piece."

Hellen turned away and stared into the river.

He put a hand on her arm. "Are the rumours true?"

"What rumours?" She did not turn her head.

"That you've fallen for some chap who was staying at the Ashtons' who lives in Hong Kong?" Calum waited. She did not answer. "Everyone's talking about it. You've been out riding with him. Just about every day, they say." He added, sulkily, "I saw you myself with him, in Sir Clancy's old banger."

"What else do they say?" asked Hellen bitterly.

"His father's Governor of Hong Kong? S'that true?"

"Uncle."

"Oh, well." Calum shrugged. He took some grass stalks between finger and thumb, jerked the seed heads off, and threw them away. He bent over and loosened the laces of his farm boots, then tied them again. "How'd you come to fall for a toff, Hellen?"

She stared into the water. When she spoke it was in a puzzled voice. "I don't know."

Calum began once more to fidget with his boot laces, pulling at them, loosening them. He cleared his throat. "Somebody said you were going to marry him."

She went on staring at the water. Staring blankly at the slow moving water.

"Is that why the Ashton woman was there, at your place?" He waited. "They say the chap's gone." He roughly grasped a handful of dry leaves, stared at them, then threw them aside. "So I s'pose it's all over." He felt guilty pushing her like this, but he had to know. "What else?" he said uncomfortably. Then, "It is over?"

Two huge tears rolled down her cheeks.

"Aw, Hellen, don't cry." He shuffled sideways on his buttocks across the flattened grass. When he was close up against her he put warm, comforting arms round her.

Her eyes were shut. Now she could smell the scents she had been trying to conjure up. The man smell that came from Oliver's clothes, and his skin. Tobacco. She could feel the strength of his arms.

Calum began to kiss the tears away, and as he did so his whole body

49

responded. "I love you, Hellen," he said gruffly. "You must know that." He had loved her for so long, and she had given him nothing. Not even an opportunity to tell her how he felt. Now the words came instinctively, right from his heart.

He kissed her again. Hellen was scarcely aware of what was happening, only that the feeling of rejection had lessened. That there was a certain warmth, a melting in her mind that overflowed and became a blossoming of the body. She cast her mind back to another day, another world, when Oliver's emotions, spilling over, had welded with hers. Now she was there again, yearning towards him. He kissed her on the mouth and felt her lips respond. Dreaming, she dreamt Oliver's mouth softly on hers, teasing the lips, bringing the blossom to flower.

Calum sensed her need and his heartbeats quickened. His fingers came in contact with the pearl button that held her blouse closed. His eyes, full of nervous apprehension and greed for her, were on her closed lids. Now, she smiled. It was no more than an upturning of the lips, but there was a sweetness there, a wholeness of loving. Tentatively, he undid the button and put his hand inside her blouse then slid it down until it cupped her breast.

His breathing quickened. Every nerve in his body signalled him to take her, now. At the same time, some instinct from the years of frustration, of standing behind the wall she had erected between them, told him to be careful. Then, without opening her eyes, she smiled, and his uncertainty went in a soaring sense of elation. That joker had roused her then left her, for him. He sensed her need for that which only he was there to give.

Hellen did not see his right hand go to his trousers. She had Oliver in her mind's eye, and in her heart. Calum's buttons came deftly undone. He jerked her to him, and with senses reeling, thrust her skirt up over her thighs. There was an explosion of shock, and the dream of Oliver slithered away. Her eyes flew wide. She opened her mouth to scream, and Calum's tongue filled her mouth, choking her. She tried to writhe away from under him, the palms of her hands against his shoulders, pushing with all her strength. One of her legs was caught between both of his. She was aware, with terror, that he was half-way out of his trousers. There was something there against her bare legs, naked and hot and hard.

He saw the anger in her face and smelt her fear, but most of all he felt, with shock, the insult of her rejection of him. His emotions flared into ruthless domination. He would have her. He would show her she couldn't play games with him. He'd tame her. He'd teach her to pass him by and cry for other men.

She felt his hand at the easy elastic of her bloomers. She fought like a mad woman. Now he was right on top of her, with one arm across her shoulders, pinning her to the ground. His strong legs had thrust hers apart. She gasped with fear, revulsion and shock as that monstrous thing entered her, then screamed aloud in pain.

"You needn't have bitten me," Calum said aggrievedly, fingering the hurt on his chin. "Look, it's bleeding."

Hellen had leaped to her feet, beside herself with grief and outrage. "How dare you! You—you—you animal," she sobbed.

"I thought you liked it," he said sulkily. "You didn't do anything to stop me. You just lay there, looking happy." His voice coarsened, became more belligerent. "You liked it. You gave me the come-on." He pulled his trousers into place and clambered to his feet.

She was like a wild cat, crouching just out of reach, frantically pulling at her clothes as though an appearance of modesty could undo what had taken place. "Don't touch me," she screamed at him.

He was sullen and uncomprehending. "I just wanted to say I'd like to marry you. I'd have asked you before, except—" The rest stayed in his head, the fact that there wasn't enough room in the house, but why couldn't they move in to Jolliffe's? There was no point in continuing, for she was running like a hare, back across the meadow towards the house. The last he saw of her, she was clambering through the fence into the orchard.

Nobody saw Hellen again that day.

"Better leave her alone," said Joe. "She's got a lot to think about, and if she doesn't want to talk it over with us, we mustn't press her. It's best she decides for herself what to do."

"I don't like her going without supper."

"She'll come down if she's hungry."

Hellen did not come down. She went to the bathroom and washed her soiled underwear. When, next morning, she hung out her bloomers, Marnie assumed she had her period. Poor girl, that must be the final straw.

"I'm going for a long ride," she said as she left the breakfast room. She went straight out to the stables, saddled Merry Astor, and not wanting to cover any of the tracks where she had been with Oliver, rode up through the village. Across the green, nestling among the elms and chestnuts that proliferated within the old stone wall enclosing the graveyard, lay the village church, a squat fifteenth-century stone pile.

Not yet knowing why, she rode towards the church, dismounted at the lych gate, dropped the reins over one of the gate posts, and went up the path between the tombstones. She had never before entered the church on a week day. The weddings she attended were solemnized on a Saturday, involving as they did grooms who worked all week. Sunday was the day for worship. That was how she saw the church.

She entered the porch, lifted the iron latch on the heavy oak door and proceeded inside, then wandered down the aisle until she found herself standing opposite the Ashtons' pew. Seating herself on their red velvet cushion, she gazed up at the stained glass windows above the altar, watching the light come and go behind them, listening to the questions that ran through her head. Why should my life be thought so trivial while Oliver's is important? Are we not equal in Thy sight? Why did You send Oliver to me, then snatch him away again? You, in Lady Sylvia Ashton's image. Then Calum, in Oliver's image? A snake in the Garden of Eden.

She did not hear a door opening, but there was the vicar, walking across the nave, looking at her curiously. She met his eyes with a baffled stare, for was he not God's proxy? He turned away, going soft-footedly about his ecclesiastical affairs. She felt the warmth of the cushion against her clenched knuckles, this velvet that supported a family without charity, without christian love to offer, except to their own kind.

She sank down on the embroidered kneeler, but could not think of a prayer that would exonerate her from what had happened with Calum; that would cancel Sir Rowan Matheson's cable; that would bring Oliver and herself together again. She rested her forehead on her hands, her mind in limbo where it had run to escape the appalling present. She was a long time on her knees. The vicar wondered uncomfortably if she had gone to sleep, or was crying, and whether or not he should approach her. When she lifted her head he moved discreetly through the vestry door, and out of sight.

"Make me strong, then," Hellen said with a surge of bitter defiance. "Make me strong enough to deal with whatever is to come." She rose to her feet and went, walking very erect, down the aisle to the door. She lifted the big, heavy latch and let herself out, deliberately leaving the door open behind her, though knowing it should be shut. The warm, sunny morning flooded in. She turned and watched, for a moment, the bright sunshine playing on the stone floor, lighting up the whole interior of the church. Then she went on her way.

For a while, Hellen behaved as though nothing had happened. She did not mention Oliver, or Lady Sylvia's visit, and no one spoke of either to her. Then one day the post boy brought a yellow envelope.

"Cable for you, Hellen. It's from Gibraltar," said the awestruck boy. "Gibraltar! Who d'you know there?"

LOVE YOU STOP HOPE EVERYTHING UNDER WAY STOP DON'T MISS THE BOAT STOP REPEAT DON'T MISS THE BOAT STOP ALL MY LOVE STOP OLIVER

Hellen went to find Marnie. Her face was radiant, her eyes shining like the sun on pools of molten silver. "Shall we go into Harland today and see Miss Sedgwick about the wedding dress?"

The P & O liner *Narkunda* moved away from Tilbury dock, edging into the centre of the Thames. Those who had come to see the passengers off turned away in various stages of distress. Hellen's sisters, Verity and Beth, clung together, weeping.

"Five years," sobbed Verity. "I just can't believe it. She could have two children by then, and no one would have seen them!" The thought was so appalling that she broke down again.

Marnie and Joe, dry-eyed, exchanged looks. Joe took his wife's arm, holding it comfortingly. They each knew what the other was thinking. Ever since Hellen decided to ignore Lady Sylvia's warning, they had been praying that it would indeed be five years before they saw their daughter again.

With his free hand, Joe patted Verity comfortingly on the shoulder. "Chicks must fly the nest, darling." They had not told the others about Lady Sylvia's visit.

"They don't usually fly that far away." And Beth, too, mopped at her eyes. The Norths were not the kind of people who went abroad. Joe's younger brothers, Corporal Len after whom Leo had been named, and Private Steve of the Queen's Own Royal West Kents, had been killed by the Boers at the Siege of Ladysmith in 1899. Abroad meant wars. It was not easy for the Norths to see the British Empire in any other light.

Leo kicked savagely at a loose plank. He was thinking that if Oliver hadn't sent all those stupid cables from every port: Gibraltar, Malta, Port Said, Aden, Bombay, Colombo, Penang (he wouldn't mind betting there was another one, even now, on its way from Singapore), Hellen might have given up. Hell! She only knew the feller for a few days. He was amazed that his parents had taken the whole thing so calmly.

Joe, who was given to offering homespun wisdom, had said no more than: "There are difficulties in being married to a man without prospects, too. You're an intelligent girl, Hellen, and young enough to take change in your stride. There's no reason why you shouldn't make a go of being. . . ." None of them liked to say out loud that

Hellen might end up as the wife of a colonial governor. It sounded too far fetched. Slightly ridiculous.

But then Joe added, "there's one thing I'd like to say, though. Once you make your bed, we shall expect you to lie on it."

Leo would never forget the look that passed between father and daughter, then. The gravity of it made him shiver. Was there something he had not been told? Calum Finn, emerging somewhat tipsily from The Cock at closing time, had said, "Tell Hellen, if she comes back, I'll be waiting."

"Tell her yourself," Leo had retorted roughly. "You know where to find her." But he had not come. Stupid ox.

Chapter 6

George Curtain

"I see that rum fellow George Curtain's aboard." Major Tandy eyed Ruth Washington through his gold-rimmed monocle. "Alone," he added. "I thought the blighter was going to marry little Kitty Burtenshaw. What happened?"

"Denzil Armitage ran away with her."

"Well, I'll be jiggered! How d'you hear this, Ruth?"

"Kitty knew I was in England. She telephoned me. She wanted me to placate her parents on my return."

"Well, blow me!" Major Tandy's red face was a study. "That'll take some doing."

Alan Burtenshaw was titular head of the hong, Burtenshaw & Jax—the Jax part had been weakened by the son's primary interests in America, and Burtenshaw virtually had control. He might not like his daughter's choice of George Curtain—and who would?—but he was a stickler for good behaviour. Once she had given her word and accepted George's ring, he would expect her to go through with the marriage.

Major Tandy settled his deerstalker comfortably over his ears. "So, what's Curtain doing here?"

"Alan sent Kitty home to buy her trousseau, and at the last moment, Denzil jumped aboard. George followed on the next steamer, but they were already married."

"What? Armitage chucked up his job! Must've chucked up his job."

"They've sacked him."

"That's fixed him, what! Silly ass is done for, now." The major stared down at the stoned teak deck, twitching his ginger moustache, uncomfortably concerned whilst at the same time telling himself not to get worked up over young fools.

Ruth Washington was a pretty woman, the daughter of a Peking

55

merchant who had, in her salad days, had the crème de la crème of the colony after her. Even at fifty, with her carefully plucked eyebrows and fair, marcelled hair without a trace of grey, she was what Harry Tandy called a "looker". People said, if she liked to crook her finger, half a dozen suitors would come running, even now. She settled herself against the rail, smoothing down her skirt as the ship caught an eddying breeze.

The Major hadn't much time for George Curtain. Didn't know him, really, but all the same, hadn't much time. There had been surprise in the colony when he landed Alan Burtenshaw's daughter for she could have had the pick of the army or the government cadets.

A Thames tug came butting upsteam with a cargo of logs. There was a deafening blast from *Narkunda*'s siren, and a black cloud came billowing out of the funnel. Ruth flicked at a piece of soot that came to rest on her sleeve, then wiped her well manicured nail on a lace handkerchief. She did not particularly care for George Curtain, either, but there was no doubt he could make himself very agreeable, and it was true women were attracted to him—although, Ruth would have said, a certain type of woman. She was never sure how he stood with men. She thought he was tolerated for his sporting abilities. He rode well, was an excellent swimmer, and the best spin bowler in the colony.

Kitty's loss to George was far more than a personal one. Neither he nor his family had climbed very far up into the colony's structured society. One never saw them at Government House, and neither did one meet them at the grander houses on The Peak. Once, Ruth had seen George labouring around The Peak roads, putting cards into letter boxes, which was the way new arrivals made their presence known. But the Curtain family were not new arrivals. They had been in the colony for years. At bridge the next day there was a good deal of game made of George's efforts with his visiting cards. The petty tyranny of Peak hostesses was greater by far than George Curtain.

Curtain père had been a tea taster in Shanghai. With the rise in popularity of the new Ceylon teas, the bottom inevitably fell out of the China tea business, and he came down to Hong Kong to start an import/export company which had not been very successful. He put his son into Lonewood & Southby, one of the bigger hongs. If they weren't accepted by now, they were never going to make it.

To be fair to George, though, girls in Hong Kong were a rare and eagerly sought after commodity. Lettice Marathon always had one eye open for a pretty one. With the battleships *Hood* and *Repulse* in permanent residence, as well as foreign navies coming on visits, there were never enough young ladies to partner the officers. Even those of slender means who resided at the Helena May hostel and did clerical work in the hongs were sometimes roped in, especially if they had a foreign language at their fingertips. One could not blame the First Lady for picking men off the top rung of the ladder when there were so many from whom to choose.

Ruth was glad Denzil had won Kitty. She did not agree with Harry that as a result of this peccadillo he would find himself persona non grata in Hong Kong. With his credentials as a friend of Oliver Marathon, and an old Harrovian into the bargain, he would get on his feet again, and prosper.

"Curtain'll be the laughing stock of Hong Kong, what!" said the Major, taking a silver box from his jacket pocket and thoughtfully pushing a pinch of snuff into either nostril. Ruth tacitly agreed. Gossip was the meat and drink of the colony. Human error was what gave the Hong Kongers something to chew on between rubbers of bridge and sets of tennis. Changing the subject, Harry Tandy asked, "Got a decent cabin mate?"

"Yes, I think so. A pretty girl. Quite young. I spoke to her only briefly."

"Fishing fleet?" It was a derogatory term used by old hands for young women who went out to the East to look for a husband.

"I don't even know her destination."

"You didn't look at her luggage labels?" He cocked an eyebrow, chuckled, and finished with a rasping smoker's cough.

"Had I wanted to be nosey," said Ruth, looking offended, "I wouldn't have had an opportunity. It was a bit like Picadilly Circus, with half a dozen of her family trying to squash into the cabin. I shouldn't think she's fishing fleet. A simply enormous bouquet of red roses was delivered for her. I'd guess she's either going out to get married, or being packed off to forget an unsuitable swain."

"I'll take you on for five bob."

Ruth was impatient with the Hong Kongers' proclivity for betting. They would bet on two flies crawling up the window. "You know my claim to fame," she said briskly. "I'm the one who doesn't bet." She lowered her voice. "Don't turn round now, but she's coming this way."

The Major screwed the monocle into his eye, and with every sign of appreciation, stared boldly. "Nice little filly," he acceded as Hellen made her way along the rail, her shining dark hair lifting on the breeze. She did not notice them. Her face was raised to the sun, and her eyes looked straight out over the bow.

They both watched her in silence. "By George," said the Major, "if she hasn't already been snaffled, I'll eat my hat."

Within a few days it became clear that George Curtain was intent upon a shipboard romance with the pretty young thing who shared Ruth Washington's cabin. And clear also, said the cynical old hands, that she was on a fishing expedition.

"Strike me," the Major remarked to Sam Palmer, a minor official in the China customs as they stood at the rail watching rocky little Malta disappear over the horizon, "it looks as though she's made a fast catch."

"I think she's teasing him. He may be serious, but I don't believe she is. Did Ruth tell you about the roses?" On a 16,000 ton steamer, everyone knew everyone else's business.

The Major pulled his Panama hat lower on his forehead in order to shield his eyes from the blazing sun. He couldn't, in the circumstances, take the roses too seriously. "George Curtain's a queer coot," he opined. Did anyone know, come to think of it, why Kitty shot off with young Armitage? According to his cook boy, Curtain had been seen more than once leaving the floating bordelloes, euphemistically called "flower boats", in Aberdeen harbour. The flower girls were not under police medical surveillance, and many a young man visiting them had contracted a nasty dose of clap. If Kitty's devoted amah heard, she would be quick to spill the beans.

Hellen, across the deck, was flirting with a young officer who had come aboard at Gibraltar. Tandy's eyes softened. If he'd had a daughter, he'd have liked her to look like that. Ah, well, he had better do his six rounds of the deck. Half a mile. He'd seen old Frobisher leaning against the rail at the blunt end, pulling on his pipe. He might be persuaded to come along. With the temptation attendant upon duty free drinks, a chap had to think of his liver.

Ruth Washington was lying back in a deck chair, her face hidden by a parasol. The exercise over, Tandy paused. "Mind if I pull up beside you, old girl?"

She opened her eyes sleepily. "Do."

"Got something botherin' me."

She dragged herself into a sitting position, shielding her eyes from the sun with one hand, looked indulgently into his face. "What can be bothering you, Harry?"

"None of my business, of course," said the Major, signalling to a passing steward to move a deck chair into the lee of the funnel beside his friend. "Getting a bit worried about the way that blighter George Curtain is making up to your young friend."

Ruth's mouth tightened.

"Wondered if you might drop a hint. Get my drift?"

Ruth exactly got his drift. Nobody wanted to be the laughing stock of Hong Kong. By stepping off the boat with a radiant new fiancée on his arm, George Curtain would silence malicious tongues at a stroke. "Who am I to put a spoke in the poor man's wheel?" she asked aloofly. "I don't, frankly, feel like taking sides."

"I just thought, she seems rather too good for him," said the Major, sounding disappointed. "Oh well, if that's your view. . . ." He tipped his Panama hat over his eyes and settled against the canvas chairback. "Just as well you didn't take me on for five bob. I might have lost, what!"

He wriggled into a comfortable position and closed his eyes, then sleepily remembered a tit-bit Ruth would enjoy. "Heard about young Marathon?"

"No."

"It seems H.E. got worried about the Eurasian girl and sent the lad home on some trumped-up errand, in the hope of getting him suitably married. His sister was alerted and got some flappers lined up, and a family friend in Kent did the same. And what does he do? He lights on some village girl, and without a by-your-leave, proposes to her!"

Ruth's eyes were like saucers.

"I tell you, the lines have been red hot. Oliver's on his way back, and the girl's been warned off. Now, if you were a betting woman, Ruth, how much would you put on young Oliver's cocking a snoot and running off with what's 'er name?"

"Lin Yan," Ruth supplied, halfway between excitement and genuine distaste. Then she added, "From what I know about him, I'd say he's too family and career orientated to cock a snoot, Harry."

"Then what's your guess?" He wriggled back up into a sitting position. "Just thought," he added persuasively, "it's not such a bad thing to put a spoke in a chap's wheel. I wouldn't like a nice young thing like Miss North. . . ." His voice trailed off. "What d'you think, Ruth? Put her off, eh? Just mention Kitty. Set her thinking, what!"

Privately, Ruth suspected Hellen was keeping herself out of mischief by playing the field. She had seen the way she held the bouquet of red roses to her heart that first evening. Even when the flowers were beyond redemption, she had refused to allow the steward to throw them out. And she had seen, too, out of the corner of her eye, though she pretended not to notice, Hellen breaking off a single rose and putting it under her pillow.

If she was miffed, she was also intrigued. Why didn't Hellen hunt? She wasn't a nervous type. Why did she never talk about people? Everybody had someone in common. There was something about her bridge game that worried Ruth, too. She was an avid player, and an intelligent one, but she did not play well. She said apologetically that

59

she was dreadfully out of practice, but Ruth knew she was too intelligent to make the mistakes she made, unless out of sheer ignorance.

The original surmise about the unsuitable liaison had gone by the board, for Hellen was not behaving like a love-sick maiden. Well, she was a mystery, but it behoved Ruth to be very careful and keep her mouth shut. Young, unmarried girls were the hostesses of tomorrow. She had always made it her policy to be nice to them. One never knew who they would marry.

Harry Tandy had begun softly to snore.

Hellen was having a wonderful time. She had enjoyed flirting with all the young men, until George Curtain froze them out, one by one. She was amused by his presumption, as well as flattered, for he was a good-looking man. Many people did not notice any more about his face than that it wore a ruddy glow of good health. His fair, almost mousy hair, which he kept neatly slicked down with brilliantine, was straight as a brush, and cut short back and sides. His dark, neatly trimmed moustache looked un-English, and would have given a smaller, more elegant man a slick appearance, but George Curtain's excellent physique over-ran any petty failing in his looks. He always seemed to be the tallest man in a group, but only by virtue of the fact that he held his back straight and his head high. He walked with the long-legged, firm gait of an athlete. People could say, as he rounded a bend in the street, "Here comes George Curtain," without waiting until he was close enough for them to see his face.

Hellen liked his sophistication and his good manners. He danced well, and was not so expert at bridge as to show her up. What was more, he asked few questions. She swam with him in the pool, played ping-pong with him, and deck quoits. Frog racing was her favourite deck game. George loyally bet on her wooden frog in every race. He had already lost ten pounds on her. She was amazed at the Hong Kong passengers' predeliction for gambling.

"We get it from the Chinks," George said. "They bet on everything." He even bet on her winning the fancy dress competition, and that was before he knew what she was going to wear.

One evening, when they were standing at the ship's rail and the band was playing "Love Sends A Little Gift of Roses', George, affecting only casual interest, lifted Hellen's wrist. The darkly glowing cabochon sapphires had caught his eye on the first night out, but it had been some time before he realised they were not fake. It had been another few days before he could swear to the fact that the leopard's head was part of the Governor's coat-of-arms.

Now he knew the identity of the relative with whom Hellen was to stay in Hong Kong, he understood her reticence about naming him. Sir Rowan Marathon had no daughters, so she must be his niece. What a sense of humour she had, though, renouncing the petty recognition that came with a seat at the captain's table, laughing up her sleeve at those who fought tooth and nail for the privilege, and gave themselves airs. Better keep his mouth shut, he decided. She would talk, if he played his cards right.

"Pretty," he said.

"It's a family heirloom," said Hellen. She tried to say, as Oliver had enjoined her, "It's my fiance's coat-of-arms and the leopard has fangs," but she was superstitious about saying the word "fiancé" out loud. Oliver, now back in Hong Kong, would have seen his uncle, and had had time to send her a cable saying all was well. But he hadn't.

"It's beautiful," said George, unnaturally aware of his voice giving away the fact that he was impressed. Je-sus! Now that he'd had a close look at it, he reckoned it must be worth a mint. He held out his arms. "Let's dance, shall we?"

That night, when the dancing was over and Hellen went to her cabin, Ruth was already in bed. Hellen came in looking wind-blown and happy. Ruth felt a twinge of conscience. She placed her book carefully on the chest of drawers by her bunk, and remarked in a friendly voice, "You look as though you've been enjoying yourself, dear."

"I really don't think I've ever enjoyed myself so much." Hellen flung down her long crêpe-de-chine scarf, peeled off the pretty dress that was one of the dozen her mother's dressmaker had made for her, and modestly pulled her dressing gown round her. "I had been told it was magic at sea, but I never guessed. . . ." She broke off on a tremendous sigh, thinking of Oliver, with whom she might have been dancing. Oliver, who should have been here with her, lying now in Ruth's bunk, with arms outstretched to welcome her; to hold her to his heart in the soft sea darkness, with the sound of the engines throbbing below, and the muted whirr of the fan in the low, white ceiling.

Ruth said, "Um—I hesitate to say this, but there are more eligible young men in Hong Kong than George Curtain."

Hellen swung round, her lips parted in astonishment. Then she laughed. "It's very kind of you to warn me, Mrs Washington."

Ruth said diffidently, "The colony's society is very close knit and, er, the Curtains are, er, perhaps not quite. . . ." She looked into Hellen's face, her expression faintly arch, drawing the girl into her "one of us" world. "I'm sure you know what I mean, dear."

"Yes," said Hellen, her voice brusque, remembering the snubs she had suffered from those who considered themselves superior to the daughter of a tenant farmer, "Yes, I know exactly what you mean, Mrs Washington."

"What I'm trying to convey to you," said Ruth stiffly, "what I don't think you're aware of, dear, is that there's a tremendous lot of gossip in Hong Kong. It's a very small place. Everyone makes a point of knowing everyone else's business. If you change your toothpaste someone will hear about it. For your own good, I'd advise you not to start off with the label of George Curtain's girl friend."

"Gossip!" said Hellen, slipping out of her shoes. She was quite terrified of this woman who, as a friend of Oliver's aunt, must on no account know who she was until she heard from Oliver that all was well.

"You may not approve of the way life is lived in the East, but you're not going to change it. You'll only make yourself unpopular if you criticise," said Ruth.

"I'm sorry," said Hellen. "I didn't mean to be rude." She turned her back, opened the tiny wardrobe they shared and carefully separated the garments to make room for her gown.

Ruth sat forward in her bunk. "Let me tell you a little tale which, when I come to think of it, could be of interest to a pretty young thing like you, for there's a very eligible young man involved, with a pedigree as long as your arm."

Hellen listened in total silence. Not once did her eyes leave Ruth's face until the story Major Tandy had related was finished. The world had ceased to turn. All the candles that had been magnificently flaring, flickered and died. All the loving cables Oliver had sent from Gibraltar to Penang lay shredded at her feet. Her heart shrivelled and grew cold.

Disconcerted by her impassive stare, Ruth wound the story down. She picked up a jar of night cream from the dressing table, unscrewed the top and with a delicate fingertip, began to spread it across her face. For heavens' sake, why couldn't the girl open her mouth and show a bit of gratitude? She was only trying to help. "He couldn't marry her without official permission until he's thirty," she finished, "and he's not going to get permission."

She put the lid back on the jar and managed a very warm smile, right up into Hellen's face. "Who knows, this very eligible young man might be yours for the taking, if you play your cards right." She waited, deflating slowly, the silence and the stony expression in Hellen's eyes stripping the smile from her face. At last she said in a sharp, offended voice, "I'm only trying to help you, my dear. I'm only

suggesting that if you're looking for a husband, you can do better."
To her astonishment, Hellen snatched up her wash-bag and towel, then swung round and without a word left the cabin, pulling the door shut with a sharp crack.

Ruth stared after her, then shrugged resignedly. What a prig the girl was! She reached for the switch and turned off the light. The cabin was hot, the fan inadequate. So that was what you got for trying to help people! You succeeded only in making a fool of yourself. And then, remembering the dreamy expression Hellen had worn on entering the cabin, she jumped with shock. Had George already proposed, and been accepted?

After a while she stopped worrying. George was very small beer. As his wife, Hellen would be a nobody. Forget it. At three o'clock in the morning, with a feeling of being alone in the cabin, Ruth wakened. She reached for the light switch. The familiar dressing gown was not there. She leant out on one elbow so that she could look up at the top bunk. It was empty.

She turned out the light. No one could say she hadn't tried. She would tell Harry Tandy to curb his fatherly concern.

Hellen sat in her dressing gown on a lavatory seat in the big communal washroom, staring at the door, her towel, face flannel and soap cluttered together at her feet. She stayed like that for a long time, suspended in shock and a kind of subdued terror. The door swished open. There was a whisper of soft soles, a lock rattled, a chain was pulled, a tap turned on and off. Then silence fell, as much silence as the busy, thumping engines would allow. Someone else came in, and later, left.

After a while an out-of-control kind of awareness returned. So everyone in Hong Kong would know, by the time the gossipy Mrs Washington had been back for a few hours, that Oliver had been recalled because he had fallen in love with her. If he came down to meet the ship, if he was going to be allowed to meet the ship, people would already be watching. She tried to visualise his dear face, drawn with despair, and saw instead a look of cool resignation. Would he, with his fine regard for duty, say merely, "You win some, you lose some," and advise her not to go ashore? She slumped against the wall, feeling sick. She was sick. Afterwards, unable to face Ruth, she put down the lavatory lid and sat on it, eyes closed. After a while she felt herself drifting into a sleep state that was black with despair.

There was a knock at the door and she jerked upright, confused, disorientated. A voice mused worriedly, "I noticed earlier that it was locked. Maybe we should call a steward. Someone could have collapsed."

Hellen moved stiffly. "It's all right. I'm really quite all right. I—wasn't well." And suddenly she was going to be sick again.

"Sorry to bother you." The voice sounded relieved. "Is there anything we can do?"

"No, really." Hellen put a hand over her mouth, holding back the bile, fighting the muscle spasms in her stomach. She heard footsteps leaving. The door swung shut. She lifted the lavatory seat and threw up.

Afterwards, she leaned down and picked up her belongings from the floor, unlocked the door, washed her face and rinsed out her mouth. When it seemed she might not be sick again, she looked at her watch. It was nearly seven o'clock. The hearties who went out on deck for a few quick turns before breakfast would already be astir. She had better get back to the cabin before someone came in and smelt the sick and asked her. . . . She shut a trap in her mind.

Ruth was awake. She looked up as the door opened. Back at last. Bold as brass! Neither of them spoke, Ruth because she was too disgusted and, it had to be said, embarrassed. She slipped into her dressing gown and went off to the bathroom, trusting her silence conveyed her very real disapproval of Hellen's morals. After all, where could she have been since midnight except in George Curtain's cabin?

Hellen climbed the tiny ladder to her bunk, rolled herself in her sheet and lay staring at the wall.

Chapter 7

George's Declaration

The *Narkunda* became a cold, inhospitable cage. Hellen was sick in her soul, and sick physically. She rose in the morning, breakfasted if her churning stomach muscles would allow, walked round the deck, played games, swam and danced. She lived from day to day, waiting for word from Oliver who had sailed on May the first; who, thirty-four days later, on the third of June, two days after she left the Port of London, was due in Hong Kong; who had now had time to confront his uncle; who could have told her by cable if all was well, yet had not. Afterwards, she knew that giving up bridge was a sign that in some part of her, she had accepted defeat.

She had already considered leaving the ship and returning home. Her family would welcome her, perhaps with relief. She mustn't think about the village gossip. Sometimes, in the small hours of the morning, when resistance was at its lowest ebb, she saw in the darkness Lady Sylvia's triumphant smile: the sly "Told you so's", of her fellow members of the hunt.

This afternoon the flat, grey coastline of Egypt had appeared. Tomorrow they would anchor off Port Said. Would she be able to find there a respectable hotel where an English girl might stay alone, whilst waiting for a homeward bound ship? Could one ask the Purser for a cabin trunk and a packing case, both labelled: NOT WANTED ON VOYAGE?

George was standing beside her at the rail. "You're not wearing your bracelet," he said.

She glanced down at her wrist.

Should she cable Oliver? PLEASE ADVISE WHETHER I SHOULD RETURN ENGLAND. That would make it easy for him to reply with a simple YES. She shivered. Why, when everyone was sweating, the men wiping their necks with handkerchiefs, easing their stiff white collars, was she so cold?

65

"You haven't lost it? The bracelet."

She jumped.

"What's the matter, Hellen?"

"Nothing. No, I haven't lost it." She was afraid to wear the bracelet. She was not certain she had the right, now. She turned round, leaning back against the rail with her elbows resting on the wood, looking at the band, seeing them only as a blur of white coats. They were playing "Till We Meet Again". It was one of the tunes she had danced to at the Ashtons', the evening Oliver proposed. She was lacerated with the pain of it.

"How would you like to leave the ship at Port Said and visit the pyramids at Giza? You should see the Sphinx."

"What?" She came back from a distance.

"Didn't you see the notice on the board? About visiting the pyramids."

She saw everything, but took in little.

"Transport has been laid on. We pick up the boat again at Suez." George's eyes were bright, encouraging.

"No, I think not. You go," she said. "I'd quite like to see the canal."

"I was looking forward to showing it all to you. I won't go if you don't want to. Let's dance." They moved off together.

"You're very quiet," he said again, sounding puzzled, or worried.

"I'm sorry. I don't mean to be."

"If you don't feel like dancing, we could play bridge."

"No, thanks. I like to dance." She toyed with the thought of asking him about hotels in Port Said, and immediately discarded it. She could not face his astonishment. She did not wish to answer his questions. Keep thinking. Keep going. Something might emerge.

Nothing emerged.

They came in to Port Said with its smells of sewage and dust; spices and sweat; oil from the ship's engine. They anchored a little way from the quay. Bum-boats came rushing out to meet them, bobbing and dancing on the water. One of them brought Major Tandy's laundry that he had dropped off at Simon Artz, the big department store, three months ago. White-gowned Egyptians with black hair and brown faces, balanced precariously in their little craft, offered black elephants with white tusks; multi-coloured rugs; prayer mats; embroidered blouses. There was a babble of excited voices.

"One English pound?"

"Two English pound, King George."

"Too much."

"How much you offer, then, King George?"

Silver bracelets, silver necklets, silver brooches. Turkish Delight. The treasures were transported to the deck in baskets dangling from long cords. George called to Hellen to come and look.

She made her way through the crowd of chattering passengers who had gathered on deck to watch the fun. George was offered the basket. He lifted out a filigree silver brooch in the shape of a crescent moon, with a star attached.

"How pretty."

"How much?" shouted George, leaning over the rail, cupping a hand to his mouth.

"Please, don't buy it for me. Please, no. You mustn't," Hellen protested.

"Six pound," called the brown man in the dirty galabiya and red fez.

"What?"

"Five pound."

She put a hand on George's arm. "Please," she protested, "you mustn't buy it for me. Really."

"Ten bob," bellowed George.

"Three pound," riposted the Egyptian.

George dug into his trousers pocket and withdrew two pound notes. "Never give the blighters what they ask. They don't expect it. Rule of thumb is one third, approx." He handed the brooch to Hellen, and put the money in the basket. As he let the rope over the side again he shouted robustly, "Two pounds."

The native's face split into a wide grin. "God save King George. You King George?" A chuckle ran through the crowd.

Hellen said with deep embarrassment, "It's awfully kind of you, but . . . haven't you got someone—"

"I want to give you a present." His hand reached out for hers, the fingertips pressing lightly.

She flushed as she pinned the unwanted gift to her dress. There was a flutter of excitement as the Gully Gully man appeared on deck, pulling chickens out of his breast pockets, from under his arms and out of his ears. Momentarily joining in the laughter, Hellen was able to forget.

"How about coming ashore this evening when it's cooler?" George asked when the Gully Gully man moved on. "I'd like to show you round. You really ought to see Simon Artz. It's very famous."

Simon Artz. Oliver had been going to take her there. He had said he would buy her a silken sari. She was to have it made into a dress when they reached Hong Kong.

"We could get a couple of rickshaws," said George.

67

A rickshaw. A kind of trap, or donkey cart, but with a man between the shifts. "You'll get used to it," Oliver had said as they sat close together in Sir Clancy's old banger on top of the ridge looking out over the moonlit Kentish fields. "It's the way everyone travels in Hong Kong."

Her first ride in a rickshaw was to have been with Oliver.

George was eyeing her curiously, wondering what had brought the gravity and the stillness back, when only a moment ago she had been laughing. Her eyes were slitted as she looked out across the turretted, minaretted, beige-coloured, foreign-looking town that could not possibly contain an hotel suitable for an English girl to stay in alone.

"Feelthy French post cards from Casablanca!" called an Egyptian in a dirty white galabiya and those red, turned-up-at-the-toe slippers that were being offered for sale.

George allowed himself to be swept away to examine the newest offering. Hellen wandered across the deck and stood within another group who were looking out on the quay. Those who were visiting the Pyramids were already going ashore in shady hats, carrying overnight bags. A tiny donkey staggered by, straining between the shafts of a cart more suitable for a shire horse. Its thin front legs buckled, and it sank to its knees. The driver, with a cry of anguish, swung a thonged whip over its head, then brought the whip down mercilessly on its back. Swung the whip again. Brought it down again. The donkey moved only to allow its head to fall, despairingly, to the ground.

Men in long white gowns erupted from everywhere, running, shouting, wielding sticks. They were angry on behalf of the donkey man. They surrounded the cart. Remorselessly, they shouted and struck, and struck again. The animal lay still.

Hellen, hands clasped tightly together across her chest, cried out in anguish: "Why doesn't somebody stop them?"

"This is Egypt." George's voice, at her side, sounded matter-of-fact.

She covered her face with her hands. All around her there were murmurings, but on the whole the colonial English took the incident in their stride. Then George was saying, "It's all right. It's dead, now." Hellen brought her hands down from her face. Her eyes were wide with outrage. Her palms were wet with tears.

"It's only a donkey," said George.

She looked up at his sweaty face in the shade of the panama hat. She did not speak, because she could not. She turned, and pushing her way through the crowd, went down to the stern rail.

He found her there five minutes later. "They're going ashore now," he said amiably. "Are you coming?"

She turned and looked at him with loathing.

He hesitated. Then, "Aw, come on," he said. "If you're going to live in the East. . . . Listen, Hellen, China is much worse than this. Maybe they're not so tough on animals, but with each other—" He sucked in his breath between his teeth. "I've seen men decapitated in the street. The Chinese are the cruellest nation on earth."

"I think I'd rather see it happen to a man," Hellen snapped.

He did not answer immediately. She could see he thought she was being silly. He was impatient with her silliness. "Come on," he said.

"I won't go ashore, thank you."

"Oh, come on. Everyone's going."

"Not everyone. Not me."

Later, sitting alone in the panelled ship's lounge, she made her decision. She could not stay in a place where people beat animals to death. She would go on. If she had not heard from Oliver by the time they reached Aden, she would cable him. The reply should reach her before they came in to Bombay. There would be hotels in British India where she could stay.

"Hello, young lady. Not going ashore?" Major Tandy was standing before her, his whisky-red face concerned.

She looked up at him with a sick smile. "I've just seen a donkey beaten to death."

"Ah, yes. Wogs," said the Major ruminatively. He screwed his monocle into the weak eye and regarded her gravely. "Mustn't mind what goes on outside England. Starts at Calais, y'know. Wogs begin at Calais. Have to make allowances. These foreigners, they don't know any better." He stamped lightly with one foot, and then the other. "You're not staying here on your own, are you? Come down to Simon Artz with Ruth and me. Do you good to get on terra firma for a while."

"Thank you, but no."

Ruth Washington joined him, looking down at Hellen on the sofa. She smiled, but did not speak as she took the major's arm. She had not forgiven Hellen for making her feel a gossip and a cat when she had been genuinely trying to help. She had not forgiven her, either, for going off in a pet and getting into George's bed. Now that she knew Hellen was an immoral girl, she did not even particularly like sharing the cabin with her. "Come on, Harry," she said.

The heat of the Suez Canal and the Red Sea was something Hellen would never forget. For part of the afternoon she would lie stifling in her bunk, because there she could rest naked—pulling the sheet modestly across her body if Mrs Washington should come in. Out on deck in the overwhelming heat where at least there was air, she would sit in a canvas chair beneath an awning, drinking glass after glass of the soft drinks the stewards brought on trays, fanning herself with the pretty fan George had brought her back from Simon Artz.

In this unreal landscape of beige-coloured sand and sparkling blue sea, relentless sun, and azure sky unbroken by even a puff of cloud, it was sometimes possible to shut off both the past and the future. The present became a kind of limbo. In the amazing cool of the evening she danced in her safe limbo, parrying questions, trying not to think.

"Your girl friend's gone quiet on us," remarked Major Tandy one day.

Ruth Washington shrugged. "She's feeling the heat."

Aden. Something had changed, but Hellen did not ask herself what it was. She only knew she was unwilling to commit herself to a cable. She had been sick again that morning. She went ashore with George and had a ride on a camel, but the relentless dry heat sent her back to the ship where there was at least a faint breeze. It was not until they were sailing in to Bombay that she allowed herself to know the reason why the cable had not been sent.

She stood beside her bunk consulting her little pocket diary. The first of May, the day Oliver sailed, was marked with a black cross. The next day, the worst day of her life, Lady Sylvia and Calum Finn had come. There was a tiny ring round the six on the calendar for May, when her next period was due, and another around the third of June, twenty-eight days later. Again, the first of July, three days before the boat was due to dock in Hong Kong.

She had always been regular. Yet, as she daily slid aside the discreetly wrapped packet in her draw in order to select clean underwear, she had not registered the fact that it was still intact. She had not allowed herself to know.

Never once, since that terrible day when Calum Finn raped her—was it rape?—had she allowed herself to consider the possibility that she might be pregnant. Now there was no shock, for tucked away in some part of her brain there had always been the knowledge that it could happen.

Calum Finn's baby! By the time the boat arrived at Hong Kong she would have missed three periods. Even if Oliver had won the battle, even if he arrived triumphant on the quay, she could not marry him. One did not foist someone else's baby on a man who, as Ruth Washington said, had "a pedigree as long as your arm". A child who might inherit an earldom. You did not foist someone else's child on a man whom you loved, and wait for that love to turn to hate.

"Hello," said Ruth brightly as she swung the cabin door open. "Getting ready for dinner? Shall I come back later?" There was so little room that they changed one at a time.

Oh, the comfort of another human being! Hellen said in an anxious, rushing voice, "No. Do come in, Mrs Washington. I'll climb up on to my bunk out of the way—"

"No, really." Ruth was surprised, even taken aback, at the unexpected welcome. "You were here first. Go ahead." She turned and abruptly left, closing the door behind her.

Hellen wanted to run after her, arms outstretched, crying, "Help me! Help me!" Instead, she said to herself with empty resignation: "If you do not give friendship, you do not get it." She had lost Ruth Washington as she had lost everything else. The forces had been beyond her control.

She did not disembark at Bombay, for disembarking meant returning to England and she was not yet ready to return. *Narkunda* was going to Australia. With those who were travelling to the Far East, she changed to *Devanha* for the China run. She thought about what her father had said: "Once you make your bed we shall expect you to lie on it." She had indeed made her bed. If she chose not to lie on it, she knew her parents would consider themselves disgraced. And Calum would hear. He knew what he had done in April. He could count the months to January. If he offered marriage, there would be no choice. Joe North, with his impeccable sense of right and wrong, would be on Calum's side. The baby should have its rightful father.

They were approaching Ceylon. There were a great many English people in Ceylon. In shipping. In tea. Might she possibly find herself a job? A clerical job of some sort? Just for a few months, until her employers guessed, and dismissed her. Would her sisters keep her secret, if she confided in them? Would they send her enough money to survive? Once the baby arrived, once it was all out in the open, someone might marry her.

Pigs might fly.

Should she simply end it all by slipping over the rail in the middle of a dark night? No one would then be hurt.

George Curtain said as they steamed out of Bombay, "You've never worn the brooch I bought you at Suez." It was between dances. They were leaning on the rail. The black waters curled away from the bow in a phosphorescent foam. The shoal of dolphins that had raced with them all day had turned away.

"I'm sorry. I'll wear it tomorrow. It was very kind of you to give it to me."

"You've got a problem, haven't you?"

She looked up at him. In the faint light of a sickle moon his face seemed kind. He seemed concerned.

"I just thought, you might like to unload it on to me."

If only she could! If only she could share this blackness with another human being. She said, "Yes, I have a problem. I am grateful for your offer, but there's really nothing you can do."

"You never know." He took a silver case out of his pocket, opened it and held it out to her. "Can I tempt you?"

She shook her head. "I've never smoked."

He selected a cigarette, put it in his mouth and turning so that his back was to the bow and the wind, struck a match. He tossed the match into the sea, took a long draw. The cigarette end glowed like a tiny beacon.

She asked diffidently, tracing a finger along the rail, "Do you know Ceylon?"

"Yes. I mean, I've spent holidays there. If you live in the east you go down to Penang, Ceylon, Singapore for occasional leaves, if you don't want to go to England."

"I'm thinking of getting off."

His head jerked up. She was surprised to see very real disappointment in his eyes. "Getting off at Ceylon! But why?"

Encouraged by his manner, she said, "I was going to get married in Hong Kong." It was a relief to let down the barrier just a little. "If I disembark at Ceylon, do you think I could stay there? I mean, do you know a place I could stay while I . . ."

"Think about things?" So that was why she had been so secretive! She hadn't been certain she wanted to go on with the marriage! He looked hard into her face, his own suddenly alight. His mind was in turmoil. The Governor's niece was in need of help, and he was here, on the spot, the only person on the whole damn boat who knew. Bloody luck! He put an expression of gravity and concern on his face. Take it carefully, George. This could be your lucky day.

"Who is this chap? Might I know him?"

"I'd rather not say."

"Meaning, I might know him?" George felt a quiver of uncertainty, not wanting to tread on toes that could kick back. But—bloody hell! Who could touch you if you were married to the Governor's niece?

He saw himself rolling up to Government House in white tie and tails. He saw his mantelpiece awash with invitations to houses on The Peak, and himself tossing one or two into the waste paper basket, because the senders had in the past ignored him. It was all he could do not to laugh aloud. In his mind the taipan of Linewood & Southby was saying benignly, "Well now, George, let's talk about promotion. I'm not certain you can keep the Governor's niece in the manner to which she is accustomed on your present salary." He saw himself

72

picnicking on the golden sands of Repulse Bay with the Governor's launch anchored off-shore.

He decided to strike while the iron was hot. Throwing the cigarette into the sea, he put an arm round Hellen's shoulders. She allowed it to lie there. It was comforting to be close to another human being. Any human being. The band had begun to play "Alice Blue Gown". Those who had been leaning on the rail moved amidships to the space cleared for dancing. George's arm steered her forward, but instead of going on to the dance floor, he headed towards the stern and the shadowy open deck. His heart was beating fast. He gave himself another moment or two to find just the right words, then stopped in a patch of darkness by a half open door.

"I think you should marry me," he said.

She looked up into his face, darkened now in the shadow cast by the door, and remembered that he had said, "It's only a donkey," when an animal had been beaten to death.

"I scarcely know you."

He laughed indulgently. "You've danced with me every night since we left England. You've partnered me at bridge, and listened to my prattle. Don't tell me you didn't notice me." His free arm came round her. She scarcely noticed he was holding her close. "I fell in love with you the moment I saw you, but naturally I couldn't say anything because—you must know there are rumours afloat that you're going out to get married. No decent chap would make up to another chap's girl," he added virtuously. "Tell me, if it's not an unfair question, why have you been so secretive, about it?"

"I wasn't sure."

"You were going to Hong Kong to have another look?"

"No. It wasn't like that. I did intend. . . ." She broke off, biting her lip.

"You can't face up to the drama? Or you're afraid he'll talk you into going ahead?"

It seemed easier to allow him his assumptions. "Something like that," she said edgily, casting around desperately for some way, at best to leave, at worst to change, the subject. "If you can't help me with regard to Ceylon, shall we dance?"

His arms tightened. "You could love me if you put your mind to it."

Out of the corner of her eye she saw the flick of a skirt and the door close by moved with a soft whoosh. She managed a little laugh, though she was vexed that someone might have heard George Curtain proposing to her. If that had been overheard it would be all over the ship within hours. "I wouldn't want to involve you in this mess," she said hurriedly, and then added, "I'd be grateful if you'd keep my problems to yourself. I'll get off at Colombo. I'll just leave. There'll be hotels—"

He cut her off with a finger against her lips. "Think about my option. Think about it, Hellen."

"I couldn't. I—"

"About the fact that I was besotted, the very first moment I set eyes on you. Think about that. Nothing else."

She thought about nothing other than being pregnant. She was sick with worry. Literally sick. She was terrified someone would come into the washroom and hear her retching.

She did not approach anyone else for help with a hotel, because now that the ship was nearing Colombo, passengers were talking about people they knew whose careers had taken them to Ceylon. Major Tandy was to be met by a planter. He would be whisked off to a plantation for the two days the ship would be in port. She did not want good-hearted passengers providing her with introductions to their respectable friends who would afterwards write outraged letters: "That girl you introduced to us, she's pregnant. . . ." Then it would be all over Hong Kong, and Oliver would hear. . . .

Sometimes she felt so boxed in by her apprehensions, so confused, that she found herself returning to her original thought of slipping over the rail and letting the warm waters envelop her. And then she thought of her family and knew she could not cause them such grief. But what was she doing to them anyway, in denying them their grandchild and refusing to return home if she could possibly find a way of staying?

One evening, when she was about to dress for dinner, Ruth Washington came into the cabin, closed the door behind her, and leaned against it. Her mouth was tight, but her eyes were concerned.

"Hellen," she said, "I've thought a lot about this, and I've decided to say my piece. It's rumoured that George Curtain has asked you to marry him."

Hellen opened her mouth to reply. Ruth put up a hand to stop her. "Let me have my say first. You've been extremely secretive with me, and I will say I have been hurt by your attitude. However, in light of what Major Tandy has told me, I must ask you to listen.

"That bracelet of yours." She paused portentously. "Harry says, and of course I should have recognised this myself, it bears part of the Marathon coat-of-arms." She softened a little, sounding puzzled. "My dear, it's almost as though we have a spy in our midst. I realise you're young, and maybe you're having a laugh at our expense, but its—simply—not—done."

"I—"

"No, dear. Please allow me to finish. The fact remains that people did recognise the leopard's head. It is now generally accepted that you are a relative of the Marathons."

"Mrs Wash—"

Ruth raised her hand again. "No. Major Tandy and I have decided this must be said. And by the way, do call me Ruth, dear.

"George Curtain is not, whatever he may have told you, a member of the set that revolves around Government House. He is not even accepted by those who live on The Peak—The Peak, as I am sure you know, is the only place to live. One has to get permission from the Governor in order to build or buy a house there. Now that the Hong Kongers know you are a relative of the Marathons—please, Hellen, I am determined to finish—they are genuinely concerned.

"George, you must realise, recognised that bracelet. You're a nice girl, Hellen, in spite of . . ." She stepped forward and took Hellen's cold hand in hers. "My dear, I cannot stand aside and see you used. The reason George is on this ship is because he was engaged to a girl who ran off with another man, and he ran after her. People were surprised that her parents allowed the engagement, but there you are. Girls can be headstrong. However, she came to her senses in time. She is now married to the other man, and George faces the bleak prospects of returning as—er—" She hesitated. "Bluntly, a laughing stock."

She squeezed Hellen's hand gently and smiled, woman to woman, friend to friend. "You know, dear, what a small colony it is, and there isn't a great deal to talk about. People can be cruel. The point I am trying to make, is, that if the rumours are true that George has asked you to marry him. . . ."

She contemplated Hellen's still face and heaved a sigh of exasperation. "We want you to know there will be no doubt in anyone's mind that he has done it for the wrong reasons. He would give his eye teeth for your connections. And he rather badly needs, at this time, to save face."

"I wasn't thinking of marrying George," said Hellen, smiling at Ruth with her mouth only. "Yes, he did propose to me. This ship must be just like Hong Kong. You said, if one changes one's toothpaste, everyone will know. You may put your friends' minds at rest, Mrs Wash—Ruth. I am not going to marry George Curtain. And thank you for the warning, but I'm perfectly able to look after myself."

Ruth could see the ice-cold sincerity in her eyes. She did not like Hellen any better for it, because she was not unbending an inch; flinging yet another of her offers of friendship in her face. But she

75

could see the girl was telling the truth. Such a shame. Such a pretty girl. And so well-connected.

Chapter 8
Singapore

"All is arranged," said George, businesslike, and at the same time, concerned. "All you have to do is wait for Mrs Washington to go ashore. Once she's safely down the gangplank, hustle along and pack your cabin bags. I've made arrangements for the big stuff to come up from the hold." They were steaming into the sea lanes off Singapore. On either side, tiny islands raised their friendly heads, here a craggy brown rock, there a mound of jungle green, and out in front, a plethora of junks, red-brown beaneath the blazing morning sun.

It was foreign, strange, beautiful, and incredibly hot. As she stepped out from under the deck awning, Hellen put her big straw hat on her head. There was no breeze to disturb hats, only the gentle movement of the hot, damp air as *Devanha* slid through a glassy sea. Over to the right a row of coconut palms reached at an angle for the sky. Behind lay the city that was to be her refuge, perhaps even her home. Looking out over the palms, she thought of it more as a jail, for there was no way, that she could see, of moving out of it, forward or back.

"If you must jump ship, then do so at a decent-sized place. I'm concerned for you, Hellen, I really am," George had said, adding engagingly that more time in her company meant more hope that she might capitulate. "Right up to the very last moment, if you should change your mind, the offer stands."

She had not even considered his offer. Allowing it into her consciousness meant opening up a whole new can of worms. Would he want to marry her if he knew she was pregnant? She knew the answer to that.

"Did the Purser protest about having to bring my trunks up?"

"Not at all. What else are pursers for, but to do the passengers' bidding?"

She did not like him when he adopted that autocratic manner. In fact, she was not certain, now she had been forced to think about him, that she liked him at all. She had accepted him carelessly when he pushed the other men away. He was a pair of feet, a pair of hands, which was all one needed for dancing whilst dreaming of someone else.

Now that he had taken her over, she was a little afraid of him, and afraid, too, that he might be unpleasant if she told him to stay away. She was puzzled by his newly acquired air of avuncular goodwill. It seemed out of keeping in a man who professed himself deeply in love. Perhaps he now saw the attraction for what it was, a kind of moon-madness. Perhaps he was really quite glad, after all, to be free, and was helping her out of genuine good nature.

This morning he had offered to give her a tour of the town. Though it seemed churlish to refuse, she had nonetheless done so.

"Oh, come on. I could give you an idea of the lay-out of the place."

"Thank you. I've decided to stay on board." She was afraid to go sight-seeing in case she panicked. When she did go ashore it would be with her luggage, so that there could be no bolting back to the ship. The terrors of Hong Kong had the treacherously delusive advantage of being a week away. Port Said, Bombay, Ceylon and Penang had failed her as bolt holes. She had to leave the ship here.

George said he would book her in at Raffles. "It's the most famous hotel in the East," he said. She had promised to lunch with him there. Her cabin trunk, the box and her suitcase would go ashore during the afternoon when the majority of the passengers were doing the town. She felt guilty about not saying good-bye, especially to Ruth and Major Tandy. Due to circumstances beyond my control, I have to be discourteous—again.

She said warmly, on the second day in port, as Ruth put on her white gloves and big hat, "Have a lovely day."

Ruth looked surprised, even faintly affronted, as though the good wishes had come rather late. "Thank you, my dear," she replied, reaching for her parasol. "Major Tandy and I are going to have lunch at Raffles." Hellen knew her presence there would serve to compound the insult of omitting to say she, also, would be lunching at Raffles, but she did not dare, in case Ruth suggested they go along together. She had to stay behind to pack. As her cabin mate went along the passage towards the companionway, Hellen began to empty her side of the wardrobe.

She descended the gangplank with George and stepped into a steamy cauldron. The air was dancing with the anxious clamour of Chinese, Malay, and Indian hawkers, stridently offering their wares. She wrinkled her nose, unwillingly smelling the scents of dried fish, sweet spices, unwashed bodies, musty clothes. It was like being in a gorgeously exotic swamp. She pushed her hair back from her face and settled her hat more squarely on her head for the sun was directly above, pressing the damp air down like a suffocating rug. Her cotton voile dress was already sticking to her body, and perspiration trickled down between her breasts.

They made their way through the noisy crowd. "Mind if I go in front and clear the way?" asked George, pushing past without waiting for an answer, waving his arms, shooing the natives as Leo, at Jolliffe's Farm, shooed the sheep into and out of, pens. Remembering Port Said, Hellen imagined a small Malay being trampled fatally underfoot and George saying, "It's only a native. . . ."

They emerged from the frantic crowd at a row of jinrickshas, all clamouring for business. "Jin, that's Malay for man," George said, knowledgeably. "Ricksha, the buggy. We call them rickshaws in Hong Kong. Hop aboard." He helped her into the hooded seat of the nearest ricksha, then set about fixing a price for the fare. "Never pay them what they ask. That's your motto." The natives in their loin cloths were desperately thin, their ribs pushing the brown skin outwards, leaving a trench between each bone. Hellen looked away, appalled. George took another ricksha. The coolies ran side-by-side along a tree-lined road. Feeling ashamed at running away, and sad, Hellen leaned forward for a last glimpse of *Devanha*. She wondered what George's answer was going to be when passengers said, "The last we saw of her, she was with you. You must know where she is."

She shivered, and drew back beneath the hood, trying to still her thoughts, failing, turning her attention instead to the emaciated hawkers shuffling alongside, persistently pushing their wares under her nose. She slipped one of them a Singapore dollar. The others saw, and closed in like a swarm of bees so that her beast of burden—she could not think of him as otherwise—was brought to a halt.

George jumped out. "What the blazes is going on?" he shouted over the babble.

Ashamed, and a little frightened, Hellen cowered beneath her hood, remembering too late what Ruth had said: "You may not approve of the way life is lived in the East, but you're not going to change it."

"Get on," shouted George, waving his arms angrily, and the hawkers fell back.

They came to a halt in the shade of flame trees and entered the hotel beneath arches, then into a hall crimson-carpeted as though for royalty, and set with bronze statues on plinths. Hellen paused to look round her at the massive carved doors, the galleries supported by ornate columns and arches, the elaborately ornamented skylight, the palms dipping elegantly over the rim of massive brass bowls.

"That's the Long Bar," said George, knowledgeable again. "It's the meeting place for up-country planters." He surveyed the line of men, mainly dressed in white suits, standing relaxed with glasses in their hands as though he might, just might, happen to know one of them. They stared blatantly at Hellen. Fashionable women in big, shady hats glanced up without particular curiosity. George indicated a table, and led her towards it.

"What would you like to drink?"

"Something cool, please."

"Lime?"

"Thank you. Yes."

They settled into the low chairs. Hellen removed her gloves. Chinese waiters in white jackets moved silently between the tables with silver trays. George gave her order. "And a stinger for me." The fans in the high ceiling whirred like frantic moths. Hellen wondered why George should have thought this a suitable place for her to stay on her own. Tomorrow, immediately after breakfast, she decided, she would set about finding a less central, more modest hotel.

"What's a stinger, George?"

"Stengah. Whiskey and soda. Everyone drinks it, here." He was making a great show of being at home in this very grand hotel. "I'm going to insist you join me in a bottle of wine over lunch. This is, after all, our last day together. Not a reason for celebration, but we could celebrate the fun we've had." He leaned towards her, legs wide apart, hands on his knees, his smile beguiling, "It was fun for you, wasn't it?"

"Yes." She smiled automatically. She had just glimpsed Ruth and Major Tandy across the lounge.

"May I have permission to propose again, for the last time?"

She should not have come. She should have known he would apply pressure, and then she would feel churlish at having to refuse. With eyes cast down, she replied miserably, "I wouldn't have accepted the invitation if I had thought—"

" 'Nuff said. 'Nuff said." Good-humouredly, George raised a hand. The waiter brought their drinks. She picked up hers clumsily, feeling irrationally nervous because George was being so reasonable.

Out of the corner of her eye she saw emerging from the archway people whose faces were familiar. George waved, deliberately attracting their attention. A little group came over and stayed a moment to chat, but George did not ask them to sit down. "We're about to go in to tiffin," he said. "Tiffin," he told her, when they had gone, "is lunch, in case you didn't know."

She noticed his eyes were over-bright. He put down his glass with a bang on the table. His hands were everywhere, picking up the ashtray, putting it down again. He crossed his legs; uncrossed them. "Let's go." He stood up abruptly. "Hello, there's old smarty-pants Crawshaw who took a tenner off me at poker the other night." He waved. "And Mrs Hazeldene. And—good God! Half the jolly old ship." He sounded very pleased indeed that half the jolly old ship was there.

Hellen smiled vaguely at the passengers from *Devanha* whom, inevitably, they passed on their way to the dining hall. Or was it the tiffin room? George slid an arm through hers. She did not look back, but she had a feeling many eyes lifted and followed them in. The room was T-shaped, of exceptional grandeur, with fine mouldings and the same magnificent columns as she had seen in the hall. Partially hidden behind a screen of palms, an orchestra of small brown men softly played a Mozart sonata.

"Filipinos," said George in that new, confident, knowledgeable way.

It was three o'clock before their tiffin was over. George made her feel she could not refuse the wine, topping up her glass more often than she would have wished. He made it clear that he would be hurt if she did not enjoy herself on this, their last day together. "Come on," he said, holding the wine bottle over her glass which she was hesitantly trying to draw away, "another mouthful won't do you any harm."

She felt a little tipsy as she stood on the verandah looking out over the traveller's palms, her edgy suspicions mellowed by the wine. She thought she was ready to face the future, now, whatever it might bring.

George pulled his watch out of his waistcoat pocket. "Now, what are we going to do with you for the next couple of hours?" he asked himself, still using the proprietorial manner he had adopted when he first began making arrangements for her to disembark. "Presumably, you won't want to go down to the quay and wave the ship away?" He laughed at the thought. "No, you wouldn't do that. No, of course not."

She swung round towards the foyer. "I'll let you go. I'd like to check on my room."

"Let me go?" echoed George in a hurt voice. "On our last day together! The room's all fixed up. Don't you trust me to do things properly?" He sounded hurt. "Don't you think I'm a very efficient chap? Mr Fix-it, that's me," he said.

"Of course. You've been very good."

He slipped his hand through her elbow, holding it firmly against his side. "Don't worry about your luggage. I'll tell you what," he pulled his watch out again and gazed thoughtfully down at the face, "the ship sails at six. I've got to call and see a chap on one of our company's trading ships. It's only a short distance along the waterfront. Just a nice little ride. Why don't you come with me? Then, I'll bring you back here and it'll be time for me to go aboard."

"I'd really rather—"

"Oh, come. Dropping me like a hot cake?" His tone inferred that she was lacking in gratitude.

She flushed. "Very well."

The jinrickshas were curled up on the ground beneath the flame trees in the shade. The two in front unrolled themselves languidly and went to stand between their shafts.

The Lonewood & Southby trader *Bangkok Lady*, standing off from the quay, was less than half the size of *Devanha*. George said she was carrying a load of indigo to Hong Kong. "And a little opium to smuggle in to Canton," he added, a conspiratorial finger to his lips as they went aboard the tender. " 'Nuff said."

Hellen, striving to stand erect in the wobbly little craft, asked in surprise, "Does your company allow that?"

"What do you think?" He winked, drawing her in with his special knowledge. They sped across the short stretch of water and tied up near the steamer's stern. George helped her up the companionway.

His friend, whom he introduced as Charlie Marsh, gripped Hellen's hand so painfully hard that she withdrew it in some indignation. "I'm too strong, that's me trouble," he said with a leer. He was a short man, squarely built, with black eyebrows bushing over eyes that had a faintly oriental look, uptilted at the sides and heavily seamed by exposure to the sun. But there was nothing oriental about his wide, thin mouth and long nose. Hellen disliked him on sight. He led the way through an open doorway into a sizeable saloon that was furnished at one end with a trestle-type dining table and some rattan chairs. At the opposite end there were four armchairs in faded covers. The saloon was grubby, smelling of rank tobacco and a little of rum. Hellen wished fervently she had stood her ground and stayed at Raffles.

Their unprepossessing host silently indicated the armchairs, and they seated themselves. He clapped his hands and a coolie appeared in the doorway. "Wotcha want to drink, Miss?" asked Charlie Marsh.

"A soft drink, please."

"Fruit? There's some good stuff here. Tropical mixes. Try one?"

"Yes, thank you." She was glad of the offer of a fruit drink, for her mouth was dry from the wine.

"And you, George? The usual? Stinger?"

"Thanks. It won't go with the wine we had for lunch," he said, still in that exceptionally good-humoured voice, "but who could refuse?" He tossed his hat down on a chair. The coolie went silently away.

The saloon was stifling. Hellen rose and went to stand in the doorway, looking out over the water. George rose also, and came to stand beside her. They fanned themselves with their hands. The boy brought the drinks on a tray. There was a tall glass for her, full of a pale yellow liquid that was a darker shade at the bottom.

"What is it?"

Charlie Marsh was watching her with an openly offensive smile on his face, almost, she thought with distaste, as though he knew something about her that George did not. Or something about George, that she did not.

"Fruit," he said. "'Ere, give it a stir." He pulled out a drawer and produced a piece of wood, pencil-shaped. "Ever seen a chopstick?"

Hellen shook her head.

"Give it a stir," he repeated. "That's passion fruit at the bottom. The rest is papaya and stuff. Good for you."

"Drink it down," said George. "Don't sip. I'm sure there's plenty more where that came from. The fruit here is wonderful."

"It's delicious." It tasted of every fruit in the world. Hellen smiled at them both. "How exotic!"

"Have another."

"Yes, I'll have another." She upended the glass. Only when she finished did she notice a very odd taste in the last mouthful. She ran her tongue across her lips; frowned.

Charlie Marsh laughed. George smiled. He took her by the arm and led her back into the saloon. She was glad to sit down. She leant back, feeling relaxed.

"What are you doing with that?" asked Ruth sharply, looking down at Hellen's suitcase.

"Tell her," said George, eyeing the cabin steward, deadpan.

"Missie want bag," said the coolie, looking nervous.

"Straight from the horse's mouth," said George.

"But she's not leaving the ship." Ruth's voice rose.

"Does she tell you everything?" George's eyes were knowing.

Ruth said afterwards, "It was true. You did not tell me anything at all."

"I wanted to," said Hellen. "I needed you. But I was afraid. Not of you. Of . . ."

"You thought I would gossip."

"You talked of gossip all the time." She could not say, "You gossiped," for that would have been rude, even unfair, since Ruth's gossip, warning her about George, had been given with the best will in the world.

The Purser watched George cross the deck, pick up his own suitcase in his free hand, then go down the gangplank and set out along the quay. The crisp English bank notes in his pocket did not touch his conscience. The Chinese had a term for it: the Squeeze. Business could not be conducted in the east without the Squeeze. Its rules were simple. You took the money, made possible what you and only you could fix, and kept your mouth shut. It was a system that worked. Back in England the Purser was buying a house on Squeeze money.

Feeling distinctly unhappy, Ruth went in search of Harry Tandy. The ship's siren gave its first warning boom. She found the Major standing at the rail looking down on to the quay, watching the late comers hurrying through a clamouring mêlée of coolies towards the gangplank. He turned as she came up beside him.

"Hello, Ruth. Saw that queer coot George Curtain going ashore with two suitcases, what! Has he left us?"

"Two?"

"Yes. Two big ones. Won't need to worry about our little girl friend any more," he said, looking gratified.

She watched the stragglers hustling up the gangplank with their parcels, all laughing and chattering. One of the white-uniformed officers said, "Right, that seems to be it," and the gangplank came up.

Passengers jostled for a place at the rail. Multi-coloured paper streamers flew through the air, their ends falling on the quay. *Devanha* pulled away, the streamers popping and floating prettily down into the water. There were cries of "Good luck," and "Come and see us again," and "Bon voyage." Ruth scanned the crowd uselessly, willing Hellen to come dashing along the quay. The ship backed into the water road, and began to turn.

"Better think about having a clean-up before dinner, I s'pose," said the Major. "Meet you for a drink, later?"

Ruth nodded. "In half an hour." She went slowly along the deck, into the lounge and down the companionway. A steward was locking her door. She called to him to leave it open. He pushed it wide and stood aside as she passed.

There was an invitation to drinks in the Captain's cabin, and beside it a cable. She picked up the envelope, wondering who could possibly

84

be contacting her, and why. It was addressed to Miss Hellen North. She stared at it for a long moment. Then, quite without conscience, she picked up a nail file, slit the envelope open, and unfolded the single sheet.

DARLING HELLEN STOP PERMISSION TO MARRY GRANTED STOP ALL ARRANGED FOR TENTH JULY STOP LOVE OLIVER.

When the numbness went, when Ruth could think again, the memories flew in, across the troubled weeks. The red roses. Hellen, her face glowing, holding them to her heart. The girl's warm, excited laughter as her wooden frog wobbled, fell, and rose again; her silver shoes flashing in a fast foxtrot; her exceptionally beautiful clothes. Trousseau clothes!

And she had gone off with George Curtain!

In an explosion of logic, Ruth knew it was her fault.

Dear God, forgive me.

When she went to join Major Tandy the tears were still in her eyes. She sat down beside him, looking into his kindly, concerned face. "If you happen to have a revolver on you, Harry," she said, her voice trembling conspicuously, "shoot me right through the heart."

Hellen wakened with a dry mouth and a thumping head. She opened her eyes, then blinked. The cabin was unfamiliar. She jerked up on one elbow and looked round. One bunk! And it was twice the width of the one on *Devanha*. There was a bare light bulb in a wire cage on the low ceiling; a tiny wardrobe in the corner. This was not her cabin! Not the same light. Not the same wardrobe. Not even the same ceiling! This ceiling was made of rough planks, with studs, or nail heads, showing. The noise of the engines, too, had an unfamiliar sound. They were quicker, noisier than those of *Devanha*. Through a porthole, foggy with spray, she saw moving clouds. No, it was the boat that was moving. They were under way.

And beneath this sheet, she was naked!

She threw the sheet back and leaped to her feet, trembling. Then something caught her eye. She stood looking down numbly at a dark stain on the white under sheet. She tentatively touched it. Make it be dry. Make the sheet be someone else's, already used. Her fingers came away damp and sticky. And now, she felt something trickling down the inside of her legs. Her heart nearly stopped beating.

The door rattled faintly, then opened, slow as an oil slick. She snatched up the sheet, holding it across her front, staring at the door, mesmerised, breath held while she waited with sick horror to see who would appear.

"Hello," said George, smiling, looking pleased to find her awake. The smile faded, a startled look came into his eyes and he bent down, taking hold of a corner of the sheet and deftly tossing it over the stain. Straightening, he put a finger beneath her chin. "Poor Hellen," he said. Shrinking from him, clutching at the sheet, she backed on to the bunk. "Poor Helen," said George again. "What on earth happened? You didn't have too much to drink at lunch, did you? I wouldn't have thought you had. And Charlie swore he gave you fruit juice."

She knew now where she was. On the cargo boat, *Bangkok Lady*, beating up through the South China Sea, going to Hong Kong, in the company of George Curtain, and pregnant with Calum Finn's child.

Yesterday flashed through her mind. Lunch at Raffles Hotel, and George's unlikely air of excitement; his deliberate efforts to be noticed by *Devanha* passengers, waving to them as they came into the lounge. His insistence that there was no need to check on her room at Raffles, or to enquire as to whether her luggage had arrived.

She looked down at the floor, saw her suitcase, and next to it, one marked "Mr George Curtain, Hong Kong".

She screamed at him.

She scarcely saw him move, it happened so fast. One arm was round her shoulders, holding her to him, the other across her mouth. "There, there, darling." His voice was soothing, but very, very firm. "We don't scream on little traders. Everyone would hear, and then what would they think?"

She hurled herself away from him, still clutching her sheet, sobbing. Through her terror and despair she was aware of his calculated waiting; he would do nothing, say nothing, until she was calm. The knowledge that he was totally in control brought her to a state of insubstantial, frightened quiet. She backed to the bunk, and sat down.

"They would think you drugged my drink." She broke down, sobbing.

He sat beside her and was gentle with her. "I didn't spike your drink," he said, sounding tolerant about her accusation. "And there's no reason in the world why the coolies should have done so. I should think it was a combination of the heat, and the wine you had for lunch. Maybe the unaccustomed food. And . . ." he shrugged. "Goodness knows. These things happen.

"Now I ask you, would you have liked me to carry you back into Raffles, slung over my shoulder like a sack of coal? I tell you, they would have shown you the door. A place like Raffles!" He turned his eyes to the ceiling, emitting an awed, "Whew! You know I was dead against your getting off at Singapore without knowing a soul. You

86

know that, Hellen." He smoothed her hair with gentle fingers. "It simply isn't done for your kind of girl to land up in the tropics on your own. I had no way of knowing if you had any money. I naturally booked you in at Raffles because it was the only place I knew, and it's respectable, but I could see you were edgy about it. I did wonder if I had been a bit arbitrary. If you really couldn't afford it, I mean," he added, looking suitably embarrassed.

"Both boats were sailing," he continued. "I was responsible for you. I had to make up my mind. I rushed up to Raffles and got your stuff, then down to *Devanha* for mine. What else could I do?" asked George the cavalier. "I thought, there's plenty of time for you to sort yourself out. *Bangkok Lady* is going to be slower than *Devanha* and no one in Hong Kong will expect you to be aboard. If you want to slip off and catch another boat home, I could arrange it. My parents would look after you. They live well away from"—they live—I mean, they're across from the island, in Kowloon." Christ! He had nearly said, "Well away from Government House!" Having collected himself, he continued, "If you haven't got the money for your fare home, I dare say I could raise it.

"At least I would be easy in my mind about you," he added. "I'd know you were safe." He bent down and kissed her very, very gently on the forehead. "I love you, Hellen. I'd do anything in the world for you. You know that."

She allowed the lies to flow over her, an unstoppable tide, and as she listened her safety net slipped, fell into the receding foam of hope, and floated away. She did not suggest that he would never have treated her this way if he loved her. She stopped herself in time from saying she did not believe her luggage went to Raffles, and nor did she believe he had even booked a room for her. There would be a small, savage satisfaction in indicting him, but would it be worth planting seeds of a poisonous fungus between them?

She looked down at the soiled bed. "Had it not occurred to you that I might like a cabin to myself?" she asked bleakly.

"There's no more accommodation. We've actually taken over the Captain's cabin. He's sleeping in his office."

Gradually, she gathered her wits together. "You put the Captain out of his cabin?" she asked in disbelief. She thought he looked evasive.

"I've got influence," he said. "Lonewood & Southby own the tub." She was silenced, the rush of doubt—"But you're only one of their employees"—sliding away, for she could tell by his manner no further explanation would be forthcoming.

George was quiet. In the silence, within her madness and shock, she asked herself if this man who had her in his clamp of deception was wicked enough to be punished with someone else's child. It was very possible, at that moment, to believe that someone who could watch a donkey whipped to death and say, "It's only a donkey," deserved what he got.

A quick glimpse of sanity, and she asked herself if she could love, honour and obey such a man; if, when his professed love turned to hate, she could be steadfast, and strong enough to find sufficient love for both of them, and for the child she did not want. He would pass as a husband. She knew from Ruth where he worked, what he did, what his father did, and that the family were that dreadful thing, socially not quite. . . On that level, at least, they had something in common.

"I will marry you, George—"Dear God, I am going mad! What am I saying? She swallowed. She had to go on. He was looking at her, his face lit up with some awful mixture of greed and desire. She could not stop now. "—since that is what you seem to want so badly." It was out. He would turn her down. He would say no, because he would hear the bitterness in her trapped voice, and know that she did not want to marry him now, any more than she had wanted to before he did that dreadful thing to her. But he did not speak. He didn't open his mouth, and suddenly some crazed voice was coming out of her mouth saying, "Perhaps the Captain could do it? It's legal, is it not, anywhere at sea, providing one is three miles from land?"

George's arms tightened round her. "Never venture, never win," Charlie Marsh had said. In the circumstances, the trite little phrase seemed crude. He thought, with immense gratitude, that someone up there must have decided, at long last, to relent and give him a break. He felt himself to be in a state of grace. From the bottom of his heart, and with a sense of new-found humility, he said a silent thank you as he kissed his prospective bride, his prize for being a clever chap, on the lips.

Chapter 9

The Pirates

Afterwards, what Hellen remembered of that joyless marriage was the Captain's navy sleeves and white cuffs with rough brown hands sticking out of them: longish nails outlined in black, on his fingers brown spots that were bigger than freckles, a few black hairs on the backs of his hands. And then, the sense of shock when George slipped a ring on her finger. Where had it come from, that ring, that evidence of his diabolical confidence? She had a feeling of the teeth of a trap closing, and grinding down.

There was white paper. A ship's log? A notebook? She never recalled the details, only the fact that a pen was put into her hand and she was asked to sign, "There." She stared down at the pen. In that moment she was fuzzily aware that in signing her name she would make Oliver's career safe; that her signature on this paper meant he would not hate her for bearing Calum Finn's child.

"Sign there," repeated the ship's Captain. She looked up, seeing his face with surprise. He was rather like a grim moose with a small, black, human being's beard. He was not pleased at having to perform this marriage. He did not like George. Without knowing her, for he did not wish to know her, he thought her trash.

"Sign there," he said for the third time, sounding brusque now, wanting the whole unpleasant business over.

She dipped the pen in the ink and wrote Helle—Her pen slipped. A great pain, stupefying in its intensity, shot through her loins. She felt as though she was coming apart. And then, slowly creeping, a warm trickle started down the inside of her legs. A feeling of amazement swept through her, followed immediately by sheer terror as her eyes met the guarded, watchful gaze of the two men who had come to act as witnesses, the appalling Charlie Marsh, and a rough-looking seaman with a scarred face and greasy hair.

"Go on," said George, his voice high and sharp. She sensed in him a trembling panic with violence at its edge. The other three, without moving, seemed to close in on her, like three black threats. In the silence she could hear their breathing, and smell the rank tobacco in their clothes. Beyond them was the bigger circle of the great inhospitable ocean, more pitiless even than they. A gull swooped out of the sky, screaming.

Her fingers stiffened. The pen dropped and rolled away as the deck lifted on a capricious wave. Someone fell on his knees to retrieve the pen. George moved closer. She could smell his sweat. She turned to him, silently begging for mercy, and met his cold, piercing eyes.

A hand pushed the pen under her nose. Without consciously accepting it, she was aware it was again between the first two fingers of her right hand and her thumb. You must sign your name; you have come to this, the silence and the man strength of them said. It is too late to turn back; it is not allowed.

The pen was impatiently taken out of her hand, dipped in the ink pot and handed back to her. "There," said George implacably, pointing. "There."

In a frozen instant, filled with outrage and utter despair, she wrote "n" to complete her christian name. Then "North".

Back in the cabin—she did not remember going—she bent over her suitcase, which had not been unpacked because there was nowhere to put her things, rummaged among the clothes and found the packet. "What's the matter?" asked George, standing in the doorway, relaxed now, ready to be amiable, but faintly non-plussed.

"Something's happened," she said numbly.

He came forward, looking down at the packet as she lifted it out of the bag, then he turned and walked out. She went along the passage to the primitive little bathroom with its wet concrete floor, its round, smelly black hole in the corner with the sinister sound of sloshing water below, and its stained basin. She did what she had to do, then came back and lay on the bed. Sweat poured down her face as pain engulfed her in great waves, taking her to the edge of reason, and back. Was there a doctor on board? She knew there was not. Did one need a doctor for a miscarriage?

Hours later, George came in. He sat on the edge of the wide bunk, looking down at her, saying nothing. It was a relief to see another human being. She did not think of him as a husband, only someone whose hand she might touch, if only to prove to herself that she was not totally alone in the world. Tentatively, she reached out, but he did not see the hand.

"Dashed queer thing to happen," he said.

The whole sorry disaster reared up and enveloped her. She wanted

90

to lean up against him and empty herself of tears. He was her sole comfort. He was all she had. But he was offering only curiosity, and showing faint distaste. She withdrew the tentative fingers and closed her eyes, biting her lips, holding on to her grief, which she must endure alone. When her lids fluttered up again, he had gone.

She lay there, bruised and despairing, lonely and homesick for Jolliffe's Farm and her horses, the black and white Muscovy ducks with the red nobs on their bills, riding all day on the leaf-shadowed pond, waddling across the grass and into the wooden duck house at night; the chickens who laid the brown eggs in boxes lined with straw, and the handsome Red Orpington cock-of-the-walk who crowed every morning at dawn. The farm dogs, and sweet Minnow, the family pet, who lived in the stable and sometimes came into the house. . . .

Simultaneously with the memory of Minnow came the blinding truth. She saw Mr Bale, the vet, standing hands in pockets, sympathetically smiling. "She sincerely thought she was going to have puppies," he said, "and went into simulated pregnancy. Nature plays tricks on us, sometimes. I've given her something to relieve her. She'll be all right, now."

Hellen stared at the low planked ceiling with its rough beams and knot holes and nail heads, trying to come to terms with the fact that the cruel and vengeful gods had caught her in a noose of George's weaving. Ship sounds penetrated the cabin walls; lusty shouts, the raucous cry of seabirds, and the muted roar of the ocean. She lay with eyes closed, comfortless and empty. And in the end, she drifted off to sleep.

She was up and dressed when George came to ask if she wanted her supper brought in. "You made a remarkable recovery," he said, clearly relieved. He took her hands, bent down and kissed her. She looked into his face for signs that he loved her; she looked for something she might love. She felt her mouth go thin and stiff. She did not kiss him in return. Her mouth did not relent.

They spent their days on deck, watching the dolphins cavorting about the bow, and seabirds that came out from the not too distant land; watching the black soot from the engines flying off into the sky; smelling the salt from the sea. They, Mr and Mrs Curtain, Hellen and George Curtain, were the only passengers.

They lived on the bridge deck with the Captain of the unlovely little cargo steamer, and his first officer, because that was the way the ship was built, the main body given over to cargo. Captain Boggis said bluntly he did not mind the odd missionary who had to find his way from one place to another, who anyway could be consigned below with the crew out of his way, or a seaman catching up with his ship, but ordinary travellers should stick to the passenger lines. That was what they were there for. Passengers.

Hellen could not help wondering how George had managed to obtain a passage from so unwilling a host, much less take over the Captain's cabin. As far as possible, Boggis avoided them. Hellen suspected his dislike of passengers was not general. She thought, had she met him in different circumstances, she might have liked him. She tried very hard to avoid Charlie Marsh, unfairly blaming him for doctoring her drink because it was unacceptable to blame George for that. For better or worse, he was her husband now.

The marriage had not, as yet, been consummated. She was forced to explain, with considerable embarrassment, that she was bleeding. She hoped George knew what she meant. She did not know if men were aware of the workings of a woman's inside.

'I don't mind,' George said.

'I do,' she snapped back. It was the only time she allowed herself to be sharp with him. She was his wife. She had to make a go of this marriage. But it had been something of a relief to let go.

'Where shall we live?' she asked the next day as they sat out on deck. She pulled her big hat, the one she had worn ashore at Singapore, the one that had, by great good luck, gone with her to *Bangkok Lady*, down over her forehead to protect her eyes. She no longer made any effort to guard her complexion. She knew from the spotted looking glass on the wall of their cabin that a glaring sum reflecting back from a glittering sea was tanning her skin. There were freckles on her nose. She did not care. In the recesses of her mind there were black vengeances that she preferred not to examine. One was that George did not deserve her beauty.

"I suppose we'll have to go to my parents to start with," George replied, looking at her sideways, waiting for her to say of course they must live on The Peak because, as it happened, her uncle was the Governor of the colony, and no doubt he would put them up meantime at Government House. He composed his face gravely, ready to show suitable amazement.

Instead, she said, "You told me they live at Kowloon. Where's that?"

"Across from Hong Kong island. On the mainland. But you'll want to live on the island, won't you?" He stopped himself just in time from adding, "On The Peak."

She was thinking, painfully—the pain was almost unbearable when she thought about how she had let Oliver down—that Ruth had said one must get permission from the Governor to live on The Peak. Hellen had a confused notion that living on the island meant, for the English, living on The Peak.

"Wouldn't you?" persisted George.

"I don't mind," she said indifferently. "Perhaps we should live near your parents."

He frowned.

Two gulls swooped on something one of the crew had tossed on to the lower deck, then winged away. "Aren't you going to tell me who you were going to marry? It's a small place, Hong Kong. You never know," George grinned, the victor considering the vanquished, "he might want to plug me in the eye. I really ought to be warned."

"There's no reason why you should know," she replied edgily. "Why you should ever know. There's nothing he can do," she said in a dull voice. "We're married, aren't we?"

He frowned, feeling a prickle of discomfort. "You're bound to feel—er—guilty," he said, "for a while." For the first time he felt an ebbing of confidence. He was not very proud of the escapade, but at least he was clear in his mind on one thing. He had had no part in her decision not to marry this buster, whoever he was. George still could not believe his luck, although admittedly things weren't going too well. Hellen was tensed up, and old Boggis, the fart, didn't help by making them feel unwelcome. But all would be well when things were on a normal footing. Crikey, he'd hotted up cooler girls than this one.

"Tell me about your horses."

"I've told you. Persimmon and Merry Astor."

"Two horses, and you don't hunt?"

"I do hunt. With the Old Forest." She had nothing to lose, now.

George had heard of the Old Forest. It was the Quorn of the south. He moved pleasurably on the hard boards, readjusting his position, seeing himself seated in the dining room at Government House, with the glittering chandeliers shedding light on polished silver candlesticks and Waterford glass. He had never dined at Upper Albert Road, but he knew Lady Marathon's dinner parties to be very grand. He heard himself saying, casually, confidently, to the visiting Admiral who was seated on Hellen's other side—Hellen looking stunning in one of those expensive-looking dresses of hers—"Yes, I ride. But my wife's the one who knows about horses. Talk to her. She hunted with the Old Forest." George longed, not so much for importance as for acceptance at his own estimation of himself.

"Why did you tell people on the boat that you didn't hunt?"

Ah, yes. There were questions to be answered. She hoped Ruth

93

was mistaken in assuming George wanted her because he thought she was related to the Marathons. She did not like the thought of disappointing him. Not loving him did not mean she wished to hurt him. Then Charlie Marsh's appearance on deck sounded a warning note, and she thought how absolutely silly it would be to risk upsetting this new husband-in-name. She did not know him in adversity and disappointment. Here, she realised with an inner tremor of something akin to fear, she was totally defenceless.

"I didn't want to look back," she said, pulling out an excuse that was more than half-way true. "I didn't want to divert conversation my way when there was so much to learn about Hong Kong."

"Listen, fathead," he patted her hand affectionately, hiding his frustration, "we're husband and wife. Don't we want to know all about each other, and if not, why not?"

Reacting with heat, because Marsh's arrival had made her nervous, she began, "You for—" then broke off.

"I what?"

She had been going to say tartly that he had forced her into this marriage without knowing anything about her, so why bother now? But she had not been forced. She must remember that. Nobody had stood over her with a gun.

"You've got what you wanted," she muttered. "Now you must allow me time to readjust."

George hitched up his flannels, rose to his feet, and wandered off across the deck, whistling. Sometimes he worried about the fact that Hellen's decision to disembark at Singapore might have been made out of a genuine desire to give herself a little more time. He didn't like admitting it to himself, but it was true that she never had said in so many words she had made a definite decision to jilt this joker. Her steamer ticket was still valid if she decided to catch the next P & O and continue on to Hong Kong.

Now he was becoming worried about her holding him off. If he didn't consummate the marriage before landfall, he was going to be on a sticky wicket. She could have him for abduction and rape—that is, if Sir Rowan Marathon would stand the publicity. And from what he knew of the Governor, George thought with very real apprehension, he'd find a way.

He shouldn't have got drunk. That was his big error. That was what she was holding against him. It was typical of George that he could so easily put out of his mind the real issue. Horsing around with Charlie Marsh, euphoric over the fact that his plan had actually worked, he hadn't stopped to think. The booze had made him randy. Oh hell, he'd decided, why not, she'll never know. But he had forgotten about

94

the sheet. Any girl would be resentful on discovering she had been knocked up while she slept.

In another three days they would be docking in Hong Kong. George lifted his head and shook back his shoulders. He was going to have to push her along. He took out his silver case, selected a cigarette and lit it, then leaned over the rail, morosely watching the foam curling away from the bow, smoking his cigarette through to the end. He tossed the butt into the water, then went through the open door into the saloon.

"Boy!" he shouted. A coolie appeared. "Get me a rum, boy, and be quick about it."

"Lime for Missie?"

George glared at him. I'll fix you, you cheeky bugger, he said to himself. Damned Chows!

It was early morning and they were approaching Lantau, the largest island in the group, when Captain Boggis sighted the lorcha. He put his head out of the wheel house to call his first mate. "Come 'ere, Mr Marsh." Then pointing to a vessel lying ahead, "What d'you make of that?"

Charlie Marsh leaned his elbows on the bridge rail, screwed up his seamed dark eyes and stared out across the grey water. It was one of those fast junks, too big for a mere fishing boat, probably engine-powered. In spite of the fact that there was a stiff breeze, her sails were lowered and she was standing still, directly in the path of *Bangkok Lady*. The first mate sucked in his breath noisily through his teeth.

"I don't like the look of it, sir. I'd say they was usin' their engines to hold against the wind."

The captain's hands tightened on the wheel. During all his years of plying the China Seas in small, and therefore vulnerable, ships, he had never yet been attacked by pirates. But he had been lucky. He knew for a fact there were dozens of caves that were pirate lairs on the outlying islands of Cheung Chau and Lantau.

"That bloody girl," he burst out, giving way to his seaman's innate superstition, "I knew she'd bring us bad luck. I should have turfed them both overboard." His stream of expletives bespattered the wheel with tobacco-brown saliva. *Bangkok Lady* was not fully armed. On the flimsy excuse that none of their vessels had been attacked for some years, that the weekly occurrences of hi-jacking occurred between Shanghai and the Pearl River delta, the ship's owners refused to take seriously the threat of pirates anywhere south of Bias Bay. The navy didn't like the kind of work that brought no glory and no prize money, and those pompous, po-faced mandarins at the Government Secretariat, afraid of offending the authorities, used the excuse that it wasn't up to them to enforce Chinese laws.

"Get everybody up on deck, Mr Marsh. Chop-chop. And out with the guns," roared Boggis. "See that anyone who can handle one, gets one." Those stinking yellow bastards probably had word of his valuable cargo of indigo even before he left Singapore. He'd long suspected there was a spy network covering all the ports in south-east Asia.

Charlie Marsh went down the companionway like a bat out of hell. There were a few repeating shotguns, rifles and revolvers stowed below. "Come topside," he bellowed to the crew. "Come topside."

"Look!" roared the captain on his bridge, though there was no one now but the Almighty to hear, and clearly He didn't give a tinker's curse. "Look out port side. Three fast junks—coming from Lantau." Fast! They were fast all right, nipping through the water with their lateen sails lowered. Any moment now the ship was going to be surrounded.

Jesus! He wasn't going to be able to get away. He'd better cut the engines and see if he could marshall those lily-livered coolies into some sort of armed defence. If there weren't too many, and his crew stood up, between them they might manage to pick off the little yellow bastards as they came over the side. Relinquishing the wheel to his second, who had come running with a gun, he strode across the deck, shouting to Charlie Marsh to get a move on. Then he stopped in his tracks, for suddenly the decks of all four lorchas were swarming with diminutive warriors, the early morning sun flashing off the naked blades of their long knives.

Numbly, Boggis returned to the wheel and put the engine to full speed ahead.

"Come on, darling," said George impatiently. "A chap can't wait forever. How do I know you're not holding out on me?"

Hellen knew nothing of the law. Neither was there any instinctive feeling in her that by withholding George's conjugal rights she was keeping open an avenue that might lead to an annulment of the marriage. She was aware only of being in a trap, and that consummation was the closing of the trap's teeth.

"I'm not ready," she repeated for the umpteenth time, grasping despairingly at another few hours of immunity from the violation she knew had to come. "Couldn't you wait until tonight? I'll probably be clear by tonight."

"I've told you, darling, I don't mind about that." He pulled the sheet down, then slid her silk nightdress over one shoulder, baring a pink-tipped breast.

"George, please!"

He hesitated, knowing it would be bad policy to force her: that it was too early to break up the gentleman-George image; but he knew in his heart he would be taking one hell of a risk if he put this off to their last night aboard. Christ! If she went for abduction and rape, and got away with it, he could go to jail.

"What excuse will you have tonight?" He spoke with affection, for he was fond of her—as fond as one could be of a wife who kept one at arm's length.

Hellen pulled up the neck of her night dress. One of the night dresses that had been meant only for Oliver's eyes. "I will not offer excuses tonight."

Perhaps she was genuinely prudish, George thought resignedly, trying his hardest to understand. Outside the sheet he put his arms round her. Her body stiffened.

"I love you, darling," he said. He kissed her long and lingeringly. "You make a chap feel randy, just looking at you." She was still as a mouse, scarcely breathing. He felt her very immobility as an insult. Wounded, he reacted with violence, grasping at the sheet, ripping it out of her fingers. Then he dragged her nightdress up over her thighs.

Suddenly there was a shot, followed by a light barrage, like firecrackers going off, and outside in the passage, running footsteps. The door burst unceremoniously open. George swung round indignantly, glaring at the coolie seaman who stood in the doorway, his face contorted with terror. "Plenty trouble topside. Plenty pirate," he shrieked. "Plenty killing." He dashed away, leaving the door open, his howls and shrieks filling the corridor.

Hellen jerked upright. George leapt off the bunk, discarding as he went the silk honeymoon pyjamas he had bought in Singapore, snatching trousers from a rail and pulling them on. "Get dressed." He flung open a drawer in the one small chest the cabin offered, snatched a sweater, and jerked it over his head.

Hellen swung her legs to the deck. She sat with palms pressed down on the mattress on either side of her, head spinning. "Pirates!" she said, wanting to laugh, though seven o'clock in the morning was scarcely the hour for playing games. Besides, George's expression was enough to freeze the blood.

"Get dressed!" he snarled. "I told you to get dressed".

Bewildered, she looked round for the underclothes she had worn yesterday. She was no longer a change-daily girl. The facilities for washing did not allow for it. She went swiftly to the tiny wardrobe, took out a blouse and skirt, and hurriedly put them on. "What does he mean, George! What does he mean by pirates?"

"He means what he says." George, his hair awry, his face haggard," said, "Put some shoes on." When she did not move, only staring at him in consternation, he snarled, "Hurry up. Put some shoes on."

She scrambled for her deck shoes, thrust her bare feet inside them, and stood erect.

"But pirates, George," she repeated, unable to come to terms with the word. Pirates belonged in pantomime and children's stories.

He said angrily, as though the pirates' coming was her fault, "Come on, for God's sake. We'd better get up on deck and find out what's happening."

What was happening was that dozens of menacing yellow men with knives, guns, lances and bamboo poles had stormed the ship and more of them were swarming over the rails, all shrieking in threatening excitement. Hellen stood frozen with horror. Charlie Marsh, clutching one knee, was rolling back and forth on the deck, moaning in agony. Blood that had soaked one trouser leg was now staining the deck.

Two seamen dashed forward, one of them brandishing a revolver, the other wielding a stout iron bar. A pirate with a half-shaven head and a pigtail, swinging a cutlass, his face creased by a grin of fiendish brutality, decapitated them both. As the two bodies fell bloodily to the deck and the heads rolled away, Hellen gave a stricken cry; her knees wobbled, then gave way. George grabbed her by the arm, pulling her to his side, supporting her.

"Keep quiet. Stand still," he hissed.

There was a clatter and rattle as the terrified crew dropped their weapons. George stood straight as a ramrod. A hugely muscled, pugnacious man, inches shorter than Hellen, noted their presence with surprise. He strode across the deck and stood staring up at her, grinning obscenely. She looked glassily back, aware also of two men standing behind him, with guns. The one in authority saw the gold watch on Hellen's wrist.

"Give it to him. Hurry up," ordered George through barely moving lips.

Numbly, Hellen undid the strap and handed over the watch. The bandit clasped the bracelet round his own wrist, then turned his attention to George. With a crafty glance at Hellen, as though he was interested to see how she would react, he punched George hard in the solar plexus. Making no attempt to defend himself, George went down like a ninepin. Hellen dropped to her knees beside him, her terror submerged by distress and concern.

"I'm all right," muttered George through gritted teeth. "Stand up.

For God's sake stand up and don't make a fuss. I'm not hurt. Just do as they say."

Keeping her eyes averted from the headless coolies and the blood, Hellen rose trembling to her feet. The pirates had produced lengths of twine and were now busying themselves tying up the remaining members of the crew. The grinning leader gestured towards the companionway and four of his men scattered amidships, then like a child with a new toy, he glanced admiringly down at the watch on his wrist. Presently, turning his attention back to George, he experimentally kicked him in the ribs.

George sat up, and unbelievably spoke in Chinese. It was the first indication that Hellen had that he knew the language. Her surprise was drowned by a little rush of relief. The pirate gestured that he should stand up. George rose obediently to his feet and stood leaning against the rail, one hand to his sore ribs, his face a mask.

There was a shout of glee and one of the pirates appeared in the doorway to the bridge quarters wearing Hellen's sun hat on his head, pulling the brim this way and that, making foolish, grinning clown faces. The sun glanced off something bright round the man's wrist and Hellen saw, with horror, that he was wearing the bracelet Oliver had given her. Shedding all sense of present danger, she leapt across the deck, arm outstretched. "That's mine! Give it back to me!"

George's eyes nearly started out of his head. The pirate, spare and wiry, a dancing cat of a man with a broken set of black teeth in a grinning brown face, teased Hellen, waving the precious object tantalisingly out of her reach. George had a sickening vision of his bride's decapitated body dropping to the deck, annihilating as it went his lovingly nursed delusions of grandeur, and he leaped across the deck, grabbed her round the waist, and dragged her back. "Can't you see they'll have your head off without a second's thought."

But Hellen was beside herself, half out of her mind. "It's not mine. That bracelet's not mine," she shrieked. "Oliver gave it to me. Don't you see," as if George possibly could, "it was my ring! I have to give it back to them, now! To the Marathons! It's an heirloom! A family heirloom of the Marathon's!"

George's face shivered into an astonished gape. "You—" He could not say it. Not, "You were going to marry Oliver Marathon?" He could not even take the fact in.

She looked up into his face, entreatingly, and saw the change come over him; saw his eyes that had been full of fear and concern, as she had thought, for her, turn brilliant with shock. There was a moment of suspended time, then his grief and his loss hardened into ungovernable fury.

"You bloody little hypocrite," he ground out. "You—you—oh God!" he cried, calling on the Deity in ragged, insupportable distress. He could not go on. There were no words for her inexplicable duplicity.

The significance of his anger was lost to Hellen on the rippling breeze that filtered between the little yellow men, across the victims, and out to the quiet waters. She clung to him. "George, I have to get it back."

Driven by vengeance, which was all that was left to him, George hit her hard across the mouth.

They turned, the monkey leader and the killer with poised sword. There was a moment's astounded stillness as they contemplated the tall, smooth-faced Englishman. Then, at a signal from the leader, two of the pirates moved together, advancing on him, the sun glinting on their wicked knives. Those who were tying up the crew, and those who were their victims, were quiet. One of the pair, tough and weathered, rendered nut-like from a lifetime of clashes with typhoons, sun and deprivation, came to a stop directly in front of George. Unarmed, impotent, George gazed directly ahead. Hellen stepped forward, one hand to her bruised face, her head still spinning, her stomach rolling with raw fear, her only conscious thought a realization of the enormity of what she had begun.

The nut man issued a threat, it had to be a threat from the way he presented the medley of tinny, high-pitched clatter. He considered his opponent for a moment, then pointing his gleaming weapon at George's chest, forced him to walk backwards until he reached the middle of the well deck.

Charlie Marsh, hunched over his wounded leg, said softly, "Don't move." He might have been speaking to George. He might have been speaking to Hellen. Or to any of the fettered crew who could not anyway have done so. Hellen held her breath, knowing with a terrible sense of inadequacy and doom that there was nothing anyone could do.

The grins on the Chinese faces were evil, lewd, a participating audience in some diabolical play. The nut-man, his lips writhing back from his darkened teeth in a fiendish grin, reached up with his left hand and appeared to tweak George's ear. George flinched. Then the chopper rose and came down, neatly slicing along the side of his head, leaving his right ear in the pirate's hand. Exultantly, he waved it high in the air.

Hellen thought she saw George blink as though in mild surprise. Then the blood began to spurt and he uttered a raw cry of pain.

Chapter 10

Escape

Oliver stood in the cabin doorway, his face a mask of resolute disbelief. "Left the ship at Singapore!" he echoed.

Ruth watched him deflating slowly. The very sight was like having a knife twisted in her gut. There was so much she wanted to say. I'm sorry, I'm sorry, Dear God! How sorry I am! She felt physically sick with remorse.

At last, Oliver asked, "Why did she get off at Singapore?"

"I don't know, dear. I know you sent her a cable, but she didn't get it. I'm sorry, she said again, in her heart. And aloud, "She didn't confide in me."

He stood there, arms hanging at his sides, looking lost. Then he turned and went slowly back along the passage.

Ruth watched with tears in her eyes until he turned the corner by the companionway, then she closed the cabin door and sank down on the lower bunk. They had not yet docked. Oliver must have come aboard in a customs launch. Outside, she could hear the excited voices, the hurrying footsteps. After a while there was a tap at the door. She rose, and went to open it.

Major Tandy stood there, looking worried. "Saw young Marathon up on deck," he said gruffly. "D'you tell him?"

"Only that she left the ship at Singapore."

"Not about George?"

"No."

"Humph." The Major looked down at his feet. "I'd have thought she'd have sent him a cable."

"I'd have thought so, too."

He put his hands in his pockets, stared down at the deck, and after a while began to make little kicking movements with the toes of his shoes.

Somebody farther along the corridor called, "We're nearly in. Aren't you coming?"

The Major's heavy shoulders lifted, then sank on a lusty sigh. "Oh, well. I s'pose you know best." He turned, and began to make his way up on deck.

Sir Rowan Marathon crossed the hall with long strides and entered the drawing room with head lifted, his hands making genial little washing movements. It was his practised entrance, meant to convey the fact that he had had a busy and successful day, "And now, it's your turn for my company. How very pleased I am to see you."

He stopped on the threshold, looking round the empty room with surprise, the welcoming mask slipping away.

"Hello, dear." His wife was sitting in a chair by the big window that overlooked the praya and the shipping in the harbour.

He came towards her, walking slowly, already alerted by his wife's tone to disconcerting news. "So what's happened?"

"She left the ship at Singapore."

He sat down in the chair facing her, hands on his knees. "how did he take it?"

"Badly."

"What—"

"Don't ask me, darling, what he said." Oliver's griefstricken outpourings were not to be shared. "He has taken it badly. He's . . ." She sought for a word. Baffled? Hurt? Inconsolable? All of that. But, "He's stunned," she said. He was more than stunned. He was in pieces.

"I'll talk to him."

"I think you had better leave him alone, dear," she warned. "He believes you sent a message to the ship."

Sir Rowan sat back in his chair, staring at his wife in astonishment. "Of course I didn't."

"I told him you wouldn't, but he was not convinced."

Her husband turned in his chair, concentrating his attention on the big white liner that was still unloading at the quay. "Why the devil didn't she send him a cable?" he asked irritably, annoyed with the girl, not only for driving a spike between Oliver and himself, but for making the lad look a prize ass, running out as he had on the pilot boat, exposing his shock to the curious gaze of every Tom, Dick and Harry on board. "There's been plenty of time."

"I'm sure he is wondering about that."

The Governor was silent, remembering. "If she is suitable, Oliver," he had said, "You may send the message—if, in your carefully considered opinion, and in the light of our discussion, you really believe her to be suitable." He could not imagine why Sylvia, such an old friend, would go to the trouble of cabling him at such length if the girl was acceptable. They had gone into that. Oliver had called Sylvia a silly cow.

"Would I want to marry someone who wasn't suitable?"

Sir Rowan said dryly, "You might well."

"You're thinking of Lin Yan, aren't you? You really believed I might marry a Eurasian? I, a Marathon?"

Sir Rowan had been so pleased, and so eminently relieved, to hear those words, after all the worry over Lin Yan, that he had given in with a smile. "You have my permission to marry your Hellen."

Now, he heaved a swift sigh. "Perhaps it's for the best." He rose from the chair. "Where is Oliver?"

"He went out." Neither commented, for neither of them wished the other to add to the weight of their fears, Oliver was bound to go where he would find comfort. Sir Rowan crossed the room and the hall, then walking slowly and heavily, climbed the stairs.

So, they were back where they started. "I, a Marathon", indeed! with ascerbic hindsight, he knew those words for what they were, the product of a sharp Marathon mind, proving only that his nephew had inherited the family genius for getting his own way.

Lin Yan lived at number sixteen Caine Road, which was at The Peak mid-levels, a neutral zone between May and Macdonnel where the rich Chinese lived in spacious homes. Below Macdonnel lived the Portuguese, the Jews, the Armenians and the less well-heeled Eurasians. And below them again were the Chinese masses of the coolie class in squalid, rat-infested, low-rise tenement buildings.

After the death of her father, the highly respected comprador of a large hong, to the consternation of her numerous relations, Lin Yan had insisted on living alone in the house where she grew up, with only the old retainers for company. In spite of her porcelain and rosebud beauty, and the money her father had left her, as the granddaughter of an Englishman she was not wife material. Several English colonial bachelors, and one or two married men had approached her, as well as rich Chinese who were able to make her very attractive offers, for polygamy and concubinal relationships enjoyed full legal status. She politely declined them all. Everyone knew about her friendship with the Governor's nephew, but no one knew how far it had gone. Some said it was purely platonic, others that they were both clever and discreet.

The family wondered if she bribed her servants to hold their tongues, paying them in excess of their own bribes to keep them informed. The eastern bribe system, that very same Squeeze that benefited the Purser of *Devanha* when he condoned George's taking Hellen's luggage ashore at Singapore, operated also at number sixteen.

Slim-hipped, supple and elegant in her bright silk cheongsam and little flat slippers—owing to the influence of her English forebear, her feet had not been bound as was obligatory in a well-born Chinese— Lin Yan was arranging hibiscus, freshly brought in from the garden, in a cloisonné bowl in the drawing room. She was able to do such tasks because she kept her fingernails short in the English way. At the sound of the door bell, followed by the shuffle of the number one boy's footsteps, she glanced with idle curiosity out of the open door that led into the hall. Oliver! She glided swiftly to meet him.

Ah Fung, the major domo of the household, was amazed to see Missie's barbarian friend, who had earlier gone down to the ship to meet the barbarian woman who was coming to marry him. Yet he was already back to see Missie, looking as though he'd been mighty disappointed in the other one. The servant faded politely away. When he was out of sight behind the lacquered screen, he scurried off to the verandah to ensure his young son, the punkah boy, kept his ears wide open. Lin Yan had not bothered to install cooling fans. She liked to have the little boys sitting cross-legged on her verandah, sleepily pulling the cords as they had in her parents' day. She was soothed by the low swish of the punkahs as they stirred the torpid air.

Lin Yan led Oliver into the drawing room. "What has happened?"

He crossed the golden Tientsin carpet and stood at the window with his back turned, looking out over the water. "She didn't come." His voice rasped as it caught in his throat. "She left the boat at Singapore. She didn't get—" his voice broke "—my cable."

Lin Yan had seen Oliver in many moods: in a towering rage after hearing Hellen had been advised not to sail; in wild triumph, waving high in the air the reply to his cable sent to Hellen's family, informing him that she had already left; raging down the newly completed Peak Road, noisy as a Cantonese in his Tin Lizzie, horn blaring, the seats piled high with possessions, arbitrarily moving from his bachelor quarters on The Peak to Government House.

"Catch me leaving Hellen to Uncle Rowan's subtle inquisitioning! Not likely. I'm moving in."

It was then Lin Yan knew the truth, that Oliver wished to marry beneath him, and she was immediately, fiercely, on Hellen's side. Now she glided across the room and put gentle arms round him, resting her petal-soft cheek on his shoulder. He held her close. "Can I stay here, Lin Yan?"

"Of course you can."

"I'll send someone to get my things. I can't go back to Upper Albert Road. I'd kill my uncle. Kill him with my bare hands."

She was shocked by the intensity of his words. "Are you sure it was him?"

"Hellen ignored Sylvia Ashton. Who, but my uncle, could make her turn back?"

"Come and sit down. Don't torture yourself." She led him to the carved blackwood settle with its lovely English cushions made especially for her at Lane Crawford, the English store, and much deplored by her family as a gesture towards decadent western living. Lin Yan disliked the bareness of Chinese houses. She hung her scroll pictures on the walls, instead of keeping them tightly rolled in a metal tube, in the Chinese way. "Try to be calm, Oliver," she said sweetly. "It is not good to be so angry. Perhaps you have not eaten?"

He shook his head. "I don't want food."

"You will think better after food. I will talk to my cook boy." She clapped her hands. "Jasmine tea and a plate of Dim Sum," she said in Cantonese. "Then to the market." She reeled off a shopping list for a substantial dinner for two.

Fah Wong, the garden coolie, was already on his way down the path to the house of Mrs Chan who lived two streets away, carrying the message relayed to the kitchen by the little spies who worked the punkahs. Ah Fung, the cook boy, had promised him one-quarter of the squeeze money that would be paid for information that Lin Yan's foreign devil looked likely to stay the night.

Hellen never afterwards remembered, with any degree of accuracy, the appalling events that followed the severing of George's ear. She was dragged mercilessly, with senses reeling, across the well deck to the wheelhouse. Here, three decapitated bodies were neatly laid out side-by-side, their heads standing grotesquely upright beside them. The dark head of the Captain was set apart from the others, as though even in death he should remain aloof from his crew. She was aware of the blood flowing through his black beard; of his terrible, staring eyes. Someone had placed his peaked cap jauntily on the side of his head.

She experienced the stomach-churning agony of dry retching. Then she vomited. Another pirate came and dragged her, floundering, away from the grotesque scene. Then rough hands forced her up and over the ship's rail. Quixotically clinging to the life she no longer wished to live, searching for a foothold, Hellen found one of her feet caught in the rungs of the pirates' scaling ladder. She scrambled down, bracing herself for the impact of water, and a fast swim to shore. Then her feet touched something hard and she recognised with

105

dismay that she was on one of the sampans. She leapt across the deck, but one of the pirates gave her an unceremonious push, and she floundered sideways. When she regained her balance she saw that they were drifting away from *Bangkok Lady* towards the open sea.

There was a moment of blind panic when she realised there was nobody but herself on board from the ship. One of the pirates stood quietly by, watching her with evil curiosity. She moved away and he moved after her, step-by-step, fingering his chopper. There was to be no jumping into the water, that was clear. A coolie in the stern, manoeuvring with his steering oar, turned the little sampan into the breeze and swung left, slicing across the bows of *Bangkok Lady*. She saw then that they were heading towards a great mountain of an island, with forested slopes.

Looking back, she saw with fear that *Bangkok Lady* was getting up steam, and was overcome by a mindless desire to hurtle over the rail. Better death than whatever it was they planned for her.

"The Chinese are the cruellest nation on earth," George had said.

Then she realised the coaster was following them in. She wondered if poor Charlie Marsh—she could think of him now as poor Charlie Marsh, with a bullet in his leg—was being forced to bring the ship inshore. Charlie Marsh had tried to help her. He had said, "Don't move." She could not think of George, who had lost an ear because of what she had done. There was enough to face, without meeting guilt half way.

Out in front lay a white ribbon of beach, lace-edged with foam, and a jetty, crowded by sampans and junks. To the right, where the sand gave way to grass and rocks, a row of shacks stood, and tied up nearby several small vessels, like water-based covered wagons, rocked gently on the swell. A knot of men huddled half way between the shacks and the jetty, their wary stance suggesting they had no part in the morning's blasphemy.

Hellen turned to look again at *Bangkok Lady*. Her decks were seething with activity, now. Scurrying figures were bringing the cargo, huge boxes, bins or vats, out into view. There was the rattle of the ship's anchor, then she slowed and ran to a stop. The sampans and junks gathered at the jetty were untied, and then they backed away, turned, and scurried out to meet the ship.

They bumped up against the jetty, and the little man assigned to guard her gestured that she should step ashore. She hesitated, and he poked her in the ribs with the handle of his knife. The jetty was a rickety wooden structure on shell-encrusted supports. She climbed gingerly on to it and stood shivering, looking back at the coaster, wondering if anyone had been left alive.

Her hesitation appeared to offend her escort. He flicked the blade of his chopper in her face. With raw terror she headed for the shore. The pier was wobbly, its wooden planks rotting. She came to the end and jumped on to the grass, her captor following close behind.

Ahead now lay a track, leading inland. She took half a dozen steps, pulled up, and swung round defiantly, thinking it was better, surely, that she should die here than disappear into the forest with her murderous-looking escort. She was alone. The Chinaman was sprinting back along the jetty. He disappeared over the end into a waiting sampan. She looked round, her nerves jumping. Two men broke away from the group standing near the shacks and came hurrying in her direction. Her first reaction was to run. But where to?

They were small, thin men, dressed in ragged tunic suits, and wearing sandals on their feet. Huge hats of woven straw sat on their heads, the brims fringed with black cloth. Their pigtails reached to below the waist. As they approached, they bowed. There was no mistaking the fact that they came in friendship. She gave them a shaky, uncertain smile.

One of them pointed down the track that led inland. The other one began to walk, indicating that she should follow. Hellen glanced apprehensively back towards the ship. The pirates were unloading the cargo into the sampans. One of the coolies, seeing where her attention lay, sliced a finger across his throat, accompanying the gesture with a gurgling sound. Mutely, Hellen accepted their warning and said a little prayer for George. Not liking him, not wanting to be married to him, did not mean she wished him to die.

They set out along a narrow path bordered on either side by scrubby bushes grown gnarled and twisted and tough through the years of withstanding salt-laden winds from the sea. Almost immediately the land began to rise and they were forced to zig-zag back and forth, forging their way through a welter of undergrowth. They climbed for about an hour, moving gradually out of the steamy heat of the seashore. In so far as she could be grateful for anything, Hellen was glad of the drop in temperature.

They rounded a sharp ridge and, still climbing, approached a cleft in the mountainside, then broke out from the stunted trees and immediately came upon a narrow stream bubbling down over rocks and stones. The guide in front leapt from stone to stone, swiftly reaching the other side, but Hellen could not resist the water. Signing to the men to wait, she kicked off her shoes, flung them across the stream, and waded in. Her clothes were sweat-soaked, and beneath the thick hair her scalp felt sticky and damp.

She flung handfuls of water over her head and arms, washed her face with her hands, dipped the front of her filthy skirt in the water, and rubbed the vomit away. The men stood on the bank, watching impassively. She waded out of the other side, and sat down on the stony ground to put her shoes back on.

They began once more to climb. At times they scrambled over lichen-covered rocks; at times, because of a cleft or landslide in their way, they took a detour round a rocky promontory, or down the steep mountainside and up again. Strong and fit though she was, Hellen began to wilt. Her skirt had long since dried, but she was again soaked in sweat. The top of her head was too hot for comfort. She looked with envy at the vast mushroom hats worn by the men. Her arms were now reddened by the sun, her face dry and burning.

They stopped to rest. Hellen leaned back gratefully against the scrub, and closed her eyes. George had said yesterday that the ship was entering the channel at the approaches of Hong Kong. Were they in fact on the mainland of China? This mountain need not necessarily be an island. It could be a peninsula, jutting out from the New Territories that lay south-west of Hong Kong, a piece of China that had been leased by the Chinese government to the British a little over twenty years ago.

She felt no rise of spirits, for in her heart she knew they were surrounded by water. The mountain had the shape and look of an island. She wondered if there were friendly villages on the other side where they could pick up a small craft and reach the New Territories, or even Hong Kong.

One of her guides spoke, and she opened her eyes wearily. He pointed to the sun, sweeping his arm down, then ahead, indicating that there was a long way to go and darkness would soon be on them. Hellen staggered to her feet. Almost, she felt, it had been a mistake to rest, for now her legs ached unbearably and her knees had grown stiff. She set out resolutely in the leader's wake.

They rested more frequently now, for the intense effort was telling on them all. The air was cold, and she was extremely hungry, for she had eaten nothing since dinner the night before. The sun was well down in the sky when at last they emerged on a grassy plateau. Above, and slightly to the right, a green peak rose, and flying from its summit, a rag of cloud. The grass here was lush, the trees, though small, and gnarled from wind and weather, appeared verdant by comparison with the rough bushes of the mountainside.

Walking side-by-side, they set out across the plateau. They had not gone more than a few hundred yards when out of the trees in front loomed an amazing gateway, with neither wall nor fence attached. Its pillars rose to double the height of the trees, and the opening was

108

wide enough to drive a horse and carriage through. Three enormous Chinese ideographs, like framed pictures, stood above the arch, and over them, an elaborately carved and tilted roof. Small metal dragons the size of a rabbit writhed, snarled, and leaped across the ridge pole.

Hellen paused, staring in amazement. One of the coolies signalled to her to keep walking. They went right up to the gate. There, at the base, was an inscription. She blinked. TO THE GREAT MONK, SING'WAI. THERE IS NO TIME—WHAT IS MEMORY? Her spirits soared. There must be English people here!

They went through the gateway and there, in front of them, lay a cluster of single-storey buildings with tiled roofs. The coolies paused. A Chinaman with shaven head and the long black gown of a monk, or holy man, emerged from a smallish building fronted by impressively carved double doors. He shuffled towards them in black cloth slippers.

The two coolies bowed in that endearing way with which they had greeted her, then, to her astonishment and bewilderment, turned and fled.

The monk said kindly, "Traveller can stay."

Shocked by her friends' precipitous departure, Hellen began a shaky explanation of what had happened. The monk lifted a hand to silence her, turned, and beckoning to her to follow, shambled off across the stony turf. Hellen hurried after him.

"English?" She looked up anxiously into his plump, impassive face. "English?"

"No English," he said, lifting both arms in their wide sleeves, gesturing to encompass the entire compound. "No English." He continued on his way.

She trailed after him. They were following a cinder path that led to one of the smaller buildings. He opened a door, went into a small vestibule, then opened another door and stood back. Hellen looked in upon a small, shadowed room, lit only from a window set high in the wall. There was a slatted trestle bed, at the foot of which lay a padded quilt, and at the head, a small pillow. The bed was covered by a discoloured mosquito net strung on a wobbly bamboo frame. "Ming toi," said the monk, or that is what she thought he said as he lifted the quilt, wrapping it round his portly body, demonstrating how it should be used.

"I am to sleep like that? I see." So this was to be her bedroom. At least she had shelter for the night. She nodded. "Thank you."

"Traveller can stay." He repeated what he had said before, and she knew with increasing despair that was his English vocabulary in its entirety.

Chapter 11
Oliver

Once more beckoning to Hellen to follow, the monk went back to the compound. Where were the rest of the monks? He could not, surely, be the only one here? The building they were approaching was marginally bigger than the others, and it had double doors, the lintel painted with Chinese characters. The monk opened one of the doors and went inside, indicating that Hellen should follow. She stood on the threshold of a large, windowless room, lit here and there by groups of candles. The air was heavy with incense.

Her guide went forward into the semi-darkness. Hellen glanced apprehensively behind. Noticing her hesitation, he gestured reassuringly. She moved in his wake, though not without a touch of very real fear. Enthroned in the lotus position on a highly ornate dais at the end of the room, an obese Buddha looked benignly down upon them. Astonishingly, bearing in mind the poverty that surrounded them, the god was covered in gold leaf. There were gold necklaces round its neck, and on its hands, gold bracelets. An exquisite little goddess made of white jade sat cross-legged below, her jade drapes edged with gold. Her sheer beauty in the flickering candlelight quite took Helen's breath away, and for a moment she forgot both her apprehension, and the gnawing pangs of hunger.

The monk moved her on. Selecting a taper from one of several porcelain vases, he pointed to a group of lighted candles. Helen obediently lit the taper at a flame, then placed it in a metal urn alongside similar sticks.

"Joss," said the monk, smiling, showing a remarkable resemblance to the fat statue on the plinth.

"Joss?" she asked, watching the pin-sized light and the incense bearing smoke curling up into the darkness. He answered in Chinese. She made a wish that Oliver would come to her, or she be taken on him. Afterwards, she knew joss to be a kind of luck, good or bad, as the gods decreed.

110

They left the temple, and continuing what she was beginning to see as a Cook's tour, crossed the open ground to a similar building, also on the perimeter of the central clearing. The monk lifted an iron bar that held a pair of double doors closed, and they stepped into a bare hall half-filled with trestle tables, each table flanked by two forms, with here and there a cuspidor. On the tables were set china bowls, each about five inches in diameter, and at the end of each trestle, a metal urn. The dining hall?

They have to eat, Hellen said to herself, with hope. Somebody has to come with provisions. At the same time, deep down inside her, she knew a monastery might be entirely self-sufficient. As they exited, she picked up a stick that was lying on the ground, and tugging at the monk's sleeve to attract his attention, marked out on the path a square about the size of an average sheet of writing paper. Then, again using the stick, she mimed some written words, and made as though to lift the paper, fold it, put it in an envelope and lick the envelope down. Turning in the direction she hoped might be north, she pointed out across the sea. The monk watched dispassionately.

"Hong Kong," she said distinctly. And then again, "Hong Kong."

"Hong Kong," he repeated obediently, but she knew with a sinking heart that he did not understand. Again using an imaginary pencil, she mimed writing on her hand. He hawked and spat on the ground, a casual exercise that had nothing to do with their intercourse, then shook his head. She thought with despair, I have lighted a candle. Perhaps some Chinese god will grant me my wish.

He moved her along again, and they went behind the dining hall. Out in front now were some stone-lined vats. The monk made washing movements with his hands and she nodded. Ahead of them now was a brick enclosure, the wall not more than three feet high, and partially shielded by the spreading branches of a scrubby tree. The monk gestured to her to go ahead alone. Before she had covered more than a dozen yards, the stench she met was more than she could bear.

Holding her breath, she entered an open door space and stood looking down with horror at a pair of holes at the bottom of a platform of sloping brickwork that was everywhere sprayed disgustingly with human ordure. She turned and hurried out. Her friend had discreetly disappeared. Well, she thought resignedly, there were plenty of trees on the outskirts of the compound.

When the monk did not return she wandered away, and led by sweet herbal scents, discovered gardens full of well-tended vegetables and flowers. She pulled a young carrot out of the ground, wiped the dirt off on the grass, then rubbed it on her skirt, and

111

feeling guilty moved on. She found smaller edifices, in the same style as the one by which she had entered with the coolies, though less ornate, and assumed they were gateways to tracks leading up to the plateau. So, at least she knew where to start if and when she decided to leave, though there was no evidence that she would be able to find her way to the mainland, for she could not see the sea from here, and dusk had now shrouded the distant hills.

She went back into the centre of the compound. There was no one about. Uncertain what to do next, she made her way over to an enormous cast iron urn standing four square on short iron legs, each decorated with a fearsomely charactered head of a lion, and roofed with a double cupola of intricately frilled iron work. Inside was a bed of sand supporting a group of guttering yellow candles. To Hellen's apprehensive eyes, it looked like some medieval shrine where one might make offerings to the gods. Standing there all alone in the eery twilight, she felt afraid.

Then a gong sounded and a group of monks, perhaps twenty in all, emerged from one of the buildings and came hurring across the grass, their shapeless black habits flowing about their ankles. They looked at her inscrutably as they passed. She did not recognise her guide among them. In identical habits, with shaven heads, they bore a remarkable similarity one to another. At that moment it was a relief, at least, to see other human beings.

When they entered the dining hall, she followed and stood uncertainly just inside the door. They each picked up a bowl and formed a slow moving line to collect their food. One of the holy men, wielding an enormous spoon, had placed himself at the head of each table beside the serving pot. Hellen took a bowl and followed. One or two of the diners glanced up, without particular interest.

The food was simple in the extreme. There were green vegetables cut up and mixed into rice, with some brown pieces added that might have been mushroom, or fungus; even dried fish. She did not find the food palatable, and nor was it easy to eat. The chopsticks slid through her fingers, the rice dropped on to the table, as well as down the front of her dress. In despair, she glanced up, looking for help and met the inscrutable eyes of the serving monk. He went away, hawking disgustingly, to return a moment later with a china spoon.

"Thank you," she said gratefully, and smiled. He made no indication that he had heard. She felt he was unaccustomed to being thanked. She sat there feeling strange and isolated while around her the chopsticks clicked through the silence. Some of the men lifted the bowls to their lips, shovelling the food directly into their mouths. She thought wryly that had she known such an abandonment of table manners was acceptable, she could have managed with the chopsticks. Another group of monks came in, and she recognised her guide, but though she smiled at him, he made no sign that they were acquainted. Her feeling of isolation grew. One by one the monks finished their meal and filed out. Hellen followed. Without a backward glance, they shuffled off in their cloth slippers, and disappeared into the temple containing the golden buddha.

She wandered slowly after them, wondering what was expected of her, then pulled up sharply as a low moan of voices, chanting in unison, came from the open door. Nervous of the unknown, wanting to make herself scarce, she hurriedly crossed the rough grass to the stone pools, swiftly and cursorily washed her face and hands, then made her way to the annexe where her room lay. There was no lock on the door. Averting her eyes from the torn and dirty blouse and skirt, despite all her anxious efforts at the stream still smelling unpleasantly of vomit and sweat, she divested herself of all but her thin underclothes, wrapped the quilt around herself and lay down on the slats, spreading the mosquito net, tucking it in at the sides and under her feet.

Sleep was a long time in coming. The slats bit into her hips. What had happened to George? Her husband? She pondered miserably on the double problem, seeing them as separate issues. Would the pirates bother to cut off his ear if they were anyway going to kill him? She tossed and turned, disturbing the net and re-arranging it again. Her shoulders felt bruised by the wood. A low hum of mosquitoes filled the room. Why on earth would a traveller come here? And how did that traveller leave? She slept fitfully. In the small hours she gave way to self pity, and wept.

She was awakened long before daylight by a tin-tinabulation of bells and chanting of voices in unison. Startled, she unrolled herself from the heavy quilt, slipped into her dirty shoes, and pulled over her head the disgusting rags that had once been her clothes. Shivering in the cold, she opened her door and looked outside, but could see nothing. For a moment or two she stood listening in the darkness. There was a wierd unreality in the ritual of the tinkling bells and the chanting. Feeling distinctly uneasy, she retreated to her room, picked up the quilt, wrapped it round herself for warmth, then hurried out again. Heaven alone knew what was going to happen, now. She felt she had to get away.

Making for the main gateway, she passed the temple. The door was open, and she could see by the flickering light of many candles, dark-robed figures moving at a steady pace round the interior. What fiendish business were they about? Her heart beat fast against the wall of her chest.

Hurrying, tripping here and there on stones in the darkness, she found the gate. There was now a faint light in the eastern sky, and she could see the solid black form of the grassy peak rearing up from the plateau in front of her. She ran forward across the damp grass, and still clutching the quilt round her, began awkwardly to climb.

The early morning air was damp and very cold, but wonderful after the airlessness of the mosquito net and her tiny bedroom. It was not so far to the summit. Still clutching her quilt, she seated herself on a rounded stone. Far in the distance, she could hear the mantras and the tinkling bells, but from here, facing the friendly, wondrous beauty of a pearl-pink sky, even they had a certain beauty.

As the light deepened and brightened, as the pearl in the sky turned to gold, strange objects took shape in the outer darkness. The sun moved higher, slashing the gold with crimson. The strange shapes grew to be great humps of islands set in a silvery sea. The beauty around her seemed to move into her, lifting her soul. With an intensity that was quite overwhelming, she felt spiritually free. After a while she found herself going back, quite calmly, over the events of the past months: the magical meeting with Oliver; the clash with Lady Sylvia; her own frail triumph, so pathetically short-lived; the strange, inexplicable intervention of Calum Finn that had coloured all the rest of her journey and brought her, through nightmare, ignorance and panic, to that strange marriage.

"I have come this far, and survived," she said to herself, feeling her heart expand a little, with hope.

She looked down at her left hand. Why had the pirates not taken her wedding ring? It did not occur to her to think of their omission as an omen. Feeling brave and strong, soaring far above that frightened creature who had run away from what was probably only some sort of daily devotional ritual in the temple, she slipped the ring off and quite deliberately, flung it far out into the misty morning. There was a strange satisfaction, again almost spiritual, in sitting up here on the top of the world, symbolically throwing George away.

She did not consider the fact that he might already be dead. One did not wish people dead, however badly they had behaved, though deep in the recesses of her mind, too far away easily to take out and examine, lay the knowledge that *Bangkok Lady* could have been sunk with all hands and the ship's log, leaving no evidence that her marriage to George had taken place.

At last she could see the bay. Where *Bangkok Lady* had lain at anchor, there was nothing. The deserted beach stretched, clear and bone white, between the green grass and the emerald sea. The empty jetty was a long black stick in the water. Hellen brushed a hand across her eyes, blinking in disbelief. It was as though this morning had cleared away the previous day.

"That," said Elliott Keane, taipan of Lonewood & Southby, speaking with the utmost distaste, "is somebody's ear. If it doesn't belong to George Curtain—and what reason have we to believe that it doesn't?—then it does belong to a white man, and therefore must be taken seriously. Young Curtain was due in on *Devanha* and has not come."

"Who brought the ear?"

"God knows." They both knew how messages crossed the water, sent by signals from junks strategically placed between the hi-jacked vessel and the mainland, but this note, in a packet containing a recently severed ear, had considerable delivery complications. There was no denying some of the Chinese junks now had high-powered engines. One of them could drop off a coolie, indistinguishable from any other Chinaman in the street. He could drop a packet in the box downstairs, and slip away unnoticed.

"But why the dickens should he change over to *Bangkok Lady*?" demanded the chief accountant, rocking himself irritably back and forth in his fine teak chair, tapping his fingers on the arm, frowning.

"That's immaterial, replied the taipan tersely. "What we have to consider is the ransom request. When we've sorted that out, I'll contact the Colonial Secretary." He brooded on the loss of his valuable cargo. "I'm going to have to talk to someone about this ear," he said, indicating the shrivelled and bloody thing that lay on the desk, discreetly half hidden by its wrapping.

"Have you told Curtain senior?"

"Not yet."

"Eighty thousand Hong Kong dollars is a helluva lot of money." The accountant's mind was already busy with ways of raising the cash.

"I'll call a board meeting." The taipan pressed the bell on his desk. His pretty Chinese secretary came into the room. "I want the Board here in half an hour," he said. "And get me an appointment with the Colonial Secretary for an hour after that." He wished to goodness he knew how his crew had fared. George Curtain was small fry. He knew what his Board were going to say. That they would be prepared to pay a lot of more if they knew for certain Captain Boggis had survived.

Mrs Harrison-Lowe, Agatha to her friends, had arranged one of her fearsome bridge affairs. It would start at one o'clock with cocktails and "small chow". An elaborate lunch would follow, then the ladies would settle down to bridge, interspersed with gossip. Tea would be served mid-afternoon, then more bridge, and finally more cocktails, the guests leaving for home about eight o'clock in the evening, exhausted with the pleasure of it all. In the kitchen the amahs were jittery, for with the influx of so many Gwei Lo, which was what they called Missie's foreign devils, without malice, behind their backs, there would be no relaxing with their opium pipes between lunch and the serving of tea.

Mrs Harrison-Lowe was neither a spiteful nor a malicious woman, but the novelty of being rich, well-dressed and important had long ago worn off, along with the conceit of living in a beautiful house situated in the select upper echelons of The Peak, and her soul cried out for sensation. Without an occasional witch-hunt, a little muck-spreading, a whisper of scandal to provide the vinegar on the bland salmon of perfection, one's parties could become thoroughly boring. Today she was bursting with a perfectly priceless bit of news.

Agatha had nothing against George Curtain. If one liked to look deeply into the matter—though why should one? It was of no importance—his parents had done him down themselves by having him educated in Shanghai, where he was born. Of course there were good schools in Shanghai, quite good enough for missionaries' children, but discriminating parents sent their boys home to public schools, where they made the right friends and the sort of contacts that led to the best jobs.

With her fine sense of drama, she planned exactly how she would deal with this gem of news that her husband had telephoned from his office in Central. Not as a hi-jack. Her friends were accustomed to hearing about the hi-jacking of ferries and small craft on their way to Canton and Macau. There was nothing new about that. Lucinda Knowles, silly woman, had only last week been stripped of her jewellery. Anyone with any sense did not even wear a watch when they ventured in small craft on the China Seas.

"So he lost an ear," she would say. "Right on top of losing Kitty Burtenshaw! Well, I ask you, how could he expect to hold a spirited girl when he couldn't even hang on to his own ear!" She could already anticipate the delighted laughter. Agatha had another quick peep at herself in the looking glass, wriggled her hips until her sash fell exactly into its correct position, then went into the drawing room to wait.

The ladies who had been shopping in Central travelled up together in the Peak tram, then hired rickshaws at the upper terminus. Those who came direct from their homes dribbled in one by one, transported by their own coolies in their own sedan chairs. Agatha delivered her bombshell over tea.

George Curtain! Ruth Washington smothered a gasp of dismay. "George Curtain!" she said, turning towards her hostess with real panic in her eyes as the flood of cruel laughter echoed through the room.

Momentarily, Agatha was astonished at Ruth's reaction. Then she remembered. "My dear! You must have travelled out with him, did you? But of course, those little coasters only go as far as Penang or Singapore. Why did he leave *Devanha*?"

Ruth pulled herself together. "I haven't the slightest idea," she said, adding stiffly, "He's not a friend of mine, as you know. I scarcely spoke to him on board." She turned back to the ladies sharing her little tea table, her nerves jumping. She had the rest of the afternoon in which to make up her mind whether to take the coward's way out and go to Lettice Marathon, or bravely face up to Oliver. One way or another, this was her pigeon now.

Ah Fung, Lin Yan's number one boy, announced impassively from the doorway, "One Missie come see your flend." Since Oliver came, he had dropped into pidgin. Lin Yan's shapely mouth circled in surprise. No one was supposed to know Oliver was at her house.

Mrs Chan, who had gratefully paid her Squeeze money to her niece's tell-tale servant then arbitrarily moved in on Oliver's heels, had seen Ruth's arrival from her upstairs window and scuttled swiftly down as fast as her five inch feet, crippled by binding, would allow. She stood very erect in the hall, formidable in her high-collared, shiny black pymama suit, with its cloth buttons and frogged loops. Lin Yan retreated in inevitable defeat. Ah Fung remained at a respectful distance, head bowed, shamelessly listening.

"I, Mrs Chan." She bowed with Asiatic politeness. "I Lin Yan's aunt."

"I would like to see Oliver Marathon, please, Mrs Chan."

"Missie, how you know your flend here?"

Ruth smiled, recognising the fierce protectiveness behind the woman's words. "I have come from Oliver's aunt. She guessed he might wish to see your niece. I assure you," Ruth added consolingly, "no one else knows he is here."

"Is not proper for unmarried girl—"

"I know, Mrs Chan. I fully understand. May I see Oliver?"

"Come." Ignoring her niece, who was now standing tight-lipped behind the impressive Ah Fung in the drawing room doorway, Mrs Chan led the caller down a passage to a side exit. "He in garden." Jerking her head to indicate the presence of the number one boy, she added darkly, "Talk in garden."

"Thank you." Ruth stepped out on to the gravel path and Mrs Chan turned to meet the bright anger of her niece.

"Am I not mistress in my own house, Auntie?" snapped Lin Yin in Mandarin, the scholarly language used in polite Chinese society.

"A young girl no have house," retorted the old lady implacably. "Your father with ancestors, I mistress here so you retain honour." Without waiting for an answer, she added, "How else you find good husband?"

She had touched a raw spot. Lin Yan turned and went back to the drawing room where she stood fulminating against fate.

Mrs Chan followed her in. "Another thing." She indicated with a dismissive flick of her long-nailed fingers, her niece's beautifully ironed cheongsam. "English dress," she said insultingly. "No iron mark." She pointed with pride to the sharply squared creases down the front of her own suit. Iron marks presented a polite fiction that the garment had only just left the tailor's box. "And short nails, like coolie girl." One of her own nails was an impressive six inches long, proving she had never done manual work. "English coolie," she said, and pleased with her inventive phrase, tottered out of the room. As to Lin Yan's feet . . . Ai-ee-e! Would she ever forgive the girl's father for refusing to have her feet bound?

Lin Yin walked to the window and stood looking disconsolately down into the lotus ponds that were strung along the stepped incline of the garden. Her family probably knew of her futile wish to marry into the English community. Whilst docilely following many of the customs of the Chinese, she had always felt infinitely closer to her English grandfather who had brought such disgrace upon the family by marrying her Chinese grandmother. Now he had gone, leaving her alone with her Englishness, and with offers of mistress, or concubine, falling into her lap like autumn leaves.

Perhaps, she had thought in the loneliness of last night with her aunt fiercely guarding her in the next room, (she would not have been surprised if Mrs Chan had curled up on the floor outside her door), and Oliver stowed into the small bedroom at the far end of the house, if this matter of the lovely Hellen came to nothing . . . Her thoughts stilled. Better not to dream.

All the way here, walking slowly from Central to The Peak tram, then in her green-topped sedan chair that was waiting for her at the terminus, to number sixteen Caine Road, Ruth had sought desperately, and without success, for the right words to say to Oliver. She must make him understand, not her own guilty part in what had happened, for the act of donning a hair shirt would not help him, but

118

the fact that Hellen was not to blame for going ashore at Singapore. She must make him see that the treatment Hellen had received from the Ashtons, combined with the fact that she had received no word from him, had quite understandably frightened her off. Ruth wished she had said this to Oliver when he came out to meet the boat. Now, there was more to say, and it was going to be a great deal harder.

Oliver was seated in the soft dusk of late afternoon on one of the hard wooden forms that lined the interior of the summer house. He rose as Ruth came along the path between the red blossoms of the kapok trees. "Hello, Mrs Washington," he said uncertainly.

"Oliver, I hope you will excuse this intrusion. Your aunt thought it best for me to come. You know, of course," Ruth said cautiously, "that *Bangkok Lady* has been pirated?"

"Yes." He looked at her quizzically, as though wondering what on earth she thought it had to do with him. "Do sit down." She settled opposite him on the slatted seat.

"And George Curtain's ear—"

"Yes. A bad business."

"Oliver, I don't quite know how to say this to you, but Hellen got off—I mean, George Curtain carried Hellen's luggage ashore."

He looked at her with baffled eyes. "Yes?"

"I mean, they went off to have lunch together. At Raffles. Then he came aboard alone, and picked up her cabin luggage."

"Yes?" said Oliver again, still looking puzzled.

Ruth studied a finger nail minutely, and keeping her eyes lidded, said, "I wondered, when I heard George had caught *Bangkok Lady*, if Hellen had gone with him." She raised her eyes, painfully, to his.

Oliver blinked.

Ruth thought of all the things she had meant to say, then managed lamely, "Perhaps he persuaded her it would be an adventure to change over to a cargo ship."

"Adventure?" he repeated, as though comprehension was totally beyond him.

If it had to be spelt out to him that Hellen had run off with George, Ruth decided, then a relative was the one to do it. She could not bring herself to shatter the trust in those eyes. "Your aunt wants you to come back to Government House, dear," she said.

"Never! My uncle tried to stop Hellen leaving England. I believe he sent her word to the ship. You can tell him, Mrs Washington, that until he undoes what he has done, and gets Hellen here—until he does that—" Oliver looked down at his hands, swallowed, then began again, "And another thing. If she has turned back, then I shall be on the next boat. And if my uncle says, what about my career, you can tell him—"

"Oliver!" Ruth held up a hand, begging him to stop, but the emotion that had temporarily silenced him had turned now to passion and he was in full spate. "You don't know if she got on this *Bangkok Lady*. Just because George Curtain got off *Devanha* and changed to *Bangkok Lady*, that's no reason to assume she would do the same. Why shouldn't he cart her stuff ashore? I expect she was jolly upset. I expect she needed help."

Ruth took advantage of his pause for breath to break in, "She didn't take her trunk, dear. And there was a packing case. . . . If she was returning to England, she'd have taken them."

He stared at her, shifted a little in his seat, then leaned forward gripping the chair seat and began rocking backwards and forwards, the knuckles on the backs of his hands showing white. His face became very still. "Thank you for coming, Mrs Washington, but I really don't think George's changing ships could possibly have any bearing on. . . ." He stopped, stared out between the hibiscus bushes to the harbour, then rose. "But if, as you say, Curtain carried. . . . He ought to know where she went . . . I mean, what hotel. . . ." He moved towards the open doorway, indicating that she might be ready to go. "I'm waiting for word from Singapore," he said. "I've cabled the consul. There should be an answer by this evening. Or, at the latest, tomorrow." They walked up the path between the flowering shrubs. "Thank you for coming," he said formally, and shook her hand.

Ruth's bearers were dozing on the pavement beside her sedan chair. As they jogged up the winding road to her home, she thought of all the things she wished she had said to Hellen. But how was she to know Hellen was that unacceptable village girl, for she was only unacceptable when judged by standards that did not apply in Hong Kong. If only she had known, Ruth told herself irritably, she could have said, "We are English. That is all that counts. Merely to be English in Hong Kong, is to be a queen."

She thought about Jack Albion, an important member of the Jockey Club, who never admitted to being the son of a small time draper in Birmingham; Milly Evesham, who lied in her teeth when she said she came of county stock. "No one would ever show her up," she would have said to Hellen had she known, "because it is essential for all of us to be important before the Chinese and the Eurasians. That we should speak and deport ourselves well, that we should have no mixed blood, is all that is asked of the English, here. Had Sylvia Ashton known the Hong Kong rules, she would not have interfered."

Yet in her heart Ruth knew that she would not have said those words out loud. They hung in the air, and seeped in through the pores, and became a part of one's life. To speak them out loud was to make a mockery of something that worked, and was therefore right. She heaved a grieved sigh. There was no way for her to help the young people. She had been a fool, and a bitch, and a suspicious old trout, and she was going to have to live with it.

One thing she knew for certain: she was never going to gossip again.

Chapter 12

Macau

"It's to the British Consul in Canton," said the Governor to his secretary. "You draft it and let me have it by early afternoon. He is to request that the Canton Government takes serious steps for the extermination of pirates, whose immunity is a disgrace.

"Remind him that we have offered full naval and military co-operation to the Chinese, but that they rejected our offers. I want it made clear that they are scandalously forgetful of the first duty of any civilised and self-respecting government—namely the suppression of piracy, brigandage, and the maintenance of law and order.

"You can also tell him . . . don't bother with notes, Peter, I'll let you have them—" he flapped the sheet of paper on which he had been working last night, against his left hand, "—that our shipping companies have spent a lot of money trying to make their vessels pirate-proof. Some of them look like floating fortresses. This should not be necessary. It is also a disgrace that the Kwok Hing Shek-ki Ferry Company should have been asked to pay fifty thousand dollars a year in protection money to a local pirate gang." The Governor tossed the notes onto the desk. "Right, you get on with that."

"The Colonial Secretary is here, sir."

"Send him in."

Peter Ackroyd was crossing the hall to the number one waiting room when Oliver came through the door like a tornado. "Where's my uncle?"

"He's busy—"

"Is anyone with him?"

"Nearly. The Colonial Secretary is waiting—"

"Hang on to him."

"Oliver!" He shrugged resignedly as the young man strode through the door into the Governor's office.

122

Sir Rowan looked up from behind his desk, his face stern. "I am expecting—"

"Uncle Rowan, Hellen may be on that ship! I've had a cable from the Consul in Singapore. She isn't there. He's made extensive enquiries. She may be on *Bangkok Lady*."

"Oliver," said his uncle with cold courtesy, "this is hardly the moment." The significance of his nephew's words scarcely touched his consciousness.

"I won't hold you up. I merely want to say, whoever is going out to *Bangkok Lady*, I want to go with them."

"We're sending in a gun-boat, and you may not go. That's an order. Now kindly leave."

"I'm sorry, sir." Undaunted, because of the second string to his bow, Oliver turned and left the room, strode across the hall and went out of the big, imposing entrance at a run. Lonewood & Southby's offices were in Central. He sprinted down Garden Road, into Lower Albert Road, and took the steps of Ice House Street at a leaping gallop. The temperature was in the upper nineties, with equivalent humidity. By the time he reached the shipping company's office his shirt was soaked and the perspiration was running down his face.

The Chinese receptionist looked up in surprise as he came precipitately through the outer door, leaving it swinging behind him. "I want to see Mr Keane, please."

"Taipan is busy."

"It's urgent, and most important."

The girl hesitated. "Taipan leave orders no one see him."

Oliver stood his ground.

She rose hesitantly from her chair. "If you give your name. . . ." She gazed at him innocently.

"Oliver Marathon," he said, grinning engagingly, well aware that she knew his identity. Everyone in Hong Kong knew the Governor's nephew, arguably the most eligible young man in the colony.

"I will see." She slid sinuously across the office, her slim little legs exposed through the side slits in her sheath-tight cheongsam, and went through the door that led to the office of the great man's secretary. "Oliver Marathon here, Oi Mei."

The secretary jumped as though a fire cracker had gone off under her desk. "Wait." With as much haste has her tight-fitting skirt would allow, she headed for the mahogany door that led to the Taipan's office.

"Oliver Marathon!" he echoed, looking harrassed. When one had deliberately acted against the Colonial Secretary's orders, a representative of the Governor was the last person one wanted to see. "What does he want?"

"He didn't say."

"Tell him I'm busy." Oi Mei left. Keane jiggled his gold watch chain between his fingers, looking out at the shipping in the harbour, wondering nervously how His Excellency could possibly have discovered that eighty thousand Hong Kong dollars of ransom money was already on its way. He did not like flouting orders from the Secretariat, but when the word "gunboat" was mentioned, he knew if he was to salvage anything from this mess, he would have to act on his own initiative, and fast. Gunboat policy was fine for government business, but no one knew better than he the sheer ruthlessness of the bandits of the China Seas, and he wanted his crew back alive.

There was another discreet tap at the door, and it opened. "Mr Marathon say is not official business. Is private. He not go until you see."

Keane ran a hand across his balding pate, considering what extraordinary circumstances would bring H.E.'s nephew to him in a private capacity. How the hell could it be private? He strode across the office, door to window, then back again to stand staring at his secretary, not seeing her. He was suspicious. Very suspicious. "All right," he said reluctantly at last, "show him in."

Keane noted with surprise Oliver's dishevelled appearance. He noted also the air of barely suppressed excitement. He indicated a chair and deliberately remained standing.

Oliver wiped the sweat from his forehead with the palm of one hand. "I want to get to *Bangkok Lady*. I believe a ransom has been asked. I am offering to deliver it," he said.

Keane managed to conceal his astonishment. "A ransom," he said, "could only be paid with the full approval of His Excellency. I have seen the Colonial Secretary. I believe he's seeing the Governor today. Presumably, a decision as to whether it should or should not be paid will be taken then."

Oliver did not know Elliott Keane well, but he was good at summing up people. The ransom had gone, of that he was certain. The truth was there in Keane's careful phraseology, in the wariness of his eyes. He flung himself to his feet. "Thank you, Mr Keane," he said politely, "I am sorry to have troubled you. We chaps are always looking for a bit of adventure."

The taipan stood watching Oliver's back as he left. Looking for adventure, my foot! H.E. was known to be a wily bird, but he must be losing his touch if he was of the opinion that young Oliver could trip anyone up with a flamboyant trick like that.

Oliver went down the stairs and out into Queen's Road, a moving thicket of carriages, rickshaws, sedan chairs and pedestrians. As he saw it, there were two options open to him now. There was the official launch, which meant getting permission. He knew, without asking, that would be refused. Anyway, it was too obvious. The outlying islands were essentially the preserve of Haaka fisherfolk and villagers. They were unlikely to talk to any Englishman arriving on what could be construed as an official mission. Or he could take the steamer, anonymously, to Macau. From there he could cross to Tai-O, where the locals were bound to know everything about a hi-jack off their shores.

He stopped on the pavement, rubbing his forehead, his mind seething with plans. He would have to take an interpreter. Lin Yan's cook boy had a Haaka wife, and she would know when the steamboat was due to leave . . . He dashed back up the hill, on his way to The Peak tram.

With the clear daylight spreading around her, Hellen looked down at her appalling clothes. She could not live day after day, week after week, smelling of sweat and vomit. Neither could she sit here in solitary boredom waiting for help that might never come.

I lit a candle to a Chinese god, whatever that means, she told herself. Now I must go out and try my luck. Across the water, in the opposite direction from the way she had come, she could see a great sweep of land. If that was China, she told herself, it ought to be the New Territories. Somewhere there it ought to be possible to find someone to help her.

How did one say good-bye and thank you to a monk who did not speak one's language? Hellen ate what she could of the unappetising mess in her breakfast bowl. Rice, perhaps, in an unrecognisable state of sludge? When the monks, in their trusty black habits, filed out of the dining hall, she approached the inevitably unknowable one who had acted as her guide. Beckoning to him in a way that seemed appropriate, she led him across the plateau to one of the smaller gateways on the mainland side. Pointing down the track, then pointing to herself, she indicated that she was leaving.

The monk said something in a high, perplexed voice. She pointed out into the far distance. "China?" she asked, looking anxiously into his face. He made no sign that he understood. With a smile, which was the only way she could think of to show her gratitude—Might one shake hands with a Buddhist monk? She thought it best not to make the attempt—she went through the small arch and began the descent. At the turning where the track would take her out of sight, she looked back. He was standing where she had left him, his shapeless habit drooping from rounded shoulders. She waved.

This side of the island was nothing like as steep as the climb had been, and the track was clear, running in zig-zags between the same scrawny, weather-roughened bushes. Within half an hour the curve of the hillside straightened and she could see the foot of the mountain. Where the land levelled out there were patches of gold, indicating a cultivated crop. Rice? Beyond, little sampans were dotted on the snuff-coloured water. Where had the blueness gone? Was it possible that this inland sea had been discoloured by the outpouring of the Pearl River that ran down through Canton? If so, she thought with renewed hope, the swathe of land before her could well be the New Territories.

It was a long walk down the mountain, the only sound the crunch of her deck shoes on the stony track, and the call and twitter of birds. Occasionally a lizard, sunning itself, leaped awake and darted into the safety of the undergrowth. Once a snake slithered across her path, but her involuntary scream sent it on its way. The sun had passed its zenith by the time she reached flat land. Here, on the edge of a paddy field, she was disconcerted to discover the track had petered out, but the narrow ridges between the plants afforded a good foothold, and they ran diagonally from the bottom of the mountain towards the sea.

Emerging from the paddy field, she found another track that led her to a walled village bearing no sign of life. The heat here, after the cool of the mountaintop, was stifling. She came upon a tiny coolie woman supporting a bamboo stick across her shoulders, a laden basket fixed at either end. The woman backed off the track to allow Hellen to pass, her face expressionless and still. She wore a mushroom-shaped hat identical to those worn by yesterday's rescuers. The sun beat down, relentlessly on the top of Hellen's head, and her arms, now, were red as a lobster shell.

It was perhaps two miles farther on that she came to the fishing village. Skirting the slant-roofed shacks, she hurried down on to the waterfront, and swiftly removing her shoes, paddled in the cool water, carelessly kicking it up on to her skirt, filling her cupped hands with it, flinging it over her face, her neck, and the top of her head.

Farther along the shore she could now see a small pier jutting out into the water. She paddled back to the shore, put on her shoes, and made her way towards it. The fisher folk had spread a recent catch along the pier.

Thousands of tiny fish, bright silver in the strong sunlight, lay on the hard surface to dry, filling the air with a tangy and faintly melodorous smell.

Hellen looked round for help. Two tiny men emerged from one of the shacks and began walking towards her, one absorbly rolling up a fishing line, the other holding the loose cord in his hands. They stared at her, their outward sloping eyes intent in mask-like faces, half hidden beneath the curtained brims of their hats.

"English?" she asked, tentatively.

One of them pointed, and glancing round she saw a ferry boat, laden with passengers, coming round the bluff of the island directly ahead. She nodded, smiled, and they want on their way. Little boats began to move out, the ferry dropped anchor, and the passengers climbed down a ladder. The smaller craft filled up, turned around, and scuttled busily back inshore.

She nervously approached and stood waiting. Black-clad fisher-women came ashore with long baskets on carrying poles, their men, thin-stalked mushrooms in their strange hats, walked unencumbered. As the last passenger disembarked and it seemed the boatman was ready to return to the ferry for more custom, she stepped forward.

"English?" she asked tentatively.

He pointed to the seats, indicating that she might climb aboard. Sculling with great skill, using his single oar, he made the short journey. As they bumped up against the ferry's hull, he grasped the ladder with one hand, steadying his little craft, then impassively held out his free hand for the fare.

With a feeling of helplessness, Hellen inverted both of the pockets in her skirt to show them to be empty. His face twisted in a spasm of anger, and to her dismay he released the ladder and kicked the boat away, leaving the gangplank teetering over the water. There was a cachophony of protest from impatient passengers waiting on the deck to go ashore.

"English!" Hellen shouted, pointing towards the mainland. The boatman hawked and spat into the water. Protests from the deck increased and were joined by a clattering, rattling tirade of staccato abuse from the boatman. "Please," cried Hellen insistently, joining in the hullabaloo, "Please! Please! You must let me go on board." Up on the ferry's deck one of the incoming passengers elbowed his way to the rail. Addressing Hellen directly, he held a finger across his throat. Hellen nodded. "Pirates!" she shouted and drew a finger across her own throat. Then, just in case the taking of an ear was an old Chinese custom, she simulated what had happened to George. A murmur of sympathy arose from the fisherfolk, and to a man they vigorously shook their fists at the boatman.

With a surly nod, he manoeuvred his craft back against the ship. The gangplank teetered across and down. Hellen grasped it and clambered aboard the ferry. The waiting passengers made way for her, their slitted eyes staring from impassive faces. A wiry little man wearing an authoritative air came forward and beckoned to her. She followed him to the wheelhouse. The Captain gazed at her with his countrymen's passive, unblinking stare. In a high, cacophonous voice, the other man explained Hellen's presence. The Captain nodded.

Hellen could only smile at him to indicate her gratitude. Then she pointed towards the mainland. "English?" she asked.

"Macao," replied the captain. "Portuguese."

With renewed hope, Hellen found a seat at the rails. According to George, Macao was a kind of liberty hall where Hong Kongers went hoping to win a fortune playing Fantan. He had mentioned an hotel called the Bella Vista. With luck, there might even be some English staying there now.

Macao was an entrancing, delightful little town. Old men, with brown faces cratered by age and exposure, sat on the pavements smoking their long pipes, and philosophically regarding the passers by. There were dark-skinned, dark-haired women, surrounded by small children, cooking rice over tiny fires in the gutters. Older children made circles on the pavements, playing card games. Here and there a man slept on his mat, impervious to the noise of passing feet and tinkling voices.

Hellen set out to walk, keeping within the shade of a row of banyan trees. She walked slowly, following a graceful crescent by the shore, all the time looking round her, alert for a tall figure, an English face. She walked the length of the waterfront and back without seeing anyone who looked remotely English. Feeling a little desperate, she approached a dark-skinned, respectable-looking man unmistakably enjoying an afternoon stroll with his wife. He shrank back, then hurried on his way. The woman with him turned and spoke to Hellen in a foreign tongue, angrily gesturing to her to move off the pavement.

"Bella Vista," she shouted after them. They hurried on. "Bella Vista?" she repeated in despair. She looked down at her torn and dirty clothes, at her shoes that were covered in dust and dirt, and remembered that her hair had not been brushed for two days. She began to be frightened.

To her right now, a narrow street ran up from the waterfront. There were houses here, prettily painted in soft colours. She decided to try her luck. Away from the trees and the water the heat had gathered between the walls, and the sun burned up from the cobbles. Her head was aching. She examined carefully every coloured front door, but there were no English names, and nothing to show the nationality of the people who lived behind them.

She had covered perhaps a hundred yards when an elderly man appeared out of a side-street and began making his way towards her, walking with a stick. He was tall! An Englishman? Her heart began to beat fast. As he came nearer she saw that his skin beneath the sheltering panama hat, though sallow, was paler than any she had so far seen here. She stepped forward. He drew himself upright, his eyes surveying her with faint distaste.

"Please," she said, automatically extending a hand to stop him should he step aside, "are you English?"

"I am Portuguese," he replied.

"Tell me, please, where can I find the Bella Vista hotel."

"Are you sure it is the Bella Vista you want?" he asked, in heavily accented English, too kind, too courteous to brush her aside, but clearly wishing to move on.

"I have come from *Bangkok Lady*," she told him. "Did you know—"

"My dear," he was immediately concerned, "I'm so sorry. So terribly sorry. I thought—"

His immense warmth melted the last of her resilience, and Hellen burst into tears.

"There, there, my dear," she heard him say kindly. "It's going to be all right."

She knew it was going to be all right. An immediate rightness that would carry her a little further on her way, but she was unable stop crying. He comforted her. "Here, take my handkerchief. Poor little girl," he said.

Hellen mopped at her face. "I lost my . . ." She began to cry again, for she had lost not only handkerchief, but everything, and most importantly, Oliver.

"Come, my dear," said the stranger gently, "I'll take you to my daughter's house. My goodness, and to think I took you for a beggar! I am most dreadfully sorry." With an arm through hers he began to lead her back along the street.

"Celeste lives nearby. I was on my way to visit her. How did you get here? And all alone! Now really," he chided himself, "I must not ask questions. First, we must clean you up and get a message to Hong Kong."

Hong Kong! Oliver! Hellen broke down again. She arrived on the doorstep of Dona Celeste's pretty pink villa with its ornate, lion-headed knocker with tears once more streaming down her cheeks. She did not see the look of horror on the face of the old man's daughter as she stumbled into the shaded interior, but she felt her familiarity as a westerner, and sensed her kindness.

The old man said something in Portuguese which brought a gasp from his daughter. Dona Celeste did not ask questions. She, too, spoke accented, though near perfect, English. She urged Hellen to sit down on a wooden seat in the hall while she sent a servant for warmed buffalo milk—explaining apologetically that there were no cows in Macau. The old man went away, and returned carrying a bottle. Dona Celeste sat down beside Hellen while she drank the brandy and milk, holding Hellen's hand on her knee, patting it with her cool palm in thick, soothing little gestures, saying, "Never mind, dear. Never mind. We will soon arrange everything."

Hellen pushed her sticky hair back from her face and sat up straight. "I'm terribly sorry. You're very kind."

"Kind? No. It is nothing."

She told them briefly about her escape.

"You were lucky. But you know, Chinese don't ill treat women."

She shivered involuntarily, remembering it was after George hit her that they cut off his ear.

"When did you last eat?" her hostess asked.

"This morning, but not very much. Something like overcooked rice."

"Congee." Madame Celeste grimaced. "It is the staple Chinese breakfast."

"You were right to leave," said the man. "Those monks were most probably illiterate. They are a very isolated community. It was brave of you to tackle the walk to Tai-O alone, though." He smiled at her. "All's well that ends well."

"My cook will prepare for you something that will be as familiar as it is possible to make," Dona Celeste said with bright concern and goodwill. "You like fish? That is quick to prepare. Fish is very good in Macau."

"Thank you. I don't want to be any trouble. . . ." Hellen's eyes once more filled with tears, and she could not go on.

"There, there," said her hostess soothingly. "You are not any trouble at all. You shall have soup, for there always soup on the stove, and vegetables cooked in the English way—we have many English friends. Now, let me take you to the bath, and I will find some of my daughter's clothes for you. And some cream for that sunburn."

There was an immense white bath in a bathroom decorated, walls and floor, with blue-and-white Portuguese tiles. Hellen lay back in the hot water, her hair floating, soaking the grime, the sweat and the misery away, drowning the uncertainties and the very real fear of the future. Never had water felt so soft, nor scented soap so luxurious. She gave herself up, hedonistically, to the kind of comfort and safety she had known all her life, wondering how she could ever have taken it for granted.

There were no questions to be answered. She sat in a pale blue nightdress and velvet robe belonging to Dona Celeste's daughter, eating ravenously. As the strain, the fears and the shocks of the day took their toll she had to fight to keep her eyes open. Only when Senor Marques, for that was his name, asked, "But should we not send a message to Hong Kong saying you are safe?" did her drooping eyelids open with fear. Dona Celeste whispered, "Let her rest, Papa," and relief flooded in.

She was tucked into bed in a big, airy room, and the shutters closed against daylight and heat.

She fell asleep immediately.

There was a big dressing table, a heavily carved mahogany wardrobe, some holy pictures in gold frames, a tiled floor. Hellen sat up in bed looking round the unfamiliar room. Macao! The present came in with a shock. She put her feet to the floor, slipped into the velvet gown and flung the shutters wide. There was a sky of birds' egg blue and a skyline broken romantically by a ruined cathedral façade, pink and gold in the morning light. There were birds chirruping in an acacia tree close beneath her window, and a flock of sparrows bickering and chattering in the dust. A sweet, strong voice arose from somewhere below, singing an aria in an unfamiliar language.

A young voice called, "Hello, there. I'm Isabel." Standing in the courtyard, looking up, was a pretty, dark-haired girl about the same age as herself. "You can certainly sleep," she said, speaking in only faintly accented English, affecting awe. "I understand you've been at it since yesterday afternoon."

Hellen shook back her silky, clean—oh, so beautifully clean—hair, and smiled. "I was very tired," she said. "I'm sorry about this." She slid her fingers along the sleeve of the robe.

"That's perfectly all right. I love to loan my clothes to ship-wrecked damsels in distress. Look in the wardrobe, and take your pick. Mama says you're a bit taller than I am. I hope something fits. Your underwear has been washed. You'll find it laid out on the big chair. I took the liberty of creeping in while you were asleep and having a look at you," Isobel said engagingly. "I've never seen a shipwrecked lady before."

Hellen laughed.

"Feel free to use the brushes and combs," said Isobel generously.

"Come down when you're ready. There's a whole lot in the morning paper about the shipwreck, but nothing about you. Do you exist?" she asked, her dark head set on one side, and then without waiting for a reply, "They found *Bangkok Lady*, but the pirates had disappeared into thin air, taking the loot with them."

Hellen's heart began to thud. She had to ask, even knowing the answer, whatever it was, to be unacceptable. She cleared her throat, then cleared it again. Her voice came as a queer croak, with a tremble at the end, "Was anyone left alive?"

"Yes. Some of the Chinese crew, and an Englishman whose ear they used as a ransom note. I presume you know him? George someone . . ."

Hellen withdrew and sat down on the underwear so carefully laid out for her, head in her hands.

Down in the breakfast room, Isabel examined her guest critically. Seeing her from the courtyard, Hellen had appeared rosy and strong. Now, it seemed from the way her hands trembled, from her listless manner as she toyed with the food, that her misadventure had indeed taken its toll. She leaned forward in her chair, saying kindly, "Maybe you would rather eat something else? Just say, and we'll be able to produce it, I'm sure."

"No, please," Hellen protested. "I'm not hungry. I mean, I did make rather a glutton of myself yesterday. I was starving when I arrived."

Dona Celeste bustled in and sat down in the big, studded leather carver. "Now, my dear, what are we going to do about letting the authorities know you're here? We really should have sent a message yesterday. Papa was quite worried about it." She added, her eyes puzzled, "There's no mention of you in the paper."

Hellen looked down at her uneaten toast. "I was not supposed to be on *Bangkok Lady*."

"You mean—you were a stowaway!" Isobel sat bolt upright in her chair, clapping her hands with delight. "A stowaway!"

Her mother frowned.

"No. I wasn't a stowaway. I was travelling on *Devanha*. I left it at Singapore, to finish the journey on *Bangkok Lady*."

They stared at her in open astonishment.

"A little adventure," said Hellen feebly. There was a moment's silence as they contemplated her daring, or perhaps her inexplicable foolishness. To cover the awkward silence, she asked, "When does the ferry leave Macau for Hong Kong?" Then, lest they return to the subject of sending a message, she added, "If you would be incredibly kind and loan me the money for my fare, I'd like to catch it."

"Of course."

They were so trusting, so kind. Their anxiety to help reminded Hellen agonisingly of how Ruth, also, had tried, with equal goodwill, and been treated to the same lack of candour. "My family have sent funds for me direct. I shall pay you back immediately," she said, staring at the sugar bowl so that she did not have to meet their puzzled eyes.

"Please. . . ." They waved her promises aside as inconsequential. "We are only too happy to help."

Heaven alone knew what they were thinking as the ferry pulled out carrying this odd stranger wearing Isabel's dress, her ticket paid for with their money, and a little sheaf of their Hong Kong dollars in a wallet in her hand. They waved her good-bye with puzzled goodwill, and wished her luck. She stood at the rail until they became tiny figures in the distance. As the ferry headed across the water she went to the bow and stood looking out at the little islands, scarcely seeing them. She would go to the Hong Kong Hotel, she decided, simply because it was the only hotel she knew. She would be able to contact Ruth from there by telephone. Now, she wondered with apprehension what kind of reception she would get.

"If you had been a bit more friendly on the boat you wouldn't be in this mess."

In her mind's eye she saw Oliver, mistily.

Chapter 13

Hong Kong

The lower deck of the ferry was packed with Chinese. There were only a handful in first class. They steamed through a myriad of featureless islands, some barren, others richly green and apparently uninhabited, except at the water's edge where there were fishermen's shacks. Several hours out they passed a ferry going in the opposite direction. A man who could have been Oliver stood in the bow, staring straight ahead.

Hellen closed her eyes.

She wondered if she might go home and let George divorce her for desertion. Then she remembered, with a sense of shock, her father's warning: "Once you make your bed, we shall expect you to lie on it." A contract was a contract, he would say, and for heaven's sake, if she did not want the man, why had she married him? Ah! That precluded explanation.

She tried out the humiliating, scourging relief of confession, turning it over her tongue. "I was raped. I married George because I thought I was pregnant."

No. There would be no cloudy-edged confession, no blaming others. She would see this through with her pride intact. The sun beat out of a leaden sky. The hat Isobel had loaned her kept the worst of the sun's rays at bay. She leaned on the rail gazing at the islands.

She was unprepared for the magnificence of Hong Kong when it loomed out of the mist, a layer cake of an island, rising from the elegant colonial buildings on the waterfront, to where tier upon tier of stony escarpments and jutting rocks fled upwards to a cloud-obscured summit.

Two cathedrals dominated the lower slopes of the mountain, one consciously gothic in the catholic tradition, one classical and stark white. St John's Cathedral, where she and Oliver were to have been married? Between the two, rising elegantly on a mound of parkland, stood a big-windowed, square mansion. Hellen stared at it stonily, seeing it as the millstone round Oliver's neck, and the tripwire, setting in motion all the events that had brought her to this.

"Government House is just across the road from the cathedral," Oliver had told her. "If brides walked, you could walk, but they'll expect you to go in style." She gazed from one to the other, and wished with all her heart that Oliver should have been a lowly clerk in the Colonial Secretariat or a shipping office.

They steamed past high-pooped junks with tattered sails stretched on frail-looking bamboo ribs; junks whose decks were strewn with fishing nets, cooking pots, dog kennels, wooden tubs, ropes. Tiny sampans tossed like discarded kites on the choppy waters. As they approached the shore an all pervading medley of odours, putrid fish, rotting vegetables, dead animals, filled the air.

They passed a squat boat with canvas after-awning. On deck, an infant tottered amongst the household clutter, perilously close to the side. A woman with a baby supported by a red net strung across her back, plied a single oar that extended over the stern. On the foredeck a husband squatted, his black pigtail falling, incongruously, from the crown of his shaven head to his buttocks. The bloated carcass of a dog bounced across the ferry's bow, and sheered away, its legs wobbling heavenwards. Hellen took in every aspect of the strange and unexpected scene with awed fascination. She did not know what she had anticipated. Certainly not this medley of bustle, and beauty, and filth.

They tied up below the town and there was a rush to go ashore. Nervous of meeting a chance acquaintance from *Devanha*, she pulled her borrowed hat down to shield her face, swiftly averting her head as two young Englishmen in white suits walked past. Thankfully, they were engrossed in notebooks, consulting one another, making pencil marks in a businesslike manner. They did not spare her a glance.

The heat on the shoreline was unbearable. Already the borrowed dress was sticking to her skin. She fought her way through crowds of coolies, through the shrieky rattle of their voices, until she reached the flood of cobblestones that constituted the quay. A beggar, curled up on the ground, snatched at her skirt. A respectable-looking Chinese gentlemen, fluttering a brightly coloured paper fan, came to her rescue, threatening the beggar carelessly with his bamboo stick. She smiled at him gratefully, but he did not respond. His face, glistening with perspiration, was still, the almond eyes remote.

There were red-painted rickshaws lining the curb.

"Hotel? Hotel? Hong Kong Hotel?" chanted a half-naked chair coolie, jumping up eagerly from the cobblestones. Others closed in, coaxing, wheedling, chattering insistently in their high-pitched voices, eventually fighting for her custom like starving dogs. She was glad to slip into the nearest chair and be swept away.

The hotel building was reassuringly familiar with just a touch of exoticism, the upper storeys extending over the footpath to provide a shaded promenade. She crossed a deep open drain by means of a precarious wooden plank, and went in beneath the great stone arches, to be welcomed by a flurry of Chinese flunkies. Two boys dressed in picturesque long gowns with high collars and piped edges, swung the doors open to admit her, another led her to the reception desk, while a fourth hovered attentively close by. She smiled at them, thanking them, but their faces remained impassive and she was reminded that the passengers on board *Devanha* never said thank you to a coolie.

The lounge was dotted with tables peopled by elegant, expensive-looking women, all chattering and calling greetings to each other. In these unexpectedly elegant surroundings, Hellen was suddenly lacking in confidence. She fingered the borrowed purse nervously, conscious it did not contain the price of a room. The dress she was wearing, that she had been so glad to accept from Celeste in Macao, became ill-fitting, and embarrassingly short. The booking clerk informed her they would be only too pleased to provide her with a room, but he wanted to know about her luggage. Two svelte Chinese desk clerks in bright cheongsams gazed at her with curiosity and interest.

Tilting the brim of her hat a little lower over her eyes, flicking the side pieces of her hair forward in order to mask her features, she said, "It will be here shortly." She stood with her back to the lounge as she spoke, jumpily conscious that this was a dangerous place to be for a girl who did not wish to explain her presence. Any moment now, she could imagine herself confronted by one or more of those shipboard acquaintances wandering past on their way in or out. The Hong Kong Hotel was the mecca for curry tiffins, tea dances, tea.

The desk clerk suggested, dead pan, that she should wait in the lounge until her luggage came. She made an attempt to appear untroubled by this problem, adopting what she thought might look like a sophisticated air to hide the fact that she was terrified out of her wits because they would not provide her with a bolt hole.

"I would like you to put a telephone call through to Mrs Ruth Washington," she said, and making a pathetic attempt to look haughty, added, "I'm sure you will find her number in the book. Then," pretending there had been no reticence on their part because she was without luggage, "perhaps you would be good enough to show me to my room."

The desk clerk was immediately alert. "You are flend of Mrs Washington?" If he had been a smiling man, Hellen thought, weak-kneed with gratitude for the magic wand of Ruth's name, he would have smiled.

She did not know what she had expected from Ruth. The shriek, yes. Relief? Shock? "I'll come, dear," she said.

"I'll be in my room. And, Ruth, if you meet anyone, or if anyone is with you, would you please not tell—"

"I understand. I'll be as quick as I can." One of the boys emerged with a key from behind the desk and escorted her to a room with huge windows overlooking the street. Another, materialising suddenly and unexpectedly, switched on the cooling fans, and there was yet another, drawing the curtains that had been closed against the heat. One of them indicated such comforts as the hotel was showering upon her. The big chintz-covered chairs that might have been lifted out of an English country house; the low table where she would take her tea; the writing desk.

"Wantee char, Missie?"

"Char?"

"Wantee tea?"

"No, thank you. Not just now."

"Bath?" The boy who had drawn the curtains was standing in the doorway leading to the bathroom, impassively waiting for permission to turn on the taps.

"Later, when my luggage comes."

"Luggage come soon?"

"Yes."

They stole away, closing the door silently as they went, and she was relieved to be left alone. She laid Isabel's hat carefully on the bed and washed her hands and face at the basins, noting the luxurious white towels, wondering if she would ever again be able to take such things for granted. Then, having tidied her hair with the comb Isabel had given her, she went to a window. Leaning on the sill, she watched the crowd below where rickshaw coolies threaded their way through cars and pedestrians. A driver of a square-built, black-painted Ford, hooting noisily, narrowly missed a limping beggar who was crossing the road. Young Englishmen, in white suits and solar topees, immensely tall among the tiny Chinese, hurried along with a busi-nesslike air, all carrying important-looking papers in their hands.

Gazing down on the busy scene, Hellen tried not to think, but as the waiting time extended she grew more and more nervous. Ruth, she remembered, was a flagrant gossip. And she had resented Hel-len's neither confiding in her not heeding her advice. Was she not now

137

presenting her with the perfect opportunity to get her own back, if Ruth wished to do so?

Hellen moved nervously away from the window, back into the centre of the room. Perhaps she should simply telephone Oliver, make a clean breast of everything, and throw herself on his mercy. At least he would be discreet. She considered calling the P & O Company to book a return berth. Why not? She could send out to the bank for her funds, and hide in her room until the boat was ready to sail.

Then there was a rat-a-tat-tat on the door and Ruth, wearing a cotton voile dress and a huge hat decorated with a swirl of silk roses, came in like a whirlwind, crossed the room at a run, and enveloped Hellen in her arms. "What happened? You were on that wretched ship? Were you on that ship? With George?"

Hellen nodded, too overcome to speak.

Ruth stood back, holding her at arm's length. "Look at you! Your poor nose is sunburnt. But you've survived. Oh Hellen, what a naughty girl you are!"

Her overflowing goodwill was a shock and a blessed relief. "Ruth, I'm sorry." A stupid remark, Hellen thought even as she spoke, but meant to cover everything.

"Sorry for what? You don't have to explain. I understood everything immediately I saw Oliver's cable."

"Oliver's—?"

"He sent you a cable, dear, to Singapore." Ruth began to peel off her white gloves. "I didn't open it out of curiosity. I really don't open people's mail, but I was so worried." She fluttered her hands defensively, then flopped into one of the armchairs, in the same movement removing her beautiful hat, flinging it on the bed, patting the neatly marcelled waves in her hair. "Oh, Hellen! If only the cable had been there waiting for you when we berthed. You wouldn't have gone, would you?"

Hellen sat down in the other chair, facing her. She was trembling.

Ruth fished in her handbag and withdrew an envelope marked OHMS. "I kept it for you."

Hellen's fingers shook as she removed the single sheet and looked down at the message. DARLING HELLEN STOP PERMISSION TO MARRY GRANTED STOP ALL ARRANGED FOR TENTH JULY STOP LOVE OLIVER. Feeling sick, and distressed beyond bearing, she crumpled the paper in her hands.

"He sent it as soon as he could," said Ruth, looking anxiously into Hellen's still face. "It was a long job, talking his uncle round. Lady Sylvia Ashton is a very old friend. Sir Rowan was inclined to respect her judgment."

Hellen closed her eyes. If only George had not taken her aboard *Bangkok Lady*! The release of tension afforded her by *Devanha*'s disappearance over the horizon would surely have brought the curse. Then, with the perfectly good excuse that she had not heard from Oliver, she would have telegraphed, asking if it was all right to proceed. The agony of knowing that none of it need have happened, was sending her a little mad.

Ruth sat in puzzled silence, watching the emotions fleeing across Hellen's face. She said hopefully, "We can fix it up. We'll concoct a story—"

Hellen opened her yes. "I married George."

There was a stunned silence. The shouts of the coolies in the street outside, the whirring of the fans, were like echoes from another world.

"You what?" whispered Ruth at last.

It came in a rush, a great outpouring of words, a muddled emptying of the coffers of misery. Then she fell into a chair, put her head down on her arms, and sobbed. What George had done while she slept, what Calum had done when she was drifting between two worlds, somehow did not have a place in the dreadful outcome. "This is what happened, these are the facts," she was crying piteously, begging for a miracle. "Undo them, Ruth, undo them for me."

Ruth perched herself on the arm of Hellen's chair. She was shocked and horrified at the disclosures. Was drugging a girl a crime in the eyes of the law? Deliberately putting her aboard a boat—did that constitute abduction? Was this a matter for the courts? She had barrister friends who could advise her.

But the scandal! She was suddenly breathless at the thought of such a scandal as would rock the colony to its very foundations. And if the case came to court, inevitably, she would be involved. Better not mention either abduction or rape to Hellen, for she seemed not to have thought of them herself. She smoothed Hellen's hair, comforting her, coming to terms with the fact that there was really nothing that could legally be done. Not without upsetting a lot of important people and, to boot, jeopardising her own social position.

Hellen shook with great wracking sobs. All the misery she had suffered since that first dreadful morning when she decided she must be pregnant with Calum's child, welled up out of the depths of her and tore her apart. It was a blood-letting, but not a cleansing. There was too much guilt for that. It was a different kind of weeping from that of the day before, leaning on kind Senor Marques's shoulder in that hot little street in Macau. That had been relief. This was sheer despair.

Ruth pressed the service bell and ordered tea.

"Char," she said to the room boy who arrived with the speed of wind and as silently as snow. "A brandy, too." She helped Hellen wash her face, loaned her her own powder puff, and tenderly combed her hair. "You'll feel better after having tea' We'll talk afterwards." They sat in silence, waiting for the tea to come.

Ruth was busy with her own unhappy thoughts. This news was going to break Oliver's heart. She thought of Lettice, torn between husband and beloved nephew. Of Rowan, who would have no sympathy with such human weaknesses as Hellen possessed. Privately, she did not think Hellen, however well things turned out for her, had a hope of marrying Oliver now. The tea came. Ruth bullied Hellen gently until she had finished the brandy. When she had eaten the little sandwiches and drunk the tea, colour began to return to her cheeks.

"What we need to know," said Ruth, "before approaching Oliver, who incidentally has gone today to Lantau—" She broke off as Hellen's face crumpled.

"I saw him." She emitted a soft little wail. "Standing in the bow of the Macao ferry. I thought I was dreaming."

"Don't worry," said Ruth consolingly. "It's better, for the moment, that he should be out of the way. He'll hear about you from the stake-net fishermen who cross to Macao every day with their catch, and he'll come straight back. What we need to know, is whether George will agree to a divorce. You would be on a much better wicket if—I don't quite know how to put this, dear." Her cheeks reddened. "You have had a week's—er—honeymoon."

"Honeymoon!" exclaimed Hellen bitterly.

Ruth examined the toes of her shoes. "You know what I mean, dear." She took out an ivory cigarette holder and fitted a Sobranie into it, not meeting Hellen's eyes. She rummaged in her handbag and produced a gold lighter, gazed at the flame, took several puffs at the cigarette, delicately touched her fingers to the careful curls over her ears. When Hellen still had not replied she rose and went to the window, standing looking down on the intersection of Des Voeux Road and Peddar Street. "You've lived with him," she managed at last, without turning. "If you hadn't lived with him, you might have been able to get an anulment."

Hellen stared at her back. "You mean, if we didn't—"

"Yes, dear." Ruth turned round, her cheeks flaming. "That's what I mean, if you didn't—er—hadn't. . . ."

Hellen said bluntly, "I had the curse. We didn't."

Ruth was ecstatic at this glimpse of her own coming redemption.

"My dear, did you not know that a marriage isn't, in some curious way, totally binding until you've—?"

Hellen blinked and shook her head.

Ruth crossed the room and stood looking down at Hellen in the chair. She said intensely, "Could you swear with your hand on the Bible, that you didn't, actually, live with him?"

"Absolutely." Hellen was remembering how she had been poised on a razor's edge that morning, with George's patience at its limit. I have the pirates to thank for that, she thought with awe, and rising excitement. Then her spirits plummetted as she remembered the other thing. "I think he did it when I was drugged."

Ruth flushed, hating having to talk like this about something so rude. She said, "That was rape. He wouldn't dare admit rape. And, anyway, you weren't married. It shouldn't count. Unless it counted against him." She added venomously, "The pig." She ground out her cigarette in the ashtray and sat down, adjusting her skirt over her knees.

"You may have to go home, dear. Even an annulment, in this tiny colony, could cause a whiff of scandal, or at the best a great deal of gossip that would take some time to die down. It wouldn't be good for your—I mean, Sir Rowan wouldn't like it, and it wouldn't be fair to him."

"No, of course." Hellen's eyes were bright with uncertain hope.

"Now, what to do?" Ruth wondered aloud. "My gut feeling is to send for George and see what he has to say. He has arrived, you know. The first mate is in hospital, with bullets in his knee, and serve him jolly well right, but George has been treated and allowed home."

"There is no question of discussing this matter in front of you, Mrs Washington," said George coldly. "When you've gone on your way I'll talk to my wife. She is my wife, you know, and I have the marriage certificate to prove it." He saw the shock in Hellen's face and asked sarcastically," You didn't really think the pirates would be interested in that, did you?"

His sang froid was frightening.

"Even if they had taken it," George continued, "there's proof in the ship's log. However, since you're talking divorce—"

"Annulment, George. Hellen is talking about annulment," said Ruth, hating this gaunt, cold-looking man with his hair half hidden behind a white hospital bandage. He stood now with feet set apart, in the middle of the room, head confidently high, as though he owned the hotel. She had not disliked George before. She had never been sufficiently interested in him to bother.

He went to the door, opened it and stood pointedly holding it open.

Bristling with indignation, Ruth turned to Hellen. Hellen gave her the faintest of apologetic smiles, thinking it was better this way for Ruth would be dreadfully embarrassed when she had to say out loud the reason why the marriage might be annulled. "I'll see you downstairs shortly."

Ruth picked up her handbag and hat. With gentle fingers she touched Hellen's cheek. "I'll be in the lounge, dear." She crossed the room and went out into the passage, seething.

George shut the door, then locked it. Hellen's eyes dilated. She said in a rush, "The marriage hasn't been consummated. That's what we wanted to talk to you about. The fact that it apparently isn't quite legal. It seems, that may be grounds for annulment."

He smiled to hide the very real fear he felt. "That's your word against mine," he said, his eyes watchful.

"What do you mean?"

"I mean, what magistrate, judge or jury, would believe that a man of my type would share a cabin with a pretty girl like you, or any woman for that matter, for nearly a week, without any hanky-panky?" In spite of the suffocating heat in the room, Hellen began to shiver. In the ceiling, the fans whirled softly. George was getting his nerve back. Maybe that interfering old cow hadn't thought of abduction. It was abduction that scared him.

"But you don't love me," Hellen protested, trying vainly to keep the panic out of her voice.

"Who says I don't love you?" He asked the question unemotionally, for he was still waiting for the other thing, whether she now knew it was a criminal act to abduct her. The Washington bitch could testify to his collecting the suitcase. The Purser, who had taken his Squeeze and had nothing to lose now, could say George had countermanded Hellen's orders to send the trunk ashore. Charlie Marsh was a good friend and business colleague where there was quick money to be made, but George would not trust him as far as he could throw him if Charlie found himself in a jam. He would testify without batting an eyelid that George doctored Hellen's drink, and he'd see that the one surviving coolie who had witnessed the affair backed him up.

Hellen's eyes were wide and frightened. George's lack of love for her was written plainly on his face. "You hit me—"

"I did?" He brushed a hand across his forehead, feigning loss of that particular memory. "I scarcely remember what happened that awful day. It was all chaos, wasn't it?" And then, his very real resentment getting the better of him, he touched a finger to the

142

bandage over the place where his ear had been. "I've you to thank for this."

"No, George," she protested, "you brought it on yourself. They cut off your ear because you hit me. I now know the Chinese don't ill treat women. They didn't like what you did."

He panicked. If she told people of his bashing her out of sheer frustration when he discovered who she was, he would be ruined. "What rubbish, you silly litle scrubber! The Chinese are the cruellest nation on earth. I told you that. Chinese pirates will do anything. You saw what they did with the fools who stood up to them."

She could only think that he had called her a scrubber, and that it sounded dreadful. "What does it mean, George? Scrubber?" She needed to know precisely how he felt about her. He would not say.

He was making an unholy mess of this, his feelings getting the better of him at every turn. The trouble was, he hadn't had time to accustom himself to the fact that she was actually alive. Boggis was dead. Charlie Marsh had guaranteed to get someone to erase the marriage entry in the ship's log. He'd already agreed on a price. Now he was faced with the dilemma of her survival. It seemed to him, in his confused and unhappy state, that the closest he could get to safety was to cut the ground from beneath her feet, and do it now. The chances were she would give up, once he had established his rights, and taken them.

He looked across at the bed, then back to her, smiling. "You made me a promise, just before the attack. Promises are made to be kept. What about it now? I can't think of anything I'd rather do this afternoon than roll you round in that bed." He came towards her, and as he came, still smiling, he was undoing the buttons on the front of his jacket.

Hellen took an involuntary step in the opposite direction. His stomach muscles tightened with fear. He didn't want to use force, but if it came to that. . . "I don't want to rape you," he told her, his voice reasonable, even courteous, "but I assure you, you won't leave this room until the marriage has been, as you put it so nicely, consummated."

She made a rush for the door but he was there before her, pocketing the key. His fear subsided, diminished by the excitement of the chase. He'd tame her, once he got her on her back. She was going to love this.

"You are, of course, accustomed to rape," she flung at him.

"I've never needed it. I've always found women a push-over."

"You're bound to, if you drug them first."

He gave her an odd look, half a smile, as though it was almost a relief to have that out in the open. "It's not as though you were a virgin," he said cruelly, playing his ace card.

She turned away, biting her lips. He waited a moment, then went to stand in front of her, gazing without apparent feeling upon her humiliation and despair. His fingers were almost gentle as he lifted her chin. "I can't have the whole of gossipy little Hong Kong saying I've no lead in my pencil, which is what a divorce, or, as you call it, non-consummation amounts to," he said. "No man worth his salt is going to lay himself open to that charge. And Oliver wouldn't marry you, anyway.

"A Marathon marry a divorced woman! Not likely," said George convincingly, drowning her futile dreams in down-to-earth rhetoric. "He wouldn't merely be banished to the New Territories—he'd be sent to the South Pole. And besides," he added, "you've lost one of their family heirlooms. That won't have done you much good."

She wanted to fly at him, scratch his face, pummel him with her fists, but she knew he would not hesitate to retaliate, so she closed her eyes tightly and stood still. At least she did not have to look at him, this strange and cruel man she had married.

Her very control inflamed his desire to dominate and subdue her. "Now come on, old girl," he said, "make the best of it." She was not going to give in, he could see that. He was going to have to use force. Damn! If things went wrong, that could count against him. He thought of a brilliant compromise. "I'll tell you what, if you don't scream I'll leave you alone in the future. Hong Kong's full of obliging ladies. I don't need you. I really don't."

She opened her eyes and looked at him with loathing, feeling trapped on every side, deprived by his diabolical offer even of the right to fight. "Then let me go," she screamed at him. "Let me—"

But his hand was on her mouth. She bit his finger. He jerked his hand away and slapped her hard across the face. "I wouldn't advise you to do that to me—ever."

She turned away, trembling, and went to the window. For a mad moment she thought of ending it all by jumping into the street, into its jumble of cars, rickshaws, bikes, loaded coolies and pedestrians. Then she felt his hand grasp her elbow and he jerked her round.

"Off with your knickers," he said mercilessly, looking down at his bleeding finger.

She cast another anguished look at the door. He sighed sharply, as though dealing with an imbecile, then losing patience, pushed her roughly towards the bed. She put her hand to her mouth, feeling the bruise he had inflicted on *Bangkok Lady*. George had taken off his white jacket and was unbuttoning his trousers. Composing her face into a kind of acceptance, making her mind a blank, she went and lay down, without bothering to remove her shoes.

"Aren't you going to get undressed, my darling?" With one of his typical about-turns, George was again the professional seducer, wanting it to come easily, willing to expend time wooing her into submission.

She closed her eyes and gritted her teeth and did not move.

"Did you hear me suggest to you that you take off your clothes?" He was leaning over her, whispering in her ear. His tongue touched the lobe, then curled round inside.

Her fingers were like hard knots, twisted into the palms of her hands. She crossed her ankles, screwed up her face, stiffened her body. "Just rape me, George," she said. "You're so good at it." 'God,' she whispered as she waited hopelessly for the dreadful intrusion, 'don't let him.'

There was a long silence. Then she felt his hand on her forehead, gently smoothing the skin. Her eyes flickered open. He was looking at her strangely, almost with compassion. "There are some things you can't fight," he said. "They have to happen. And God can't do a damn thing about it. I'm not such a bad chap, you'll find, if you treat me right."

"George," she begged him, sitting up a little, leaning on one elbow, pleading, "don't do it. Please, George."

"I'm sorry, my dear. I really am. But it's something I want to do. I have a right to make love to my wife, and you're going to find it's wonderful." She had fallen back on the bed, her face full of anguish.

The insult went deep, overlaying as it did the ignominy of Kitty's turning her back on him. That was the story of his life, George thought bitterly. Not being wanted. "Now, are you going to take that dress off, or am I?" She opened her eyes and he saw the despair in them. He felt no pity, only an abasement of his ego. Ruthlessly, he lifted the hem of her skirt and jerked it up over her thighs.

Down in the lounge Ruth glanced anxiously at her watch. An hour had elapsed since George expelled her from the room. She looked down at her hands and realised she had chewed one fingernail out of shape, she who had never chewed her nails before.

Twenty minutes later they came down the stairs. Ruth leaped to her feet, took a step forward, then halted. Hellen's hat was pulled low on her forehead and her head was bent so that her face was hidden behind side curtains of dark hair. Ruth saw George's lips move, saw Hellen's head rise listlessly, as though obeying some softly spoken command. Ruth crossed the floor and stood waiting as they descended, arm-in-arm. She was shocked at the sight of Hellen's stark white and tear-stained face.

George said coldly, "I am taking my wife to my parents' house, Mrs Washington, until we can find a place of our own."

Ruth saw then that Hellen's left hand, apparently resting lightly on her collar bone, was in reality holding closed a rent in her dress. Their eyes met and Hellen's eyes filled with tears. Then George jolted the arm he held, and they crossed the foyer together, side-by-side. The "boys" stepped forward alertly to hold open the doors, and they went through.

Jogging along Des Voeux Road, not yet knowing whether she was going to The Peak tram or to report to Lettice Marathon at Government House, Ruth ruminated savagely on the afternoon's disaster. Was there no end to her bad judgment? Why on earth had it not occurred to her that George would be within his rights to order her out of his wife's room? That he could so easily settle matters by doing on the spot that which, anyway, he had a perfect right to do? Why had she not hidden the girl until Oliver returned from Lantau?

Bitter in her need to blame someone for her own lack of wisdom and forethought, she lacerated herself with the advice she had failed to give Hellen on board *Devanha*. "That we should speak and deport ourselves well. . . ." George Curtain does not deport himself well, she said to herself angrily, and that is why Hong Kong society has never accepted him. He will always be an outsider.

She could not know that when George used brutality to box up the luck he had to grasp out of the air, deep down inside him, tears flowed. Neither bloody Denzil Armitage, who had taken his girl, nor Oliver Marathon, would ever know what it was like to be lightly and thoughtlessly excluded from so many things they took for granted. It would be said, if Oliver did not keep his mouth shut as a matter of pride, that George had taken his girl out of sheer bravado, but that would be wrong. George had grown up among the Chinese and a good many of their characteristics had rubbed off on him. To a Chinese "face" was paramount. Whatever else he had lost, along with his self-respect, in returning to the colony with a bride on his arm, he had, at least, saved face.

Chapter 14

Kowloon

"I really don't understand," said Marcia Curtain, bewilderedly, "why you didn't tell us when you arrived, that you were married."

She stood in the middle of her stifling drawing room, a big-bosomed, square-shouldered woman with untidy hair, amid the clutter of objets d'art, big armchairs, pictures, all brought from the spacious house in Shanghai. She had bundled them haphazardly into the bungalow, unworried at the time because number twelve Nathan Road, cool amidst the rustling foliage of great banyan trees, was a pleasant enough temporary stopping place, but it was far too small to consider as a permanent home. Neil, they were confident, would soon find his feet and they would be able to move to more stylish surroundings among the right people.

By the time she realised her husband had not the knack of business, that in fact this rather small bungalow was going to be well suited to their new circumstances for without money "standing" was something one could not transfer from one place to another, her possessions had merged with her memories of the palmy days, and could not be relinquished.

"Frankly," George selected a cigarette from a box on the piano, wondering irritably why large women, who were so impressive in command, should look crumpled and unattractive in low water, "I couldn't be certain I was still married. The last I saw of Hellen, she was being carted off in a sampan. I didn't give much for her chances."

Marcia gasped.

"You know the Chinks." George looked annoyed at her reaction. "They could have marched her into the scrub and amused themselves cutting her into little slices." He flicked the lighter and sucked at his cigarette.

"George!"

"Mother, be realistic. It would not exactly have brightened your

147

day to hear you might have had a brand new daughter-in-law, except that—"

"George!" She stood there in the small space between the brown leather armchair and the cushioned rattan sofa, covering her ears with her large hands. It occurred to him to wonder, with idle distaste, if Hellen, who was as tall as his mother, would fill out in middle age. George liked diminutive women. They made him conscious of his size. Kitty Burtenshaw and the frail Chinese girls in their form-fitting cheongsams. Women who used a lot of scent, and had small feet. His mother's large feet, in their flat-heeled shoes, reminded him of the squat boat women on the sampans in Causeway Bay.

Marcia Curtain slowly lowered her hands to her sides. George, standing there with his thumbs in his braces, cigarette on his lower lip, eyes narrowed against the curling smoke, head thrown back, was looking at her so critically that she glanced down at her dress. She nervously straightened the skirt over her ample hips, then patted her hair. She was aware of her habit, when startled, of running her hands through it. And startled she had been, to see George standing there at the front door with an exhausted-looking girl in a torn dress, saying coolly, "Mother, I'd like you to meet my wife,' he who had left the house only an hour or so earlier, to all intents and purposes a bachelor.

"I'm sorry I was not at my best when you came," she said, smiling at him nervously. She liked to please George, and she was determined to love him. "If you had telephoned—"

"She didn't want to hang about. She was upset."

"What about?"

George laughed harshly. "What about?" he echoed. "I've told you what happened to her. And you ask me what she was upset about! Come, Mother."

"Yes, all right dear," said his mother hastily. "Let's forget I asked. Tell me about you and Hellen. Where did you meet? In England?"

"On the boat."

"She was on her way to Hong Kong?" Determined not to let it appear that he had crushed her, Marcia smiled at him. For a big woman, she had surprisingly small teeth.

He hesitated fractionally. "Singapore. She was going to Singapore." He wished he had remembered to instruct Hellen to say she had been on her way to Singapore. If he said she was coming to Hong Kong, his mother would ask whom she was visiting. He was not going to have it said he had snatched an easy catch from the fishing fleet. With a bit of luck, Oliver would go off on the rebound and marry that half-breed of his. Then no one would ever know anything about anything. George was pretty confident Oliver Marathon, every-body's darling, was not going to admit in public, or even in private, that George Curtain had taken his girl.

"So you were married at Singapore?"

"No. She got off there, to visit—er—friends, but I persuaded her back on to *Bangkok Lady*."

"You mean, you let *Devanha* sail without you?"

"I was besotted," he said, smiling wryly, acting out a little human foolishness. "I knew *Bangkok Lady* was due out within a day or two, so I got off, too, thinking I might still talk her round, in time for both of us to catch the other boat. And I did. We were married by the Captain." He lifted his head, laughed a little, pretending he didn't know damn well his mother was as suspicious as a cat. It showed, not in her large girlish face, but in her shrewd eyes. "It was rather romantic," he said.

Marcia did not believe a word of it, but since she was unable to say so, she thought she had better change the subject. She glanced covertly back towards the door, checking that it was closed. "May we ask—you didn't write at all. We don't know what happened—about Kitty."

"She married Armitage," George snapped, glancing round the room, feeling irritated by its clutter and its heat, remembering the cool spaciousness of *Devanha*'s public rooms.

"Oh." His mother felt there was something she ought to say, but he looked so forbidding. . . . She fiddled with the lace on the corner of her handkerchief, then settled for, "I'm sorry, dear."

George took a long draw at his cigarette. "Why be sorry? I have a beautiful wife whom I love devotedly, and who loves me."

She said abruptly, "I'll go and see how Hellen's getting on." She turned in the doorway. "What is going to happen about her luggage? Was it found?"

"They're sending it—what's left of it, if there's any left." His mouth hardened as he remembered the monkey with the bracelet, and automatically he put a hand to his wound, hating the bitch for what she had done to him. His eyes accidentally caught sight of his mother's face, the broad, shapely lips tightened over those ridiculously small teeth, the eyes watchful, and he turned swiftly.

Marcia opened the door and went off down the passage, feeling distressed. George went to stand at the window, looking out into the ghost forest made by the banyan tree, hands in his pockets, the cigarette teetering on his lower lip, the smoke curling lazily through the heavy air.

He was accustomed to those long, steady stares. His mother was

149

adept at them. He had ceased to allow them to matter to him. He knew he disappointed her, but what about the fact that she had, much more pertinently, disappointed him? He was never going to forgive her for the smothering devotion that had resulted in her keeping him at her side instead of sending him to England to be educated at a public school. It was not just bad joss that he was an outsider in Hong Kong. It was entirely her doing.

He wondered if she realised that very same decision had set, validated and confirmed her own social position when they came to Hong Kong. It had been different for them in Shanghai, because, as a tea taster, his father had an acclaimed profession. And also the people among whom they lived had known George since he was a baby. But he had come to Hong Kong as an adult, bearing the social stigma of having been educated in the East with the children of missionaries. The Hong Kongers naturally accorded him the social status of a missionary. Nothing was ever said, of course. He simply was not one of the boys.

Marriage to Kitty Burtenshaw could have rectified his problems. Marriage to the Governor's niece, and he would have been set for life. The non-existent Governor's bloody niece! God, he could laugh, if it wasn't so tragic. Well, he'd gathered together what pieces there were to salvage. There was nothing left to do now but push on.

Marcia went to her room and changed out of the cotton house dress into her tussore silk, pinning the big bow carefully above her massive cleavage. She thought the bow feminine-looking, though she would be the first to admit she lacked taste when it came to clothes.

She took the pins out of her hair, brushed it and twisted it into a coil, then pinned it up again. Now she felt better, somewhat redeemed. She was genuinely sorry to have embarrassed George, but she felt his wife had probably not noticed her untidiness. Hellen's first consideration, at her age, and in the circumstances that she was meeting her new in-laws, must have been the kind of picture she herself presented.

Neil would soon be home. Marcia went to the kitchen door and instructed Ah Ho to set out the drinks. There were no summoning bells in the bungalow. With a swift glance at herself in the looking glass on the wall to ensure she did not look too bad—the young seemed to find the middle-aged unattractive, she could not think why, for it had not been so in her young day—she proceeded further down the passage. Her tap on the door elicited a bleak summons to enter.

Hellen was sitting in the ratten chair by the window. She had moved it so that she could look into the garden. Her back was to the door. She did not turn her head.

"I came to see—"

She broke off as Hellen, looking flustered, jumped out of her seat. "I'm so sorry, Mrs Curtain. I didn't expect you."

"I came to see if there was anything I could do for you, dear," said Marcia, swiftly veiling her dismay at the reception that had been waiting for her son. "George says he has sent down to *Bangkok Lady* for your luggage."

Acutely embarrassed that her mother-in-law should have been the recipient of this demonstration of her outraged feelings, Hellen did not meet her eyes. "I don't suppose there's any left. One of the pirates was wearing my hat. Do you think they might take my clothes for their wives?" Without waiting for a reply she rattled on nervously, "A kind family in Macao took me in, washed my underwear and loaned me this dress." She glanced down at it, flicking her fingers against the creases. Somehow, it had finished up under her on the bed at the Hong Kong Hotel. "Luckily, their daughter wears the same size shoes as I do. But I've nothing to change into. And now," her face crumpled dangerously, "I've lost the comb they gave me, so I can't even comb my hair."

"Then we shall have to get you fitted out as swiftly as possible," said Marcia briskly. "I'd happily loan you a frock but I'm twice your size and you would be quite lost in it. Meantime, I'll get you a comb." She turned, glad to give Hellen a chance to pull herself together.

She went to her room, feeling distressed, trying to tell herself that the girl, being young, would soon put the unpleasant experiences of the past few days behind her and rejoice in the fact that she was alive. She picked up a comb, washed it and dried it carefully. Then she went and stood uselessly in front of her wardrobe, examining each garment in turn, knowing perfectly well that slim creature could not wear any one of them. Then, walking slowly and heavily, she went back to the guest room. This time Hellen looked comparatively tranquil.

"Thank you, Mrs Curtain."

The distant formality of the words seemed to accentuate her air of solitary withdrawal. "Would you like to call me Mother?" Marcia asked kindly.

"That's nice of you. No." The answer came quick as a snap. There was an awkward silence. Then Hellen said apologetically, "If you don't mind."

"You're Mrs Curtain, too." Forgetting she had tidied her hair, Marcia flapped one hand around her forehead, loosening the short pieces as she always did when she was disturbed. "Think about it, dear." Her weighty lingering on "dear" pointed up the affront. "Two of us with the same name."

Hellen felt pressured, as though Marcia was trying to push her into a box from which, if she gave in, she would emerge irrevocably as George's wife. She looked down involuntarily at the third finger of her left hand, remembering the act of throwing her marriage off the grassy cone on Lantau Island. She wished she could explain to George's big, sympathetic, insensitive mother that one did not acquire a parent like that. Not by walking in at the door and borrowing a comb. She had felt more at home with Dona Celeste in Macao.

There was an element of forgiveness in Marcia's smile. "George told me you were married on board ship. He must get you a ring at the first opportunity. You don't look married without one."

"Oh, I'm married, all right. Oh, yes, we're married," Hellen repeated, speaking with bright hopelessness, feeling a little mad as she had been ever since she came into this small room and saw the double bed which she was going to have to share tonight with George. It was all she could do to stop herself from screaming, "And the marriage has been consummated! Consummated, do you hear?" As though such bad behaviour might help to rid her of the memories of violence and pain and humiliation.

She was in the grip of some sort of wierd death wish. She actually wanted this woman to ask, "Why did you marry my son?" so that she could reply, "An explanation would do neither of us credit," putting the ball into both courts, where it belonged, for if she was to make anything at all of this marriage, she must not lose sight of the fact that the appalling disaster it represented was in part her fault.

She made herself say, "I hope we will be friends. It's very good of you to take us in."

"It's a pleasure," Marcia replied, baring her little teeth in a brave smile as she tried to come to terms with the snub. Perhaps she had been a little hasty, though goodness knows she had spoken with the greatest possible goodwill. "We're delighted to have you, and of course you may stay as long as you like, though we will quite understand if you want to get settled in your own home."

Our own home! Hellen's face was still.

"We will be able to help you," Marcia blundered on good-naturedly. "This house is excessively over-furnished. We would be only too pleased if you would take some pieces." The girl did not respond. Perhaps, Marcia thought, ruffled, she had already decided their taste was not up to her standards. She was distressed that things were going so badly. A good mother, sure of herself, sure of her son, would have been able to project a welcome that was so spontaneously affectionate the girl would feel immediately at home. But it was not in her any more to be spontaneously affectionate. Her motherly gestures had too often been repelled. And besides—oh, besides, besides, besides. . . . She heaved a sharp sigh. She would do her best. Hadn't she always?

They made their way together to the drawing room. George had disappeared. Ah Ho, shuffling along in his cloth shoes, was making a great play of setting out glasses and bottles on a silver tray. He focussed unblinkingly on Hellen, then expressionlessly asked his employer, "Missie want small chow?"

Marcia nodded. "When Master come."

He shuffled out of the room, a comical diminutive creature with a tuft of hair sprouting from his crown into a long plait that hung to his knees, his short black trousers exposing rope-thin ankles.

"Why do they shave the front of their heads, yet wear this long pigtail?"

Marcia held up a warning finger. "You must call it a cue. They would say they are not pigs. It is a custom forced on them by the Manchus, originally a sign of subservience. The Manchu dynasty fell, as you may know, nine or ten years ago." She shrugged her strong shoulders. "I suppose they have become accustomed to it."

Manchu. . . . It was only a name to Hellen, culled from school history books. She looked round the dark, over-furnished room. There were good pictures on the walls, in gilt frames. A set of hunting prints. Automatically, she crossed the room to examine them.

They were early-eighteenth century, when artists drew horses with ridiculously small heads on long, thin necks. All those so familiar top hats! The lovely, rolling hills, washed with gold. The Englishness of it, viewed from a background where little men in pigtails—cues—brandishing sharp weapons, cut off a man's head for fun! The ladies in the picture, adorned with bonnets and wrapped in rugs, were comfortably ensconsed in a curricle. Cherished. Hellen felt tears very close. Ghastly pictures crowded in. George hitting her. George raping her. George drugging her drink. She wanted to snatch one of the pictures off the wall and hold it to her heart. She wanted to go home.

Marcia said, "They're nice, aren't they? They belonged to my grandfather. He was the first of the family to come to China. My parents were both born in Shanghai. Neil's, also. We went home to school. We met when Neil was at Cambridge. I was nineteen. I was glad to come back to Shanghai. We would have been there still but for the bottom falling out of the tea business. It was lovely in Shanghai, though of course very cold in winter. Do you like Chinese art?" She indicated a large picture of mountains shaped like tall thimbles, their summits shrouded in mist, with a misty lake in the foreground.

"I haven't seen any before." Hellen thought it beautiful. "So many

153

waterlilies. Do they really grow like that, on long stalks?"

"Yes, they do. And they're called lotus flowers. It's painted on silk. That's the Chinese way."

Hellen took a deep breath, turned her back on the hunting prints and mentally faced the future. History, a new, strange, undoubtedly barbaric history, was all around her, and the beauty of clouded thimble mountains. She was not going home. There was no way back. But perhaps there was something to be salvaged from this vale of sorrows, if only she could come to terms with it.

"There is a great deal for me to learn," she said, moving to the window and looking out into the gloom, trying to exorcise the hunting prints from her mind, and hold the thimble mountains there.

"I expect there is," said Marcia. She, too, glanced out of the window. "Would you like to see the garden? It will be dark, soon. Unfortunately, at this time of year, it's often hotter in the evening than in the daytime. July is a dreadful month, except for those who live on The Peak." She spoke, Hellen noticed, without the envy and ill-feeling that was endemic in George's voice when he spoke of that area of privilege.

Marcia unlatched the insect screen attached to a side door. The door itself was folded back against the wall. They crossed a small paved area, then stepped on to some coarse grass. The garden was full of an insistent rasping chorus of cicadas. The dying sun, low over mainland China, filled the garden with shadow, except where a low shaft of light caught a million tiny, frantic insects and a riot of purple bougainvillaea, drooping from the timber walls of the house.

"It isn't easy to keep a garden going," Marcia told her. There's a chronic water shortage."

"Is that why the islands are virtually uninhabited?"

"Yes. We've had some rain lately, but sometimes, in mid-summer, things become terribly difficult. We often have to ration ourselves to a basin full of water for a bath. It's something you grow accustomed to. Now, where on earth has George gone? I thought—Ah! There he is."

George was coming towards them, his shirt foggy white in the gloom, his face indistinct. "Admiring the estate?" His voice was dry, but not without a certain ironical humour. "She's an outdoor girl, Mother," he explained. "She hunts in England," adding, "with the Old Forest." His mother had probably never heard of it.

"That's nice," said Marcia. She turned to Hellen. "You're a country girl, then? You will have to tell me all about yourself."

Hellen saw, then, the reason for George's ironic look. She had been in his company for nearly a week, yet he still knew virtually nothing about her. "I am Kentish born," she said, the words exploding in short, sharp bursts. "My father is a tenant farmer. My mother came from Yorkshire. Her family there are engaged in trade. My two sisters married into trade. My brother helps my father on the farm. I suppose you might call him a farm hand. Don't get the idea that, because I hunted with the Old Forest, I am anyone of note, Mrs Curtain," she said, looking very directly at George. "We're quite an ordinary lot."

If the cicadas had only stopped for a second, Hellen thought, her senses spinning, you might have heard a pin drop. There was a long wait before George found his tongue.

"Confession is good for the soul, I suppose," he said lightly, at last, lifting her wrist, which after all was now one of his possessions, slipping her arm through his elbow where he surreptitiously squeezed it so hard it was all Hellen could do not to cry out in pain. "Mother will tell you we're not likely to take you into the kind of society where you'll feel out of place. I believe I heard the gate click. That will be my father returning from work. Come and meet him. He'll like you. He'll say, if you treat him to that spiel, you're a woman after his own heart. He never pretends to be what he isn't, either, and a fat lot of good it has done him."

Marcia stayed rooted to the spot as they walked away, crushing a hibiscus blossom in her hand. Dear God! What had George done?

Hellen liked Neil Curtain on sight. He was only as tall as his wife, a slender twig of a man with a small moustache, wide cheekbones and a crinkly smile. His dark hair, in spite of being cut short, had an unruly look. His kind face was full of astonishment as his eyes surveyed Hellen, arm-in-arm with his son.

"Married!" he ejaculated, his very dark eyebrows shooting up. "When did you get married?" Then, "Why the dickens. . . . What's the secrecy about?" To George, "Why didn't you tell us you had a wife?" To Hellen, "Where've you been, my dear?"

She told him.

His head was thrown back in shock and horror, a hand covering his eyes as though that would serve to block his imagination. "Are you all right?" He took her hand and looked concernedly into her face. "Did they treat you—you poor kid. Gosh! You poor kid."

She sat on the arm of his chair while he downed that odd sounding drink, a gin and it. What was "it"? Small chow, she discovered, could be termed cocktail savouries, Chinese style. Tiny fried sardines, rice pastry, dumplings stuffed with shrimps or pork. Something learned.

"The pirates were really very kind," she said.

There was an ejaculation from George. They looked up. He pointed angrily to his ear.

Hellen flushed. "I was talking about how they treated me. They did treat me well, George."

"Do go on."

Marcia and Neil were looking to the floor.

She began again, but uncertainly, for George's intervention had robbed her of poise. "One of them escorted me ashore and left me on a track that led to a monastery." Out of the corner of her eye she could see George studying the drinks trolley, picking with his fingertips at the seams of his white duck trousers, looking irritated, as though the beer had disappeared, which it had not.

Gradually gaining confidence, Hellen told them about the two little Haaka fishermen who had laboured up the mountain with her. George returned to his chair with his drink and sat, eyes lidded, listening without any sign of emotion to the happy tale of his wife's survival. She told them how the monk had taken her in; about the kindness of the Portuguese family. She told them everything George had not felt he needed to know.

"And here I am," she finished. George looked up, met her eyes with a bleak look, and the light went out of her voice. "So here I am," she repeated flatly.

"And we're very pleased to have you," said Neil Curtain warmly, lifting her hand and squeezing it between his own. "You have undoubtedly had a very bad time. Both of you." He glanced at George with very real sympathy, then addressed his wife. "A daughter, heh? Isn't that nice, Mother?"

"Very nice." Marcia wished she had Neil's ability to accept people and events at face value. She was glad he and Hellen had taken to each other. That was something to cling to. She had an intuitive feeling that Hellen's refusal to call her Mother went deeper than a mere snub. The girl wore a transcient look, as though she was passing through. Marcia found herself coupling the empty third finger of her left hand with an insistent fear that she did not belong to George at all.

That night when they went to bed, George said, "I've got to go out and see a chap." When Hellen returned from the bathroom, he had disappeared. He brought her a cup of tea in the morning. "Where did you sleep?" she asked, not caring but smiling because she was grateful to him for leaving her alone.

"Try that," he said, nodding towards the cup, ignoring her question. "I may have been a bit heavy handed with the sugar."

Later, exploring, she saw there was a day bed draped in mosquito netting at one end of the back verandah. A handkerchief, bearing an embroidered letter G peeped out from under a cushion. She picked it up and took it into her room, then ruffled up the side of the bed that had not been used, wondering cynically why she should bother. George's parents would have to be blind and deaf to imagine this marriage was made in heaven.

Her suitcase was delivered intact, except for the jewellery she had worn on *Devanha*, her pearl choker and its matching ear-rings. The clothes had presumably been discarded as unsuitable, and certainly, if one could judge by the height of their spouses, her dresses would be too big for any Chinese bandit's wife.

The diamond pendant and ear rings, Sir Samuel Porchard's wedding present, had been stored in the trunk, along with her frost-white wedding dress. George, in not keeping his word to have the trunk and the box unloaded at Singapore, had done her that unwitting favour, though what use were they going to be now? She considered, bleakly, the fact that the Governor would not, after all, have an opportunity of judging for himself if she was a suitable bride for his nephew.

"I suppose I wasn't," Hellen said to herself, considering that was what it amounted to, in the end. "Perhaps Lady Sylvia was right. I did let everyone down."

And herself most of all.

She did not cry. It was far too late for tears.

When her trunk and the big packing case came from Government House, Marcia asked in astonishment, "Why Government House? Why on earth would they go there?" She was staring at the box, wondering why a girl going to meet friends in Singapore should take all that with her.

"You may well ask," said George, lifting his shoulders to indicate there was no end to the inefficiency down at the docks.

Hellen told Marcia there was nothing she would require until she and George acquired a home of their own, so Marcia instructed the servants to put the box and trunk in a shed in the garden. "They will be perfectly safe," she said, still staring at them, perplexed.

Hellen turned abruptly and went for a walk in the sweltering heat, losing herself among the banyan trees of Nathan Road. She would no doubt find an opportunity, when Marcia was out, to open the trunk and take out the necklace which certainly should not be consigned to a shed in the garden.

Neil talked openly and chattily about The Peak, as George, carrying a chip on his shoulder, could not. "It's the colony's visible manifestation of class and position," he explained. "The taipans of the great hongs—if George hasn't told you, hongs are what we call business houses out here—live on the upper reaches with their staff.

And leading civil servants. There are messes where the young bachelors of standing live."

George had never been a bachelor of standing. Oliver lived in a mess on The Peak.

"Everyone who lives there knows everyone else who lives there, and they don't know anybody else," Neil said. "You get invitations to Government House, and an overdraft at the Hong Kong and Shanghai Bank; you have a pew close to the altar in St John's Cathedral, with your own name plaque and the sole right of use. You join the Hong Kong Club." He looked up at Hellen, blinking, with a half smile. "And the Governor will come to your wedding."

For a dreadful moment she thought he knew, and the breath seemed to leave her body. But he was looking at her kindly, and now she saw in his face what she had sensed in his voice, a certain wry amusement at the waywardness of human beings, and the implacability of the gods. "How does one reach these exalted heights?" she asked, planting an expression of amusement firmly on her face.

"Your place in Hong Kong is defined according to race, nationality, position, accent and education, my dear."

"So why do you not live on The Peak?" She was sitting on the arm of his chair, as had become a habit. Without wishing to take her father's place, he was her father, now. A kind of Joe, better educated, and with enormous resilience. She sensed he would not have said once she made her bed he would expect her to lie on it. She ruffled his hair affectionately, wishing George could have taken after him, knowing that if he had, she would not be here now. "You seem to have all the credentials."

"My job doesn't warrant it," Neil replied simply. "We couldn't afford to keep up."

"If George becomes a high executive in Lonewood & Southby, shall we move there?"

"Oh, yes, you might well." He could not say that George would never become a high executive in Lonewood & Southby, now that he had lost Kitty Burtenshaw, for there was no one of influence to speak for him. He smiled at Hellen. "You will be very good for George," he said. "I am so glad he married you." He squeezed her hand, noting without allowing himself to attach any significance to the fact, that it had gone limp.

Chapter 15

Ruth

"You will forget about this girl. You cannot, and will not, make a prize ass of yourself by getting involved with someone who is married, do you understand? Married, like it or not, to another man. Are you so stupid that you cannot see what's at stake? Your whole career—"

"Damn my career!" Oliver read correctly the expression on his uncle's face, and hesitated.

Sir Rowan advanced slowly across the room. Though he was virtually the same height as Oliver, he had never seemed so tall. Lifting both arms, he slapped the palms of his hands down heavily on his nephew's shoulders, saying in the voice he was accustomed to use when commanding his Grenadiers on the battlefields of France, "A Marathon does not damn his career, young man. Our family are born to public service. They serve their king, and their country, while there is breath in them. They do not toss in the towel for a woman—any woman—much less for some flibberty-gibbet who anyway has proved she hasn't the moral fibre of a fly. That kind of woman does not make a Marathon wife. She has proved herself deficient in the attributes Marathons expect of their wives."

"You heard what Mrs Washington said." Oliver stood square-shouldered, head high.

"Mrs Washington did not give me a reasonable explanation for the marriage." Sir Rowan dropped his hands, turned away, then back again. "I'm not being inhuman, Oliver. Hang it all, I know about moonlight on ocean liners. A great deal can be forgiven in certain circumstances. But when I hear someone has gone through a marriage ceremony, and signed on the dotted line, I find it dashed queer that you should believe she did it against her will. Many of our colonial women have faced up to tougher issues than this."

"She was frightened, Uncle Rowan. You heard Mrs Washington

159

say she was frightened. She was one woman among some pretty tough men—"

"She was in the care of a highly responsible, respected sea captain, one of Lonewood & Southby's best men," retorted his uncle tersely. "Now listen to me—there are questions you might ask yourself. Why was she aboard the ship in the first place?" He paused briefly, then continued, "If it's true Curtain drugged her, why did she not go to the Captain immediately she came round, and request protection? You don't marry chaps because they put something in your drink, Oliver, if that is, in fact, what he did. The girl's got no moral fibre."

Lettice, looking up from her listening seat in the deep chair by the window, felt the lines of grief in Oliver's face cutting like knives into her heart. She wished she could go to him and put her arms round him, but fifteen years as Rowan's consort, and the acquired discipline of life as the First Lady in the colony, had given her precise knowledge of when to speak and when to remain quiet.

The Governor's voice softened fractionally. "I'm not saying this girl is scum. We've been into her background and allowed it to stand. But I am saying, quite categorically, that the circumstances are such that I want you to overcome your feelings and forget her." His hands dropped to his sides. He turned, and crossing the room, put a comforting arm around his wife. "I could do with a cup of tea before I see His Nibs," which was the way he referred, in his private capacity as an Englishman, to visiting firemen possessing a different coloured skin from his own. "And none of that flowery rubbish, daisy, or dandelion, or whatever it was that Ah Sam tried to poison me with yesterday."

"Red lychee, dear."

As he bent his head to kiss his wife's forehead he whispered, "Take Oliver upstairs and listen to him for a while. Then see he gets back to work."

The newly weds took one of the spacious Victorian colonial houses in Tsim Sha Tsui, on the Kowloon side, an area of wide, tree-lined streets where Europeans, working mainly as dockyard supervisors, marine engineers, police, prison officers, sea captains, lived. George did not wish to reside on the island unless he could have a house above May Road on The Peak, May Road being the dividing line between the English and the Others, but it went without saying that there was no question of asking the Governor for permission. Minden Row, off Mody Road, was as exclusive a site as Kowloon could offer. The south side of the peninsula housed the docks and go-downs, as well as the streets of prostitution; the north end, the wicked walled

160

city, where opium was openly bought and sold; but in Tsim Sha Tsui there were large, gracious houses with leafy gardens. From upstairs verandahs, if there were no treetops in the way, one could often glimpse the water.

Hellen wrote to Dona Celeste in Macao, repaying the money loaned to her, and to Isabel, apologising for the dress which George's mishandling had rendered unwearable. She sent a sum of money which she hoped would compensate. She wrote also to Senor Marques, thanking him for taking her in off the street in such a disreputable state. She said she hoped to visit them all one day, or perhaps they would come and visit her, when she was more settled. She did not mention George.

It occurred to her, as she put the letter on the hall table for the number one boy—the number one boy was the delegator of tasks—that she had created for herself a vacuum in a world where friendship had been offered on all sides. Yet she clung to her cold isolation as she clung to a delicate thread of hope. She never stopped thinking about Oliver, who made no attempt to get in touch.

Marcia was kindness itself in generously unloading furniture sufficient to make the house, for the moment, habitable. She was clearly surprised that George should choose such a large dwelling, and surprised, also, that he could afford it, but she had long ago ceased to ask questions of her son. She found Hellen a cook boy called Ah Wong, and a frail little sparrow called Ah Saw, who was to be the wash amah.

"She does nothing else but wash and iron linen and clothes?" asked Hellen in disbelief, thinking there would be very little laundry necessary for a two-person household.

"She will find plenty to do, I assure you." And indeed, owing to the damp heat, there was a great deal of laundry done, for George wore to work white suits that had to be scrupulously clean, and changed his shirts twice a day. When the heat grew unbearable, Hellen took cold baths while the water lasted, and changed her underwear three and four times a day.

The wash amah worked uncomplainingly, perhaps calling on an inner strength germane to her class. Hellen never stopped feeling guilty at employing someone of such poor physique, keeping her standing all day in the sweltering heat, rubbing linen on a board, using coarse bars of soap and cold water; heating flat irons over a fire. There was no juice in her for sweat. Ah Saw manifested, in her papery skin and fleshless bones, generations of starvation suffered by the underprivileged of China.

"Don't expect Ah Wong to do anything other than cook, go to

161

market, answer the door and see guests off," Marcia advised.

What guests? Hellen wondered. George did not bring friends home. Had he any friends? Life in Tsim Sha Sui was a far cry from the world of which Ruth had spoken, of tea-dances, bridge, cocktails, and dinners galore.

"Your number one boy will stay up until three o'clock in the morning for the privilege of seeing guests off," Marcia informed her, "but you will outrage him if you ask him to do other than top jobs." Cooking was a top job. "If you were so foolish as to suggest he clean the kitchen floor, or even wipe up something that had been spilt," she warned, "you wouldn't see him for dust."

Ah Ping, the makee learn, swept and cleaned. She was the lowest of the low. Hellen was not expected to deal with her at all. Then there was the garden coolie, Fah Wong. Marcia's garden coolie had the same name. One did not talk to Fah Wong (or the Fah Wong if the name meant gardener, or handyman) for he apparently was not expected even to understand pidgin English. His orders, also, were given to the number one boy, the major domo, to hand on.

"What does Fah Wong mean?" she asked George.

"He's the garden coolie."

"Our garden coolie? Or everyone's?"

"Just call him Fah Wong."

Hellen understood the Curtains considered themselves a cut above those who lived in Tsim Sha Tsui. They were Peak people, really, though without the qualifications. She thought wryly that in some ways her life had not changed. But four servants! There was nothing at all for her do to.

Her loneliness increased. Sometimes, in the evening, she would walk to the waterfront and stand watching the ferryboats, lit up like fireflies, nimbly running to and from the island. Then she would allow her eyes to travel, in the secret dark, up the slopes of the great rock mountain whose flanks reared sharply from the harbour, and she would wonder which of the myriads of light came from Hillcrest, the bachelor mess at number 114 The Peak, and which one of those particular lights came from Oliver's bedroom window. She would scourge herself, thinking that Oliver was sitting alone, trying to come to terms with what she had done.

Some mornings, before the sun rose too high and the air heated up like a Turkish bath, she would stroll across the peninsula into Canton Road that ran behind the docks and go-downs to the harbour edge. When she saw a stately liner coming in to berth, she would ask herself if one day she might simply walk down here, climb aboard and return to England. Then she would remember, always with a new shock, her

162

father's pronouncement that once she had made her bed they would expect her to lie on it, and she would consider how she might beg for their mercy.

But when she thought about Joe and Marnie with their narrow view of life, their gentle righteousness and virtue, their innocence, she knew they would not understand, and she recognised, deep down, that she must never embarrass them by returning. Yet time after time she stood, as though turned to cold stone, watching a liner sailing away magnificently into the South China Sea. When it finally obliterated itself behind the little islands she would still be there, not blinking so as to hold on to the last puff of smoke from the funnel, until, inevitably, that disintegrated into the mist. She had not yet written to her parents. It was one of the hurdles waiting to be tackled, and she would tackle it soon.

When she had worked out what she could say.

Where did those who lived in Tsim Sha Tsui meet people? Marcia did not offer introductions. Hellen sensed George's mother wanted her friendship, first. Would George introduce her to people if she gave him love? Sometimes, glancing up, she would surprise him watching her, an odd expression on his face. She would glance swiftly away and the next time their eyes met he would be wearing the familiar look of cool detachment.

Aloof, she kept a delicate balance of safety.

They did not share a bed in the big-roomed, big-windowed, verandahed old house, typically a Victorian family dwelling, which, for all its faded grandeur and spaciousness, was not a home, for there was no heart beat there. The drawing room was a receptacle for Marcia's cast-off furniture, no more than that. The bedroom was bare of all but essentials, for Hellen had no desire to make it attractive, though George had offered her money and told her where to shop.

George slept across the hall—"Where I won't disturb you when I come in late," he said. He would return in the evenings for dinner, then quietly disappear. She never asked him where he went, for that would have established her position as a wife, with rights. She did not want rights for herself, as she did not want them for him.

As the weeks passed her mother-in-law dropped in less frequently, then ceased to come at all. She heard nothing from Neil. Hellen sensed they were waiting, on the perimeter of her life, for her to make friends with their son. Or perhaps they did not wish to have confirmed what they suspected: that in the evenings they would find their new daughter-in-law alone.

She took to walking, in the early morning and in the evening. Nathan Road was lined with a ribbon forest of banyan trees, fascinating monsters whose gnarled and massive branches sent sprouting laterals down to the ground where they formed smaller trunks that helped support the branches' weight. The trees, and the road, ran for three miles. You would walk to Imperial China along Nathan Road, if you turned right at the end, except that they would not allow you in.

George said the Chows, Chinks and Chinamen called their country the Middle Kingdom, and generally believed it was situated in the centre of the earth, surrounded by four seas, beyond which lay a number of islands inhabited by red-haired barbarians who came to trade. "Arrogant bastards," said George. Hellen was gradually coming to the reluctant conclusion that George did not particularly like anyone for themselves. He did not accord other people the right to their own dignity.

If you turned left at the end of the road, you would find yourself in the New Territories. But English ladies did not walk. They travelled in sedan chairs and rickshaws. Except in the New Territories, where one could walk or ride, but for that she needed an escort, and George did not care to go.

One day, Hellen told herself, she would climb aboard a train at the red brick, pillared railway terminus near the Star Ferry Pier, and ride up to the Shum Chun River. Not much of a river, according to a map she bought, more like a creek. But it had an importance beyond its width, for it constituted their boundary with China. The purple hills and the country beyond were troubled by recurring civil wars and the disruptive ambitions of a man called Sun Yat Sen, whom the British Government viewed with some suspicion.

She ventured one day in a rickshaw as far as the walled city of Kowloon, a six-acre enclave preserved under nominal Chinese sovereignty by treaty, that was a bolt-hole for criminals and secret societies. Law enforcement being minimal there, it was full of opium dens, Chinese brothels, thieves and murderers so dangerous that even the police did not dare to venture into its labyrinthine alleys. The wall ran up a steepish hill with rocks and boulders on either side. Within that, there were ramshackle lean-tos clinging to tier upon tier of terraces. Shivering with some unrecognised fear, Hellen turned her attention to the hills behind that rolled away to China.

Then one day George handed her a letter addressed to Miss H. North, and postmarked Macao.

"Miss H. North?"

Looking up into his waiting face, she said, "I didn't tell them about you because I didn't know if you were still alive."

"Touché," he said, cynically amused.

And then came a day when Ah Wong announced in his quaint

164

pidgin, "One Missie come your door." Ruth, hatted and gloved, looking formal and vaguely nervous, was standing in the hall.

Hellen hurried forward, holding out her hands in a spontaneous gesture of affection. "I thought you had given me up."

Ruth encircled her in her arms. "Given you up? I was too—" she was going to say "deeply ashamed", but there was no resentment in Hellen's manner, so she shelved her guilt. "Too busy. What have you been doing?"

It had never occurred to Hellen to blame Ruth for bringing George to the Hong Kong Hotel. That disaster had settled in her mind as an Act of God. Hellen led her into the big sitting room. Standing on the threshold, Ruth was reminded of a small indoor barn into which some unwanted chairs and tables had been dumped. Marcia's furniture was not enough for the big room. It seemed merely to point up the emptiness.

"I haven't been doing anything much," said Hellen. "Walking. Learning about China. Mings and Sungs and war lords and all that. Learning about Hong Kong. Feeling homesick. Feeling hot. Learning to like Chinese food. That's what I've been doing. Not much." She took a deep breath. "I don't really exist, you know. You will have seen George's interviews in the *South China Morning Post* and the *Hong Kong Telegraph*. He didn't mention a wife. Do you realise that if I had died at the hands of the pirates, my family would never have known what happened to me? Do sit down." She indicated the rattan sofa, and in the same sweep of her arm, an over-stuffed chair and the bare wooden seat by the enormous windows that looked out into the shady garden. Seeing the room suddenly through Ruth's eyes, she was embarrassed by its bleakness. She rang the tinkling bell for Ah Wong and ordered tea.

Settling on the sofa, Ruth proceeded to remove her hat and gloves, then fluff up her hair with her hands. She fiddled with the frills on her parasol, keeping her eyes lowered, wishing to goodness she had come earlier. "Doesn't George take you out?" she ventured at last. "He must have friends." Though who they were, she could not imagine. Those he had made as Kitty Burtenshaw's fiancé would have every excuse for giving him a wide berth, now.

"Has he? George goes out alone at night."

Ruth began absorbedly ironing her gloves across her knees with the palms of her hands. Then Hellen staggered her by adding, "We don't, as you would say, 'live together', so I presume George looks elsewhere. I'm not complaining. I got myself into this. It's just that—" suddenly the mask of indifference dropped, her face crumpled and her voice trembled "—there doesn't seem to be a way out."

Ah Wong came in carrying a silver tray given to Hellen by her mother-in-law. On it was arranged the porcelain tea-set she had bought in Mody Road. She had not unpacked her own china—that china meant for the home she and Oliver were to share. Hellen proceeded to pour the tea. "I presume you like Jasmine? I love the China teas. I'm sorry I haven't got a cloth. I—" With a nervous gesture, she brushed the dark fringe back from her forehead. "As I said, I haven't had any guests. And I haven't wanted to use—" She burst out, "Have you seen Oliver?"

It was the moment Ruth had dreaded. "No, I haven't." Nobody had seen Oliver, except those with whom he worked. "I think it would be better if you forgot Oliver, and set about making a life for yourself, dear. As you said, there doesn't seem to be a way out." She smiled brightly, pretending she had not seen the raw pain in Hellen's face. "Have you signed the book at Government House?"

Hellen paused with the teapot held in mid-air. Her mouth sagged open with shock. "Me, go to Government House!"

"You are obliged to, you know. As a British citizen. It's just a formality."

"George didn't say."

"No. . . . Well. . . . But I'm surprised your parents-in-law haven't acquainted you with the rules."

"I don't think they're very sociable." Hellen put the teapot down and carried the cup across to her guest. "I'm sorry, I haven't any occasional tables." She spoke in quick, nervous spurts, thinking about going to Government House, of possibly running into Oliver who might turn and walk away—or glare at her with contempt in his eyes.

She said in a fevered rush, "I really will have to go out and do some shopping." She looked down at the tea she had spilt into Ruth's saucer and her eyes filled with tears. "I'm sorry about that. And I'm sorry there isn't a table. Do you mind holding this on your knee? Oh, I'd better empty. . ." She went back to the tray and poured the tea from the saucer into a bowl, then returned it to her guest.

Ruth put the tea cup down on the floor at her feet. Hellen gazed down at it, dreadfully embarrassed that there was no table. "I'm sorry," she said again.

"It's perfectly all right," said Ruth. She took a deep breath and asked, "Do they—George's parents—know—"

"That I was to marry Oliver? Not unless George has told them, and I hardly think he would. Or unless," she looked directly at Ruth, her mouth trembling with anticipated hurt, but needing to know if her only friend had let her down, "this sorry business is common knowledge in Hong Kong drawing rooms."

Ruth bristled. "I'm sorry you should think that of me, dear. So far as I know, only the Marathons, Major Tandy, and I are in on it, and I hasten to say the Major is the sole of discretion. And, if I may add, an admirer of yours. I had to talk to someone at Singapore, so I talked to him."

Hellen went to sit on the bare wooden window seat with her tea cup in her hand. "I'm sorry I said that. It's just—I'm a little unnerved. I haven't had anyone to talk to. I don't really know anything," she said forlornly.

They sat in silence. Ruth lost herself in dismal thoughts of the gossip that was doing the rounds of Peak drawing rooms regarding George, who had picked up a girl in Singapore, and was now openly patronising the flower girls on the floating bordelloes in Causeway Bay.

"There's something I would like to ask you." Ruth started as Hellen spoke. "I've got to do something or I shall go mad. I've decided I'd like to learn to speak Chinese. How do I go about finding a teacher?"

"Why on earth? I believe it's awfully difficult."

"I'd like to be able to communicate with the servants."

"Oh, Cantonese," replied her guest dismissively. "It's not necessary. None of us know more than kitchen pidgin. It's enough. They should learn English."

"I want to learn the language."

"You mean Mandarin, then. That's the scholars' language."

"No. Nobody speaks Mandarin in the south. I'm not thinking of becoming a scholar. I merely want to be able to communicate with the ordinary people. Not just the servants. People in shops. People I might come across."

Ruth said with dismay, "But—one doesn't."

"I want to." Hellen's voice held a faint hint of desperation.

"What does George say?"

"It's nothing to do with George." She did not want to say she had received an identical reaction from him.

Ruth said gently, "I agree you have to make a life for yourself, dear, but this is not the way to go about it." She saw now, with compassion, that the room's emptiness indicated a cry for help. She said impulsively, "Let me help you furnish. That would be fun for both of us. And by the way," a simply brilliant idea lanced through her mind, "I'm having a cocktail party on Saturday. That's actually what I came to tell you. I want you and George to come." There was time to send out the invitations, if she got down to it right away.

"Will Oliver be there?"

167

"Hellen!"

"No, well, I was just asking." Hellen looked down into her cup.

"It wouldn't be right, dear. I would get into no end of trouble with Lady Marathon."

"Will she be at the party?"

"Er—no."

There was a long silence. Then Hellen said, "I don't think I need to obey the rules by signing the book at Government House." She smiled over-brightly. "I seem to have broken most of the rules already, so another one won't really matter. I don't think Lady Marathon would feel it was a great indiscretion. After all, she isn't going to ask me—us—to anything, is she? But, yes, I would love to go to your cocktail party, and I hope George will, too."

Ruth asked diffidently, "Are you a friend of Sir Samuel Porchard, the north country industrialist who was knighted a few years ago?"

Hellen blinked.

"You sent a letter to him, from the boat."

Hellen smiled and Ruth flushed faintly. "He's my grandfather. Trade and industry. Is that acceptable in Hong Kong? It didn't do a thing for me with the Old Forest hunting set."

Ruth said briskly, "We're none of us county. I should play it for all you're worth, if I were you. The title, I mean, and perhaps the industry. Forget about the trade." She did not add, because she did not know if this was what Hellen wanted, that George would love her for having a knight in the family.

"Before you go," said Hellen, "since, as you say, we're being so outspoken, perhaps you could answer this. Why is George—I think one might call it—persona non grata in Hong Kong?"

Ruth fiddled with the frills on her parasol. "Do you really want to discuss your husband with me?"

"I would like you to answer this question about George," replied Hellen, dead pan.

"It's really up to oneself," said Ruth, weighing her words carefully. Wild horses would not drag out of her a criticism of George, to whom, as she saw it, Hellen was now irrevocably tied. She added, "Providing, of course, one has had a good education."

"Meaning, English public school?"

Ruth looked round for her hat. "I'm sure George had a good education in Shanghai," she said cautiously. She picked up the hat and set it carefully on her head. "I must go now, dear. See you at the party, then, if not before."

As she jogged down the road in her rickshaw, holding her parasol at the ready in case one of the coolies at the harbour side leaned too close, she wished she had been able to bring herself to say, regarding George, that even among Peak snobs, charm and the right kind of behaviour had been known to work miracles. She had every intention of redeeming herself by helping to make this marriage a success. But she was not certain Hellen was yet ready to try to influence George. A cocktail or two. . . . A little water flowing under the bridge. . . .

"That's very civil of Ruth," said George, looking pleased, flicking the invitation that had arrived that morning between his fingers. "Good-o."

"Have you been invited to her place before?"

He grinned cheerfully. "No. But now, you see, I've got an influential wife." He put a hand lightly on her shoulder, looking down into her face. "We were friends, once," he said tentatively. "We used to dance, and play bridge, and look at the moon together."

Only because you were the pushiest man on board Hellen remembered. She said aloud, "That was before some quite unforgiveable things happened." She moved away and his hand fell to his side.

"Are you going to hold that against me for the rest of our lives?"

"Very likely," she replied bleakly. "One does not forget humiliation."

"I just thought you might not realise people have a habit of finding things out in Hong Kong," George replied lightly, pretending to himself he had not heard the word humiliation. "If we're to become social, some cat might tell you that people are saying behind your back that your husband goes—"

"I can guess," she broke in. "There's no need to go into detail."

"You would not consider such gossip humiliating to yourself?"

"I prefer gossip to rape."

"Oh, come on, Hellen. It doesn't have to be rape."

"It would be," she replied.

"Have it your way," said George coldly.

It was a complicated journey, that evening, from Tsim Sha Tsui to The Peak. They left the house by rickshaw, crossed the harbour in the Star ferry, then took a chair to the lower terminus of The Peak tram. The tram was cable drawn with wooden seats and a wooden roof. They stepped aboard and Hellen made a dive for the front.

"Not up there," warned George, restraining her with a hand on her arm. "The first two seats are reserved for the Governor."

Hellen stiffened. "Ruth hasn't asked them."

He steered her to a seat half way down. "It's kept vacant in case he wants to use it. The summer residency is up here." Another couple stepped aboard. George nodded to them. They acknowledged him distantly in return. When they thought Hellen was not looking they treated her to stealthy glances. She smiled openly back. The woman's mouth moved uncertainly towards a smile. The man pretended he had not noticed.

"You're looking very pretty," said George affably, leaning back in his seat, eyeing her speculatively. He had been extremely amiable since the arrival of the invitation. She was wearing a cocktail dress for the first time since her arrival, a pretty, dusky pink voile decorated with tiny bouquets of daisies, and she carried a beaded handbag that matched the colourful band she wore across her forehead.

"You look fine yourself." George did, in fact, look well in his white dinner jacket of tailored Saigon linen.

"Where'd you get that head band?"

"In Jordan Road. There's a tiny shop where they will make anything you want while you wait, or at least by the next day." She had discovered the Chinese had a genius for intricate work.

"Pity about your pearls." George's eyes rested on her bare neck. "Would you like me to replace them."

"Now that I've got a husband, I doubt very much if anyone else is going to give me jewellery," she replied with a little smile. Whilst not wanting anything from him, neither did she wish to spoil his mood by rebuffing him.

"Who gave you the pearls the pirates took?"

"My grandfather."

"The one with the jewellery shop?"

"Jewellery shop?" she frowned.

"You said your family was in trade. I should keep it under your hat," said George, maintaining the outward geniality. "You may not be interested in getting in with The Peak set, but it could help me considerably."

"Shall I tell them my grandfather is a knight?"

George laughed. "You're quite a girl, aren't you?"

She glanced round the interior of the tram. Another half dozen people had boarded. A man in riding breeches, looking hot. Several English couples dressed as they were, the men in boiled shirts and black ties, the women in flounces and the new style head bands. There were no Chinese. She remarked on the fact to George.

"There's no reason for Chinks to go to The Peak."

"What about the servants of the residents? They must come and go. And the water coolies? Ruth said there's no water up here. Coolies have to carry it up on their backs."

"There are tracks for them," replied George carelessly.

Looking ahead at the steep rails running up the mountainside,

170

Hellen asked in amazement, "You mean, you make them toil all that way with those great drums on their backs?" She had seen the water carriers in the town, bent nearly double under the vast weight of their loads.

"I don't," replied George, remembering just in time Hellen's extraordinary reaction to the sight of the overloaded donkey in Cairo. "I don't live on The Peak."

"You're splitting hairs."

"You've got used to the wash amah," said George in that same careless voice. "You'll get used to the water carriers, too. We're off."

Clanking noisily on its steel rails, the tram dragged them up the immensely steep mountainside through foliage that brushed against the windows, obscuring the view. At the top, while their fellow passengers haggled with the waiting rickshaw coolies, they climbed into the comfortable sedan chair Ruth had sent for them, and were borne by four bearers along the winding footpaths of the green wooded heights. The air up here was wonderfully cool and fresh, scented with the damp foliage and musty bracken.

They were set down outside a pair of wrought iron gates. A coolie gate keeper moved out from beneath a rattan shelter to let them in. The path to the house was lined with tree ferns and camelia bushes. Half way along Hellen paused to look round her. Ruth's house, set on a jutting spur, held a commanding view of the harbour. Seen from here, the water was a fairyland. There were the winking lights on the Star ferry, and the small riding lights on junks. The anchored ships were all decorated with glowing necklaces from funnel to funnel and bow to stern.

"How beautiful!" she exclaimed in delight. "No wonder everyone wants to live up here." The people George had acknowledged on the tram came walking up the path behind them. She smiled, and now they both smiled back.

Ruth ran across a broad verandah to meet them. "Ah! The guest of honour."

Hellen looked behind her and was about to step aside when Ruth, putting her arms round her, said warmly, "You, dear. The new bride is the guest of honour. Come in and meet my friends."

171

Chapter 16

The Pearls

"Why didn't you tell me your grandfather was Sir Samuel Porchard?" asked George looking like a cat that has swallowed the cream. They were sitting in their seats waiting for The Peak tram to start it descent.

"I didn't know you knew him," replied Hellen, teasing him for his silly snobbery.

It was on the tip of his tongue to say, "Provocative bitch," but he would have to use a fond voice to get away with it and he couldn't, quite frankly, be bothered.

"Sorry, George, but I don't think it's quite the thing to say, 'I am Hellen North, granddaughter of . . .' It's more honest to say 'daughter of', and as you may remember, you weren't very impressed by that."

George looked out into the rock cliff on the inner side on the tram line.

"He's not a knight in shining armour, by the way." Warmed by Ruth's generosity and the friendliness of the guests, she was happy, and in a mood to tease. "Just a rich one who bought his title with the money he made in the dark, satanic mills." She turned the quote over her tongue, looking quizzically at George from under her lashes. "Dar-r-k sat-an-ic. They keep the North family in comfort, and we're very grateful to them. It occurs to me, it's what you get accustomed to, isn't it? Like using a Chinese as a beast of burden." Without giving George an opportunity to reply she hurried on, "It was nice to see Major Tandy again. He is a dear." The Major had taken her into a corner and, showing fatherly concern, asked her if she was happy. He said he had grown fond of her on *Devanha*. She responded with an effort to put his mind at ease, saying, yes, she thought she was happy. That Hong Kong was fascinating.

"Remember I'm here," he said then, and slipped her his card. She had been deeply touched.

172

George didn't want to talk about Tandy, who treated him as an outsider, and besides, her teasing had rubbed him up the wrong way. It held rather too much truth for his liking. He put a hand to the scar on the side of his head where his ear has been, an automatic reflex action now, when he was disturbed. "I hope you enjoyed yourself," he said stiffly.

"Ah yes, I did. I did." On The Peak she had felt nearer to Oliver. Down in Central, she had seen the Colonial Secretariat where he worked, and also the imposing mansion which was his uncle's by right of tenure, but the young bachelors' quarters at 114 Peak Road were where he ate and slept and had his being, and though she dared not ask, she felt he must be somewhere near. She sensed his nearness. All evening, in spite of Ruth's saying she did not intend to invite him, when a man taller than the rest came into the room her heartbeats quickened. But he had not come.

Looking around the tram now, Hellen noted that though the guests had dispersed all at the same time, none of them boarded the tram. Then she remembered what George's father said, that everybody who lived on The Peak knew everyone else on The Peak, and nobody else. Those who had ascended with them earlier must have come on from attending to affairs in Central.

"What road do you live in?" people had asked, assuming she lived, as did everyone else, above May Road and below the summer residency. When she replied, "Minden Row, Kowloon," a frisson of surprise went through the group. One woman actually walked away. Someone said, with a laugh, "I thought only bachelors lived in Kowloon." At Hellen's baffled look, she added, "It's a joke. People say, 'Are you married, or do you live in Kowloon?' because – I suppose you'd say, it's easy to keep a concubine there."

One woman asked baldly, "Can't you get a place on The Peak?" as though, Hellen thought, amused, she could only make a friend of me if I conformed.

She had countered the question by saying, "We're not quite settled yet." It was as though Lady Sylvia, in that world she had left behind, should ask, "But does you father have to be a tenant farmer?"

The men had been kinder. "I met someone called Toby Ayre," she remarked to George. "Do you know him?"

"Lives in the road beyond Ruth," George replied. Everyone seemed to know exactly where everyone else lived, even if they were not on visiting terms. "Works for Jardine's," he added. They knew where each other worked, too, and the strata of their job. Hellen had a feeling, though nothing had actually been said, that George's job was not up to much. She puzzled about it, remembering he had sufficient influence with Captain Boggis to commandeer his cabin.

"Toby rides most mornings at Happy Valley," she said. "One can hire a horse. He invited me to join him. Apparently there are Mongolian ponies there, looked after by white Russian mafoos. What's a mafoo?" Without waiting for a reply, because she was excited at the thought of riding, she rushed on, "You have to sit low in the saddle and lift these ponies along with your legs down. It's more strenuous than riding short. It sounds exciting. I'd really like to go."

"At five thirty a.m.?" George snorted. "That's when he goes."

"I'm quite capable of getting up at five. Anyway, that's only because he has to be in his office by 8.30. I don't have to ride with him, I'm sure." She gave George a sideways glance. "You could come with me." George did not respond. "The point I'm making is that I can hire a horse. A Mongolian pony."

George shrugged.

Later, while she was undressing, he came in to her room. He was wearing the blue silk pyjamas he bought in Singapore for the honeymoon, and his feet were bare. His hair was still tousled from the harbour breezes, and he was standing very straight, looking athletic and strong.

She snatched up her dressing gown, slid into it, tied the sash firmly round her waist and began furiously to brush her hair.

"If there was a chair in here I'd sit down." George wandered across to the bed, bent down and thumped the mattress with his fist, as though testing it. He looked up at Hellen. "Or would you rather I got into bed?"

She glanced round at the papered walls, a riot of wild-looking orange nasturtiums running up painted trellises, still unadorned by pictures, bare of looking glasses, photographs, the normal paraphernalia of a woman's boudoir. She said in a panicky rush, "I'm sorry. I didn't quite know where to start – decorating – I mean furnishing. Ruth is going to help me. I'm sorry there isn't a chair."

George made a sound like, "Hh-h-phhh," mostly through his nose. An amiable sneer. "You strike me as an efficient girl who wouldn't need too much help with anything."

She began again furiously to brush her hair.

He sat down on the end of the bed, staring at his knees. Hellen went on brushing. He looked up. "Why did you marry me?"

She put the brush down on the dressing table. It landed on its side, tottered, then rolled over on to the floor. She stared at it. Then she picked it up. She placed it carefully on the dressing table top, and swiftly turned. "If there's going to be an inquisition," she replied with a desperate show of spirit, "let's start with the fact that you married

174

me because you thought I was related to the Governor."

"Attack," acknowledged George in a bored voice, "is the best defence. This isn't an inquisition. Just a simple question."

"I was frightened." She leaned against the dressing table causing it to rock with her weight. The comb went sliding to the floor. She crouched with her back turned, slowly picking it up. George eyed the slim waist, accentuated by the wide sash; the curved hips; the provocative little rounded bottom. Slowly, she rose to her feet and placed the comb beside the brush. She carefully straightened the dressing table. "You're right," she said with a nervous little laugh, "we do need chairs."

"Of what?" asked George. "Of what were you frightened?"

"Of what might happen to me."

"You thought of me as protection?"

She picked up the brush again, frowning at its silver back, considering the word. She turned a little towards him. "Shelter," she said at last, knowing there would have been no shelter with George for a woman bearing someone else's child. Involuntarily, she shivered.

George eyed her narrowly. "Someone walking over your grave?"

She put a hand to her brow. "I'm rather tired. I'd like to get into bed."

"Yes, why not?" He pushed the mosquito curtain aside, carelessly flicked back the corner of the sheet. "I'd like to get in with you." He smiled at her with very real warmth.

There was a long silence. "It's normal for married couples to sleep together," he said encouragingly, at last. "Don't you know that?"

"I don't see this as a normal marriage. A normal bridegroom doesn't humiliate his bride. It isn't easy to forgive humiliation. I've said that before. That one doesn't, in fact, forgive humiliation." Her fingers trembled on the sash at her waist, tightening it, and tightening it again as though that would keep him, George Curtain, who was strong enough and ruthless enough to do with her anything he wished, from violating her body once again.

"I'm sorry," said George wearily. "I'm sorry that the circumstances should have warranted it. The necessity to humiliate you, I mean. It would not have happened if you had agreed to relax and enjoy. I really don't know what you expected me to do. In the circumstances, I mean."

"If you have convinced yourself you had an excuse for what you did in the Hong Kong hotel," she said, her voice high and jumping, "let me remind you that the humiliation began when I discovered I had been drugged and seduced on *Bangkok lady*."

He stared at her, faintly frowning.

She managed to bring her voice under control. "You must be very lacking in understanding, George, if you think a girl could love you for that."

"Love?" queried George, picking delicately at the cut edge of the mosquito netting. "Who mentioned love?" When she did not reply he lifted his head and added robustly, "Rolling around in bed is a very pleasant pastime. Why not look at it that way? Good exercise. Fun."

Hellen put the brush aside and went to the window. Outside, the hot air was ruffled by a faint breeze that stirred the net curtains.

George heaved a little sigh and climbed to his feet. Crossing to her side, he rested a hand on her shoulder, then slid it down her silky sleeve until it came to her fingers. He intertwined them in his.

Hellen held her breath.

"I shall keep away from the flower boats," he said. "That's my part of the bargain."

"I haven't made a bargain."

"Oh, but you have. A marriage is a bargain to love, honour and obey. Obey," George repeated. His head came up. He might have been a general, commanding his troops. "I want to sleep with you. You, my wife. I expect you to obey."

Outside, a night owl hooted in the banyan trees.

"Come on," he said persuasively. "It mightn't be the best marriage in the world, but whose is? Forget and forgive." He slid an arm round her, pulled her close up against him, pressed his hard belly into hers, smoothed her hair with his free hand.

"Living together," she said, her voice trembling conspicuously, "is a demonstration of love. I understand you might not see that, since you live with women you don't know, as you say," her voice was suddenly hot, scathing, out of control, "for the exercise."

"Oh, come on!" He gave a sort of laugh.

She ignored his interruption. "I can get plenty of exercise riding one of those ponies in Happy Valley."

George let her go. Biting back the abuse that rose to his lips, he turned and without a word left the room, slamming the door behind him. Standing staring out of the window into the darkened garden, hands in his dressing gown pockets, he gave vent to his feelings. George could swear in Mandarin, Cantonese and English. His vocabulary of abuse was filthy and extreme. He swore very softly under his breath, until he had himself in hand again. When he was calm he considered what was best to do. It was not long before he came up with an idea.

The next evening, when he came home from the office, he was genial and full of goodwill. "Well, and how have you been amusing

176

yourself today, my dear?" he asked, divesting himself of his jacket, loosening his tie.

Hellen looked up from her book. "I went shopping. Ruth and I bought some furniture. I hope you will approve."

George jerked at his collar stud. The surprise on his face was genuine. "Tell me, and I'll tell you if I approve." He looked full of good-will, bent on approving.

"We bought a sofa and two chairs—a suite—from Lane Crawford. And some occasional tables. Two little chairs—"

"For the bedroom?" George leaned towards her. His voice was warm and encouraging.

Hellen sucked in her breath. Of course it was going to begin again. He would not give up so easily. "For the drawing room. I've had quite a busy day," she said briskly. "First things first. I'll get round to the other rooms in time."

"I hope you will," said George, smiling fondly, reaching for her hand. "A woman needs a pretty bedroom. I don't care very much for that bed cover. I seem to have been looking at it all my life. Mother had it on her bed for years."

"It's a very good cover," protested Hellen, attempting to withdraw her fingers without being too obvious. "Replacing it would be an extravagance."

"We can afford to be a little extravagant."

"Can we?" asked Hellen. She lifted her eyes to his face, searching it. "I don't know anything about your job."

His eyes slid away. "Buy the best," he said expansively, ignoring her question, "and get them to send the bill to me." He glanced down at his office clothes. "I had better change. Ah Wong will be announcing dinner any moment now."

She followed him with her eyes as he left her, thinking about the fact that his parents lived in a very modest way; about Marcia's surprise that she and George should move into such a large house; about Marcia's saying, when pressing her excess furniture upon them, that she and George were young, and must cut their costs according to their cloth; about the fact that she had a distinct impression from the drift of her conversations with Ruth, that George's job was nothing to write home about. Ruth had evinced surprise that she spent so much on the furnishings.

On Ruth's advice, Hellen had invested in a collection of fine porcelain. A chow-fan bowl for rice, tiny porcelain cups without handles for the red lychee tea which she loved, or the rice wine George sometimes drank, but which she found too strong. The cook boy made the rice wine himself, boiling poor quality rice, then adding yeast and water and allowing it to ferment for twenty days with pork fat to help the maturing process.

She bought an assortment of different sized bowls for sauces, and a big plate for the intriguing Dim Sum, a varied mixture of steamed dumplings, crab claws, and other small foods. Ah Wong made tissue-thin wheaten pancakes which he wrapped round minced squab. That was her favourite. Dim Sums were a never-ending source of delight. She would eat an entire lunch of them.

She was learning to eat with chopsticks because George used them all the time. She did not find them easy to hold. The food overbalanced, dropping back into the bowl, sometimes even onto her lap. She refused to shovel it into her mouth as she had seen the monks do on Lantau, though George declared it was quite acceptable, even in polite society. She thought he must be talking about polite Chinese society. It was not always possible to tell. Growing up as he had in Shanghai, he often did not differentiate between Chinese and English customs. She could not imagine Ruth eating Chinese food that way.

This evening Ah Wong had set the table with a cloth Marcia had given her—the best one, made of embroidered Irish linen. Either he, or George, had lifted down from the mantelpiece a little bowl of flowers she herself had picked from the garden. She was amazed when the first course of lobster ball sauté with dried salt bean sauce arrived. That was the kind of dish one would use for very special occasions. It was followed by a cutlet of garoupa. Garoupa was a highly prized fish, and George's favourite. Then, spiced goose, web-feet and wings. Hellen had never eaten it before. She thought it ambrosial. It bore no relation to any goose she had ever eaten. And then the penultimate, the highly acclaimed shark's fin soup, followed by melon. Melon was a fruit for hot days. It was thought to have a cooling effect on the system. The delicious mangoes and lychees, the cook boy informed her, were served in cooler weather.

It was indeed a banquet! Each dish a surprise. She looked at George questioningly several times as the meal progressed, but he avoided her eyes. Sitting opposite her, his hair spruce with pomade, his face shining, his small moustache neatly trimmed, he was behaving like a host with a very important guest. Hellen grew more and more restive. She was not in the habit of setting the menu. Ah Wong knew what dishes they liked, and those they did not, but he had never produced such a grand meal as this one. There was no doubt in her mind that George had chosen it. He must also have given the cook boy extra money for marketing.

"You can leave after the shark's fin soup," George told her good

178

humouredly as Ah Wong set soup bowls before them. "Remember that. Not before. Never before."

"Would I want to?" Hellen asked, puzzled.

He shrugged. "Maybe not, since most of the ex-pats serve it in the usual English way, first."

"What's an ex-pat?" she asked.

"Ex-patriates. You. Born and brought up in England."

"You're not one, then?"

He hesitated, and a shadow crossed his face. "If I'd gone to school in England—" he began, then broke off.

Regretting her question, Hellen changed the subject. Any mention of school put George on edge. "Why do we have the soup second to last?" she asked. "I'd prefer not to."

"You're the boss." George was genial once more, leaning across the table and squeezing her wrist. "Just tell the boy."

She had been glad to get away. His unaccustomed geniality, and the banquet produced and eaten without explanation, made her nervous. She opened the big glass doors and wandered out into the garden. The heat seemed to have lifted, at least to a degree. The crickets were creating their usual din. The moon was almost full, the sky glittering with stars. Through the floral scents of the garden drifted the salt smell of the sea. Over the treetops she could see the topmost lights of The Peak, where Oliver lived.

She glanced back at the house. The drawing-room windows were wide open. She could see George sitting on the sofa turning over the pages of the *South China Mail*. There were flying beetles buzzing round the light. Her apprehension deepened. Why was he staying in tonight? She walked along the little path between the crimson, long-tongued hibiscus. She stepped off the path on to the grass, losing herself in the darkness created by the tall shrubs.

She was somehow prepared when she heard a footstep on the path, but pretending she had not heard, she strolled on, moving out of the darkness into the moonlight, not wanting to appear to be hiding. George came up behind her and put an arm round her shoulders.

"Come inside. I've something to show you." She allowed him to lead her back through the French windows, then across the room to the carved mahogany table. In the centre of the table lay a folder covered in gold brocade.

"A present for you," said George expansively.

"How very kind." The banquet, and now a present! Feeling trapped, Hellen broke open the metal clasp on the folder and turned back the lid. A creamy pearl necklace, virtually identical to the one taken by the pirates, glowed from a white satin background. A pair

179

of matching pearl ear-rings lay in the centre. "How very kind of you," she repeated.

"Is that all?" he asked, sounding indulgent, though he wanted her to know, his tone implied, he was faintly hurt. He turned her round to face him. She moved stiffly under his hands. He kissed her, running his tongue across her closed lips, pushing with the tip. His arms tightened. She gasped, and he put his tongue inside her involuntarily opened mouth. When he released her there were bright tears of anger in her eyes.

"What an emotional creature you are." George was still being hideously indulgent. "Here, let me put them on." She stood quite still, anger warring with very real despair as he took the pearls from their bed, undid the gold clasp, and placed them round her neck. One of the angry tears fell and rolled down her cheek.

Ah Wong appeared in the doorway. "Number two Missie Master come your door," he announced.

"Ooo-o hoo! It's only us, dears."

Marcia! Hellen snatched a handkerchief from her pocket and wiped the tear away.

Her mother-in-law entered first, big and jolly in a floral print dress and lisle stockings, exuding goodwill and the confidance of one arriving by invitation. Neil followed, looking pleased. Marcia pulled up precipitately, the smile on her broad face fading. "What's the matter?"

With his arm round Hellen's waist, George led her forward. He said, in that unbearably indulgent voice, "I've just given my dear wife a present, and she's having an emotional little weep."

Feeling vulnerable, exposed, and trembling now with fear and rage, Hellen moved sharply away from him. Mutely, she indicated the necklace.

They smiled, immensely relieved. "How pretty," said Marcia. "A pearl necklace! What a lucky girl you are."

She wanted to scream at them that she was not lucky at all. That she would not have lost her own pearls—she thought of them as her own pearls—if their son had not drugged her, abducted her, and raped her.

"Do sit down," George said to his parents. "We're going to have this place set up in two shakes, and then you can have that sofa of yours back."

Marcia protested they could have everything that was already here, as a gift. "You know I have far too much for our little bungalow."

"Good of you," said George, adding affably, "Nice of you to come," as though their visit was a surprise.

Then Marcia ruined his cover by replying, "It's nice to be with you again, dear. We don't like simply to drop in."

There was a flash of annoyance on George's face, wiped off by a smile.

Hellen crossed the room with swift steps and picked up the bell. "Tea?" she asked the guests in a brittle voice. "Or a drink?" The air was poisoned by George's stupid behaviour.

"Tea," said Marcia, settling her bulk comfortably on the sofa.

Neil was watching her. Hellen could feel his eyes, but all she could think about was the fact that George was using his parents, as he had used the banquet, to set a scene. When, an hour or so later, Marcia said, "We really must be off and let you two young people get to bed," she replied, sounding desperate even to her own ears, "Don't go. Do stay a little longer."

But she could not keep them. They had to go. She went to her bedroom and closed the door, knowing she could not keep George out, for there was no key.

He came in that brief moment when she was standing naked, pulling her nightdress over her head.

"I think it would be nice if you were to knock," she said sharply, jerking the silk down over her hips, turning away from him.

"I don't know that one should have to knock on one's wife's door."

She swung round angrily to face him. "Everyone has a right to privacy."

Looking athletic and strong, George went over to the bed, jerked the mosquito net out of the way, then flung himself down on his back, holding out his arms.

She strode furiously across the room. "Get up, and get out."

With one hand, he grasped at the skirt of her night dress. "Come on, darling. It's time."

She flung herself away from him with a kind of violence.

In one stride she was at the dressing table. She picked up the satin folder contaiing the pearl neklace and with all her might she flung it at him, then swung round and leapt through the door, slamming it behind her. She looked to right and left. Where to go? She sprinted down the passage to the room that held her cabin trunk and the big packing case, spun inside, locked the door behind her and stood leaning with her back against it, trembling with anger and grief.

Gradually, as she realised George was not coming after her, as she had expected, to shout and bang on the door with his fists, as her heartbeats slowed and the trembling ceased, she went to the window and stood looking out towards The Peak, casting a prayer across the harbour, sending it spinning up to the heights.

Bring him to me before this dreadful thing happens. Bring him to me.

If George rapes me again, she thought, I will kill him.

Please, God, save me from that.

She stayed at the window for a long time, watching the lights and the stars and the big, smiling moon. Gradually her fear left her and her anger dissolved. Later, she turned on the light and taking the key from where she had hidden it above the curtain rail, opened her cabin trunk.

For several moments she stood looking down at the useless array of her beautiful trousseau. She lifted a fluffy cotton towel to her cheek, feeling Oliver's nearness in the silky embroidery of his initials and hers, entertwined. When she put the towel back it was damp with tears. With loving hands and a heavy heart she lifted the wedding dress out of its tissue wrapping, shook the heavy silk folds, smoothed the Brussels lace with tender fingers, and held it to her heart. On an impulse, she removed her nightdress, slipped the wedding gown over her head, and returned to the window. The lights were still there, high up on The Peak where Oliver lived, glowing like fireflies.

Oliver, I am here. With all her strength, she willed him to come.

The sun was coming up pinkly over the South China Sea, and the top of The Peak was shrouded in mist when at last she rose to her feet, took the dress off the folded it back into its tissue, then placed it reverently on the upper shelf of the wardrobe, the only piece of furniture in the room. She looked round tiredly, picked an armful of the larger towels out of a trunk, and placing them in a folded row on the bare boards, stretched out across them, and fell asleep.

When she wakened it was eleven o'clock. The sun was streaming in at the uncurtained window and she was damp with sweat. She lifted herself up from the pile of towels and went back to her bedroom. The pearls were on the dressing table, the bed neatly made up. The house was silent. She bathed, dabbed some lotion on her arms where a mosquito had bitten her in the night, took a pale blue voile dress from the wardrobe, dressed swiftly, donned the big straw hat she had bought in Lane Crawford, picked up her gloves and parasol, and went down the stairs. As she reached the hall she could hear the thin alto voices of the servants chattering in the kitchen. She let herself quietly out of the house.

Fah Wong (or the Fah Wong) was asleep beneath a tree with his broom lying across his skinny knees. He did not move as she passed. She had no clear idea of where she was going. She was following some deep, inner impulse. She walked the short distance to the waterfront where she was immediately accosted by a rickshaw coolie. Without bothering to haggle for a good price, she stepped deftly over the shaft handle and rode to the Star Ferry pier. The astonished coolie showed rows of bad teeth in a grin as she paid him the exorbitant two dollars he asked for the tiny journey, then she stepped on to the waiting ferry.

Central, the business area of Hong Kong, was always busy. Hellen's athletic strides, so unlike the short steps of the small Chinese, brought her up through Royal Square with its statues of the English monarchs, past the Tai Wah Medicine Company, the Ying Fat Ivory Factory, and a shop that sold fluttering birds in cages. Whatever the unrecognised force in her, it knew the direction, for she went straight.

On Battery Path, directly below the cathedral, she slowed. There was a row of beggars, curled up on the pathway, emaciated, half naked, all with the shallow eyes and pin-point pupils of the opium addict. She fished in her handbag for some coins. Above her and to the left, Government House rested elegantly on its knoll, smiling out on the island-studded harbour; below, the imposing façade of the building that housed the Colonial Secretariat, where Oliver worked. Where Oliver, if he happened to look out of a window, must surely see her, now. To her right lay the stately edifice where she and Oliver were to have been married.

As she stood there, mid-way between all that was to have been, she felt a wash of warmth, and it seemed as though she was on an upward flight, in floating swirls of warm mist. She moved on, her footsteps taking her in to the cathedral yard. The white building was surprisingly small, now that she was close to it, scarcely cathedral size, as she knew them—Westminster, Salisbury, York.

Near the door she turned back to look across the road to Government House, and in a waking dream, saw herself stepping out of a big, black car, feeling the swish of silk round her calves, the delicate tug of the embroidered veil on her forehead and smelling the scent of the tuber roses and stephanotis in her bouquet. She went slowly up to the door. Inside, she stepped delicately along the broad aisle, made holy beneath her feet by a brown cross, and there was a pair of slim hands, exquisitely wrought in smaller tiles outstretched in warmth and welcome. The organ was playing.

She stood looking round at the laddered, stained glass window, all open to relieve the damp heat, listening to the organ rendering with some uncertainty a rough version of "Onward Christian Soldiers". The interior of the cathedral was spacious. From behind the altar a rosy Christ on a blood red cross looked down on her with sadness, the golden roofs of Jerusalem at his feet. There were high white arches in the side aisles; wooden chairs with cane seats and cane backs; overhead, huge candelabra bearing golden lights.

Behind her there was the sound of soft footsteps and then a hand slid into hers. Without looking, she knew it was Oliver, for had she not conjured him up, all through the long night? Had he not drawn her here, out of his need? He said softly, with a break in his voice, "Hellen. Oh, my darling." His hand was warm and strong, sending its strength into her, filling her with faith and hope.

"I knew you would come," he said. "Last night you were very close." He bent and kissed her, with the utmost tenderness, on her lips, and her heart swelled until it seemed ready to burst, while the practising organist, with a flurry of wrong notes, ground "Onward Christian Soldiers" to an end.

Of one accord, they took a couple of cane chairs and sat entranced, not talking, simply feeling—merged, Hellen thought afterwards, in the most deep and exquisite fashion, one being, as they would have been made one, if only things had been different; if Fate in the shape of Lady Sylvia Ashton had not been so unkind. The organist was having a tentative go at "There Is A Green Hill Far Away". A nostalgic tear welled up, broke loose and ran down Hellen's cheek, for was that not how it had all begun, on a green hill far away?

Oliver whispered, "We could go to Mountair Lodge. There's absolutely nobody there. I have to let go of your hand. I can't bear it, but I have to let go of you. We mustn't walk together. Go to The Peak tram, and I'll follow, but if there's anyone else aboard, don't speak to me. Get into a rickshaw at the top and ask for Mountain Lodge, but don't let anyone overhear. I'll catch you up. There are forty-three acres of grounds. We'll be perfectly safe when we get there."

There were half a dozen people on the tram. Hellen sat at the back watching with fierce jealousy while Oliver chatted to a young woman who accosted him. She thought she would die if she did not soon have her hand in his again, die if she could not feel his lips on hers. George Curtain was gone from her life, as though he had never existed, leaving neither gap nor memory.

There were the rickshaws with their sad, hopeful coolies vying vengefully with each other for the privilege of being turned into packhorses. Hellen settled into a seat, for the first time without a thought for the lot of the poor creature who carried her. He trotted off up the road, chanting his coolie cry, "Hoo-hoo, hoo-hoo."

It was as though they were going through a public park, except that they passed pretty dwellings surrounded by emerald green lawns, and flower strewn gardens, on roads leading from one level to another; through cuttings lined with whispering bamboo that gave on to magnificent views of the sea, with its crouching islands shading into a damp heat mist. Then Oliver's rickshaw coolie caught up and they travelled side-by-side, smiling at each other as they slid beneath huge-leafed monsters that grew out of the hillsides and overhung the path, with vine rampaging amongst the branches. Above and around, now, were beautiful mansions set like eagles' eyries among granite peaks and frowning precipices.

They came to the lodge gates and stepped down. "We'll walk now." Oliver paid both coolies, or overpaid them, Hellen thought, loving him for his warm generosity as they turned grinning faces on her, showing rows of sparkling gold teeth. Even their teeth are gold today, she thought dizzily.

Oliver spoke to the lodge keeper in Cantonese, or Mandarin, or whatever it was the cadets learned, and handed him some coins. "The price of silence and discretion," he whispered, sliding an arm through hers. "I wanted to walk with you here. It's magic. A paradise." He bent and kissed her on the lips, considerably less gently then he had in the cathedral, and she thought she would die of happiness.

"I can't believe I've got you again," he said, as though he had, as though she did not belong, by the proof of *Bangkok Lady*'s log, and the confirming stamp of the colony's consul, by a spider's web of not-to-be-broken laws, to George Curtain Esq. of Tsim Sha Tsui.

They wandered along a path bordered by azaleas and red hibiscus, that gave later on to shaven lawns, and tennis courts, then a riot of summer garden. Two and a half acres of it! A little plateau of grass led up to a great square mansion with enormous windows, peaked roofs and verandahs.

"Oh!" said Hellen in awe. She had not expected such grandeur.

"It's awfully damp," said Oliver deprecatingly. "Half the time it's hidden in fog, and the bed linen has to stay all day in the hot cupboard. My uncle is trying to persuade Lloyd George to let him build a holiday house in the New Territories. Thank God he hasn't won the battle—yet. Today, we need this." They went up some stone steps, into a stone porch. He pressed a bell and a wizened old man who was nonetheless a "boy", came to let them into a cool, brown wood hall. Oliver spoke to him briefly, some more coins changed hands, and they went towards the stairs.

"That's Ah Chow. I gave him a couple of dollars. A fortune. But beware. If my uncle were to suspect, and give him three . . ." They laughed softly, with delicious dread, as they proceeded hand-in-hand to the upper floor.

Chapter 17

Stolen Fruit

"No one is going to take you away from me," said Oliver fiercely, careless of the fact that George Curtain had already done so.

The velvet softness of her skin beneath his fingertips, the trembling of her lips against his, the silky stream of her beautiful hair falling across his cheek, filled him with a sense of joy beyond belief. Nothing had ever been like this for him before. It was emotional ecstasy at its peak.

The big, sunny room pulsated with the joy of their loving. He lay back, and closing his eyes tightly, lost her, for the sheer excitement of finding her when he opened them again. He leaned up on one elbow and looked down in wonder at the long, curved beauty of her body, then back to her face. She was peeping at him from between those little black rolls of lashes, her grey eyes full of exotic knowing.

"Hello," he said.

Her mouth trembled. "Hello." She was listening to his thoughts, wrapping herself in the love that flowed out of him, passionate, overwhelming, and above all, triumphant. It was as though the whole world was poised on their heartbeats, rocking in ecstasy. Her fingers stole up to his face, caressed his nose, the line of his cheek bone, his eyelids that were once again closed, in bliss. She knew with intense clarity why he kept closing and opening them. She read it in his eyes, felt the shout of joy that went through him each time his lids lifted to look at her. "You're here! You're really here!"

It would be with her forever, that great rush of awareness as they came together, the seeing, the feeling, the understanding of what had been beyond understanding before, that George must not invade her because what she had to give, oh so fulsomely and with such infinite love, was crystallised into a gift for Oliver. So precious a gift that no suffering in the world, no endurance, would be too great in her efforts to keep it inviolate. Now Oliver lay back on the bed and she leaned up on one elbow, bending her head, kissing him again with the utmost tenderness, sealing the kiss with her blessing. He breathed contentedly against her cheek. Her lips, like a butterfly's wing, fluttered across his eyelids.

"Why didn't you tell me there might be trouble, darling?"

"I was so sure it would be all right." Sure of his uncle, whom he believed thought as he did, and had the same values.

"Didn't you suspect you were being recalled because of me?" Her lips moved to his cheeks, his chin, his neck. She touched his adam's apple with her fingertips, ran them round the firm flesh of his jaw, kissed his ear.

"Great heavens, no. I had to go back. King's Messenger, remember? Chased off by the Whitehall mandarins." His arms tightened round her, holding her to his heart, that was full of the bitter-sweet knowledge that though he had indeed won this round, he had, in reality, lost. But she was his to love. He clasped her to him in an exultance of loving. "My darling, we belong, as we didn't before. It's a start. It's a start.

"Who needs the jolly old archbishop and orange blossom and full fig!" he demanded. "Who needs it, I ask you?" His triumphant words were smothered in her neck, lost in the impetus of his return to the bottomless well of feeling in each other. "Kiss my toes. . . . Kiss my neck. . . . Kiss here. . . . And here. . . . And here. . . ." They laughed together, secretly, breathlessly. Their love was an unquenchable thirst, a seeking, a hunger that invoked fantasy and yearning and a mad lust for possession.

In the late afternoon they stood at the window, arms entwined, looking out over the lonely heights where the mountain slopes fell away from this, the ramparts of Nirvana, to the sea. From far below the magic silence was broken by the fitful call of a barking deer foraging upward through the thickets and Chinese pines. On the distant horizon the mouse-shaped islands dozed on the sun-glittered water.

Oliver asked, "What are we going to do?"

"What can we do? I've thought so much about it. There's only one way, and that is for me to go home and wait for George to divorce me." Oliver opened his mouth to protest but she held a finger against his lips to silence him. "Think about it."

"I have thought about it. He may choose not to divorce you. What then?"

"There is another matter." She swallowed. Already the words were catching in her throat. "He says you would not be allowed to marry a divorced woman."

"I shall marry whom I wish," averred Oliver stoutly, reaching out for her, hugging her hungrily, flesh against flesh, kissing her breathless until they both collapsed in ecstatic laughter.

In the next quiet moment she said fiercely, "Your career—they all talk about your career as though . . ." She wanted to shout out aloud in defiance, "As though careers are more important than human beings. They are not," but she stayed quiet with her certain knowledge that careers were merely the support of people whose function was to love one another. That was something her mother had known when she stepped out of a mansion to marry a penniless tenant farmer. That was a truth Lady Sylvia would never see with that blind eye of hers.

"It's one of the pitfalls of the foreign services—of any office worth having," said Oliver soberly. "That's what we have to think about. I must be able to provide for you."

It was her turn to protest, and this time it was his finger against her lips. "I have it clear in my mind," he said. His mouth twisted wryly. "My uncle has made certain I have it very clear in my mind. I have to be able to provide for you. But meantime, we can see each other. I shall find a room, somewhere in Central, where we'll meet." He put a finger beneath her chin and lifted her face. "Would you think that sordid?" He looked close into the grey depths of her eyes.

"With you? Sordid?" Her arms tightened round him. She buried her face in the soft dark hairs of his chest, kissing the skin wherever her lips touched.

"Outside of our happiness at being together, it would be sordid," Oliver acceded gravely. "You have to accept that." He picked up his gold watch that was lying on the bedside table and read the time with something of a shock. "I have to explain why I left the office and did not return. You have to say something to George." He grinned, put the watch back, took her once again in his arms. "Something other than, 'I have been in bed with Oliver Marathon at Mountain Lodge.'" They laughed together and were merrily, exultantly, lost in each other once more.

"We mustn't come here again," Oliver said as they prepared for their return to real life. "There would be hell to pay if we were caught. I'll find a way of getting in touch with you." He took her hands, clasped together over her breast, and lifted them to his lips, kissing each finger in turn. "Leave it to me. I will find a way. And in the end, all will be well."

They were both so certain, deep in their inmost hearts. How could it be otherwise, when fate, the all-seeing, all powerful, had brought them together, crowned them with thorns, caught them in traps, heaped disasters on their heads, yet allowed them to come together again. Ah! That was the portent. The fact that they had been allowed this brief ecstasy. Was She so idly fickle as to allow all that, then carelessly bring down the guillotine?

"I promise," said Oliver gravely, still holding both of her hands, "to love, honour and cherish you all the days of my life. Repeat after me."

"I promise."

It was their most holy moment.

"Where Missie?" demanded George, distinctly disquietened to find Hellen gone. He spoke Mandarin fluently, having picked it up as a child in Shanghai. His Cantonese, learned by the hit-and-miss method of association with flower girls, and disreputable Chinese with whom he did business, was no more than adequate. Anyway, he preferred to speak pidgin to the servants. That's what everyone else did.

He had returned early from the office after a vaguely uneasy day. He had some half-baked ideas that teetered insensitively between taking Hellen out to dinner at the Hong Kong Hotel—it did not occur to him that she might consider it a symbol of torture—and reading her the Riot Act. He preferred the latter. He had an idea he might just let her know he was within his rights to lay down a few basic rules that included obedience and seemly behaviour.

"Missie come back by 'n' by."

"When?"

The boy shook his head. "No say, Master."

George returned upstairs. He went into the bedroom they were meant to share, smarting as he did every time he came here from the insult of Hellen's having made it her virginal own. Smarting, also, from the memory of having his goodwill gesture thrown back in his face. The pearls were still there, where he had placed them last night, on the dressing table.

Now that he knew Hellen was well connected with money, he sorely regretted not only that slap on the deck of *Bangkok Lady* but raping her in the Hong Kong Hotel. If only he had been prepared for the possibility of her survival, he would have plotted a strategy. But getting that telephone call right out of the blue, he had panicked. He had been furious about his ear, too. He had wanted to punish her for that, and for the fact that she was Oliver Marathon's girl. God! He would never have gone near her in the first place if he had known she was even thinking of marrying Oliver Marathon.

George had not given up hope of bettering himself in the colony.

"Get rich," he had said to himself. "Don't worry about the ethics. Just get rich. Then they'll listen. Nobody cares where money comes from, once you've got enough to throw your weight around." He stamped over to the window and looked across at The Peak, craven envy in every line of his face. Oh, hell! He could have seduced her that day, he told himself, if he had been prepared to spend the time. If he hadn't had that bloody Washington woman downstairs plotting God knew what.

But what about Hellen? he asked himself resentfully. What about that inexplicable outburst on trade, in front of his mother? And totally inexcusable, in view of the fact that one of her so-called tradesmen was a bloody great industrialist! Sheer bad temper and spite. He'd been down to the library the day after the Washington party and looked up Sir Samuel Porchard in *Who's Who*. The man existed all right. But how the hell had he been expected to know? Why hadn't she told him?

Above all, why had she married him? He hadn't forced her. Not . . . really, though he felt a prick of conscience when he remembered that queer moment, half way through the ceremony, when she seemed loath to sign her name. What a goat he'd have looked, in front of Charlie Marsh and bloody Boggis! Talk about losing face! It didn't bear thinking about.

He moved agitatedly once more round the room, picking up the pearls that were supposed to fix everything, slapping them down again. He straightened his shoulders, stretched his neck above his stiff collar, assumed the dominant stance that suited him so well. He'd just have to convince her that she'd cop it from him in more ways than one if she didn't come to heel. With the Washington woman pushing it along for them now, things could be pretty bobbish if they played their cards right. During the brief period he had been engaged to Kitty, people had been as nice as pie.

He pulled out his watch. Five-thirty. Where the hell was she? He went along the passage and flung open the door of the room where Hellen had slept last night. He stood staring in at it, at its bedlessness, which was the part he did not like, the proven strength of her rebellion. His shoulders jerked automatically. It wasn't going to happen again. He'd see to that. He took the key out of the door and pocketed it.

There were only three objects in the room. The wardrobe, that huge cabin trunk, and the packing case. He knew jolly well what they contained. A girl coming out to get married would bring a trousseau. Well, he thought aggressively, she was married to him, and it was about time she started using it. Why should he provide sheets and towels, and whatever else brides traditionally brought to a marriage? That was her part, her with her pearls and her rich grandfather.

He stepped further into the room, advancing on the trunk belligerently, as though it might be alive. He had looked at the padlock on several occasions. He had even considered breaking it open. Somewhere, there were cutters that would make short work of this. And the box, too. Gaining confidence, he stood looking down on the intricate metalwork of the cabin trunk as though it were an easily vanquished enemy. It was then he saw, to his astonishment, that the padlock was not in place.

"Boy!"

Ah Wong came running. "Yes, Master."

"Come topside. Chop chop." George went back into the room. He had thrown his white coat over the opened lid of the trunk. His collar hung by the back stud, and his tie dangled down the front of his sweat-soaked shirt. In spite of the whirring fan overhead, the room was hellish hot.

Ah Wong pattered up the stairs. Master was standing with a pile of household linen at his feet. The Chinese's slit eyes widened. There were the sheets, towels, pillow cases, doilys, antimacassars, tea cosies and tea cloths, all the things that should be filling the mysteriously empty linen cupboard. Ah Wong showed his decayed brown teeth and his single gold one in a grin of pleasure and relief.

"Takee tailor." George pointed out the embroidered initials on sheets, towels and pillow cases. "Makee undo. Savee?"

Ah Wong nodded.

"Givee wash amah after. Putee topside cupboard." Ah Wong bent double, lifted a pile of sheets in his arms, then hurried out and down the stairs, calling in his high-pitched voice to the makee learn to help. Ah Ping came running. He spoke to her in Cantonese and she, too, pattered up the stairs. The Master was down on his knees on the floor—actually on the floor—unwrapping packages. There was wrapping paper all over the place. Why had Master not asked Ah Wong to unpack? A foreign devil down on his knees! Ah Ping could scarcely contain a little giggle of surprise.

George heard the soft sound of her cloth slippers and without bothering to turn, pointed silently to piles of towels and pillow cases, table cloths and napkins. But her eyes had moved to the window where there was a great shop window of treasure—a gold clock, a canteen of cutlery, china and glass, silver cake stands. . . . Ah Ping had never seen anything like it, although Ah Wong had talked to her about other houses where he had worked, that contained all sorts of

191

treasures. "All same Chinese house here," he had said, with scorn. "Empty."

"Chop, chop," said George harshly. "Takee bottom side."

Ah Ping jumped, dragged her eyes away from the booty and braced herself to pick up one of the piles of towels. Clutching it tightly in her skinny arms, she pulled upright and obediently hurried out of the room, rocking blindly along the passageway. Leaning against the banister for guidance, she pattered down the stairs. Ah Wong was already starting up again for another load.

George was standing, hands on hips, stretching his long back. He pointed to the objects beneath the window. "Takee bottom side, putee sideboard, table, dining room, mantelpiece. Chop, chop." He felt a rush of blood to the head at the thought of Hellen returning and catching him in the act, dishevelled and sweaty; guilty as a small boy caught pulling wings off butterflies. He must be bathed and changed and cool. Master of the house with a drink in his hand. The stuff should be spread around in suitable places when she walked in. A fait accompli.

George was not caught in the act. By the time he had bathed and changed into a tussore suit, the linen had gone to the tailors and the boxes been carted off to the garden shed. He went downstairs and poured himself a beer, looking with satisfaction at the crystal Ah Wong had set out in his mother's glass-fronted cabinet, at the quite magnificent gold-faced clock on the mantelpiece.

He had no sense of shame for what he had done, only relief for the fact that he had not been caught doing it. He rehearsed what he would say, rehearsing also his method of saying it, first stretching his chin above his clean starched collar and squaring his shoulders, standing tall, master of the house.

"My dear, you can't keep your past locked up in a box." Or, and perhaps this would be better, spoken in a very reasonable voice, "Why should they not be used? It's a trousseau, isn't it? You're a bride, aren't you? Well. . . ." As to the linen. "Hang it all, we can't use stuff with those initials on. Is that why you didn't bring them out? Because of the initials. Well," he would make indulgent noises, "it's done for you now."

He finished his beer, pulled out his watch again, frowned. Where the dickens was she? Surely she would not have gone to his parents? No. She was not at ease with his mother, and his father would only now be coming home from the office. Might she go and tell her troubles to Ruth? He went out to the hall and stood looking at the telephone on the wall.

He reared up mentally. Hell! What troubles? He was all at once

192

aggressive within himself. When your husband gives you a pearl necklace, you'd have to be off your onion if you thought you could get sympathy from even the most biased old trout. And, God help him, Ruth Washington was nothing if not biased against George. He stretched his chin again, fiddled with his stiff collar.

She'd come back, he decided. Her wardrobe, so far as he could discern, was intact. He'd had a good look round her room and couldn't see that anything was missing. Now the tantalising smells of spiced chicken and sweet and sour fish were seeping through from the kitchen. Should he eat alone? He was dashed hungry, and too restive to stand around. Besides, it might be better to greet her on a full stomach.

"Boy," he shouted. Ah Wong appeared in the doorway. "Servee chow. Chop, chop."

Hellen descended from The Peak in a haze of happiness. Oliver had stayed behind, deeming it wiser now that they should not be seen, even sitting apart, on the same tram. It was not until she emerged from the terminus on to Albert Path that the plateau of careless ecstasy tilted. It was nearly half-past five. George would be home by now.

She climbed into a rickshaw, forgetting again the cardinal rule to fix the price, and sat back, listening to the coolie's cries of "Hoo-hoo, hoo-hoo, hoo", as she jogged towards the Star Ferry Pier. Now she must think what she would say to George.

"I've been shopping"?

"I've been to see Ruth"?

"I've been walking"?

The heart's ease she had found cloaked her like silk. She was not ready to have it ripped off by confrontation with George. She rocked in it sweetly as the little ferry boat bore her across the water.

She stepped on to the Kowloon pier. Ignoring the beseeching eyes of the rickshaw coolies and the agitation of outstretched hands, she set out to walk. Very slowly, she went up Salisbury Road, then turned into Nathan, where one could lose oneself among the banyan trees.

It was hot here, where the sea breezes did not penetrate, suffocating after the fresh cool of The Peak. Her dress was already sticking to her skin. Strange how the heat so often descended in the evening. She wandered, twisting in and out of the trunks and laterals, listening to the noisy cicadas, pausing to rest a hand on the warm bark, dreaming until in time she came to the intersection where Mody Road cut in. She hesitated on the corner for a long time, then reluctantly turned.

But outside her control, her footsteps slowed and slowed again until, on reaching Minden Row, they were scarcely footsteps at all. From here she could see the big house with its gracious verandahs and wide open windows. Assailed by sudden panic, she swung round and headed towards the harbour.

When she was out of sight and sound and smell of everything that was George, she allowed her footsteps to slow again. There were evening gulls over the harbour, plaintive, friendly, haunting in a way. The lights were going on all over The Peak. She went right down to the sea wall and stood looking at the water, listening to its whispering, dreaming to herself. Now, with the strength and power of Oliver's love in her, she knew she could write home, though what she would say she did not yet know. It was enough that the future held a mite of hope.

She would be able, at last, to talk to them about Oliver. She would not tell them about the pirates. There was no point in upsetting them. She would say the marriage could not take place just now. That she was living meantime with a family in Tsim Sha Tsui. And because their reply would come addressed to Miss Hellen North, she would give them a box number. It did not occur to her to wonder how long she could carry on such a deception, or in fact why she should deceive them. She was thinking only that now she had a purpose for being here, she could get in touch.

It was an hour or more before she achieved a sense of resignation sufficient to allow her to go back to Minden Row and face up to that part of her life which must go on. With luck, George might even have gone to Causeway Bay. Prostitutes proliferated also in Kowloon. She had seen sailors, often the worse for drink, staggering off down Canton Road which ran behind the docks and go-downs on the other side of the peninsula. Kowloon had everything, except the pristine exclusivity of The Peak. That was why the right people did not live here. It even had a hostel for single working girls, affording some of the good Peak ladies, missing the charity work that filled their days at home, an opportunity to censor their library reading and deliver moral lectures.

She went up the path between the hibiscus trees and rang the bell. Ah Wong came swiftly to let her in. "Missie velly late," he declaimed, looking relieved. "Master eat chow." The cook boy gestured towards the door that led off the hall and into the dining room.

"That's all right, Ah Wong." She smiled at him, handed him her hat, and still holding handbag and gloves, crossed the hall to the dining room door.

George was sitting at the table, chopsticks poised, his eyes steadily fixed on the open doorway. Hellen saw his expression, recognised the stillness as unfamiliar, then her eyes caught the unexpected glow of gold on the mantelpiece behind his head.

"Close that pretty mouth of yours," said George brusquely. "It's unbecoming." Even as he spoke, he knew he'd blown it. God, what a fool! Why hadn't he stood up as planned and reeled off one of his rehearsed phrases? The chopsticks fell from his fingers, clattering against the place setting of newly unpacked silver and Royal Doulton dinner plates. He pushed back his chair.

Hellen was standing as though turned to stone. Only her eyes moved, slowly taking in the pair of Staffordshire china dogs her cousin Hettie had given; the tiered silver cake stand; the table spread with a fine embroidered linen table cloth trimmed with Nottingham lace; the Doulton soup tureen and vegetable dishes. Stunned, she could only stand and stare, not considering George's graceless behaviour in appropriating those precious things that she and Oliver were meant to share, only seeing, and feeling, a violation that was close to injury.

"And where have you been?" George asked, truculent with a new and unexpected sensation of guilt.

She blinked, dark lashes coming down on parchment cheeks then rising on eyes glazed with disbelief. She gestured weakly, encompassing the room that contained so much that was dear to her, and private, with the hand that held her white gloves. One of them slipped out of her grip and fell to the floor.

"I thought," said George recklessly, "it was about time one of us made a move. It was pretty clear you weren't going to do it, so I did."

She turned and began to walk, in a kind of daze, towards the stairs, leaving the single glove on the floor.

"Hellen!"

"Yes?" She turned round slowly, trancelike, and looked at him as though she did not see him.

"Shall we . . ." George hesitated. "Er—let's talk, old girl, shall we?"

Talk? She could not have spoken then if her life depended on it. She revolved slowly back again and began to climb the stairs. At the top she turned right, making her way to the room where she had spent the night. It was empty, quite empty, except for the wardrobe in which she had placed her wedding dress. She stood before the mahogany doors with their oblong looking glasses, steeling herself for the discovery that the dress, too, had gone, consigned to some wicked bonfire of George's making. She took the frail key down from its hiding place on the curtain rail, put it into the lock, and turned the key.

There was the pile of tissue lying on the shelf, exactly as she had placed it the night before. Coming swiftly, defensively alive, she slammed the doors shut and locked it, pocketing the key.

George was standing in the doorway to her room. "Shutting the stable door after the horse has gone?" he asked, one eyebrow raised, not mocking her, rather pointing out the foolishness, as he saw it, of the operation. "Come on, old girl, let's have a heart to heart and clear the air, shall we?"

"No," said Hellen, her voice steady, her eyes fierce. "We won't have any heart to heart. There is no way of making the air clear between us. I accept what you have done, but I find your way of doing it unacceptable."

"You'd never have unpacked it yourself," said George defiantly. "You know damn well you wouldn't."

"For once, you're right."

"Well, what was I supposed to do? Leave it there while you play at Miss bloody Haversham?" he blustered, surprisingly invoking the classics.

She walked past him into the big, empty bedroom. "I don't know what you were supposed to do," she replied wearily. She put her handbag down on the bed, stared, frowning, at the single glove, dropped it on top of her handbag, and went to the dressing table, still the only item of furniture in the room apart from the wardrobe and bed. She stood with one hand resting on the polished mahogany surface, looking down at the brushes. When she had clear in her mind what she wanted to say she turned round and looked up at him, her eyes steady.

"I have a proposition for you," she said. "I will act as your wife in public, and as your hostess here, if you should wish to invite people. I will furnish this place completely and make it into an attractive home for you. But if you feel you need some 'exercise', as you have put it to me, I shall expect you to find it elsewhere. Why don't you take a concubine? I believe it's quite usual for single Englishmen to have a concubine. Perhaps even married ones, for all I know. If you find it too great an expense, I have a small allowance from my grandfather, which I would willingly contribute."

She heard the faint hiss of his indrawn breath, hesitated only a second, then added, her voice dropping but the words enunciated still with crystal precision, "Bear in mind, also, that if you attempt to molest me, I will either kill you, or leave you. I don't think you would like me to leave you. It wouldn't do your standing any good. And as for the other, it really depends on the barbarity of the molesting. But don't underestimate me, George."

196

He said angrily, "You bitch! You bloody, rotten little bitch." He lifted his hands and would have crashed them down on her shoulders. Then, as though reminded by her expression of the threat she had made, he allowed them to fall to his sides. "Why did you marry me? Tell me that, you sadistic little trollop?"

At least she could give him a simple and truthful answer. "Because you drugged my drink, then took advantage of me while I was unconscious."

"You vindictive little scrubber! You would marry me for that, then hold me off?" George took an involuntary step forward, towering over her. "Why, you're as twisted as a corkscrew. You're mad!" he bellowed. "I've a good mind to—"

George's brutish insult broke through the soft shell of her tolerance, exposing the grit-hard strength that had taken her, head high, over snubs and innuendoes that were an integral part of being Joe North's daughter and at the same time, a member of the Old Forest hunt.

"Living with a woman means loving her. You do not love me, George. When you forced yourself upon me that first time, it was for self-gratification, for what can a man give to an unconscious woman? The second time was for dominance, and ratification of a contract for your own ends. You did not think twice about humiliating and hurting and insulting me. It was of no importance against the possibility that people would say—" she paused, brought splintered glass into her voice, then added—"you had no lead in your pencil."

"Jesus!" He slapped the ball of his palm against his forehead in very real despair. "You married me for spite."

"Not for spite. I told you before that I married you because I was frightened. I needed shelter, at that time. It was a cold-blooded decision which I immediately, and bitterly, regretted, but it seemed right, then, after you had gone to a great deal of trouble to convince me that you loved me.

"By the way, what have you done with the household linen?"

He swung away from her, reached the door then turned, hurling the insult of his behaviour at her with triumph. "Everything with initials on has gone to a tailor who will remove them. The unmarked stuff has been put away in cupboards. Ah Wong will show you where."

With tremendous fortitude, she managed to say quietly, "You've been very thorough." She picked up her hairbrush, squeezing the handle hard between her fingers, bringing every muscle of her body into play in an effort to cease the trembling.

Without a word, George turned and went off down the stairs.

197

Chapter 18
Lady Marathon

It was with a feeling of dutifully serving George that Hellen went out and bought curtains, carpets, occasional tables. She used George's money expertly, but without pleasure. She made her bedroom clinically functional with a suitable chair and a small mahogany desk. Methodically and tastefully, she relieved the bareness of the building. The house, looking for love, withdrew its warmth.

Now that she knew the lay-out of Central, she would wander by the hour among the narrow, dark shops. One day she found a Chinese medicine store, smelling of a hundred different aromas: musk and coriander, rotten eggs, liquorice, ginger, incense, seaweed. A wizened little man with a long, silky beard and wire-rimmed glasses, bent over a stone mortar and pestle grinding his potions, reminded her of those carved ivory figures in the antique shops.

Being George's wife in name only, she would not use his money to buy treasures such as ivory figurines, at which the Chinese craftsmen excelled, but sometimes, out of her own pocket, she bought trinkets: a set of wind bells, an inexpensive bone statuette, or a handful of thin silver bracelets to tinkle on her wrists.

With Ruth helpfully at her side, Hellen edged warily into Hong Kong society, that gossipy enclave of well-to-do hostesses and single girls whose conversation centred round tea dances at the Hong Kong Hotel, picnics on the beach, or lunching at the Repulse Bay Hotel. The latter meant one's escort owned a car. One could go there by donkey cart, but there was an airy splendour in being able to say, "We came by gasolene." Such a different snobbishness from home. All that was asked of a girl here was that she should be pretty, and well dressed. That her father, if in the services, should be of high rank; if in business, that it thrived. Those working in the Colonial Secretariat were beyond reproach.

New gowns would be ordered for the races from the Army and

Navy stores. Everyone worried lest they should not arrive in time. Girls dared one another to have their hair shingled. They discussed who was going home on leave; who was on the way back. And whether or not a mother would ask to dinner that nice young man who had come to work at Jardine's, but who appeared to have no credentials at all. Such excitements could take up an entire morning.

When someone slyly brought up Kitty Burtenshaw's name, Hellen affected not to hear. When asked where she had met George, she told them what he had decreed: she had been travelling to visit friends in Singapore. In reply to enquiries as to whom she intended to visit, for so many Colonial Service people knew one another, she replied merely that her friends were passing through. She acquired a reputation for being a dark horse. Well, she thought matter-of-factly, I am.

Sometimes, she and George picnicked on the beach at Repulse Bay, taking Marcia and Neil with them. George was an excellent swimmer and looked well in bathing costume. She would search the beach for Oliver, but he never came. Sometimes they went to the Cricket Club in downtown Victoria where the ball boys were called Tadpole Wong and Tadpole Chou because they were always fishing boundary balls out of the water. While George played she watched for Oliver, but he did not come.

Toby Ayre took her riding at the Happy Valley racecourse and she discovered a mafoo was a Russian cavalry officer turned groom who had escaped the revolution via a route to Shanghai, then on to the Crown Colony. There was more than that to discover about Happy Valley, and not all of it good. Hong Kongers admitted it was plagued by bad joss. Accidents occurred there more frequently than could be attributed to coincidence. In 1919 the main stand collapsed and one old coolie, dragging his foodstall away in a panic, upset his charcoal stove, causing a blazing inferno. It was carnage, but only for the Chinese.

They laughed when Buddhist priests were brought in to perform rites of exorcism, dipping leaves into holy water and solemnly processing round the course to drive off spirits that had taken possession of trees, brooks, stones and animals. When abandoned babies were found there, the English shrugged, for they were Chinese babies from the overcrowded tinderboxes on the slopes above the valley. What future was there for them anyway?

Riding with Toby became a regular pastime. She enjoyed crossing to the island as the sun came up over the sea, then the jog in a rickshaw through empty streets. Hoo-hoo. Hoo-hoo-hoo. The air was not cool and fresh in Happy Valley as it was on The Peak. The thick mould of vegetation on the ground stank of the valley's swamp history, and the mosquitoes were enormous. George said it was more than likely she would go down with malaria. Being ignorant of the effects of a poisonous bite, she considered the riding worth the risk.

Toby's nice wife Wanda was unperturbed by this daily assignation Hellen had with her husband. "I may take a leaf out of George's book, and join you when it's cooler," she said. Hellen had told them George considered it was too hot at present to ride, but in fact he was seldom at the house when she left. His door would be open, the bed untouched. If he was building a nest with his concubine, he had indeed moved with speed. Hellen cherished the thought that Oliver might hear of this early morning gallop and come along to join them, but he did not.

Then one afternoon, as she was standing by the French windows, thinking about him—did she ever think about anything else?—and watching a magpie digging in the sheltered garden for worms, Ah Wong appeared. "Missie," he said impassively, "one Eurasian Missy come."

Hellen's cheeks flamed. High class Eurasians, she knew, were the material of concubines. Would George send his to humilate her?

"I show her in?" asked Ah Wong in his high, thin voice, focussing on his mistress those unreadable, unblinking eastern eyes.

"I go." Hellen composed herself as best she could to meet with dignity this new hurdle.

The girl was like a beautifully wrought figurine. She had a rosebud mouth, and her eyes were black almonds, widely spaced. She was dressed in a form-fitting silk cheongsam slit up the side and buttoned high at the neck. Her glossy black hair was arranged high on her head, and she had the exquisitely unreal complexion of a china doll. She stepped forward, smiling, holding out a hand. Hellen's back was straight, her head high, her eyes cold.

"I am sent by your friend," said the girl.

Oliver! Hellen was at once giddy with excitement. She extended her hand to meet the delicate fingers, then swung round and led the way into the big drawing room. "Oliver has not spoken of me?" asked the visitor. "I am Lin Yan." She delved into a silk bag and withdrew an envelope. Hellen's hand trembled as she took it.

"Do you mind if I read it now? I'll ring for tea. Please sit down." She indicated one of the new Lane Crawford chairs.

Lin Yan seated herself elegantly, with back straight, knees together, her small feet neatly side-by-side. Caressing the envelope with her fingertips, touching the paper Oliver had touched, smiling down at his flamboyant writing, Hellen went to the window. The name on the envelope was "Hellen". Just that, as though he would not write to Mrs George Curtain because she belonged only to him.

Darling Hellen,

I have found somewhere for us to meet. It's horribly sleazy, but the sleazier the safer. Number fourteen Ladder Street, Central. Ladder Street runs up the side of the mountain below Government House. Very steep flights of steps flanked by shops. Meet me there, if you can, when George goes out the day after tomorrow. I shall be there from seven o'clock. Don't be put off by the entrance. I shall have someone watching for you.

Lin Yan is a very good friend, but don't tell her about Ladder Street. It's not that I don't trust her, but I don't want her to have the responsibility of knowing.

Tomorrow, Lin Yan will take you to Upper Albert Road. (My uncle is safely in the New Territories.) I want you to meet my Aunt Lettice. She will accidentally pass through the hall, be introduced by Lin Yan, and take you to the private apartments for tea. I could come across from the Secretariat, but I think it better for my aunt if I don't. I don't want to get her into trouble.

With All my love

He had signed with one enormous, flamboyant "O".

Hellen folded the paper and looked up, her eyes dewy, her heart full of fear. Ah Wong came into the room bearing a silver tray on which was set out the tea service given to Oliver and herself as a wedding present. She had taught herself to live, not always unflinchingly, with this ever present insult. She rose and crossed to the tea table. She had ceased saying thank you to the servants. It only confused them. She lifted the tea pot with a shaking hand. Some tea shot out of the spout.

"It is usual for English people, when they arrive, to sign the book," said Lin Yan.

Hellen swallowed.

"It is not different for you," the Eurasian girl added comfortingly.

But it *was* different, Hellen thought agitatedly as she poured the tea into Royal Doulton cups that would never, if Kitty Burtenshaw had not jilted George, if Lady Sylvia Ashton had not interfered, if George had not drugged her, have seen the light of day in Tsim Sha Tsui.

She put the teapot down. Another gout of tea ejected itself from the spout and another stain spread across the cloth. How could she go up to Government House—bold as brass, as Oliver's uncle would undoubtedly think—and sign the book in the expectation of receiving an invitation to some official function? She picked up the cup with a trembling hand. It wobbled dangerously. "Sugar? Lemon?"

The visitor shook her head.

Hellen put the cup and saucer down on the new blackwood table obediently purchased for George. Why did Lady Marathon wish to see the girl who had, to all intents and purposes, thrown Oliver over for George Curtain, who was not on the Government House guest list?

"We are to be there at four o'clock tomorrow," said Lin Yan.

Hellen glanced automatically at the clock on the mantel. Why four o'clock? Was this a trick? Had Sir Rowan discovered that she had been to his Peak-top residence with Oliver? Was he going to rush in from the New Territories at four o'clock, and warn her off? She poured a cup for herself and went to sit on the sofa. The magpie, growing tame on cake crumbs, plodded delicately to the French windows and stood head to one side, looking in. Hellen pulled up one of the carved tables and rested her teacup on it.

"Half-breeds," George had told her scornfully, "are scum." Why would the Governor's lady invite a scummy Eurasian to tea? The feeling of being tricked intensified.

"Do you know Lady Marathon."

"Everyone knows Lady Marathon. I think you mean, does she know me? Chinese and Eurasian of good families are sometimes invited to Government House functions, though an Englishman is not allowed to ask a Chinese or Eurasian girl for more than two dances. The governor's ADCs keep count." Then, with a hint of mischief in those dark almond eyes, she added, "I go to parties at the bachelors' messes on The Peak. The ADCs are not on duty there."

Hellen rose, faintly smiling, went back to the window and threw the magpie a biscuit. If Lin Yan's appearances at Government House were the result of official government policy, then she must believe Sir Rowan would not use her as a decoy. She turned to look at her visitor. Lin Yan's face was sweetly innocent. "I'll come with you," she said. She hoped, most fervently, that Oliver's trust was not misplaced.

Lin Yan said sweetly, "I love Oliver very much. I hope you will be my friend, too."

Hellen knew then that if this invitation was a trick, Lin Yan had no part in it. She clasped the girl's hands, saying impulsively, "I have a parcel—it's to do with Oliver and me. I don't want George to find it. Could you possibly—would you be willing to take it home with you and keep it safe?"

Lin Yan nodded.

Hellen ran fleetly upstairs, took down the wardrobe key from the curtain rail, and removing the precious wedding gown from its hiding place, carried it downstairs. "It's very light," she said, bouncing it in its rustling tissue wrapping on the palms of her hands. "I'll get my cook boy to wrap it up."

Ah Wong, with the fearsome chopper in his hand, was standing at his work table contemplating a very dead chicken. There were feathers all over the floor. "This one you makee proper parcel," she said.

"Blown paper and sling?"

"Yes."

The makee learn appeared in that silent way the servants had of materialising, and proceeded to sweep up the feathers. Hellen smiled at her, receiving an impassive stare in return. She went back into the hall.

"You have asked one of your servants to accompany me," said Lin Yan, as though confirming a fact.

"What do you mean? That you would like to be escorted home?"

"Your servant could bring the parcel," Lin Yan said.

Hellen went back to the kitchen for help. "Missie say you takee parcel."

"I send makee learn with Missie," said Ah Wong.

Hellen breathed a sigh that was part exasperation, part amusement. So, it was all a matter of "face". If Ah Wong would lose face by carrying a parcel, how could she expect Lin Yan to take it! As she went back into the hall, she wondered wryly if she had lost face in her visitor's eyes by running upstairs and bringing the dress down.

"The makee learn will go with you," she said, meaning three paces behind. "I will tell you, some time, what's in the parcel."

"I think," said the Eurasian girl sweetly, "it is your wedding dress. I will take the greatest care of it."

"Tomorrow afternoon," said Oliver, leaning across the small table in the private dining room on the first floor of Government House, "Hellen is coming to sign the book."

Lady Marathon's hands fluttered nervously, but she managed, with a great effort of will, to keep the dismay out of her voice. "In her capacity as a married woman, dear, what has that to do with you?"

"Nothing, dear Aunt Lettice. It has to do with your total and unassailable devotion to me," he replied gravely. "She will be here at four o'clock. I want you to cross the hall at that time. You will recognise Lin Yan, who will be with her, so you will pause and be introduced. Then, since it will be dead on tea time, it will be only civil to invite them both up for tea."

"Oh, Oliver!" No wonder this wretched girl had fallen in love with him. Could anyone resist that charisma? But the boy was playing with dynamite. "I've a bridge party tomorrow afternoon," she said firmly.

"Where?"

She brushed back the tendrils that curled softly on her forehead. "With friends of mine."

"Actually, Aunt Lettice," Oliver smiled beguilingly, "I've done you a very good turn and got you out of that bridge party. I heard you were playing with the Empress of China and the Brothers Karamazov. I've taken it upon myself to put them all off. The Empress said, anyway, there was an execution in Canton, and that she'd really rather go there to watch. And the Brothers have to go back to Russia. You know I don't like you to be lonely, so I've fixed you up with company for tea."

"Oh, Oliver!" said his aunt again. "I can't. I really cannot. If Rowan should discover—"

"Why should he? None of the staff knows who she is, and it will make their day to catch a glimpse of the beautiful, unattainable Yin Lan. Both Roger and Jock are madly in love with her."

"Both of the aides have gone with your uncle to Kam Tin," Lady Marathon told him, wondering, not for the first time, if Lin Yan's unattainability was due to the fact that she was Oliver's property. What a mess it all was.

"Good," said Oliver with satisfaction, leaning back in his chair. "That'll keep them out of temptation's way."

Lady Marathon extended her hands beseechingly. "Darling, where will this lead us?"

Oliver said gravely, "You will know her, Aunt Lettice. That's where it will lead us. I merely want you to know her."

Lettice Marathon gazed thoughtfully at her husband's nephew. He was so sweet, so determined, and in affairs of the heart, so very unworldly. "Oliver, dear, I do hope there isn't going to be any trouble."

"I don't know," he replied gravely. "I really don't know."

She reached across the table, taking his hand. "Dear one," she said, "you must accept this marriage. Hellen is not yours."

"I accept that the marriage has happened," he replied fiercely, "but not that she has ceased to be mine. She will always be mine. That's why I want you to meet her. I want you to understand. When whatever has to happen . . . happens." His brilliant blue eyes clouded. "I want you to understand," he repeated.

"Please, Oliver, I beg of you, don't do anything foolish."

"Foolish. What is foolish?"

"It is foolish to do what you are doing. To cling to the hope of something you can never have."

"It is not like that," he replied stubbornly. "Not hoping for something I can never have."

She was shaken by his foolishness. "You're talking like a romantic with your head in the clouds." Her voice took on an unaccustomed edge, and she let go of his hand. "If Hellen had felt as you do, she would not have married that man."

He said impatiently, "You don't understand. You don't know what she was going through."

"Do you?" Lettice asked gravely. "Do you know exactly what happened?"

"It's unimportant." His face closed, and she recognised that he did not want to know.

"She married Mr Curtain. Your uncle is right in what he says. She need not have."

The servants in their blue satin long-gowns and white-soled boots came soft-footedly into the room. Lady Marathon and Oliver sat in silence while the plates were taken away. When they had gone, Oliver rose and closed the door behind them.

"You expect me to understand about Hellen," said his aunt, manifestly emotional in her response to what she saw now as sheer obstinacy. "I do not even understand about Lin Yan. I am expected to entertain these two girls, neither of which are . . . I mean . . . Oliver, I have never understood about Lin Yan."

He leaned back in his chair, his face grave, his eyes flickering. "She's a cross between a doll and a sister."

"What!"

He grinned. "If there was such a thing as a chap wanting a doll. I can't call her a Hornby train set, but that's what I mean. Endless fascination."

"Are you being fair to her, dear?"

"In giving her my friendship?"

"Don't be deliberately obtuse." His aunt's voice sharpened. "You know what I mean."

He thrust both hands down into his pockets, rocking the blackwood chair dangerously on its rear legs. "She meets plenty of chaps through me. Who knows? One of them might marry her. At it's bleakest, you could say I've given her a social life. She's having fun." He saw the gravity, the very real concern in his aunt's face, and added, "I'm aware that she's a problem no one can do anything about. I'm doing what little I can. One day, things may change."

"Not in our lifetime, Oliver. And not in hers."

He shrugged. "Eurasians are like poverty—they're not going to go away. I know what you think, that she should take the best option.

You think she should be a concubine. She's not concubine material, Aunt Lettice."

"Can I be awfully blunt?"

"If you must."

"Your uncle Cecil is not going to survive to inherit the title."

Oliver burst out laughing. "So that's what's on your mind. That I'm involved with two unsuitable women, me who is likely to end up with the earldom. Well, it's not going to be for a long time. Father's only fifty-two, and we're all long livers. Besides, Uncle Cecil has been going down hill since the Germans got him in 1915. For a dying man, he's doing jolly well." Oliver's eyes again crinkled in a smile. "He's fathered another daughter since the doctors gave him his death sentence. It's not easy to get rid of us Marathons. I dare say, any moment now, Aunt Penelope will start having a son."

"Oliver, dear, things don't happen just because you want them to."

"I should know." His mouth was so twisted with bitterness that, after all, she was sorry she had spoken. In an abrupt voice, he said, "In case it should occur to you to mention this matter of the title to Hellen, I'd rather you didn't."

She wondered if he thought it might put the girl off. "I won't mention it," she promised.

But maybe there was something she could say to Hellen. Perhaps, at the very least, tactfully refer to the impetuosity of young men.

Chapter 19

The first typhoon

Hellen chose to wear a dress of dimity material cut with a demure neckline and flounced hem. Her straw hat was trimmed with blue ribbon tied in a bow with the ends floating over the brim. She had found the hat in Lane Crawford's department store. They said you could buy anything in Lane Crawford, from a tin-tack to an elephant. On her feet she wore white shoes bought in London, beautifully polished by whomsoever the cook boy should choose, a matter that was not supposed to concern her. The heat having lessened, it was now possible to wear white kid gloves without her hands breaking out in sweat.

Her painted sunshade, a delicate object of oiled paper on a bamboo frame, she had bought in a street market. It was far more efficient at keeping the sun at bay than an English parasol, and it also kept out the rain. What was even more important, it was considered acceptable. Hellen was fast picking up the notions of what was acceptable and what was not.

The heat pressed down through a layer of ash grey cloud. Up on The Peak, the rich hostesses would be blanketted off behind dripping walls, their bed linen tucked away in heating cupboards, while silver fish ate their way into books. Hellen often wondered wryly if it was such a privilege to live there. As she went down the path Fah Wong was desultorily picking off faded flowers. She smiled at him and he gazed inscrutably back.

In Mody Road she could often pick up a ride. She had stopped worrying about the poor emaciated rickshaw coolies as she had stopped saying please and thank you to the servants. Rickshaws were her only mode of transport, and the coolies needed the money. Besides, Neil told her the rickshaw was invented by a Shanghai missionary who had a servant tow his invalid wife in an old perambulator with shafts. "The Japanese, with typical ingenuity, improved and patented the invention," he said. "And so the rickshaw puller was born."

"A man-of-God, get that!" George intervened to say. Her concern for the coolies annoyed him.

More and more, Hellen discovered, to understand was to condone.

That morning, carefully casual in face of George's startled reaction—a gulp of the adam's apple, a forward jerk of the chin—Hellen had told him she was going to Government House to sign the book. "I understand it's expected of new arrivals," she had added. "It would seem I have been remiss. I should have done it sooner."

George pushed back his chair from the breakfast table, rid his palms of toast crumbs and replied heartily, "Good." What he meant, even he could not have said. Good try, perhaps, though Oliver Marathon would no doubt be consulted before any guest list was ratified by Her Ladyship, and if he got in a wax about it. . . . Still, Hellen was game, he'd give her that.

He thought, as he legged it down Minden Row, that if this came off. . . . With good joss he could be in the sort of scene he'd been working up when that tick Denzil Armitage had spiked his guns by running off with Kitty. Remembering Kitty always made him aggressive. As he rounded the corner into Mody Road, he told himself he would get Hellen into bed, if it was the last thing he did. So, he had made a few mistakes. He'd admit it. But, crikey, she ought to be able to forget and forgive! He'd work on her. Nothing so obvious as the pearls, next time.

As he came to the harbour wall his mind exploded with an idea of such brilliance that he nearly stopped in his tracks. What about a visit to that Chink herbalist in Cat Street! Rhinoceros horn was one hell of an aphrodisiac. He bounded ahead at full lick, the future flaring brilliantly in his mind's eye.

Hellen emerged from the Star ferry with the crowds spilling into Central. Lin Yan was waiting for her. Here, in the bright sunlight, the Eurasian's skin had the luminosity of porcelain. She was dressed in a silk cheongsam printed in peacock colours—bright rich blues, greens and gold. Hellen thought wryly no wonder the Chinese despised the English for their big feet and hairy bodies. For the first time in her life, she felt enormous, and rather untidy. Lin Yan's hair was impeccably arranged as before, high on her head, but today she wore in it an ivory comb trimmed with jade. No wonder the English men at Government House balls were allowed only two dances, Hellen thought with awe.

"Are you all right?" Lin Yan asked concernedly.

"No," replied Hellen with a breathy little laugh, "I am not at all right. I'm scared out of my wits. I think it's a trick. I think Sir Rowan Marathon is going to burst in just when I've got the tea cup in my left hand and a dim sum in my right—"

"You will get an English tea."

"Oh, yes." Surrounded as she was by the cries of the coolies, smelling the aromatic, dusty, spicy, scented air of the town and the salt of the sea, Hellen often had to make an effort to think in English terms. "Thank you for coming with me. I could never have done this on my own."

They climbed into a sedan chair and the chair coolies set out up the hill with their now familiar trot-walk. "Hoo-hoo. Hoo-hoo." They turned into Upper Albert Road where the gilt-iron gates of the Residency were guarded by Fusiliers, awe-inspiring in their red and gold dress uniforms, and magnificently crowned with plumed shakos. The chair coolies lowered their shafts and the girls stepped out. Hellen looked through the bars with dread. There was a wide drive encircling a lawn surrounded by decorative bushes. The air was full of the scent of frangipani.

They walked up the drive side by side, their feet crunching in the gravel. Two fierce stone lions roared silently at them from either side of the steps. "Daniel," Hellen muttered, "coming into the lion's den." Lin Yan smiled encouragingly.

They went up the steps and into a pillared hall. There was a magnificent crystal chandelier and a royal coat of arms with its lion and unicorn. Dieu et mon Droit. Hellen stood there on the cool marble floor, oddly disconcerted, vastly overwhelmed. If Lady Sylvia Ashton had come through the white-painted double doors ahead shrieking, "What is that gel doing here?" she would not have been at all surprised.

The First Lady of Hong Kong, in the comparative sanctuary of the secretary's office, waited beside a door left discreetly ajar as the two girls drifted in. Her first sight of Hellen with her Attic quality of purity and simplicity, the stylish walk, the gracefully held head, confirmed what she had suspected all along but been unwilling to accept. Oliver would not be attracted by the wrong sort of girl. "Common," Sylvia Ashton had said. There was nothing even artificial about this girl, nothing either chic or elaborate. She was so right, so absolutely, heartrendingly right for Oliver. Oh dear. . . . She took a deep breath and followed them.

Hellen turned, and their eyes met. Expecting a cool survey, Lettice was dismayed to encounter raw fear. "My dear," she said kindly, forgetting everything but the girl's discomfiture, "I am so glad you have come."

They followed her up the stairs and entered a pretty sitting room. They could have been in any comfortable country house in England, except that there was not the familarly worn look one might expect in an English house. The carpet on the floor was Chinese, its colours complementing the soft blues, the leaf greens, the shaded pinks of the English chintz.

Hellen went to the window and stood looking out over the praya and the island-dotted harbour. Her chest was so tight she could hardly breathe.

"Do sit by the window if you would like to," said Oliver's aunt kindly. She signalled to a musical-comedy servant, white-booted and long-gowned, who had followed them in. He brought over the chairs and a table, placing them in a group by the window.

"Do sit down, Hellen," repeated Lady Marathon.

Hellen heard the words with the shock of knowing she had heard them before, without reacting. Lin Yan had seated herself elegantly, with a straight back. Lady Marathon was sitting opposite, smiling, looking composed. Hellen's knee joints gave way and she found herself in the cushioned chair the servant pushed forward. Another servant bought tea on an enormous silver tray. There were two kinds of bread and butter, white and brown, slim tomato sandwiches, caraway seed cake, and little Yorkshire tea cakes.

If one did not look out at the harbour, or listen to the incessant whirring of the fans, if one was not conscious of the oppressive heat, it might have been tea-time in Kent, with the same embroidered Irish linen tea cloth and dainty napkins, the same starched doilys, the same food. It was as though a fluffy, sun-lit English cloud had settled itself familiarly over the room. You are on English soil, it said. Feel at home. She looked across at Lin Yan, a Chinese doll taken down from the shelf of a department store. From Harrods, whence only the finest china came. The doll was wound up, speaking in a pretty, musical voice. "It is very kind of you to ask us to tea, Lady Marathon."

"It's a pleasure, my dear."

The First Lady reached for the silver pot. "I do hope you like China tea, Hellen?"

"I love it." She jerked round nervously. Was that a man's footsteps in the hall?

Lady Marathon noticed. "Do close it. I'm sure you've discovered for yourself that coolies are incapable of shutting doors."

Hellen rose precipitately and crossed the room. For a shaky moment she battled with the temptation to slip out of the door and fly off down the stairs. She closed the door quietly and returned to her seat. Lady Marathon addressed Lin Yan directly. They discussed the typhoon season that was already upon them, but which they had so far been mercifully spared.

Then gradually and skilfully, she steered the conversation Hellen's way. "Oliver tells me you're a very good rider."

"I rode with the Old Forest." Now she could speak of the hitherto unspeakable, for Lady Marathon was certainly not going to ask her if she knew old So-and-so. Lady Sylvia Ashton had seen to that.

"I rode with it once or twice myself, in my young days, when Rowan and I were on a visit to the Ashtons. Oliver tells me you have lovely mares, Merry Astor and Persimmon," said Lady Marathon, unwittingly showing the extent of her caring. "Are you going to bring them out?"

"I don't think so." George would have to pay for their transportation, and she could not allow that.

"You can hire ponies at Happy Valley, and indeed in the New Territories, which is good equestrian country."

"I have been riding. I go—" Hellen shut her mouth like a trap. Lady Marathon must not know she rode early in the mornings, for then she would guess if Oliver went to Happy Valley before work.

There was a sound from the passage outside. Hellen started and again glanced towards the door. Was that a footstep?

"Do eat up, dear." In the most natural manner, Lady Marathon said as she passed the cucumber sandwiches, "My husband will not be back until the day after tomorrow."

Hellen flushed.

Lady Marathon tossed the conversation back and forth between the girls. "If you get a mosquito bite, a mixture of quinine and gin is a very good medicine. The Chinese, I believe, use measured doses of opium. Is that not right, Lin Yan?"

"It is a cure for most bodily ills," replied Lin Yan gravely.

"With good joss, one doesn't get bitten," smiled Lady Marathon. "You have learned about joss, Hellen?"

Hellen remembered where she had first heard that word, from the monk on Lantau when he suggested she light a candle. "Joss is luck?"

"It's a corruption of the Portuguese word 'Deos', meaning God. The Chinese don't believe in luck. Is that not right, Lin Yan?"

She nodded. "Prayer and hard work will bring good joss."

Hellen's eyes were cast down. She had prayed for Oliver. Prayed that he might be hers.

They talked about Chinese cooks. One of them had produced this very English tea. Gradually, Hellen relaxed.

"It never occured to me to ask Ah Wong to make an English cake,' she said, and found herself smiling.

"They have to be taught," Lady Marathon told her. "We all keep Mrs Beeton's excellent manual. You can buy it in the town. Read it to your cook boy. Most of them need telling only once."

When the girls rose to go, politely on the stroke of five, it was almost with a sense of regret.

"It was not so bad, was it?" asked Lin Yan as they parted in Central.

"It was not bad at all. Why do you suppose she wanted to meet me?"

"Oliver wanted her to meet you. He and his aunt are very close."

"Oh!" Hellen felt elevated, in a way transported, as well as a little frightened by this demonstration of Oliver's confidence and love.

At a shop in Central she bought a copy of *Mrs Beeton's Book of Household Management*, wondering as she tucked it under her arm if her cook boy would be shocked that she should carry it herself. She took it anyway. Crossing the water to Kowloon it occurred to her that her newly found friends might not want to travel by sedan chair, Peak tram, rickshaw, Star ferry and another rickshaw to Tsim Sha Tsui to take English tea with her.

George was alredy back from the office. She found him in shirtsleeves and braces, sprawled on the sofa in the drawing room, his celluoid collar dangling from his back stud, reading the *South China Mail*. He pulled himself alertly into a sitting position, and dropped the paper on to the carpet. "So, how did you get on?" In his anxiety to know, he forgot to greet her.

Hellen peeled off her gloves. She did not want to tell him she had had tea with Lady Marathon. That was private. Part of her real world. "I bought *Mrs Beeton's Book of Household Management*," she said. "It's quite a size. Tell me, George, should I have carried it home, or had it sent?"

"You know what I mean," he growled. "How did you get on at Government House?"

"I signed the book."

Provocative bitch! He didn't want to put her through a catechism, but this was pretty emotive stuff, bowling up to Government House as though she hadn't married George Curtain instead of the Governor's nephew.

Hellen saw the tension manifested in the tightened sinews of his neck, the deep clefts that ran from either side of his nose to the corners of his mouth, and knew why he had come home early. She considered the fact that he might, he just might, this being as he said, "gossipy little Hong Kong", hear that she had taken tea with Lady Marathon, and then he would put two and two together regarding herself and Oliver. She had better tell him.

"I had tea with Lady Marathon," she said.

By God! George felt a rush of high excitement that had his mind and heart racing. Tea with Lady Marathon! Suddenly his mouth was grinning, his eyes shining.

"No hard feelings, then?" he asked, holding back the eager questions crowding one upon the other in his brain, wanting it to appear that tea with the Governor's lady was no more than he had expected of her.

"None at all."

As though suddenly finding himself in the presence of an important guest, George pulled his collar round, replaced the stud, and buttoned his shirt. "Why don't we go out to dinner?" He was expansive. His mind was already whirling over a selection of people whom Hellen had mentioned as having invited her, in spite of her ambiguous status as a resident of Tsim Sha Tsui, to play bridge or tennis. He heard himself saying to Wanda Ayre, "I don't think my wife's very hungry. She had a rather late tea with Lady Marathon." Lord! But things were looking up.

He jumped to his feet. It suddenly seemed to him that, by good joss, he had invested in a genuine treasure of a wife. There was an old story that in Hong Kong one could acquire anything from a thirteen-year-old virgin to a thirteen-hundred-year-old T'ang Dynasty statuette, and that both might be genuine. It was all he could do not to laugh out loud. He'd invested in Hellen, and she was genuine, all right. God! If only he hadn't cocked things up by bashing her in front of the pirates. . . . He could kick himself every time he thought of that. Loss of an ear! Loss of conjugal rights! None of it should have occurred. But nothing was ever so bad it could not be put right. He'd made it with her up to Singapore. He'd get her on his side again.

"Won't Ah Wong have the meal ready by now?" Hellen asked.

"We'll be doing him a favour. He'll get a good price for it down in the market." George was jovial. Full of goodwill.

"What?"

"Didn't you know leftovers are the cook's perk? Food won't keep overnight in this weather. Where d'you think the other half of the chicken goes?"

"I thought they ate it themselves."

"You've a lot to learn, old girl." His voice was warm with very real affection.

By God, when he got on to the Government House guest list, he'd show the world! If his next deal came off he'd have enough money to throw his weight around. He could do it now he had Hellen as a screen against curious questions. She hadn't volunteered details of the allowance her grandfather made her, and privately he suspected it was little more than pocket money, but what did that matter? Once people heard she was on tea terms with Lady Marathon, whatever she said they would think she was merely being modest. He was at last going up in the world! He clasped his hands above his head, stretched himself to his full height, grinned happily. It was all a matter of good joss and timing, as the Chinese said, and living by one's wits. He stood for a moment, thumbs in his braces, contemplating his pretty asset with immense goodwill.

She was in the middle of removing her hat, her hands raised, holding the brim, her body defenceless. He crossed the room swiftly and put both arms round her. She jumped, and the hat fell to the floor. He kissed her hard on lips, exercising the utmost self control in keeping his hands well above her waist, avoiding any suspicion she might have that his mind was on anything more exciting than a kiss. Lurking in the back of his mind was the happy knowledge that he had a little packet of finely ground rhino horn hidden upstairs. If they went out tonight there would be no opportunity to use it, but tomorrow he'd somehow find a way to plant it in her food.

After breakfast the next day Hellen went over to the island to look for Ladder Street. It was a narrow lane full of high, shadowed buildings, steep as a staircase, with overhanging verandahs of rattan or iron. Creaking signboards hung everywhere splashed with Chinese hierographs in hard, earthy reds and yellows. Tarpaulins, dragged awkwardly across flimsy bamboo struts, served as verandah roofs. The entrance to number fourteen was half hidden in an alley between a noodle shop and a food store. Afterwards, she wandered through narrow alleys where the air was aromatic with the Eastern smells; woodsmoke, garlic, corainder, dried fish, soy sauce.

At one o'clock she went with a light heart to meet Ruth for tiffin. She had thought she would never again walk through the doors of the Hong Kong Hotel, but it was the mecca of society and she could not avoid it. Everyone went there to see and be seen.

Ruth was bright-faced and pretty in a big hat and floral voile dress. "You're happy now," she said. "It's so obvious." Her eyes roved over Hellen's face, noting the warmth, the new softness. "I'm glad. I knew you'd make the most of—well, you're sensible, and there's no point in—I mean, if you're stuck with something. . . .' She hugged Hellen's arm. "He's not such a bad chap, is he?"

"No," said Hellen, her eyes glimmering softly as she steeped herself in longing for Oliver, her body liquid, like a stream, drifting and flowing towards evening.

"Why, I declare you've actually fallen in love with him," said Ruth.

"If you can't beat 'em, join 'em. George is a lucky chap." She wanted to add, as a last self-indulgence before setting about learning to like the brute, "I'm sure you'll make something of him," but decided against it. Leave well alone.

The afternoon rattled by, an eternity of clatter. Friends and acquaintances of Ruth's came and went, as well as new friends Hellen could call her own. When at last it was time to go home and have dinner with George, the Jordan she had to cross before paradise, she parted from Ruth with a kiss, demonstrating the new affection they held for each other as well as the new warmth in herself. She picked up a rickshaw outside the hotel, and set out for the Star ferry pier.

The wind had risen. Outside the harbour the sea was rough. Little sampans, running for shelter, were bobbing and dancing, rearing up and sinking out of sight in great watery troughs. Though his skeletal frame could provide little wind resistance, her rickshaw coolie was bent almost double. Hellen held down the brim of her hat, protecting her face from the grit-laden wind as it swirled through the hood. She came up the path with skirts flying, rocking on her feet, sticky, dusty, and hot.

The makee learn swiftly ran her a cool bath, as though, Hellen thought wryly, and a little impatiently, she was incapable even of turning on a tap. She bathed and changed into the honeymoon underwear, then dressed inconspicuously in a dark blue dress and put ready a dark coat and a cloche hat that would hide her hair.

She asked Ah Wong to serve dinner early, then went to sit on the window seat in the dining room with her legs curled up beneath her, willing the time to pass in a great rush, dreaming of sweeping up Ladder Street and into the sweet haven of Oliver's arms.

George arrived home as affable as he had been the evening before, when, a little drunk on Athelbrose, he had boasted, "She's pretty well connected, old boy. She hunted with the Old Forest. It's littered with close friends of the Marathons. Don't underestimate my wife. She moves in only the best circles." Not since that blow to her jaw on the deck of *Bangkok Lady* had Hellen underestimated the strength of George's ambitions, but she was surprised to find him capable of cloaking them with humour, and a certain élan.

George crossed the room, and bent down to kiss her on the mouth. Poised like a statute, and as still, with eyes cast down, Hellen steeled herself not to react. Unmoved by the rebuff, for did he not have the evening's winning card, George straightened. "Looks like a bit of excitement tonight," he remarked, drawing the curtain and glancing out of the window. The wind had penetrated the sheltered garden, swirling the palms, sending the bushes into a frenzy. "They've hoisted two cones on Observatory Hill," he said.

"What do you mean?" Hellen leapt to her feet.

He took her reaction for fear, and reaching for her hands, pulled her towards him. "Don't worry, my love. It's only a little typhoon at the moment. Your husband will look after you. And we don't have to go out."

She withdraw her hands, trembling. It had not occurred to her that George might stay in tonight. He went out every night. He must go tonight.

He saw the expression of dismay on her face and misread it. "Don't worry, I said." He gave her fingers a squeeze, then walked back across the room, shedding his white duck jacket as he went, loosening his collar. "I can't think of anything I'd like better than to settle down to a cosy evening listening to the wind. I'm off to bathe and change, then I thought we'd have some rice wine."

"Ah Wong has the meal ready," Hellen said, her panic transposed to a rising inflection in her voice. George wore an air of such confidence as to strike terror to her heart. His manner threw up memories of the Hong Kong Hotel on the day of her arrival in the colony; of Singapore; of the gift of pearls. She knew—had never been so certain of anything in her life—that he planned to devote this evening, Oliver's evening, to some unspeakable wickedness.

"Ah Wong will have to wait," said George carelessly. "We're not in a hurry." He turned in the doorway, smiling at her, then disappeared into the hall.

She went with quick, nervous footsteps to stand at the glass doors looking out into the garden. The light was fading fast. Some frail bushes were bent almost double in the wind. It occurred to her that if the storm worsened the Star ferry would stop running. She swung round, crossed the room at a run, then took the stairs two at a time. Pausing on the landing, she looked along the passage towards the bathroom. Its door was closed. There was the noise of water, coughing and gurgling, as it did when the pressure was low.

Her handbag was lying ready on the bed. She snatched it up, pulled the hat low down on her head, slipped into the dark coat, and went fearfully back to the door. The tap had stopped running. The house was an eerily silent oasis within the roar of the wind. She tiptoed towards the stairs, descended with stealth, and left by the front door.

Even knowing the storm had worsened since she came in, she was unprepared for the sheer brutality of the wind. It flung up stones from the path, tore at her hat, somehow infiltrated her coat and seemed about to lift her off the ground. She let her hat go. On every side was the unnerving crack and thump of the wind in the trees. In the eerie twilight the palms in Minden Row, with their fronds wrapped round them, looked like telegraph poles. The next moment they were whirling like dervishes in a mad, slapping dance. She arrived in Mody Road and turned towards the harbour.

Ferry boats were sturdy vessels, she told herself, and the harbour was sheltered. After all, that was what Hong Kong was all about, a sheltered harbour where trade could continue in spite of the exigencies of the weather. But she knew, fearfully, that no one took chances with typhoons. She must get to the pier before the ferries ran for shelter, or battened down, or tied up, or whatever it was they did. It did not occur to her that if the ferries stopped after her arrival on the island, she would be unable to return tonight. Perhaps not for some days. She could only think that she must be with Oliver. She must be made safe from George, in Oliver's arms.

As she emerged on Chatham Road—she hoped she was on Chatham Road—she recoiled as a huge palm leaf came hurtling by, missing her by inches, whipping itself into a frenzy in the air. Grit and dust slapped into her eyes and stung her skin. With her mouth tightly closed, and her eyes slitted, she fought her way on.

Suddenly there was water everywhere. It struck her in a great wave, head-on, knocking her off balance. Then it sucked away, slapping round her ankles as it went. Soaked, bewildered, desperately frightened, she realised she had run up against the sea wall. She turned inland. Another great wave came flying vengefully through the air, hitting her in the back. Running, tripping, searching for something stable to grasp and hold on to, she came up against a paling fence and clung to it.

The ferry could not possible run through this! She would have to return to the house. If there was one thing certain in this dreadful night, it was that she could not stay outside. Buffetted, blind, disorientated and half mad with disappointment and despair, with her wet coat slapping round her calves and salt water running down her back, she somehow found her way to Minden Row and staggered up the path towards the front door. There was a flash of light at her bedroom window. George appeared framed in the opening. As she stood there with the wind screaming round her, he hurled up the window, then reached out pulling the shutters closed.

There was appalling significance in the fact that George was closing off her bedroom from the outside world. Hellen lurched off the path, and staggering among the bushes, headed for the unsafe safety of the back of the garden. At the far end there was a small wooden shed with an iron roof. She could already hear the sound of its door crashing

217

back and forth. Bang! Cr-a-a-sh! Bang! Cr-a-a-sh! Blindly, led by the noise, she found her way towards it. She caught the door as it flew wide, and dragging it behind her, staggered into the hut. The door hurled itself vengefully shut again.

Chapter 20

Marnie

It was not possible to secure the door of the hut from the inside. It crashed backwards and forwards in the raging wind. Crawling around among the garden implements on the pitch dark floor, Hellen found a basket of firewood and managed to drag it out on to the grass. The wind caught at her coat and slapped her wet hair across her face. She inched the basket along until she had pinned it close to the wall. Now the wind swirled round the interior, but its pace was broken, its strength dispersed. Hellen collapsed into the corner and, shivering with cold, drew up her knees beneath her chin, encircling her legs with her arms.

The garden shed rocked perilously, its iron roof screaming against the sitting strength of its lead-topped nails. A dazzle of lightning showed unidentifiable objects as they flew through the air. The basket, dislodged by the force of the wind, rolled across the doorway, spilling its logs. The door swung in again, crashed back again. Hellen curled herself more tightly, head on her knees, hands clasping her elbows, shivering. The sea water had run down her neck, and her coat was soaked.

The door crashed open, then shut. Open. Shut. A branched snapped off and danced across the roof. She lifted her head, watching the doorway with apprehension, praying that the shed would remain intact. Suddenly a torch shone in her face.

"What in the name of all that's holy are you doing here?" George grasped her wrist and forced her to her feet. Half mad with cold and fear, Hellen jerked frantically, uselessly, to free herself. Walking backwards, holding the door open with his free arm, George jerked her out on to the grass, kicked the logs away with his foot, and secured the bolt. The torch beam dived in among the whirling, dancing branches as he picked his way across the garden, dragging her with him. He did not let her go until they were inside the hall.

"Jee-sus Christ!" he exclaimed then, sucking the air in sharply between his front teeth as he surveyed her bedraggled form. "Jee-sus Christ! Take off those shoes." She could only look at him in mute terror. "Take them off," he shouted, "or I'll take them off for you and hit you with them. I'll tame you, you stupid bitch, if it's the last thing I do."

She kicked off her shoes and ran like a deer up the stairs. The key had gone from the bathroom door! She turned away in shock, but George, coming behind, pushed her forward, put the plug into the outlet pipe, and turned on both taps. Then, without another word, he strode away, banging the door behind him. She dropped her soaked clothes on the floor and climbed thankfully into the warm water.

Ten minutes later the door burst open and George entered bearing a steaming glass, sat down on the stool and with one of those quick about-turns that were so typical of him, smiled. "If you can't look after yourself," he said, "I shall have to do it for you. Drink this."

"What is it?"

George took a sip, licked his lips, and rolled his eyes. "Ah Wong set it up. It'll warm you."

She knew immediately he was lying. That he had made the drink himself. "Put it down," she said. "I'll have it when I get out." She added stiffly, "I'd like some privacy, if you don't mind."

"Come on," George urged her affably. "It's got to be drunk hot."

Hellen lifted herself on one elbow, took the proferred drink and slid back into the water, taking the drink with her. "Drugging me then raping me is not going to help you," she said, emptying the bath water from the glass and handing it back to him.

George's face was a study.

"You did it once before."

Affecting an engaging air of confession, he said, "If you want to know, there's not much percentage in poking an inanimate body. But there was something in that that would have made our evening very pleasant, and set our marriage up nicely. Just a little aphrodisiac."

"Aphro- what?"

He frowned. "Leg opener. For an experienced woman, you're remarkably uninformed, old girl."

"Get out!" She would have slapped his face except that she knew he would slap her back.

"I can't keep a concubine, if you want me to be respected by your friends." He was looking at her breasts.

She laid a protective arm across them. "Plenty of businessmen keep concubines."

"The very rich, and those in unassailable positions. I've only got an average job."

"Average? Does an average job pay enough for the kind of furniture we own?"

He was silent, his eyes uncertain. "I've got savings," he said at last. "But I can't keep a concubine on savings." He rose, and with an air of delivering the last word, said, "I'm afraid you're going to have to be a proper wife, my dear."

"I will. In every way but one. You shall have your concubine, George. I'm sure you can afford her. I'm sure there are some that are less expensive than others."

He turned and went out, banging the door behind him.

She reached for her towel, rubbed at her hair, and stepped out on the floor. Looking down at the bundle of wet clothes under the basin, at the pale silk underwear streaked now with blue dye from her dress, she felt an overwhelming sense of despair. Then she reminded herself that she had survived the dreadful marriage, and the pirates, to drink at the overflowing cup of Oliver's love. She would think of herself as a cat with nine lives. Count out the typhoon and the aphro- what? There were still five to go.

She opened the door and pattered barefoot across the hall to her room.

Marnie had worried herself down to a splinter; Leo was truculent; Joe grew more and more silent; Verity and Beth laid tearful blame on their husbands for not introducing Hellen to suitable bachelors. They retorted that they had tried. "One day she's nice to them, the next she's forgotten their names. A chap knows when he's not wanted," said Dudley Reid. "The reason Calum Finn stayed friendly with her, was that he wasn't in a position to ask for her hand."

Only Marnie understood, for that was how it had been with her. She had scarcely noticed young men before meeting Joe. Even after nearly thirty years she could not have explained what it was that had attracted her to him. She remembered the overflowing sense of excitement in her as he stood at the other end of the tennis court. She, who was not an accomplished player, had served a ball that went straight to him, as though some power beyond her control held it on course. She sent the ball to him again. And again. It was as though the ball had become a barque, taking them both on board.

Now the sight of the envelope with its foreign stamp gave Marnie quite a turn. It was the first communication since the happy letter posted from Gibraltar. Night after night they had lain awake, worrying. But for Lady Sylvia's warning that Hellen should not sail, they would have cabled Government House. There was no other address.

Joe, who had been fixing a leaking outside tap, hurried in through a side door. Leo came, half-sliding, half-jumping down the stairs in his stockinged feet. "Read it out to us, Mother."

It was a surprisingly short letter in the circumstances that there must be a lot of ground to cover. Hellen described the house where she was staying, large and square in the Colonial style, with verandahs on both floors. She described the beauty of the colony; the tiny, hurrying Chinese who ran round practically naked and wore amusing, cone-shaped hats. She talked of the glamorous Hong Kong Hotel; the grandeur of the houses on The Peak.

She said there were a few cars—Government House had had one for ten years—but even Sir Rowan Marathon rode, or so she had been told, on ceremonial occasions, in an ornate sedan chair with eight coolies to carry it, and a string of bearers in bright red liveries, white gaiters and mutton-pie hats with red tassels. She described the servants, decked out in blue satin, with pigtails that must be called cues, reaching almost to the floor.

She said she had been to Macao, a little bit of Portugal on mainland China. She said Hong Kong was in some ways English, in others foreign and strange. She said she was settling in. And at the end she mentioned Oliver. In passing, they realised, their eyes widening, their apprehension growing. Oliver was busy. Just that.

"There's no question of a wedding at the moment." Joe looked out of the windows at the ducks idling on the pond, repeating his daughter's words aloud. Leo looked across the lawn to the stables where Hellen's hunters lived, daily exercised by himself and Ben. Marnie looked down at her hands.

"If she's not going to marry him, then she had better come home," said Joe. "She can't stay there without a chaperon.'

"She says she's with friends?" Marnie's statement was a question. As though any of them could explain.

"What friends?" Joe's question was uncharacteristically aggressive.

"She would have made friends on the voyage out." Leo made an attempt to lighten the tension.

"Then why doesn't she say so? Why doesn't she name them?" Joe examined the letter carefully, as though better news might be hidden between the lines. "She says he, the man of the family, is in the import/export business. T-s-i-m S-h-a T-s-u-i. It isn't even in Hong Kong. She doesn't mention getting the letters we sent to Government House."

Leo said abruptly, his mind grappling with the long, foreign name that his father had spelled out, "She can't be living with a Chinese family. How could she?"

Joe looked stricken.

"And why does she give a box number, instead of a street number?"

Joe and Marnie knew, though they did not care to say so out loud, that one could not send someone to call at a box number. That if a girl wanted to hide behind one, it was perfectly possible.

Lady Sylvia was critically examining some delectable-looking cakes, home made by Mrs Piddick at the Old Forge. Mrs Honeywell had set them out on the counter on three-tiered stands under glass domes bearing an impious similarity to those used to house artificial flowers on gravestones in the local churchyard.

"I'll have the sponge cake with the pink icing," she said with a flash of her large teeth. "Cook has been struck down with a tiresome summer cold." She had scarcely finished speaking when she caught a glimpse out of the corner of her eye of that woman whose outrageous daughter had rushed off to Hong Kong in hot pursuit of dear Oliver. She swung round to face the door as Marnie walked innocently through.

Marnie would certainly have hurried on if the Rolls had been parked outside, or if she had recognised the two black labradors sitting alertly on their hind quarters with their leads hooked over the railings. Unwarned, frail from the shock of Hellen's letter, she stepped into the lion's den.

Knees aslant, Lady Sylvia advanced. Her bony hips brushed against an untidy fall-out of penny dreadfuls, sending them sliding to the floor. "Do tell me what news you have of your gel, Mrs—er—North," he brayed. It was one of her affectations to convey the fact, without acrimony, that she did not bother to tax her memory with the names of those she considered of no account.

"Hellen had a very pleasant voyage, thank you, Lady Sylvia." Marnie, with Hellen's letter folded and refolded, read and re-read, in her handbag, could see by the expression on her inquisitor's face that was not enough. Not nearly enough. Marnie moved towards the counter and found her way blocked by drums of treacle. Oh dear. To run into this woman whose path through life was so smooth, so permanently laid down, whose background was so unassailable—to be besieged, she felt genuinely besieged—was the final straw. Marnie despaired, wishing she had not left the house.

"I thought you would have news from the Marathons," she hedged. Those gimlet eyes were boring their way right through the soft leather of her bag. Any moment now she would say, "Is that not a Hong Kong postmark on the envelope?"

"We haven't, actually," Lady Syliva returned impatiently. Her eyes took on a malicious gleam. "Surely the gel would send a cable to you, though, if a wedding had been arranged."

"They didn't intend to marry immediately," Marnie said with great dignity. "After all, the young people didn't know each other very well."

"Precisely. That is precisely what we all said. He really did not know the gel. Well, I tried to stop her. I did my best." Lady Sylvia's voice warmed with a suggestion of triumph. She began to turn back towards the counter, indicating that this rather regrettable confrontation was over, then pulled up in surprise at Marnie's next words.

"Hellen would be very foolish to rush into marriage without taking time to accustom herself to such a very different life. Also, to get to know Oliver better."

Her Ladyship's eyes bulged.

Marnie drew herself up, just a fraction taller. "It's one thing to be head over heels in love, Lady Sylvia. It's quite another to take such a very final step."

Her Ladyship made an odd little sound, full of irritation and impatience. Was this impertinent woman actually suggesting that the girl should stop and think before marrying a Marathon?

"And, of course," Marnie continued bravely, looking down again at the treacle tins, wondering if it would be possible to step over them, "If Oliver's parents couldn't come to England because of trouble in the Malay States, they wouldn't be able to go to Hong Kong either."

The disturbances weren't as bad as they at first thought." Her Ladyship gave the game away in the careless manner she used for people whose feelings did not count.

"You have heard from them then? From Oliver's parents?"

"Er—not actually." Lady Sylvia's mouth tightened. The woman had not only turned the tables on her, she was speaking, audaciously, as though they had mutual friends.

Mrs Honeywell leaned more comfortably against the counter, listening with enormous interest, her chin on the heels of her hands, her bosom sagging close to the mixed biscuits. If you asked her, if Hellen married this gentleman, it wouldn't be too far off suitable. Not too far at all. She was a lovely girl, was Hellen.

"I'm sure you will hear in due course," said Marnie, sounding quite insultingly comforting. She managed to project her head round the human barrier blocking her way. "I've come for some matches, Mrs Honeywell. Could you possibly hand them across?"

Lady Sylvia looked down at the mess of penny deadfuls under her feet, then with an air of distaste, stepped off them. Ignoring the fact that Marnie had already asked to be served, she demanded the cake with the chocolate icing as well the sponge. As she left the shop Mrs Honeywell eyed Marnie with compassion, but she made no comment. A body couldn't be too careful what she said in this village. Especially when a body was in trade. Anyway, she acknowledged to herself, she never knew quite how to talk to Mrs North, who was virtually a lady herself.

It was three days before the winds went on their way. It was not a bad typhoon as typhoons went. Inevitably, there were outbreaks of fire and some loss of life on the hillsides above Happy Valley for the poor Chinese cooked over naked flames, so when the flimsy rattan shelters blew apart they inevitably caught fire. The meagre possessions of the coolie families were strewn everywhere, to be swept away by the floods that followed.

Ah Wong, angrily sweeping the kitchen floor, which was a task far below his dignity, explained to Hellen: "Ah Ping clying. Glanfather die in fire. First sister and second bluther burn." Ah Wong did not care to have his routine disturbed. It was Wednesday, and on Wednesdays the silver had to be cleaned, whether or not it seemed necessary. Every night the kitchen floor had to be scrubbed, dirty or no. One of the servants going to pieces was a major catastrophe.

Hellen, distressed, gave him a blanket and some money to give to the little makee learn, and told him to send her home to her family.

"You gave her a blanket!" echoed George incredulously. "Are you mad?"

"Some of her family have died in the fire. And they've lost everything."

"Good God! If we gave away a blanket every time the wind blew, we'd be the ones living under rattan shelters. You're taking one helluva long time to learn the ropes, Hellen."

"I'm sure if I put my mind to it I could be cold-hearted and uncaring."

George said irritably, "This is colonial life, and you are a part of it." Momentarily, she was full of excitement and apprehension, thinking he was going to say, "If you don't like it, go home," but he didn't, and she walked away.

She was jumpy and miserable as the days went by. Had Oliver taken the typhoon's arrival as an omen? Had he been seen waiting in Ladder Street? Had Sir Rowan, putting two and two together, sent him to another colonial outpost? She could only wait.

The animosity between George and herself settled. At the Hong Kong Club, waiting for the softly padding servants to bring their drinks, Hellen would search hungrily among the leather armchairs and fluted columns for a glimpse of a tall man with dazzling blue eyes and brown hair. He did not come.

She went to Lin Yan's house and was shown her treasures, delicate water colours mounted on silk, dream-like, exquisite. Lin Yan told her with pride they had been painted in A.D.1180 by Fu Tsing, a court lady, the second concubine of Ko Chung. "Of course you realise if they were not so valuable, they would be on my walls," she said, rolling them up and replacing them in their metal tubes, indicating her Englishness with that sweet air of defiance that Hellen found enchanting. To please her, Hellen tried to think of Lin Yan as one-quarter English, and to treat her as she would an English friend, but it was like treating a kitten as an Alsatian dog. Her way of prettily fluttering her fingers, her high, tinkling voice, the frailty of her bird-like bones, were all Chinese. Only her almond eyes were wider than those of a full-blooded Chinese, and her features less flat.

Hellen would have liked to repay her many kindnesses by taking her to champagne tiffins at the Cricket Club, as well as to watch George play, but though the Cricket and Yacht Clubs were livelier than the Hong Kong Club, the same rules of exclusion prevailed. "Please do not worry," the Eurasian girl protested when Hellen apologised for not being able to return her hospitality. "It is no use to be annoyed. It has always been like this."

"If you were to marry an Englishman—"

"We would both be excluded, and my Chinese relations would disown me. When my English grandfather married my Chinese grandmother, it went very badly for them. Neither the English nor the Chinese accepted them."

"I saw you in Central with Oliver's Eurasian friend," said Ruth one day, her eyes bright and beady with curiosity. "Does this mean you've seen him?"

"It means Oliver sent her to visit me," said Hellen. "Was that not kind?" She was developing two faces, one for the safe truth and one for the half truths.

She was growing very strong.

Hellen was finding she could sit in the Peak tram, with the exclusivity afforded to her race, and watch with resignation emaciated coolies, their muscles shrunken beneath their parchment skins, their poor thin backs bent double, going up Old Peak Road lugging coal, luggage, and often great loads of ice. She did not lose her compassion, but she learned to live with the differences.

226

There was no percentage, as George would say, in protesting. "You're on to a good thing," he said to her once. "And we're giving them work. That means food." George could justify anything. "Besides, plenty of them are skinny because they spend money on black rice instead of food." Black rice was the opium that made the existence of the poor endurable. There was never enough money for that as well as food.

At last Lin Yan brought a message from Oliver. All that day Hellen walked in a rosy cloud, her feet scarcely touching the ground. She was to meet him this time at noon. She had told Lin Yan that George could no longer be relied upon to go out at night. There were times when he left the house looking worried, and returned wearing an expression of relief. More and more she came to think he was not going to a woman.

She never asked him where he went. Strangers, even living in the same house, had a right to privacy. She decided, contemplating the expensive furnishings she had bought, ostensibly on George's savings, that he must be running a little business on the side.

Chapter 21

Forbidden Fruit

There was no sign of Oliver when Hellen, in a flurry of excitement, reached Ladder Street. On one side of the doorway, protected from the fierce sun beneath the jutting first-floor rooms of the old building sat a cobbler, twine in mouth, needle in hand, his hammer and last on the pavement beside him. He squinted up at Hellen without curiosity. She stepped into a narrow passage, blinking rapidly until her eyes grew accustomed to the dimness, and was immediately aware of a strange yet faintly familiar smell. On the right lay a doorway curtained with colourful beads, and from somewhere beyond came the click and rattle of mah jong tiles.

Tentatively, and very carefully, she moved several strands of the beads aside. The room was full of Chinese seated at tables with tiny porcelain tea cups at their elbows. In an alcove, on a low stool, a very old man sat hunched over a wooden pipe from which a thin spiral of smoke arose. Now she could place the distinctive smell that pervaded the building. It reminded her of Macao where opium was smoked so commonly in the streets that its strange odour hung in the air. "Sordid" Oliver had said. She was fascinated, thrilled, and faintly repelled.

A man looked up and caught her eye. Flicking his tiles with his fingertips so that they fell face downwards, he rose from his seat. His companions' eyes, slitted, dark, intensely curious, turned her way. Hellen receded. The beads rustled aside and the man emerged. Though he could not have been more than seventeen, and wore the look of a high-class Chinese, his grey face and the pupils that were mere pin-points in shallow pebble eyes showed him to be an addict.

He said, "Your fiend come soon. I take you." They went together down the passage and climbed a dark staircase, scarcely more than the breadth of a man's shoulders. The smell of opium was stronger here. The upstairs passage was lined with single bed spaces where skeletal Chinese lay like stick insects, more limbs than body.

They reached the end. The boy inserted a key in a lock. There was a clatter of heavy footsteps on the stairs. Hellen swung round, every nerve in her body coming alive. A tree of flowers rose from the stairway, frangipani, oleander, hibiscus, their fragrance overpowering. Then Oliver's arms came, encircling the flowers. He lowered the giant bouquet and his dear, dear face emerged, rueful, laughing, apologetic.

"I'm sorry. I'm so sorry." He strode towards her, projecting his amazing offering in front of him. "I was held up. One can't say to a big-wig, 'I've got an assignation.'"

Her guide faded discreetly away. Hellen swirled into the room, floating on the perfume of all the flowers, with Oliver's scent of tobacco and man intermixed, and her head spinning with his nearness. Kicking the door shut, he flung his arms wide and high, sending the lighter blooms exuberantly into the air to float down over her, like exotic confetti falling on a bride. "I meant to get here first and decorate—" He broke off abruptly, surveying the squalid little room with shocked eyes.

Hellen encircled him within her arms, leaning a tear-wet, laughing face against his cheek. "How I love you." He held her close. They might have been in Atlantis instead of Central Hong Kong with opium smokers only a low cry distant, rattling their mah-jong tiles.

"It doesn't matter about the room. It doesn't matter about anything, except that we're together."

He buried his lips in her neck, kissed her eyes, her hair. "It shouldn't have to happen like this," he said fiercely. He pulled off his jacket, undid his tie and collar stud, then his watch with its gold chain, a vicious reminder of the transiency of their togetherness. They did not undress each other. There was not time.

Hellen dropped her hat and handbag on the floor, kicked off her shoes, and pulled her dress over her head. They stood naked and young and slender, their arms extended, then Oliver picked her up and laid her tenderly on the bed. The heat was suffocating, for there was only peeling paper where once there might have been a fan on the ceiling.

It was such a short interlude, so tantalising, so incomplete in essence as to make them impetuous, rash, greedy with a new kind of rage for what they could not have.

Oliver said as they hurried into their clothes, "We can't live like this. I can't bring you back here. I thought of it only as somewhere I wouldn't be recognised. We can't come here again," he repeated. "Divans are for fornication, and whoring." Neither of them wanted to expose the miracle of their loving to such momentary, sterile reprieves. Even the flowers lay like disappointed wraiths upon the floor.

He did not say, "I'll think of something," because it was a moment of lost hope. Hellen held his face tenderly between the palms of her hands. Their hearts were welded, their love divine, but it was now one fifty-five and Oliver must be at his desk in the Secretariat at two. They parted in the doorway, Oliver going on ahead, taking the steps two at a time. The old shoe mender stared at her without interest. She wandered down the hill, thinking soberly how close they were to Government House and the Secretariat, how close even to shops where she might meet someone she knew.

Nonetheless, as she reached the bottom step it was with a sense of shock that she heard a familiar voice.

"What on earth are you doing here?" and looked up into Marcia's big, puzzled face. "Sorry to startle you," she added. "What on earth did you find up that sordid little street?"

Shocked, totally unprepared, Hellen could only stare at her. Marcia's smile faded and a shadow of suspicion came into her eyes. "I was wandering. That's all."

"Up those steps in this heat?"

"It's always hot. One day is as good as another to climb steps."

Marcia said huffily, "Oh, well, I had better be on my way. Why don't you come with me? I'm taking some shoes to be mended. A friend told me there was a good little man somewhere here."

Hellen froze. Then self-preservation came to her aid and she lied swiftly, "I believe I saw one down a little street over there." She pointed in the direction of the harbour. "Come, I'll see if I can find him for you." Walking at Marcia's side, obliquely in the direction of the water, guiding her away from the old shoemender who might show some sign of recognising her, she felt infinitely depressed. She hated having to lie to this nice woman who wished her nothing but good. For better or worse, she was now caught in a web of deceit.

Lin Yan brought Hellen a tutor, a wraith of a man who might be picked up and whisked away into the sky by the wind in his sleeves. His skin was the colour of old ivory, his fingers tapered down to almond-shaped nails. With his Mephistophelean beard and the fine corkscrew of whiskers quivering on his wrinkled cheeks, he looked like a mandarin from a scroll painting.

He would come up the path shaking hands with himself outside his wide cuffs, then as he neared the door, with great ceremony, he would clasp his hands before his face, and bow. Hellen would bow gravely in return. Though Ah Wong brought a spitoon which he set on the floor beside the tutor, he did not use it. Neither did he hawk. He cleared his throat, when necessary, in a very acceptable manner. Lin Yan introduced him as Sin-shaang. Sin-shaang meant teacher, or wise man. As with the gardener, he shared his name with his profession. He brought Hellen a Cantonese primer, a small book of radicals, a writing brush, a black stick, and a palette for mixing the stick with water in order to make ink. He spoke in a high-pitched, gentle voice with the stilted diction characteristic of Hong Kong's English-educated Chinese, slurring his s's, using incomplete vowels. Hellen was enchanted with him. Ah Wong brought him rice wine in tiny porcelain cups.

"Ho, ho," he would say. "Ho, ho, ho." Very good.

He taught her a great deal, not all of it about writing. He told her she must never bang her fist on the table when there was a Chinese in the room, for they would assume she was banging them on the head. He taught her never to tell a Chinese he is wrong, for this would cause him to lose face. He gave her a list of common orders for the servants in Cantonese and as she acquired a tentative and simplistic grasp of the language, she became more at ease with them. When the high-pitched sounds of the coolies' squabbling infiltrated from the kitchen, she was able to cope in a manner that suited her, and which she felt gave them a semblance of dignity. Marcia had taught her to say, "Too muchy bubbery. You savvy? Go topside and fixee beds."

"And what is Cantonese for "Hurry up?" she asked.

"Faai-di Tso," he supplied, adding with a wry look, "English—Chop-chop."

Hellen flushed. In part, she knew, it was the way George spoke those words that made them sound particularly offensive, but she could not bring herself to use them, so she never asked the servants to hurry. "Faai-di Tso." She nodded, pleased.

In the beginning, Lin Yan came, gravely listening, drinking green tea—Hellen had discovered that jasmine was not the only, or even the most delicious, tea on the Chinese market-indulging her English fantasies with the *Weldon's Ladies Home Journals* that the expatriate ladies passed from to hand.

The pictures in Lin Yan's house of birds among blossoms, fish among reeds, insects delicately poised on bamboo, inspired Hellen to buy rice paper and a fine brush. They were so simple in essence that she was certain she could copy them, but it proved not to be so. She gave up after two or three unsuccessful attempts. Lin Yan was amused by her friend's first tentative efforts at the complex strokes of the Chinese ideographs, for Hellen let them go to her head in wonderful sweeps of the writing brush, as though she was indeed painting. Her tutor would look at her quizzically over his wire-rimmed glasses. His own elegant strokes were made with impressive dignity.

It was Wanda Ayre who told Hellen that Denzil and Kitty Armitage were returning to Hong Kong.

"Poor chap, he hasn't been able to get the right sort of job in England. And Kitty, as you may know, is an only child. She misses her parents. But, my dear, how very awkward!" Wanda's eyes were slyly watching for Hellen's reaction.

"Are you insinuating that George is still in love with her?" Hellen leaned back in the big chair, crossed her ankles and carefully placed an amused expression on her face.

Wanda giggled and patted the kiss curl on her cheek. "Don't you mind? Her coming back, I mean?"

"Why should I? She's married. George is married." Later, Hellen felt a flicker or sympathy for George, wondering if he was still in love with this girl. She had briefly met Kitty's parents at a party, after which they made a quick, embarrassed exit. There was a flare-up of chatter then, with women gossiping behind their fans, casting surreptitious glances towards George and Hellen.

Ruth said, with a touch of malicious amusement, that it had been shameless of the hostess to invite the Curtains and the Burtenshaws together. Hellen did not mind. She had long since learned that booby-traps were the meat and drink of their enclosed society.

Wanda said now, sounding disappointed, "We'll see," then she glimpsed a friend, waved happily and the fleet little inquisition was over.

The next day, when Hellen and Toby were leading their mounts out, there was the noisy clamour of a car approaching, and a model T Ford came racing towards them. It skidded to a stop and Oliver leapt out, lean and casual in jodhpurs, shining brown boots and a silk shirt. Hellen stood rooted to the spot, her face alight.

"Oliver Marathon! I might have known," said Toby indulgently, looking pleased.

Hellen walked to Oliver, her feet half way off the ground. He held out his hand and she extended hers. Her fingers clung.

Oliver looked down at her with infinite love.

"Come and join us, old chap," called Toby, vaulting into the saddle, amiably recognising that Hellen and Oliver were friends. Then a smartly uniformed groom came forward leading a lean horse quite sixteen hands high, snorting and dancing on a short rein, dwarfing and disturbing the lively Mongolian pony the mafoo was holding for Hellen.

Hellen assessed with her practised eye the gelding's elegant lines.

"This," said Oliver with pride, "is Ransom. He belongs to my uncle."

"I hope you don't expect us to keep up," said Toby sheepishly, shortening his reins as his own mount, disturbed by the projection of pent-up energy from the newcomer, swung round in a circle, stamping his hooves.

"He's lovely," breathed Hellen.

"Ride Merryman," suggested Oliver. "He's more your style than that pony." And so began their daily gallops together. Of course word filtered through that Oliver Marathon, Mrs Curtain and Toby Ayre rode together. It was a measure of the distance between George and other men that no one teased him about handsome Oliver Marathon meeting his wife every day. Nobody mentioned the matter to Sir Rowan, either. His grooms assumed she had permission.

Happy Valley racecourse lay in a U-shaped basin facing the sea. Toby free-wheeled from The Peak on his bicycle, a coolie servant running down the road after him in order to perform the tedious task of pushing the machine back up the mountain to his house. It was only courteous for Oliver to offer Hellen a ride from the Star ferry landing in his Tin Lizzie. "It will save you a quarter of an hour," he said, speaking casually before Toby, "if I meet you at the pier."

He would be at the ferry building when Hellen arrived. Neither of them showed more than carefully schooled politeness as they said "Good morning," and "How did you sleep?" and "What a lovely day!" for the benefit of anyone who might overhear them.

But they did shout, "I love you!" and "Darling, is this really you? Are we really together again?" over the noisy throbbing of the engine and the rushing wind, as they tore inland to the race track. They were careful not to hold hands, though, for the hood was always down. Someone might notice if Oliver drove with one hand on the steering wheel. This delicious nearness, circumspectly controlled, generated a particular excitement of its own. Hellen would descend from the car walking on air.

The hills round Happy Valley rose on three sides. Precarious shanty-towns composed of Heath Robinson-type corrugated iron and rattan shelters clung to the more desolate and craggy areas, but where the dry scrub ended there were hardy evergreens, tough, embattled and tornado-proof. Once, when the gods, smiling on the lovers, allowed Toby to sleep in after a late night, Hellen and Oliver left the race track and rode up the slope. They spread their inadequate saddle cloths over the cold mulch and drew each other magically close. Those were blessed moments, with the rustling greenery round them, the early birds twittering and fluttering in the branches, and the sun leaping over the crouching islands to filter its golden light through the leaves.

They did not delude themselves that such enchantment could return. They came to accept each moment that was offered to them, spellbinding themselves into it, knowing with a lingering sense of sorrow that it might never happen again. Hellen would float through the remainder of the day with the mustiness of old leaves in her nostrils and her feet half way off the ground. Neither of them spoke of the future. It was as though they did not dare.

Hellen's days now passed swiftly enough. She wrote again to her parents, to her sisters and her grandfather in Yorkshire. Having broken the ice with that first feeble letter—she saw it now as feeble, and frightened—she expanded on the very real excitements of living in Hong Kong.

She had reckoned without her grandfather's penchant for calling a spade a spade.

"Now look here, young lady," he wrote with typical north country directness, "I want the story now, and I want it straight. Are you or are you not marrying this man?" He had looked up the shipping news. "This letter will, God willing, catch the *Alipore*. You'll have it by the thirtieth of September. *Delta* sails three days later. Three days is enough time to write a letter, if it's the truth you're writing, and I expect nothing less. I anticipate hearing from you by the ninth of November."

Even had it occurred to her to ignore her grandfather's demands, Hellen would not have done so. Sir Samuel was the head of the family. He loved them, watched over them and spoiled them. When necessary, he bullied them. "Some men are providers, and some are not," he had said early on to Joe, "and I expect you to use your commonsense." Joe did, knowing how much pleasure Sam had from providing his daughter and grandchildren with an allowance.

"There has been no change in our feelings for each other," Hellen wrote. "Lady Marathon has been very kind, but we can't marry just yet. However, there is no question of returning home."

She was amazed that it should have been so comparatively easy.

"I've never given you an engagement ring," said George.

"There was no engagement." Hellen went to stand at the French windows, looking out into the bougainvillaea that flared orange, pink and purple on the wall. There were butterflies fluttering all over the garden.

His voice, coming from behind her, was firm but kind. "I'm conscious, in public, that you're the only woman not wearing one."

It was as though fine threads were coming out of the air and winding themselves round her body. They came down from the walls and in from the garden, creeping up to her throat, choking her. She must not allow herself to sink any further into George's debt. But more than that, an engagement ring was not a string of pearls—a ring was a token of love. A promise. She thought of the engagement bracelet Oliver had given her, that the pirates had stolen, and wanted to cry.

"I think you should have a ring," said George.

She turned to face him. "Very well," she said, laying the decision precisely at his door, "since I don't wish to embarrass you in public, you may buy me a ring."

Unexpectedly, he smiled. "Give me your wedding ring for size." She removed it from her finger. George had insisted on replacing the one she threw away at Lantau. He slipped it into his waistcoat pocket, then dropped his watch after it. He crossed the room and, bending down, kissed her on the forehead, then left.

She felt miserable all that day. Drained. The heat was suffocating. Wanda telephoned to say she was cancelling her tennis party because the clouds had come down so thickly on The Peak that the court was soaked.

Hellen said, "There seem to be some advantages to living in Tsim Sha Tsui."

Wanda gave an embarrassed little laugh. In its aftermath Hellen felt edgy and out of sorts. She felt she would go crazy if she did not find something to do. She decided to ask Marcia and Neil to dinner. Chinese servants did not need notice. They could produce a dinner for eight in several hours, including time spent at the market.

The cook boy was on his knees before the shrine he had made for the small, carved figure of the kitchen god, holding a chopstick, dripping with honey, to the creature's mouth. This god was said to compile a comprehensive dossier of the behaviour of a household, and to report on them to his superiors in heaven at the time of the lunar New Year.

"What you do?" asked Hellen sharply.

The coolie looked up. "Putee sweet on Tsao Kwan mouth," he said. "Makee sweet leport."

Normally, Chinese superstitions left Hellen feeling mid-way between enchanted and appalled. Today she felt angry with a severe Englishness. And angry with herself for not being able to translate her reprimand into Cantonese.

"I no likee food on floor," she said, signing to the coolie to put the honey back on the kitchen table. "Rats."

"No lats, Missie." He looked at her with veiled hostility.

She swung round sharply, and going up to her room stood at the window looking out on the vast white cloud that hid The Peak as far down as mid-levels. All the fans in the house were whirring, helpless against the great weight of the atmosphere. She decided to issue the invitation in person. Ah Wong, by the time she returned, should have recovered.

She picked up her handbag and hat, and went downstairs. There were roses in bloom on either side of the path. She felt vaguely irritatated by the blaze of colour, and again because Fah Wong was dozing, broom in hand, beneath the acacia tree. Everyone said the heat would lessen, but it only lessened for a few days, then returned. She wished for the sight of a Kentish landscape, white with snow. As she turned into Mody Road she began to cry because there was no way back and no way forward, and like an omen, George's insistence on the ring seemed to be an indication that the ground beneath her feet was sinking.

Chapter 22

The Burma Ruby

His Excellency's secretary stood before his employer's desk with a sheaf of papers in his hands, waiting patiently while Sir Rowan vetted the guest list for the forthcoming ball. Peter Ackroyd had lived all his life, apart from his school years, in the colony, and followed his father into the Hong Kong Government. When his predecessor was forced to return home a year ago, after suffering frequent and debilitating attacks of malaria, Peter was seconded to take his place.

It was jokily accepted, and inexplicably true, that children born in the East acquired an eastern look, which they shed back in England. Nobody had ever said this of Ackroyd who was the quintessential Englishman with a pink and white Anglo-Saxon skin and a mass of unruly golden hair. The high-class Asian girls who came to Government House adored him for his chubby Englishness, his clipped, military type way of speaking, and his disarming manner.

"I see," said Sir Rowan thoughtfully, "there's a Mr and Mrs Curtain on the guest list." He waited, without looking up.

"Mrs Curtain is a new arrival," said Ackroyd. "She signed the book when you were in the New Territories."

"Ah!" murmured Sir Rowan. Without looking up, he asked, "You have met her, Peter?"

"Yes. I've met her."

"At the Hong Kong Hotel? Mmn?" Sir Rowan continued to give the impression his main attention was concentrated on the list.

"I actually met her here, when she came."

"To sign? With her husband? Mmn?" Sir Rowan's concentration remained apparently unbroken.

"Actually, she came with—or rather, escorted by—that Eurasian girl, Lin Yan."

"Ah." In Sir Rowan's alert mind the pieces dropped swiftly into place. He sat back in his big chair, friendly as a teddy bear. "Where's my tea?" As his secretary moved swiftly to call Chan Mei, he raised a hand to stop him. "Don't worry. I'll have some with my wife. By the way, Peter," he picked up a pencil, stared critically at the point then put it aside, "do you know George Curtain?"

Ackroyd hesitated. "Yes, I know him."

"Bit of a bounder, isn't he?"

"Perhaps he'll change, now he's married." Sir Rowan's staff were adept at the diplomatic answer.

"Ah! She's that type, is she?" The Governor projected his personality warmly, smiling up from his desk, implying they were two chaps who understood each other: who could discuss, strictly between themselves, the intriguing characteristics of women.

"Sir?"

"The reforming type. Mmn?"

The secretary smiled back, but warily. H.E. was a past master at drawing on to the tip of one's tongue the answer he wanted to hear. "She seemed nice—I mean, certainly very attractive. I scarcely spoke to her." He was about to add that Lady Marathon had whisked her away. He stopped short. If Sir Rowan knew about the girls taking tea with his wife, he would have addressed the questions to her. "If you're doubtful about Mrs C., sir—"

"Doubtful? Not at all, my dear chap. Not at all." But he waited, watching Ackroyd's face.

Ackroyd cast round in his mind for something innocuous to say about the lovely Mrs Curtain. "As I understand it, sir, Curtain has done very well for himself."

"Ah! Is that what the gossips say?" Sir Rowan shed the teddy bear aura and dropped like a cat on a mouse. "That he has done very well for himself?"

"Curtain was engaged to Mr Burtenshaw's daughter," Peter said diffidently, "and she went off with Armitage. Left him looking a bit of a Charlie. This girl . . . she's rather more favoured than Kitty Burtenshaw."

"Favoured?"

"She's very pretty. Er—" Ackroyd shifted his papers from one arm to the other. "You know Denzil Armitage, sir."

"I know him well." Sir Rowan stared thoughtfully at his silver ink stand, leaned forward, picked up a pen, examined the nib, shook an ink drop on to the leather-backed blotting pad, then replaced the pen in the well. "Damn' good bat, young Armitage," he remarked conversationally. "Made a century that year Oliver played in the Eton and Harrow match at Lords. He's blotted his copy book now, silly ass." His Excellency looked up. His eyes were very direct. "So, Curtain picked up this girl on the rebound? Mmn?"

"I don't really know." It was gradually dawning on Ackroyd that there were other things H.E. did not know. For instance, that Mrs' Curtain was riding his horses every morning on the Happy Valley racecourse. "Shall I have your tea sent upstairs, sir?" he asked, sounding busy, looking down once again at his papers, edging towards the door that led into the main office.

Sir Rowan rose. "Yes, do that." He went out of the opposite door and climbed the stairs slowly, with his eyes on the treads.

The door leading to his wife's sitting room was open. He entered and closed it behind him. She was at the window, working on her petit point. The sun, filtering through the curtains, lit up the gold as well as the early strands of grey in her hair. Odd, he thought, how Englishwomen improved with age. Lovely when young, a bit messy in the thirties and forties, soft and pretty in their fifties, then magnificent in old age. His wife was only forty-eight, but she already had the elegance, the poise and the mature beauty of an older woman. He wished he had the family diamonds to bestow on her. It scared him witless to think where they might end in Oliver's hands, and Oliver was going to get them, in the long run, because poor old Cecil wasn't going to make it to the earldom.

She was wearing buttercup yellow, with a replica of his regimental Guards badge, set with small diamonds, tugging at the soft material of her dress, exposing the cleft between her breasts.

"Hello, darling," she said, looking up with her soft, pretty smile.

Sir Rowan pushed his hands down into his pockets and came slowly across the room. "Oliver has been in touch with the girl."

There was no point in denying it. Besides, she was ready. There had been time to work out her reply. "Yes, dear," Her Ladyship replied composedly. "Of course he has. He couldn't leave the matter in mid-air."

"I made it quite clear to him—"

"Yes, dear. And he understands his position perfectly. But you must acknowledge that they had to meet. They had to meet once, if only to discuss—" She stared down at the picture clamped tightly in her embroidery frame: the leopard's head of the Marathon coat-of-arms incorporated in a swirl of bamboo canes and long, slender leaves; the wall of a temple; lotus flowers. It was to be a fire screen, commemorating their Chinese experience.

"To discuss her reasons for marrying Curtain. Yes." Sir Rowan, giving way to impatience, finished the sentence for her. "I've ordered tea up here." He set a comfortable chair directly across the low table

239

from where his wife was sitting. "Why did she marry him?"

"I don't know, dear."

He frowned. Lettice would defend Oliver to the last ditch, but she was not untruthful.

"I don't think he knows, dear."

"Of course he knows. She has to have given him an explanation. Of course he knows," Sir Rowan repeated.

Lettice knew this mild manner only too well. Part of her husband's success as a career diplomat was his ability to ferret out facts without his victim realising he was being pumped. It was why he had a governorship and a knighthood, whilst his elder brother, starting on the same rung of the diplomatic ladder, was a mere resident general.

The door opened and a servant entered carrying a silver tray. Her Ladyship put aside her work and proceeded to pour the tea. Sir Rowan rose automatically, crossed the room and closed the door. "The Curtains are on the guest list for the ball."

"Why not? I'm sure you would be interested to meet Hellen."

"Hellen?" He came back across the room, head down, the ball of one hand against his chin, frowning at his black boots, hand-made in Jermyn Street where his father had his footwear made, and his father before him. He watched the colour rise in his wife's face.

"Hellen is her name, dear."

Sir Rowan sat down, knees apart, stared at his teacup, then leaned back in his chair. "Yes," he said. "That's her name." He waited a moment. Mutely, his wife offered him a cucumber sandwich. "I am not interested in meeting her," he said distinctly.

He sipped his tea, then replaced the cup in its saucer. "I regret very much the fact that she came here, for if I have them crossed off the list now, there will be a confrontation with Oliver. No girl who has done what she has done would have the gall to come here and sign the book, unless explicitly requested to do so." He swallowed the remainder of the tea down at a gulp, and stood up, six feet two with the straight back he had acquired during his service with the Guards. "Have Oliver in for dinner tonight," he said.

"We are already eight, dear."

"Get another girl to even the numbers."

He rested a hand on her shoulder, massaging the soft flesh through her thin gown. "I have to confront him, Lettice. You know that." Sometimes he wondered if it had been right to leave Oliver here when he took over the governorship. But even the Colonial Office had thought moving the lad would be an unwarranted interference in his career. And his own boys had only just gone home to school. Lettice

240

was missing them. Now, she would be the one to suffer if things went wrong.

"Try not to worry," he said.

"What will you do, Rowan?" Lettice asked, trying to keep the apprehension out of her voice.

"I will talk to Oliver, and if he is carrying on with the girl, I will send him away. There is nothing else I can do. You know that."

The ring George brought home was an astonishing ruby, surrounded by diamonds. The sun was slanting through the window. Helen held the silk-covered box in her hand, turning it in the sun's rays. Through, and outside the deep red, there were other colours. Flashes of green, then white, then black. She moved the box into the shadow of her body. The stone became blood red.

"It must have cost the earth!" she blurted out.

"Good God!" said George. "Is that all you can say?"

"You didn't have to . . ."

"I understood you to say I should buy the kind of ring I would like to see on your finger. I'd like to see a Burma ruby on my wife's finger. Put it on."

She did not want to put it on. She thought it might be stolen, or bought with money dishonestly acquired.

A memory from the past seeped in. Her mother meeting her off the train from school and taking her shopping. New hockey boots, and some plain underwear. Afterwards, in the book department, Hellen bought a volume of Longfellow's poems. As she dropped the package into her basket, she noticed an unfamiliar shape lying on top of her other purchases. She lifted the edge of the brown paper and peeped inside. Silk, trimmed with expensive lace. She looked round with a queer feeling, thinking that someone had stolen this garment, then losing her nerve, dumped it. She had an overwhelming desire to plant the package on the counter and hurry away.

"It's mine," said Marnie, reappearing, smiling at Hellen's foolishness. "What a goose you are. It's a new night dress. I came to show you, but you were so absorbed in your book buying, I dropped it in the basket then went off again without disturbing you."

Hellen had the same feeling now, of being mistakenly in possession of someone else's goods.

"Put it on," said George, impatient now.

She slipped it on her finger. The sun caught the perfect little diamonds. The ruby glowed. The white flash came then the black, and the green. It was alive with light. She was mesmerised by it. Frightened by it.

241

"Made for you," said George, running a forefinger across his small moustache, showing his white teeth in a smile.

"Thank you, George," she said. "It's very beautiful. None of the women I know have a—such a—" Recognising a note of protest in her voice, she stopped.

"Bully for you," said George, sounding aggressive. "You'll be able to cock a snoot."

She knew then the ring was his answer to those with homes on The Peak.

In the morning, after George had gone to work, she wrapped the ring in paper, made a little slit in the stitching of her mattress, and hid it in the kapok. Each evening, immediately before he was due to return, she took it out and put it on her finger. One day when she was shopping with Ruth, she asked, though without hope, if precious coloured stones were easy to come by in the colony. If they were perhaps inexpensive because of being mined in the East.

"I don't think so. Certainly there's more choice. Much more choice. Why do you ask, dear?"

"George wants to buy me a ring."

Ruth shrugged. "It depends on the stone, I suppose. What were you thinking of?"

"A ruby . . . perhaps."

"You've plenty of scope, there. You would be able to get a pretty stone well within George's means. You don't have to have a Burma ruby, do you?" Ruth asked, laughing at the thought. "But the setting can make all the difference, and Chinese workmanship is superb. You can get away with a very modest stone, if the setting is good. But why not let George choose it, dear? He knows how much he can afford."

Hellen could only think that asking Ruth had been a mistake. She lay awake that night staring at the ceiling, worrying about the fact that Ruth knew, probably everyone knew, George's salary did not run to a Burma ruby. In the early hours she had an almost uncontrollable desire to dress, go down to the harbour, and throw it in the water, as she had thrown her wedding ring off the peak at Lantau.

Drifting off to sleep, her heel slipped over a dream cliff. She floundered and was wide awake again, breathless with shock. She was afraid to go off again, in case the cliff was still there, waiting for her. Old worries surfaced. Captain Boggis had not wanted George and herself aboard *Bangkok Lady*, yet he had given up his cabin for them. She thought about George's unlikely friendship with that rough seaman, Charlie Marsh. Once, coming home, she thought she saw Charlie Marsh limping out of Minden Row, heading in the direction

242

of the go-downs in Canton Road that ran behind the docks.

She wakened knowing that she had to face George. She would approach the questions systematically, one by one.

Charlie Marsh.

Their large house.

The ruby.

One, two, three, in that order.

That evening the shark's fin soup came and went. They had soup at the beginning of the meal now. She was ready to broach her problems when Ah Wong left the room, but he came back quickly, forestalling her.

"Missie like pigeon?"

"Missie like everything," said George, answering for her, looking pleased with himself, glancing across the table at the beautiful blood red ruby ring. Ah Wong told them a long story about how he had beaten down Goko Jai for the most delicious mangoes Missie and Master had ever eaten. Missie and Master would be amazed. George, in benevolent mood, teased him, saying he must be the terror of the market place.

Ah Wong brought the mangoes and placed them on the sideboard. Hellen joined in the banter, relieved at not finding an opening, worrying about not finding it. The mangoes were so lush that the cook boy had to bring in a second set of hot damp towels to wipe up the juice. It dribbled down from their mouths, over their hands and up to their wrists.

"Well done, Ah Wong," said George, sitting back in his chair. "Worth getting half drowned."

Ah Wong left the room looking, in his impassive way, very well pleased with himself. As he went out of the door George tossed his towel down on the table. "Why are you staring at me?" he asked disagreeably.

Hellen jumped. "I'm sorry. I didn't realise."

"You've been staring all evening. Got something on your mind?"

"Yes," said Hellen, meeting his eyes with outward calm, though her heart was beating very fast, "I was wondering where you go in the evenings."

George's face closed. He pushed back his chair so that only his hands and wrists lay on the table, arms extended. He shuffled his napkin ring back and forth on the white, white cloth. Ah Saw, with her coarse bars of soap, cold water and flat iron, did a wonderful job with linen. He cleared his throat. "I wondered how long it would take you to acquire an interest in my affairs," he said. He gazed absorbedly at the napkin ring, as though it was new, or intricately marked, which it was not.

"You mean, you would have liked me to acquire an interest before? Is that what you mean?"

"I should think your average wife would have been curious." He spoke as though he had been hurt by her lack of interest.

"I thought it was none of my business. I thought that was what you would say, if I asked. That it was none of my business." She glanced up nervously, rose and went to the door leading into the passage. She closed it firmly and returned to the table. "In the beginning," she said, "I assumed you were going to your concubine."

"I haven't got one." He spoke with soft violence. "I told you that was impossible, now."

"So where do you go?"

"I have some private business."

"What kind of private business?"

His eyes were lidded. He turned the napkin ring on its edge, then back on to its side. He rolled it with one finger, watching it closely, as though performing an intricate trick. She suddenly decided that if he did not explain his private business she would return the ring to him. She hoped he would not explain. "Do you want to tell me?" she asked.

As though he shrewdly recognised the fact that she was delivering an ultimatum, he raised those hooded eyes and said mildly, "Import."

"What do you import?" She willed him to say he imported precious stones.

But it was not precious stones. It was This and That. "And by the way," he added, "Lonewood & Southby aren't very keen on their chaps doing a bit on the side, so I wouldn't want you to spread it round your tea parties." He flipped the napkin ring into the air, tossed it from hand to hand. "In the east," he continued, "more or less anything goes, so long as you're careful. The fault lies only in getting caught."

"I don't much like the idea of your doing something illegal," she said.

"I told you," flared George in one of those quick change of mood she had come to know so well, "it's perfectly all right. You don't much like being married to me," he added. "That's the truth of it." He turned on her a very intent look. "What makes you suddenly so curious?"

"This ring." She lifted her hand from her knee and placed it on the table. "I think it's very valuable. I don't know what you earn, but I got the impression—"

"Got the impression, did you?" He leaned across the table, his eyes

244

full of displeasure. "And just how did you get the impression? You're living in damn' sight better circumstances than most people of your age. Better than your farmhand brother, I'll be bound. Better than your tenant farmer father."

There was a waiting pause.

It was a moment to explain that silly outburst made in the presence of his mother so shortly after he had raped her. She still saw it as rape, not thinking of herself as his wife, who could be raped by law with impunity. But explaining meant telling him all about Oliver and herself, Lady Sylvia and the county set. The story of her life, to which George had no right, because she was only his wife by virtue of a forced signature on a dotted line. She was clearer in her mind about that now. Hemmed in by Boggis and Charlie Marsh and George, in the middle of the South China Sea, she knew now, with certainty, she could not have refused to sign.

"We're not on The Peak admittedly," George began again, indicating with a quick little sigh of impatience that he was tired of waiting for her to reply, "but whose fault is that? You're the one with influence at Government House. So where did you get this impression of yours? This impression about my job."

"Please, George."

"All right. If you want to know, I picked up that stone donkeys years ago when I was on holiday in Burma. I didn't pay all that much for it. Burma rubies, especially if you found them up country, were two a penny at the time. A lot of old dames in Hong Kong have big stones like that. Those who've lived in India or Burma."

"Two a penny?" She frowned.

"You know what I mean."

She wished she did. She looked down at the ring on her finger, wondering if it had graced Kitty Burtenshaw's hand for a while, and if not, why not? Kitty had, after all, been his fiancée, as she had not. Then it occurred to her that maybe George had a collection of precious stones for which, donkeys years ago, as he said, he had not paid all that much. "Have you any more?" she asked. "Tucked away, I mean?"

"Sorry. That's our fortune. You'll have to be content with it."

She hated the way he had of turning the tables on her, twisting her words, pretending he misread them. She could only hope that the ruby had come back from Kitty Burtenshaw. People would recognise it, if that were so, and there would be sly innuendoes, but better that than finding another explanation. And if Kitty and her parents accepted that George could afford such a ring. . . .

She remembered, then, that Kitty had run away.

Chapter 23

Opium

The next morning brought the invitation to the ball at Government house. George fingered the gilt-edged card, his cheeks reddening with pleasure.

"Well!" he said. He took a long breath and turned to Hellen, smiling. It was as though the smile filled the room. "I think it would be a graceful gesture if you were to wear your pearls," he said.

"I will wear my best jewellery, of course." Hellen was thinking of the diamond necklace. She would have liked to tell him about the diamonds. He might be pleased. He might feel they gave him, as her consort, social cachet. On the other hand, she felt he would guess they were intended specifically to be worn at her marriage.

"By the way," he said, "I think we should talk about this wedding—"

"It's nothing to do with you, George."

He tapped an impatient forefinger on the invitation. "I'm talking about the fact that breaking off the engagement wasn't a mutual decision. And yet, you're getting this treatment." He again tapped the card. "Is there something I ought to know?"

"Everyone who signs the book gets an invitation," hedged Hellen. "Your parents did, when they came down from Shanghai." She took the invitation from him, placing it beside the gold-faced clock on the mantel.

"Only to a—I s'pose you'd call it a reception."

She smiled tautly. "P'raps they've changed their policy."

George came towards her, walking slowly. Placing a hand on either shoulder, he bent and kissed her on the cheek. Involuntarily, though she did not mean to, for it was clear he was showing gratitude, she stiffened. He turned and left the room.

Marcia Curtain came to Minden Row with the express intention of asking Hellen outright if she needed help with her dress for the ball.

"I'm sure you understand it will be a very grand affair," she said diffidently. "Neil and I would like you to look nice, dear. If there's anything we can do to help, please don't hesitate to ask."

Hellen smiled at her, nervously. "That's very kind of you, but I had a number of evening dresses made for the boat trip. I knew there would be dancing every night."

"But wouldn't you like a new dress, dear? I hardly like to say this to you, but if you have danced every night in. . . ."

"No, really. It's very kind of you." Hellen felt discomfited by Marcia's insistent kindness.

"So long as you're sure, dear. Neil and I, as you know, live thriftily. We're quite able to help you."

"Thank you," Hellen said again. And again, "You're very kind."

Marcia began to turn away, a good-natured, large woman, inexplicably rebuffed. "You'll wear the pearls George gave you?" she asked uncertainly.

"I expect I will." The words were meant to be friendly, but they sounded, even to Hellen's ears, unintentionally patronising. They hung in the air between them, pushing them apart. In a nervous effort to make amends, she added, "I've several pieces of jewellery. It depends on what looks best with the frock. Do stay to tea. I'll get Ah Wong to bring it out into the garden. It's nice today. Not too hot." She gestured towards the French windows. "Do go on ahead. I'll speak to Ah Wong." She could have tinkled the bell, but she wanted to give her mother-in-law a moment or two to settle down. It occurred to her then that Marcia would know the ruby if George had—donkeys years ago—brought it back from Burma where rubies were two a penny. And Hellen would know from her air of embarrassment if it had formerly graced the hand of Kitty Burtenshaw.

She hurried into the kitchen. Ah Wong was seated on a stool beating eggs with two bamboo chop sticks held apart by the forefinger of his right hand. The air was full of the smell of burning joss sticks which she sometimes suspected were used to camouflage the pungent smell of opium. A plate of wunton, the pork dumplings at which Ah Wong excelled, stood on a shelf, and a bowl of pineapple buns.

She gestured towards them. "Fetchee char." At such moments she forgot her newly acquired Cantonese.

She ran upstairs, took the ring from its hiding place, and slipped it on her finger. Yes, she thought, she was going to be embarrassed in public if this had been Kitty Burtenshaw's ring.

Marcia seated herself on a bamboo chair in the partial shade of the bauhinia tree, feet inelegantly apart, her cotton dress sagging into a basin between her large knees. She stared down at the grass between her feet, feeling distressed. She had so looked forward to having a daughter-in-law whom she could help, and in whom she might confide. She puzzled as to how she could tactfully convince this awkward girl that the women guests would judge her on her clothes. That those with very little to do, except gossip, could be very cruel.

Hellen arrived back as Ah Wong was setting out the tea. Marcia saw the ring and her eyes bulged. Suddenly, everything fell into place. The packing case, the enormous trunk. She had known girls to come East with the fishing fleet, confidently bringing their trousseau with them, cheeky things, but she had never heard of anyone bringing her own engagement ring. Besides, she did not see Hellen as a member of the fishing fleet. There was nothing predatory about her. In the ring, she decided, was the answer. Hellen must have been going to Singapore to marry another man. The engagement had been broken and the dishonest creature had kept his magnificent, most valuable ring.

"George calls it my late engagement ring," Hellen said.

Marcia looked coldly down at the beautiful jewel, knowing George had not bought it.

When it seemed her mother-in-law was never going to speak, Hellen said deliberately, "He got the ruby up-country in Burma. They're two a penny there."

Marcia found her tongue. "No, dear," she said, the words squeezing out of her like lemon pips. "Rubies like that are not two a penny anywhere." That was telling the minx.

Hellen put the teapot down. At that moment she had an overwhelming desire to confide in Marcia and ask for help, but her mother-in-law was looking at her as though she hated her.

On the morning of the ball Hellen retrieved her diamond necklace from the vaults of the Hong Kong and Shanghai bank, and carried it back to Tsim Sha Tsui. There were emerald cut diamonds in the centre, stepped one against another like matchsticks. The rose cut diamonds were attached individually to the chain. They sparkled up at her in the shaded light. She looked down at them with tears in her eyes.

She did not think of George that evening as she stood before the looking glass surveying herself in the elegant crêpe-de-chine gown that had been designed and made especially for the pre-wedding reception at Government House, where she was to have met all those who mattered in the colony.

Only Oliver mattered in the colony. The dress had been made for him.

The door opened. George came into the room and stood looking down at the necklace. His stillness was intense, but unstable.

"Are they real?"

"It was a gift from my grandfather."

"A wedding gift?"

She hesitated. "If you like."

"Take it off," said George.

She lifted her head and quite fearlessly met his eyes. "You have no right to ask me to take it off."

"So that was what you had up your sleeve, you devious bitch. Take it off and put on the pearls."

"This necklace is suitable for the occasion," she said.

"I'm surprised you're not going the whole hog and wearing the bridal gown, which I presume is tucked away somewhere."

Hellen went to the window and stood gazing steadily out, seeing nothing.

"I asked you to take that necklace off," said George.

"No." There was something quite terrifying in the thought of making an enemy of George. But she was not going to give in. She was dressed for Oliver. She became a hollow ice form, with an engine beating remorselessly in her breast.

"As my wife, you shall not go to Government House decked out like bloody Oliver Marathon's bride," George said. "I know your sinister little game. You got off at Singapore because he threw you over. And so you married me. I fell for that one, did—I—not! Hook, line and sinker," said George, as though he had played a purely acquiescent part. "Now, you think you're going to flaunt yourself in front of him to show him what he missed. I've got news for you, Mrs bloody Curtain. You're going to take those diamonds off, and if you don't do it toot sweet, I'll make you change that dress as well. And by the way, where is the ring I gave you?"

"I don't wish to wear it."

"No," said George heavily, "of course you don't. It's not part of the picture, is it? I've got further news for you. You are going to wear it. Get it out or I'll rip that dress off your back, and the necklace too."

Suddenly she knew she had a card to play. She lifted the bed cover, reached into the hole in the mattress, and in silence brought out the package containing the ring.

George said rudely, "I thought stuffing valuables in mattresses was strictly for senile old ladies. You've come to it early. Now, put it on your finger. And take the necklace off, and put on the pearls."

Accidentally, she was sure, it was accidental, she dropped the ring on the floor.

249

He took a step towards her. She held up her hand and he stopped. She was not surprised that he stopped, for at that moment the strength in her was greater by far than George's bullying anger. She said, "If you touch this necklace, I will set about finding out what it is you import that allows you to buy Burma rubies."

"Opium," said George.

She realised then that she had known all the time. Nonetheless, she gasped.

"I thought that would ruin your evening," George told her with cold malice.

"You blackmailed Captain Boggis. Charlie Marsh and you, between you, got the opium off *Bangkok Lady*. That ring was bought with the money you made."

"With some of the money," he corrected her. He came a step closer. "You're an astute baggage, aren't you?"

"Don't you realise everyone knows your job doesn't run to that kind of ring?"

He fingered his moustache, looking suddenly sly. She had never seen George looking sly before. It made her feel cold. "They'll think you bought it yourself. A girl who owns that kind of necklace," he indicated the diamonds with a flick of his fingers, "come to think of it, could easily have bought her own ring. Yes, do wear the necklace," he said. "Poor George!" he continued, derisive now. "Captured by a member of the fishing fleet who came with her own ring as well as her trousseau. At least they'll say he did very well for himself. Now, pick up that ring and put it on your finger."

She stayed where she was.

"Remember what I said I would do to your dress," said George softly.

She went down on her knees and picked up the ring. She put it on the third finger of her left hand.

"That's a good girl," said George. "Did you not know this entire colony was founded on the sale of opium?" Hellen did not reply. "The original wealth of the great hongs came from forcing opium on the Chinese at gunpoint. Is it my fault they have a taste for it? Back in 1845 three-quarters of the Indian opium crop passed through this harbour, much of it in P & O ships. Don't you know most of those mansions up on The Peak were built on poppies? I can't imagine what anyone here has to be holy about."

"It's now illegal." She looked down at the ruby with loathing and fear.

"Listen to me," said George. "There are seventy retail shops in Hong Kong selling government opium under licence at fourteen dollars fifty a tael. It's still our precious government's greatest source of revenue. Only the rich can afford it at that price. I sell it to the poor, at a very reasonable price. That's what's illegal—making bearable the miserable lives of those rickshaw coolies you're so sorry for. Opium to the Chinese is no more than a relaxation," George went on. "A whisky or gin to the rich. A pint of beer to the working man. At the end of a day's work, the Chinese coolie needs his puff or two on the old hookah. I do more for the poor than the missionaries." He flicked back the long tails of his coat, put his hands on his hips, and looked down at her with a confident, cold smile. "Get that, Miss Virtuous. More than the missionaries."

"I've seen them dying in the streets," she spat at him.

"That's their problem," returned George hard-heartedly, "if they want to indulge themselves to excess."

There was a sound of light, shuffling footsteps and they swung round, both of them disconcerted. "Number two Missie Master come see," announced Ah Wong, standing in the doorway in his white coat and black trousers and little cloth slippers, his impassive face giving away nothing of his feelings at this astonishing sight of Missie looking like the great Empress herself. George nodded and he went away.

Then Marcia called from the stairs, "I hope you two don't mind our coming to see you off."

Hellen picked up her beaded bag, walked past George and out of the door. She went down the stairs with her head held high. She was going to see Oliver this evening. Think of that. Concentrate on that. Don't think of anything else.

Neil said mildly, "It's really not our affair, my dear. And George needs this particular kind of triumph. He desperately needs a wife with the right connections. And she has got the right connections, no doubt about it. People don't get invited to a ball at Government House simply by virtue of signing the book. Didn't she look wonderful?" He picked at a leaf hanging low over the path, flicked it away with his fingers. "It's lucky you thought better of suggesting we help her with her dress."

Marcia had forborn to tell him about the rebuff she had suffered from Hellen. She seldom told Neil about matters that hurt her. She thought him insensitive because he took life as it came, and expected her to do likewise. When she remembered how she had offered to help fit Hellen out she went hot and cold with embarrassment. "There's something I haven't told you," she said, and repeated Hellen's outburst on that first day at Nathan Road.

"Her brother a farmhand! Her father a tenant farmer!" Neil repeated in disbelief. "Oh, come."

"Then why did she say it?" Marcia asked defensively.

He pondered the matter, his expression quizzical.

"I didn't imagine it. That was what she said. Please walk more slowly, dear. It's dreadfully hot." Marcia lumbered to a stop, took a handkerchief from her pocket and wiped her brow.

Neil shrugged. "That was a bad day. Who knows what they had both been through. I should forget it, if I were you. Forget about the ring, too." They were turning into Nathan Road. It was pitch dark now beneath the banyan trees. Neil steered her into the middle of the road. "George must have agreed to use the story. She wouldn't tell you he had bought the ring if she wasn't expecting him to back her up. The chap, as you say, is presumably in Singapore. I must say, though, from what I know of Hellen, she doesn't seem the kind of girl who would do a bunk with George and the ring. Of course I know it's been done before, but it doesn't seem the kind of thing Hellen would do."

"You can't read people like that," said Marcia. "I wish you could."

George has done very well for himself," said Neil. "Concentrate on the credits. Now that we know who pays for the house, and who bought those carpets and curtains and the china and silver, I feel a lot more easy in my mind about him."

Marcia's skin began to prickle as it always did when they spoke about the side of George they did not know. "You mean, she pays?"

"Who else? I thought an intelligent woman like you would have worked that out. George never saved anything. His trip to England chasing that wretched little girl must have taken everything he had. Let sleeping dogs lie, I say."

Marcia was vexed with herself for not having realised Hellen was paying for that big house, but she was mollified by the fact that Neil had called her an intelligent woman.

"Next year, we'll probably have a grandchild and it'll be all water under the bridge." Neil slipped an arm through hers.

A grandchild! that could change everything. Life could begin again.

Chapter 24

The Ball

The squat white structure of Government House had been transformed into a crystalline fairy palace. A gaudy paper dragon danced among the trees, capering sideways, bounding high on fifty pairs of brown legs. Its red-painted jaws grinned gleefully beneath eyes popping over hidden lanterns: Chinese musicians dressed in shrieking reds and yellows sounded drums, gongs, pipes, and flutes. High above the rooftops an orange moon nestled in the Nine Dragon Hills beyond Kowloon.

Hellen, dismounting with George from the sedan chair along with the other guests from the Washington dinner party, was enchanted and awed. Behind her enormous, ostrich feather fan, Ruth gave her a sideways look. What a silly girl! When one thought all this could have been for her, it was hard to believe she had tossed it away for George Curtain. Well, she had, and that was that. Ruth tucked her right hand through Major Tandy's arm.

Already the big entrance hall was awash with men, the army officers resplendent in scarlet, the navy spruce in white. They milled up and down watching the entrance eagle-eyed, their prey the single girls. With two hundred male guests and a hundred women, one had to be ready to pounce. Oliver milled among them tossing a friendly word here, a smile there. He saw Ruth's party approaching, Ruth and Major Tandy leading, and Hellen coming behind them. He did not see George, though he stood tall, in that impressive way he had of standing that made people notice him. For Oliver, he did not exist. He moved swiftly through the vestibule to take his stand at the top of the flight of steps.

Outwardly calm.

Hellen came forward with her head held high, her gown, silver and blue, swirling and eddying from her hips. She began to ascend the steps. Some power within Oliver, beyond his control, moved him forward. He raised a hand in greeting, encompassing the party in a warm, Vice Regal welcome. Then, with his inbred courtesy and sense of occasion, he managed without offence to by-pass Ruth and Harry Tandy.

George said loudly, "Good evening, Oliver."

Hellen sensed something, transient as a shadow, between them. Then Oliver replied, "Nice to see you, George," and softly, "Hello, Hellen." Now she was close up against him where she could touch him, if she dared. Now, she was where she belonged. He looked into her eyes, expectantly enormous, smoky grey, black-fringed, and soft with love. Then, with Oliver walking at Hellen's side, with Hellen at George's side, they followed, moving through the throng beneath the glittering chandelier in the pillared hall.

Ruth and the Major, safely hemmed in by the crowd, exchanged glazed looks. What fools young people are! thought Tandy, and Ruth felt an uprush of wicked excitement. She loved human error, for it was the food of gossip. Oliver's hand brushed Hellen's and her fingers automatically curled round his, then nervously released them.

"How did your dinner party go?" he asked.

Somebody said, "You should have been there. It was fun."

He grimaced. "I had a dowager on one side and a visiting admiral on the other. Why do important guests have to be so jolly old?"

Hellen's eyes shimmered up at Oliver. She felt no constriction because of George's presence at her side. The faceless crowd flowed beside them. As on another level, she heard the staccato rap of laughter and swift, meaningless chatter. She might have been in the midst of a flock of disturbed birds.

Ruth's dinner guests, excited by the novelty of this special treatment, walked with pride. Wanda Ayre, in answer to a startled question, whispered behind her fan that Hellen knew Oliver at home. "She exercises Sir Rowan's horses." Wanda was exultant that her husband's innocently good-natured offer to introduce Hellen to Happy Valley had brought this splendid reward. "Poor Toby has no end of trouble keeping up on his cob."

Overhearing, Oliver flinched. He knew full well how such a comment could jump like a frog through the crowd. People derived a spurious kick from Vice Regal tattle. He ignored George's startled glare, turned first on him, then on Hellen. In the east wing they entered a flower-filled passage that ended outside the ballroom in a little flight of carpeted steps where the Governor and his lady stood.

Sir Rowan, in spite of looking endearingly like Oliver, was the most impressive human being Hellen had ever seen. Behind him, on a pillar, stood a magnificent bowl of arranged flowers, somehow giving

254

him an air of unreality, as though he was more a painting than a man. She could not take her eyes off him.

They moved forward. The aide who had been announcing the guests' names, glanced questioningly at Oliver. He shook his head and they were allowed to pass. As Oliver introduced Hellen her heart began flailing unmercifully against the wall of her chest. It was as though they were alone, she and this handsome, formidable statue of a man—he was a statue now, rather than a picture, for he had gained strength and power in greeting her. And he had shed the Oliver look.

Totally.

He was His Majesty King George's plenipotentary, greatly esteemed on his high pinnacle, with the ribbon of the K.C.M.G. round his neck, and his chest magnificently decorated with tiny rainbow orders. With the confidance of greatness thrust upon him, and eminence achieved, he was addressing her.

"Mrs Curtain." His eyes roved over her face, but more than that. He was looking intrusively right into her brain, reading all about her love for Oliver as he held her hand. His own fingers were cool and very, very firm. There was no question of withdrawing. Not until he wished to release her. He had her soul, and with courtesy and charm he was saying things he did not mean, though what they were she never afterwards remembered.

Lady Marathon, looking faintly formidable in this official setting, said she hoped she and Hellen would have an opportunity to chat. She spoke as though they had not had tea together. They were miraculously released to move on.

"Mrs Wash-ing-ton," bellowed the aide, returning to the job in hand. "Major Tandy."

Hellen stumbled, and Oliver grasped her hand, squeezing it, winding his love into a protective scarf around her heart. The world came right again.

In the ballroom, where hundreds of candles flickered in crystal chandeliers below a ceiling richly decorated with ornamental plasterwork, the band was playing the latest tune to hit the colony, "Let The Rest Of The World Go By". Guests stood around in groups, chatting. A woman, idly glancing their way, saw Oliver's hand in Hellen's and her startled eyes lifted to Hellen's face. Oliver released the hand. The woman leaned towards her husband, whispering.

Oliver said, "Your programme, Hellen, please, before the other chaps get to it." To George, "You've got to share her. The men are two to one."

George made no sign that he had heard.

255

Hellen delved into her bag. "I'm co-opted as an extra aide at times like this," Oliver said to George.

George, prickly as a hedgehog beneath the confident exterior, muttered under his breath as Oliver took the programme and wrote his name, "Patronising bastard." Surprised expressions seen on the faces of people who knew him had set his nerves on edge. One loud-voiced tick had said, "Look! There's George Curtain," and there had been a telling whisper in reply, "It's his wife. She's in." Yes, everyone who was here was in. Had been in while he was out. Well, he was in now, and they could stuff their surprise.

"I've got to go,' said Oliver, "before my uncle with his eagle eye catches me attending to matters not strictly in the line of duty." Handing the programme back, he surreptitiously squeezed Hellen's hand. Ruth saw, and felt again that uprush of excitement. What fools! What fools! "I've got all the secretaries," Oliver went on, as though quite unaware of George's vengeful eyes. "Defence Secretary, Colonial Secretary, Secretary of Chinese affairs, and all their middle-aged wives. Registrar of the Supreme Court. Chief Justice. Elderly wives." With the Marathon ease and confidence, he was laughing at himself for being what he called a dogsbody.

Hellen's eyes shimmered and her mouth trembled. It did not occur to her that they were playing with fire. She was intoxicated, enchanted, outside the realms of real life where people were punished for loving.

George asked, "What's the matter?" Hellen was looking forlornly at her programme, wondering why Oliver had signed for only two dances. His eyes followed hers, puzzled. Then Major Tandy moved forward saying, "Can an old buffer claim one dance, my dear?" and tentatively held out his hand for her programme.

"Of course."

He said kindly, "Please feel free to cross me off, I'm sure you're going to be very rushed, but I would like a dance if you can spare one."

Then a man with deceptively sleepy eyelids and a shock of hair materialised before her. "You won't remember me," he said. "I met you when you came to sign the book. I'm Peter Ackroyd, H.E.'s secretary. May I claim a dance?"

"Of course I remember." She did not. On that tense afternoon she had been aware only of someone courteously checking the nib of the pen, dipping it in the ink well and then Lady Marathon had appeared, scattering her wits. "Yes, please do," she said, offering him her programme.

At her side, George shuffled his feet impatiently. He said in a voice that was carefully goodnatured, but with annoyance throbbing through, "I presume I'm to be given the first dance?"

"Of course."

"Finished, Ackroyd?" George gestured impatiently.

As he returned the card, Peter Ackroyd gave George a straight look, then he disappeared into the throng by the big windows where fans whirled over tubs packed with ice, and a group of Asian girls, impeccably coiffed, glossy as plumed birds in brilliant cheongsams split to the knee, were shyly giving up their programmes to a jostling crowd of Englishmen. In the forefront was Lin Yan, demurely smiling, as her programme was snatched from hand to hand. Hellen waved her fan, and she smiled back.

"Who's that Chink?" asked George, then he saw it was Lin Yan and did a double take. "How d'you know her?"

'I met her,' said Hellen, "somewhere."

George thought as he fished the white glove out of his pocket, that she could have only met Lin Yan through Oliver. Let it pass, though. Let it pass for the moment. He remarked distastefully as he pulled on the glove, I'm surprised to see so many Chinks here."

Hellen stiffened. "It's their country."

"Oh no, my dear, it's not." They moved on to the floor. "It's ours. They're here by courtesy of us. When we came in Hong Kong was a barren rock with a few fishermen's shacks. So what's this about riding with Marathon?"

The band was playing Irving Berlin's "Nobody Knows". Hellen was surprised to find George so light on his feet. "One day when Toby and I were going out, Oliver turned up to exercise his uncle's race horses. As he has two, I begged him. . . ."

"Begged him, did you?" asked George. "I got the impression you were rather taken with the ponies."

"So I was. But—"

"Do go on," he said saracastically.

"Don't spoil my evening, George. If you're offered a race horse, you don't turn it down for a Mongolian pony."

"No," agreed George, "I don't suppose you do." He was feeling savage about the way things had turned out. He'd been thinking of himself as having made it. The new George Curtain. Now it seemed he was merely trailing only in his wife's wake.

Why? In the circumstances that she had ditched Marathon, why? Bloody why? George's curiosity was fuelled by fear. He was well aware that the machinations he had employed at Singapore would not go down well in Government House circles. Now that the marriage was proving such a disaster, he could see that if Hellen let the story

257

out, what he had done would be seen, at the very least, as a pretty low trick. At the most? Criminal.

What particularly frightened George was that whatever was going on behind his back appeared to bear the stamp of H.E.'s approval. He tightend his gloved hand, pressing cruelly with his fingers against Hellen's spine.

Through the huge windows Hellen could see umbrella trees hung with fairy lanterns, with slatted seats beneath, ready-made for lovers to whisper together. Where was Oliver? Beyond the garden, on the black pitch of sea, ships lay at anchor flaunting their outlines in strings of winking lights. The tune changed to "Chong, He Came From Hong Kong". Their footsteps quickened.

"George, you're pressing too hard. You're hurting me."

He relaxed his fingers. "Doesn't it strike you as odd, Mrs Curtain, that your husband didn't even know you'd met H.E.?"

She glanced round swiftly to ensure George had not been overheard. "I met him tonight for the first time."

"How come you're riding his horses, then?"

"George, please! We're here to enjoy ourselves."

"Are we? Is that what we're here for?" The music stopped and he pushed her away a little, looking down at her, demanding an answer, bullying her with his waiting silence.

She turned her head so that she did not have to look at him. A man standing close by said affably, "Hello, George. May I claim a dance with your lovely wife?"

George shrugged.

"He's not going to introduce us," said the man, not minding about George's rudeness. "My name is Don Coleman."

"Mine is Hellen." Grateful for the interruption, Hellen fished the programme out of her bag.

"He's a bit of a dark horse," said Coleman good-humouredly, flicking the silk tassel on the pencil George's way, managing with the same gesture both to excuse and dismiss him. Men came in from all sides, claiming acquaintanceship with George, asking to be introduced, filling Hellen's programme with their names. George grew more and more edgy.

The Governor and his lady took to the floor. His two aides, released, sped across the room, introduced themselves and pencilled in their names near the bottom of the list. Roger Cadman. Jack Lovell. "When, hopefully, our official duties will be over," Lovell said.

George led Hellen away from the centre of the floor. He was getting thoroughly fed up. The wary glance, the careful avoidance of the scar where his ear had been, the brief, "Hello George," from men he had known for years, before their fatuous faces split into smiles for Hellen. He knew jolly well what they were saying behind his back. Something a damn sight more stringy than the jovial, "He's a dark horse," that had been Coleman's public comment. More likely in private it was, "What's George Curtain doing with a rich girl in a bloody great diamond necklace? And a friend of the Marathons to boot?"

He relinquished Hellen to one of the men who did not want to talk to him, and went off, without much hope, to see if any of the Chinks had a dance to spare. Even as he approached they were being snatched away. But the very last one was still standing. He dived, and was beaten to the post by a cocky little major with a perspiring face as red as his bum-freezer jacket. George moved off holding his head high, pretending it hadn't happened.

The next dance was Oliver's. Hellen felt a glow begin deep down inside her and spread through her whole body. Then the crowd parted and Sir Rowan was standing before her. His appearance was so sudden that she remained stock still, expressionless, like a child uncertain of what the grown-ups expected.

"Ah!" he said, "Mrs Curtain," and then, while her mind skittered alarmingly, he was asking to see her programme. "Perhaps you would be good enough to spare me a dance?" She recognised his question as an order.

She fished once more in her bag and produced the card, standing mutely while he looked down the full list, sending up a little Thank You to God because the card was full.

"I'll have the next one," he said, pointing, "if I may. My nephew won't mind."

My nephew won't mind. My nephew won't mind. A great wave of despair enveloped her. The governor's eyes roved over her, reading the misery behind her glassy smile, not caring. Then the aide called Roger Cadman, with a dead pan expression, scored out Oliver's name and their host moved, leaving her standing like stone, stranded, in a crowd of whispering, laughing, chattering revellers.

"I say, you are favoured, my dear," said Mrs Harrison-Lowe archly.

They all smiled, with immense warmth. She was no longer that odd girl who lived over Kowloon way, but someone with whom to be on quite intimate terms.

"She's a friend of the family."

"She rides his horses."

She seemed to hear it being shouted all over the room that she rode the Governor's horses. She was the cynosure of all eyes. She was dying inside. She wanted to rush screaming into the garden with Oliver at her side and hold him close in the moon shade of a blossom tree as they had held each other that night, so many years ago it seemed, at horrible Lady Sylvia Ashton's dance in Kent.

When Oliver came to claim her the grey eyes were almost colourless behind a film of tears. Innocently, he extended his arms. Then the aide appeared from nowhere, and laughingly, with the intimacy of good chums, he pushed Oliver's arms down to his sides. "Sorry, old chap. This is your uncle's dance."

"The hell it is." Oliver's head came up. The blue eyes blazed.

Hellen mutely held out her programme, showing the line scored through his name.

He stared at it, his face white with fury, but all he said was, "I'll escort her, Cadman," and Roger, who had become Cadman, stood back while Oliver slipped an arm through hers. Holding it very close to his side, his fingers recklessly entwined in hers, he led her to where Sir Rowan was standing with his lady.

"You don't mind, do you, Oliver?" his uncle asked, avuncular, benign.

"I do," said Oliver, releasing Hellen's arm and backing stiffly away.

The pain in his face, the bewilderment and hurt, cut Lettice to shreds. She held out her arms. "Dance with me, dear." Without waiting for acceptance, she moved close. As they waltzed away, Oliver said, outraged, "He ordered me to book only two dances. Ordered me! He treated her as though she was Asian! Two dances, he said. And then he takes one. Is he going to take the other, Aunt Lettice? Tell me that. Is he?"

"Hush, dear. People will overhear. You know your uncle. He has his own way of doing things. Be careful not to provoke him. He overheard someone say you ride with Hellen. You have been very indiscreet."

He whirled her savagely through the throng. He could not speak, he was so angry. He kept looking across the big room, pinpointing that distinguished dark head among a host of other heads, and close by the ear on the side of that distinguished head, the shining cap of dark hair which was all he could see of Hellen. "What's he saying to her?" Oliver asked when he could trust himself to speak again. "Is he warning her off? Is that what he's set out to do? Warn her off?"

"You know he wouldn't do that, dear."

"I don't know anything, Aunt Lettice, except that I have to—"

"Hush, dear," she said sharply, glancing round, smiling at her guests who smiled back at her, pleased to be noticed by the First

Lady, innocently pretending they did not wish to listen to a private conversation.

Over by the window Marian Keane, wife of the taipan of Lonewood and Southby, said to her husband, "Did George Curtain introduce you to his wife?"

"He did."

"What do you make of that?" Her husband recognised "that" meant the whole situation, not the girl. The beautiful, expensive gown. The diamonds. The ruby glowing on the third finger of her left hand.

"What can one make of it?" Elliott Keane shrugged. "He's done very well for himself. I'd heard he had. I'm surprised she's so good-looking. I should have thought a girl with her obvious advantages could have done better. But then, as I always say, there's nothing so funny as people." He looked faintly wry. "Perhaps there's more to George Curtain than meets the eye."

Raising her painted fan to her face, Marian murmured behind it so that she could not be overheard, "People are saying she bought her own engagement ring."

"George didn't buy it, that's certain. Not on what we pay him."

Ruth had been puzzling all evening about the ring. She resolved not to ask questions. There was no doubt, for a nice girl, Hellen was an odd creature in some ways.

H.E. was not a smooth dancer. Given the bagpipes playing a Scottish reel and he'd be away, kicking up his legs with the best of them, kilt and sporran flying. But ballroom dancing! He had a healthy suspicion of men who slid round the floor hanging over their partners, mauling them. He thought it pretty undignified stuff.

Sir Rowan's idea of a decent, self-respecting Englishman, was the man he himself represented. A good tennis player, for a start. He had built two courts at Upper Albert Road. As a young cadet in the Colonial Service, stationed at Singapore, he had gone on from the rudimentary lessons begun at Eton and reached damn' near perfection in the art of fencing. He rode well and played golf to a very respectable handicap of five, though, to be honest, six was nearer the mark. When he was stationed in Berlin, just before the balloon went up in 1914, he had distinguished himself as wing forward in a rugby team the embassy put together. But ballroom dancing? One got on with it.

"You seem to be no worse for your misadventure, Mrs Curtain. Sorry, did I bump your foot?"

"No, really. Yes, I have recovered."

"Piracy is something we have to live with out here, I'm afraid. If you go up to Canton, or across to Macau, be sure you leave your jewellery at home." H.E.'s expression was quizzical as he looked down at the diamond necklace. "Did you lose any valuables?"

Automatically, she touched the chain. "This was in a cabin trunk that stayed on *Devanha*."

"That was lucky. So you didn't lose anything?"

Hellen's brain went into a state of paralysis.

"Mmn?" Sir Rowan waited.

"Nothing much," she managed to say, her voice croaking with fear. "My clothes would be a little large, I think, for Chinese women."

He kicked her toe again, apologised again.

"That's all right," she said.

Then, abruptly, he changed the subject. "I'm told you're a good rider. Mmn? I'm told I needn't worry about my horses missing their exercise. That's good of you, my dear."

She felt as though he knew everything about her, or could find out, if he wished. She wanted to rush away and hide before he told her he knew about Calum Finn, and the reason she had disembarked at Singapore; the fact that she was living with Oliver, had three times lived with Oliver, once even with his own horses looking on, before breakfast, among the trees at Happy Valley; that she had never lived with George. Not willingly. Only by rape. She felt unstrung.

The urbane voice went on, "Oliver, of course, is a good rider, too. So who wins, mmn?"

She cleared her throat in an effort to dislodge something large and dry that any moment now was going to prevent her swallowing. Possibly choke her. "We ride as a threesome," she said. "The third horse is not so fast."

"You mean you're not exercising my horses at full stretch?" Sir Rowan was good-humouredly indignant. "That won't do at all," he said, shaking his head, reducing her to the standard of a child with a pony on a leading rein. They came to a corner and he concentrated on getting her round it on the slippery floor without bumping into anyone.

"The races are coming up," he began again when, as he would have said, the track was clear. "I'm hoping for a win. My horses will have to be in very good fettle. I've got some excellent chaps who ride like the wind. Those mafoos were Russian cavalry officers—so they say, and I believe them." He smiled at his tiny joke.

Hellen tried to think of an answer, knowing he did not need one. He had wiped the floor with her. With incredible ease and finesse, he had delivered the last word. She was not to ride his horses. There was no answer to that. With those few words he had cut her off from

Oliver. The music stopped. The Master of Ceremonies announced the super waltz.

Sir Rowan said genially, "I must deliver you to your husband, and then find my wife. He's a tall chap, your husband. Easy to see. Ah! There he is. Thank you, my dear, for the dance." He slipped a hand through her elbow, and holding her at a distance, began to walk her across the room.

Chapter 25

Backlash

"A word, Oliver, if you don't mind." The last guests had gone on their way.

Lettice said hurriedly, "I'm off to bed." Sir Rowan signalled to Oliver to follow her. They went up the stairs in silence, Indian file. Lettice paused in the upstairs hall to say good-night to Oliver. Surreptitiously, she squeezed his hand as he kissed her. Sir Rowan went ahead into their private sitting room. The house was very silent. The room was pleasantly fresh and tranquil after the heat and the noise of the public rooms.

Sir Rowan settled in one of the comfortable chairs, gesturing to Oliver to do the same. He leaned back, stretching his neck, moving his chin from side to side, running a finger round the inside of his high, stiff collar. Oliver went to the window. The curtains had not been drawn. Outside, the moon rode high over the darkened bay. Stars glittered in the east.

There was a tap on the door. Ah Sam entered bearing a silver tray on which stood a bottle of whisky, two glasses and a crystal jug half-filled with water. Oliver looked at the whisky and his apprehension deepened. Sir Rowan gestured to the servant to put the tray down on the table. Oliver followed Ah Sam to the door, closing it behind him.

"By jove, it's been quite a night," said Sir Rowan. "Be a good fellow and pour me a stiff one."

Oliver removed the cork from the whisky bottle, poured out a measure and turned the water jug round so that its handle faced his uncle.

"Aren't you having one?"

"No thanks."

Sir Rowan slowly and carefully poured a little water into the glass. "Mrs Curtain," he said.

264

Oliver's nerves jumped. Even when you knew exactly the kind of threat you awaited, you could be thrown by its presentation. After all, he poured himself a small whisky and left if neat.

"Sit down, old chap."

Oliver lowered himself gingerly into the chair opposite.

"You gave her a bracelet." Sir Rowan's voice was pleasant, conversational.

Oliver's head reeled. How did he know?

"A Marathon heirloom, perhaps?"

"It was mine to give."

He might not have spoken for all the notice his uncle took of his reply. "Sapphires and enamel? On gold?" Sir Rowan held the whisky glass close under his nose, frowning into it as though a small insect had found its way there.

Oliver thought defiantly, an heirloom that was anyway going to pass his uncle by was none of his business, but to display anger would be a fatal error. He took a gulp of his whisky and blinked as it caught at his throat.

"It's a long time since I saw it," Sir Rowan went on, still in that mild, conversational tone, "and I don't clearly remember what it was like. Mother used to wear it when I was a boy. A leopard's head, perhaps? Did it have a leopard's head?"

"Yes."

"And you gave it to Mrs Curtain. Dangerous thing to do, in the circumstances that she married someone else." He took a sip of his whisky, engendering a deliberate silence, offering it to Oliver to fill.

Oliver cleared his throat. "I'll get it back." He was not going to get it back. He already knew that. He had searched the antique shops of Macau, Kowloon and Hong Kong. He had made discreet enquiries wherever he could uncover dealers and second hand jewellers.

"It isn't really yours," his uncle went on. "You're only its caretaker. Marathon valuables don't belong to us. We only have the use of them."

"Yes."

"And you're a responsible young chap."

"Yes," said Oliver.

"Although, seeing a woman who is married to another man is scarcely the act of a responsible person." His uncle's head came up and those very blue eyes of his met Oliver's squarely.

"I don't think you would understand. We went into the matter before, and you didn't understand. So there isn't much point—"

"Let me put it this way." His uncle leaned forward in his chair, very intent. "Has she decided she made a mistake? Or are you pressing

265

yourself on her in an endeavour to disrupt the marriage? Those are the crucial questions. Who is at fault?"

"Neither of us is at fault. I said, I cannot give you an explanation that you would understand."

Sir Rowan looked down at the back of his left hand that was lying on the arm of his chair. He lifted his eyes again. "Did you happen to dance with a woman called Wiley? Mrs Janet Wiley."

"No."

"Do you know whom I mean"

"No."

"Fair hair. Green dress. Youngish. Thirty-fiveish, with a much older husband. Guests of Mr and Mrs Broughton. Humphrey Broughton, comprador of Martin & Fair."

Oliver waited. His uncle was playing an all too familar game. Cat and mouse. The kind of power game that one played only with the certain knowledge that one was on the side destined to win. "I've said I don't know her." He pronouned the words politely, with careful goodwill.

"I merely wondered if you had noticed the bracelet she was wearing. Gold. With a leopard's head. Sapphires and pearls."

Oliver ran his tongue over his dry lips.

"Perhaps Mrs Curtain forgot to tell you," Sir Rowan went on, leaning back again, elbows on the arms of his chair, his hands together, the fingers steepled, "either that she sold the bracelet you gave her, or else that the pirates took it from her and sold it themselves. Mr Wiley found it in a junk shop in Macau."

"The pirates took the bracelet," said Oliver. "Now we know where it has ended up, I'll go and see this woman. If I explain the circumstances, I'm sure she would allow me to buy it back."

"I've no doubt her husband paid the beggars a goodish sum for it. Chinese dealers are not fools." Sir Rowan paused, allowing his words time for maximum effect. "Of course the bracelet must be returned, but the husband will have to be reimbursed. Do you think you could afford to buy it back?" He was calm, unruffled, apparently not particularly concerned.

"I think I know where I could raise some money."

"In the event that I should prefer you didn't go to your grandmother for money, and considering that my intervention may carry a little more weight than yours, I intend to deal with this matter myself." Sir Rowan's voice sharpened. "You have put me in this dashed awkward position, Oliver. I hope you are aware of that."

Oliver was aware only that the bracelet would now be in his uncle's hands. He considered the fact, in relation to the knowledge that he could not, anyway, give it back to Hellen. Not while she was tied to George. "Thank you," he said stiffly. "That's very good of you."

"I shall put it in the bank," said his uncle, immutable in his expectation that the owner would meekly hand the bracelet back. "Now, there is the little matter of jumping the reception line."

Oliver grinned disarmingly. "Nobody minded."

"Of course nobody minded. Nobody is in a position to mind the Governor's nephew taking advantage of his position of privilege."

"I'm sorry, sir."

"I can only assume you were carried away by emotions which, in the circumstances that Mrs Curtain is irrevocably married, you have no right to feel, much less display."

Oliver looked out over the darkening bay where the riding lights on the stationary vessels moved gently up and down.

"You will understand that I have no recourse but to forbid you to see her again."

Oliver knew there was a way to have Hellen. There had to be. But this, he recognised with a new kind of fear, was not the moment to seek it.

"Do you understand what I am saying, Oliver?"

"I understand." He managed to say the words firmly and quietly. He even managed to look into those steely blue eyes as he spoke, showing nothing of the heartbreak and the pain.

Sir Rowan rose to his feet. "Time for bed," he said pleasantly, glancing at the clock. "It's late for you, too, old chap. Time you were on your way."

Lettice was already in the big four-poster, her thin silk nightgown with its rows of inset lace falling away at the neck to expose the still firm curve of her breasts. Her hair lay round her shoulders, softly waving. She put the brush down on the mahogany bedside table as Sir Rowan came into the room.

Irritatedly, he began battling with the onyx studs on his shirt front. "It was irresponsible of him in the extreme to give that bracelet to a girl he scarcely knew," he said. "I hate to think what's going to happen to our heritage in Oliver's hands. The boy's an ass. An irresponsible ass."

"He was very much in love with her," said Lettice gently, forebearing to remind her husband that he had given her a family ring before departing for South Africa to fight the Boers.

"Was?" queried her husband impatiently. "Was? What do you mean, was?" without waiting for a reply, he went round to his wife's side of the bed and thrust out an arm. "Help me with these links, before I break my fingernails." She took the board-hard cuff between finger and thumb. "Was?" he repeated, watching her face as she straightened the gold clasp into a peg and forced it through the narrow slit.

She smiled gently. "Of course he was."

He allowed the diplomatic answer to pass. "Did you see him tonight? Did you see his face when he was looking at her? By God, it will be all over the colony tomorrow. I'm going to sent him to take young Sinclair's place in the New Territories. And I'll make jolly sure he gets away without seeing her again."

His wife looked up at him in distress. "You said yourself that's a post for a married man. You said even for a married man, it was lonely."

"A little time on his own might bring him to his senses. He can take plenty of books. He used to be a reader, before he lost his wits," Sir Rowan growled. "I don't propose that Government House should be involved in a scandal, and scandal there will be if he remains here."

He did not say it out loud, because he was never crude before his wife, but frankly, he thought Mrs Curtain had behaved like a bitch on heat, and Oliver like a randy pi-dog.

George said, "What with you behaving like a bitch on heat, and Marathon doing everything short of mounting you, what conclusion did you expect me to come to? Je-sus!"

Hellen took her night dress from under the pillow. "George, I'm very tired. I would like to go to bed."

"Yes, wouldn't you! And with Marathon," said George savagely. "You've been riding with him. What else have you been doing with him? Eh? What else?"

Hellen undid her necklace and carefully put it away in the leather-covered box. George moved two steps forward. She could hear his breathing. Long, deep breaths, through his nose. She could feel the power of his emotions, and she was afraid. Not that he would hit her. It was a greater fear then that.

"Sexy little bitch you are, after all," said George.

Hellen crossed to the other side of the bed, moving away from him. She heard the hurt and bitterness in his voice and sympathy for him warred with this new feeling of fear. Real fear. She was drenched with it. "We both need sleep," she said.

"I'll tell you what I need," said George aggressively. "I need my conjugal rights. Don't think I'm going to keep you for no return, Miss Pretend-Frigid. There's nothing frigid about you. If you two haven't been rooting like rattlesnakes, I'll eat my best Panama."

Hellen clasped her hands tightly together to stop their trembling, and raised her eyes to his. "You don't have to keep me. There's a hostel in Kowloon for single girls. I would be quite happy to go there."

"The Helena May hostel! The Virgin's Retreat," scoffed George. "And who do you think would pay for you, even if they would take you, which I doubt?"

"I could use my allowance to cover my board, and I could work at the Nurse Matilda hospital on The Peak."

George's eyes popped with astonishment. "You've got it all worked out, haven't you?"

"No. It suddenly occurred to me. As you say, you are keeping me for no return. Why should you?"

George walked round the bed until he stood directly in front of her, looking down at her. It seemed an age that he stood there, without speaking. She could not have looked up if she had wanted to. Without the partial screen of her lids, she knew he would see right into her soul. He would see her fear, and his confidence would blossom; he would see her love for Oliver, that diminished him.

The mattress springs creaked as he slowly lowered himself on to the bed. "Because you are my wife," he said distinctly. "That's why I keep you. As my wife you will not go to the Helena May hostel, and neither will you go out to work." He waited. Still Hellen did not look at him. He began again, softly, persuasively, "We're in a cleft stick, old girl. You're never going to get Marathon back. Let's try and make something of what we've got."

She lifted her head and with tears in her eyes, cried piteously, "You know I love Oliver. There's nothing I can do about it, George. I can't make something of this—this—" She gagged on the word "marriage". "I can't, because I love Oliver. I'm sorry, George, but there's nothing I can do about it. I love him."

George's eyes seemed to glaze over. He asked with soft violence, "You're going to cuckold me?"

Hellen saw what was in his heart written plainly on this face, the sick anger, the desire for revenge. She felt cold sweat prickle on her forehead, and on the back of her neck. George rose slowly from the bed. The very pace of his movements was a threat. "You can't make anything of our marriage because you're in love with Marathon," he repeated, then paused. "Let me tell you this, then. I'll divorce you, and name him. He'll be drummed out of the Colonial Service, and then he'll be drummed out of the clan. The Earl and Countess of Stradlock will be a little less smug about their lot by the time I've finished with their gilded grandson. I'll make mincemeat of him," said George with cold relish. "Mincemeat. I'll have the divorce plastered over every newspaper in England and here. His name will be mud, and so will yours.

"They're going to hate you for what you've done to him, and so is he, when the lust cools. Don't forget, Hellen, that you're the one who doesn't count. People like the Marathons get where they are by jettisoning people like you. People who don't count." He repeated the words calculated to produce the greatest impact on her morale. "There's no way you and Marathon are ever going to get together without total chaos, and no Marathon is going to disappear in total chaos. Marathons and their like are winners by nature. Under all that charm, they're ruthless and clever and tough." He paused, gathering the hurtful words once again on to the end of his tongue, injecting them with a full complement of venom before repeating them for the third time, "You're the one who will be destroyed, because you're the one who doesn't count."

He turned and took two steps towards the door, then paused. "Just in case you're thinking of running away," he said, "I'd like you to know you couldn't embark without my being informed. I know a few bribeable people down at the docks."

Hellen stood still as death with eyes cast down. George turned and went with a heavy tread to his own room.

On the Tuesday following the ball, after George left for work, Lin Yan telephoned asking if Hellen could come to her place. She went in a great hurry, snatching up her sunshade and hurrying out into the road, away from the comfortable cage furnished with George's wickedness, from which there was now no escape.

They talked in the summer house where there was no chance of the servants overhearing. "It has happened," said Lin Yan. "Oliver has been sent away."

She could not believe he would go without getting in touch with her.

"He has gone to the New Territories," said Lin Yan. "He asked me to tell you he has been forbidden to get in touch with you. Forbidden," said the Eurasian girl portentously. "He said that means, if he does contact you, much worse will happen. He cannot write to you, because if George finds the letters and takes them to Sir Rowan that really will be the end for you both."

Hellen was drowning in despair.

"Last night," said Lin Yan, "Peter Ackroyd came and brought this for you." She fished in a slit pocket in her cheongsam and drew out a flat packet. It contained a piece of jade on a gold chain. On either side of the clip there was a tiny gold plate etched with the figure nine. "It is

270

the most lucky number," said Lin Yan. "He wishes you to have good luck. The jade is for good luck, too." The way she said the words, Oliver's wish had a final ring. As though he was saying good-bye.

Lin Yan smiled comfortingly. "He is not so far away. Did you not know you were very indiscreet at Government House? Everyone was looking at you."

Hellen said wanly, "I can't help it. When Oliver is near I . . ." She could not say to Lin Yan that she was alight, like a star. Afire, in a great conflagration. "Something happens to me," she said, enfolding the magic of Oliver in prosaic words more easily understood by those less honoured by the gods. Less damned.

"You will have to learn," said Lin Yan gravely. "He will come back here. You will meet him in public. But if you do not wish him harm in his career, then you must learn to behave differently."

Hellen undid the clasp and put the chain round her neck. Her fingers fondled the smooth stone. "If you are well and happy, the jade will glow," said Lin Yan. "If you are ill, it will grow dull."

"Is it expensive? I mean, could I have bought it myself?" She was thinking of George, wondering if she could keep the precious stone from George's eyes. Wondering how to explain it away.

"Not expensive. No. You could have bought it yourself."

Lin Yan extended her hands warmly. "Come with me. I am to have lunch with my aunt. This will be novel for you, a meal in a Chinese house, and it will help to take your mind off things."

"I doubt if I could eat anything."

"Oh, but you must, otherwise my aunt will think you are unfriendly. Or that you are sickening for a contagious disease that she and the other guests might catch."

"For heavens' sake!"

"It is the Chinese way of thinking," said Lin Yan, disassociating herself from such foolishness.

"Then let us hope it's a light lunch."

"Twenty-five or twenty-six courses. Each course will be small. A mouthful."

Hellen managed a wry smile. Twenty-five or six courses to swallow over a lump in her throat the size of a pigeon's egg!

Mrs Chan's house was built in the Chinese fashion with spacious courtyards filled with a blaze of flowers that were growing in stone urns. Sitting at her table listening to the tinkling wind bells dancing on golden branched plants, smelling the perfume of incense, Hellen was for a little while able to feel less pain. The warmed rice wine they drank between dishes lifted her spirits. The food was delicious. There were pieces of duck in soy sauce and mustard, chicken giblets, lotus

271

seeds, lychees and melon pips. She lost count of the courses. The soup came near the end, followed only by fish and rice. Now she understood what George meant when he said a guest was not obliged to stay after the soup. She left feeling exhilarated by the new oriental experience, and better able to face the world.

"You are so kind to me," she said gratefully as she and Lin Yan strolled together towards the tram.

"You know I love Oliver, too. But I cannot have him. I could never have him. I must content myself with trying to make him happy. Your joss will change."

Would it? Hellen tried not to think about the future as the tram carried her down the mountainside. She thought about the sadness in Lin Yan's eyes as she said she, too, loved Oliver. Well, neither of them could have him. That was what it amounted to.

Oliver had gone, like a blown out candle. They were dismal days that followed. Only in studying Cantonese could Hellen lose herself, and even that took on a sense of futility, because in order not to be thought eccentric, she had to keep her new-found knowledge a secret, not only from George, but from her bridge and tennis playing friends. She looked for pleasure in the work for its own sake, and for the fact that it helped, for short periods, to blank out her loss.

Sometimes she thought George would detect the strange smell of Chinese ink that pervaded the corner of the drawing room where she had her lessons, but he never noticed. Sin-shaang answered questions she hesitated to ask Lin Yan, who did not care to associate herself with Chinese ways. After Mrs Chan's lunch Hellen asked him about the series of small mirrors set low on the outer wall of her house.

"They are there to divert the evil spirits, who fly low and always in a straight line. They see their own ugly faces and are frightened away." He taught her gravity and respect for customs that would bring hoots of derision over the tea cups in the lounge of the Hong Kong Hotel.

There was very little grammar to learn. One symbol indicated meaning; another, sound. A mark on the right side of the water symbol indicated cold. She could now leave a note for Ah Wong telling him if she required the water to be heated.

"Twins?" he said to her one day, his boot-button eyes crinkled with amusement. "I do not think you have twins."

"I said that?" Hellen looked astonished. "I said I have two horses at home in Kent."

"Then your tone drill is faulty. Tone drill is important. That is why we spend seventy per cent of the time on it. Depending on how it is spoken," said Sin-shaang, "'Ma' can mean a mother, a horse, a wharf, twins, linen, a yard measure, or to scold. In pronouncing 'Ma' wrongly, you have told me you have twins. You have no children?"

"No." She fingered the jade pendant at her neck.

"Your husband has given you a present, I see."

Automatically, her fingers closed over the stone, curving round it, protecting Oliver's gift from shadows of George. She said, "It was given to me by a very dear friend."

The tutor looked at her quizzically over his wire-rimmed spectacles. "A man?"

"Yes. A man I was not able to marry."

"May I ask why?"

"Because, I suppose it boils down to—"

"Boils? You have a saying about ketting into hot water. You have ton this with a very dear friend?"

She tried not to laugh about his g's and t's. "You could say that. You are helping me along a difficult path, Sin-shaang, and I am grateful. This man—"

"This boiling man? Perhaps raging? Perhaps passionate?"

She laughed so much she spilt the ink and had to call Ah Wong to wipe it up, though of course it was little Ah Ping, the makee learn, who wiped up under his instructions, for he was too grand for such a menial task.

"I was considered not good enough for him," she said when the servant had gone. That was putting oh, so many mistakes, misunderstandings, misconceptions, errors of judgment and human weaknesses into a nutshell, but in the beginning, it had been true.

Sin-shaang nodded sagely, the curly whiskers on his cheeks shivering delicately as he moved his head. "Confucius said, 'The good man does not grieve that other people do not recognise his virtues. His concern is that he should fail to recognise theirs.'" His little black eyes were sombre. "When the Manchus invaded China, forcing men to wear the pigtails that symbolise submission, the Imperial Dragon shed tears of sorrow that petrified into jade."

"This is a tear of sorrow," she said, caressing the jade, and a tear of her own rolled down her cheek.

"It is also a link between heaven and earth, life and immortality."

"Immortality," she said softly, feeling a sudden glow as she remembered that first time her eyes met Oliver's eyes across the courtyard at the hunt meeting in Kent. "Do you believe that if one has known someone in another life, that love can continue?"

"To make this life perfect, as we would have it?"

She thought she detected a note of wry cynicism in Sin-shaang's voice. "For perfection, you have to pay, Mrs Curtain. Only those who are perfect themselves get something for nothing. But if you were perfect, would you be here? There is an old Chinese proverb which says the highest towers begin at the ground."

She walked out on to the coarse grass of the lawn and looked up towards the Nine Dragon Hills behind which they, omnipotently, had hidden Oliver. Sing-shaang shuffled off down the road, head bent, his tunic falling flat on his narrow hips, taking along with him his wisdom, and her momentary hope.

Chapter 26

Happy Valley Races

The New Territories, acquired from China in 1898 on a ninety-nine year lease in order to meet possible attack from Russia, Germany or France, all of whom had already moved into Indo China, was a fascinating place for a young man to be. Except that it was indescribably lonely. Oliver had that morning taken the Sinclair family to the Fan Ling station and seen them on to the Kowloon-Canton train. They were now puffing their way through the swampy marshes and yellow bamboo on the shores of Tolo harbour, through the Lion Rock tunnel and the lovely Shatin Valley, towards the pillared Victorian railway station at Kowloon.

The bungalow, stripped of the children's impedimenta, the happy chatter of the family, the patter of running feet, was awesomely empty. Oliver wandered from room to room, hunch-shouldered, his face as long as a pole. He did not blame his uncle for what had happened. He had been a fool. Hot-headed, careless, over-confident and arrogant, committing the same offences as when he had forced Hellen on Sylvia Ashton and the county set.

He had considered the implications of tossing in his job, sweeping Hellen up and taking her home, for home it would certainly be. There would be no question of a transfer, even to one of the less desirable areas of the British Empire. It would be Scotland, or, if the family refused to take them in, England. Society would brand Hellen the scarlet woman who had ruined him. If George Curtain chose not to divorce her, her sins would be compounded as a kept woman. Kept with what? he asked himself bitterly. Who would give him a decent job, he who had been trained specifically for the Colonial Service?

Then there was the other matter, the one of which Hellen was as yet ignorant. One day, if his Uncle Cecil did not survive, and nobody thought he would, if he could not marry Hellen, if George never divorced her, there would be no heir to the Earldom of Stradlock. A black headline printed itself starkly in his mind: "Family ne'er-do-well comes without heir to ancient title. The new earl and his mistress, Mrs George Curtain. . . ."

He stepped out on to the verandah and stood scowling across the acres of rice paddies, the fish ponds, the rooftops of the little Haaka village huddled behind its moat and its high stone walls; at the tall mountain in the distance, pine clad and swathed in mist. The land was beautiful with its delicate, waving bamboo, its pretty acacia trees, its pink and gold earth that appeared where tree roots failed to hold and the land slid away; its wild orchids.

He went through the gate in the picket fence, then strode across the rough fields, making his way towards the village and the bay. A bride was being carried across the fields in a brightly painted sedan chair. His limbs seemed to lock with pain. He did not move on until the party had gone out of sight. A chow dog, lying in the dust on the side of the village moat, pricked up its ears at his approach. Two buffaloes, plodding patiently before a small boy, turned in at the village gates.

He crossed the road that led round the inlet. A withered old woman in black, sitting on a rock peacefully smoking her long-stemmed pipe, stared up at him. He paused, greeting her in Cantonese. She answered in a dialect he did not understand. Coolies in big hats were fishing from a tiny boat in a pond. A browsing buffalo lifted its head. He skirted it gingerly, for they did not like the smell of a white man. He went on down to the water and stood looking up the beautiful Tolo channel, watching the fisherfolk draw in their nets prior to going home to their wives. The loneliness crept into his bones.

They were a mixed community with whom he was to work, Hakka, Hoklo and Tanka, each with their own distinctive dialect, customs and creeds. The Cantonese farmers had established clan villages in the eleventh century, on the best available land, then the Haakas, the nomads, originally from northern China, hardy, frugal people, content to farm such land as was ignored by the industrious Cantonese, gradually moved south. Haaka meant guest people. They were still guest people, with different customs, separate lives. They neither bound their feet, nor intermarried with the Cantonese.

Tankas were fishermen and seafarers. Sea gypsies. They were the people he was to live among; to get to know; to settle their differences by the Englishman's creed. "I am supposed to know how to run lives," he said bitterly to himself, "and yet I cannot manage my own." He ached with the misery of his loneliness; of his half life.

He moved on, walking, walking. He was only fifteen miles from

Tsim Sha Tsui. He could walk there in a few hours. Four miles an hour, for three and three-quarter hours, and he would be with Hellen, the ache appeased. But it was not going to happen. If you loved a woman you did not expose her to the kind of life that would ensue from such impetuous silliness. The sun went down over China. He returned to the lonely bungalow in deepening twilight and sat on the verandah drinking whisky, listening to the cicadas, and the occasional high whine of a mosquito.

Racing was the closest thing to a common religion that Hong Kong possessed. Happy Valley racecourse with its picturesque grandstand supporting a thatched roof, verandahs and sunblinds, its well-watered lawn, its paddock alive with snorting, dancing horses, was the only place to be that day. Women were lovely in the new gowns that had come in from Harrods and the Army and Navy stores. Men were dressed, as for Ascot, in morning clothes.

Temporary private stands and tiffin rooms had been erected over some of the stables. Languid English ladies, seated in basketwork chairs on the lawns, held court beneath pretty parasols. Uniformed Chinese ushers hurried to and fro attending to their slightest whim.

Everyone knew everyone. They came from Canton, Shanghai and Macao. Where the Chinese disported themselves were stalls dispensing food cooked on charcoal stoves, those very same stoves that had caused the blazing inferno of 1919. There were Chinese jugglers running swords through little boys; dentists pretending to draw teeth, then reinstating them; deformed dwarfs; ducks with three legs. Sir Rowan Matheson and his lady came in style, heralded by the band, and were seated grandly in a box draped with clouds of bunting.

It was a cool day, but clear, exactly the kind of day everyone would have prayed for if they were praying people, but they were betting people, so they had a few dollars on the weather instead. Kitty Armitage came nervously on Denzil's arm, for it was certain George and his bride would be there. She hoped very much that he, like the taipan of Lonewood & Southby who had taken Denzil back—on probation to be sure—would forget and forgive. Kitty was a small girl, fair-haired and pretty. People referred to her as an English rose, though she had been born in Hong Kong and lived outside it only for the school years.

"Don't look now," said Ruth to Hellen, holding a glazed smile on her face. "The Armitages. She's small. Blonde. Enormous hat with poppy trim. Do you wish to be introduced?"

Hellen said lightly, "I'm sure George isn't going to effect an introduction, so, yes. Why not?"

Ruth revolved slowly, glancing over the crowd until her eyes were on a level with the Armitages, when she allowed an astonished expression to leap into her eyes. She moved forward with hands outstretched, crying, "Why, Kitty! Dar-ling! And Denzil! How very nice to see you." She kissed them both, then turned to Hellen. "You'll have heard George is married?"

Hellen said, as warmly as she dared in the circumstances, "I hope we'll be friends." George was standing not far away talking to a large and rather flamboyant woman wearing a hat decorated with a mass of flowers. Her gown, with its lace trim and braiding, could have moved right out of a Paris fashion plate. At that moment she laughed up at him and playfully wagged a finger in his face. Hellen started forward, but Ruth put a restraining hand on her arm.

"I wouldn't, if I were you."

She was vaguely aware of eye contact between the others, and then Lin Yan, stepping out of the crowd, broke the tension. She shook hands with the Armitages, then asked, in her gentle, demure way, "May I take Hellen away? There's someone I want her to meet."

As she led Hellen off, she said, "Oliver is here. He's waiting in a tiffin room that's given over to visitors, so you should be reasonably safe. You will have to be careful, though. I beg you, Hellen, take that expression off your face."

She could not. She was aglow, walking ten feet off the ground. Out of control. Oliver! She hugged herself ecstatically. Lin Yan led her to a set of steps leading up on one side of a stable block, and left her there. She ascended like a piece of thistledown, floating to the clouds.

Marcia saw Hellen come in, saw her face, and was briefly delighted that she was happy. She said to those sitting close by, "There's our new daughter-in-law, the pretty dark girl in the. . . ." Her voice trailed off. Her visiting Shanghai friends looked up. They saw the ecstasy on the girl's face, the way she held out her hands, saw them being taken by a man who was not George. Then Neil cleared his throat loudly and said, "And how are the Framwells? I'm surprised they haven't come down."

Suddenly everyone was talking at once, looking down, fingering their cocktail glasses, gazing blankly at each other, anywhere but at the slender girl in the lavender-coloured gown and the heliotrope hat. In that moment of great shock, Marcia was remembering how she had seen the Governor's nephew dashing down Ladder Street immediately before Hellen descended; remembering that she had thought her daughter-in-law looked that day like a cat that had swallowed the cream.

Hellen breathed, "You've come. Oh, darling—" and then there

was a hurried scraping of chairs close by and a delighted voice cried, "Hellen! How wonderful, you're here!" and Isabel, whose grandfather had found her in the street in Macao, was flinging her arms round her. Isabel turned to Oliver, then back to Hellen, looking down at her left hand. She saw the enormous ruby and the plain gold band. "You're married! You didn't tell us!" Before either of them could find their tongues she was rushing on, "This is your husband? I'm Isabel. Hellen came to us after her adventure. We call her our shipwrecked lady." She swung back to Hellen. "Sit down with us. Please do sit down, both of you, and tell us everything."

Hellen half-turned towards the table from which Isabel had sprung and saw Dona Celeste's smiling face. But first, as she turned, there was Marcia, large, square-shouldered, and wearing an expression of withering scorn. Hellen gave her a glazed smile. Marcia stared coldly back, then deliberately turned away.

Oliver was laughing, saving the situation with enormous panache. "I'm not her husband, I'm afraid. I'm a very old friend. We haven't seen each other for ages."

They put brave social smiles on their faces and sat down between Dona Celeste and Isabel. Only when the fanfare of trumpets sounded for the first race were they able to get away. They walked primly through the happy, excited crowd, carefully keeping a space between them, keeping their hands to themselves, walking on a razor's edge, looking for George whose presence with them would make Oliver safe.

Hong Kong threw a party each year on the day of the Hungry Ghosts Festival, the fourteenth day of the seventh moon, for the ghosts of the departed, and all the spirits of the earth, water and skies. In temples and houses the people laid out food for the ancestors and burned imitation money and clothes, believing them to fly on the warm air to the dead, ensuring they should be provided for during the year to come.

"Superstitious rubbish," said George. But others thought it was fun. The cook boy, somewhat disconcertingly, put out such Chinese delicacies as chickens' feet and entrails for his ancestors, as well as for those of the other servants.

Hellen went with Kitty and Denzil down to the typhoon shelters in Causeway Bay to watch the fleet of miniature ghost ships set sail across the bay with candles glowing in their holds. George went out on business. It must be business, for he continued to insist he had no concubine. As time passed the candles flickered and died, so that one could no longer see the prayer inscribed on the banner that hung on the mast of the rearmost boat: Hsun-feng Teh-li. Temper the wind and gain profits, as Denzil explained.

Temper the wind and send Oliver, Hellen prayed.

Curiously, a friendship had blossomed between Kitty, Denzil and herself. Although he never mentioned Oliver, and Oliver had never mentioned him, she knew Oliver and Denzil were friends. Neither did George avoid Kitty. Hellen would sometimes see a strange, brooding look on his face as he watched her.

There were other festivals in the Chinese calendar. When it came to the mid-autumn festival, celebrated on the fifteenth day of the eighth moon, the cook boy made cakes which he stuffed with sweet bean paste. The servants consumed them with artless gluttony. George said, "The sweet bean is Cantonese. In Shanghai they gave us heavier cakes, made with eggs and chestnut puree. Get Ah Wong to have a go at them."

Ah Wong agreed, impassively, to "have a go". Hellen invited Marcia and Neil, hoping to please them with the north China food, but the visit was not a success. George's mother said in a hard, bitter voice while George and his father were enjoying a cigarette in the garden, "So that's why your luggage went to Government House. You were going to marry Oliver Marathon?"

There was so much venom in her eyes that Hellen had to look away. "Yes," she said softly. "Yes, I was."

"And you are still in love with him." Marcia added in a low, angry voice, "I'm sure you know George has already had an unhappy experience."

"I do know."

"When you have a son of your own you will know how a mother suffers for a son." Marcia's face twisted with grief. "Girls can be so cruel." She indicated the ornate ruby on the third finger of Hellen's left hand. "I don't think it's right that you should continue to wear his ring. It may be that George doesn't mind, but I think it's an insult. Why do you not give it back to him? That is the correct procedure."

"George gave me this ring," said Hellen. "I did tell you that he bought the stone in up-country Burma a long time ago when they were two a penny." Afterwards, she knew her repetition of the words George had used to be a cry for help. When Marcia only glared at her angrily she said, "I think it would be better if we didn't discuss the matter, Mrs Curtain."

Offence was written clearly on Marcia's broad features. "You don't seem to realise that when parents have only one son it's doubly important that his wife should become a member of the family. 'Mrs Curtain'," she repeated with deep distaste.

"I would like to call you Marcia," offered Hellen diffidently.

"That," said George's mother, "is the most disrespectful thing I have ever heard."

"I am sorry. I didn't mean it to be so."

"What would people think?"

"They might think," said Hellen smiling placatingly, "that I had a mother of my own."

It was altogether an unfortunate evening. The guests left early. George said as they disappeared up the road, "You've offended my mother." It was a flat statement, without recrimination. George had been easier with her lately. She was grateful, but sometimes, apprehensively, she thought he wore a waiting air. The way he watched Kitty made her nervous. He went out at night as usual, but recently he had returned early, walking with a new spring in his step. Twice, she had seen a short, square seaman walking with a limp in the vicinity of the house. Charlie Marsh?

"She would like me to call her mother. I'm sorry, George, but with the best will in the world, I cannot."

"Sort out your own problems."

The next time she saw Neil he said, with an odd little quirk at the corners of his mouth, "I'd like you to call me Neil, my dear. Do you realise you don't call me anything at all?"

Hellen flushed. "I didn't know what to—"

"It's unusual, of course, but I would like it. Use 'Look here', and 'By the way', and 'I say' for Marcia. She may care better for that than 'Mrs Curtain'."

She liked Neil more and more. He had this pleasant way of ironing things out.

The weather turned cold. Not English cold, but uncomfortable, with the winds coming down from the northern states. The servants suffered from their inability to close doors. Time and again Hellen would enter the kitchen to find them huddled together drinking hot tea and gazing forlornly out into the yard while the back door flapped in the wind. Exasperated, she would close it, but the next time one of them had to go out of doors, it would be left open.

Christmas came and went.

Letters and presents arrived from the North family, and requests for news. What was she doing? Her sister Beth wrote plaintively that her letters read like a Chinese history book. They were considerably less interested in the strange goings on of the little yellow men in a country so foreign they could scarcely imagine it, than they were in the details of Hellen's day to day life. She had drifted away from them, leaving them nervously irritable with her. Hellen discovered her allowance at the Hong Kong and Shanghai bank had been doubled. She wrote to thank her grandfather, assuring him she was all right, but even as George's prisoner, she experienced relief knowing her return fare lay in the bank.

One day the number one cook boy came to Hellen with a request for money. "For Squeeze," he said.

"What for Squeeze?"

"Bad men stay away."

She told him in Cantonese that she did not understand.

"You pay Squeeze. Thieves not come."

Her meagre Cantonese did not run to questioning that. She resorted to pidgin. "We before not have thieves."

Ah Wong went away, his face expressionless.

A few days later she noticed the silver inkstand had disappeared and spoke to Ah Wong sharply.

"Thief, Missie." The cook boy's face was impassive. "You no pay Squeeze."

Hellen remembered then, with apprehension, that some of her underwear had not come back from the wash amah. Ah Wong had said he would enquire of little Ah Saw, but had not reported back. Now she remembered mislaying a pair of white kid gloves. Usually the servants would find such things, but the gloves had not turned up.

"Ornament gone too," said Ah Wong sadly, pointing to the mantelpiece where now only one Staffordshire figure stood.

Hellen telephoned Ruth for advice. Ruth, with her ten servants, could give an answer to most household problems.

"George will have to pay," she said. "I give my gatekeeper fifty dollars a month to keep burglars away. It's and old Hong Kong custom. A tax, you might call it, levied by the Triads. There's a Guild of Thieves. The Guild would do an individual thief to death with a flick of the chopper. Once you've paid, you'll find your belongings will mysteriously return in the night."

"No one has broken in. There have been no windows unlocked at night."

"Your servants hand over the booty, dear. If Triads ask them for your possessions, they dare not refuse."

Hellen knew from Sin-shaang about the Triads, that most feared Chinese secret society, established in the last century specifically with the avowed purpose of overthrowing the Manchu Ch'ing Dynasty and restoring the Ming. Now its members, bound by oaths of blood brotherhood, were pledged to overthrow the foreign conquerors of their country and restore the ancient ruling house of China to the throne. Sin-shaang had inferred that the society was something sinister and evil, rather than a mystic brotherhood of man.

Hellen had asked Denzil about them. He gave her a strange look. "The Government's penalty for Triad membership is up to three years imprisonment, a branding on the left arm and deportation at the discretion of the presiding judge," he said.

She said with indignation to George that evening, "They've got some of my clothes, and goodness knows what else."

George was unperturbed. "A mere error of judgment." He picked up his newspaper. "Don't worry."

"You mean, you're going to pay?" Hellen was angry that he should allow himself so easily to be blackmailed.

"No. I am not going to pay."

She was glad at least there was someone in the colony who would stand up to them.

That evening, after dinner, he left the house as usual. When he returned several hours later he said briefly, "I think you'll find everything back in place by tomorrow." The way he said it, watching her, stroking his moustache with one finger, made her feel strange.

"Is this something to do with your opium business?" she asked, suddenly frightened.

"What opium business?" George's voice was sharp as a cutting knife.

"You told me—"

"You're imagining things. Don't start imagining things, Hellen. That way lies very serious trouble."

Lying awake in the night, she considered with fear and amazement that George had thought it worth the risk of making himself vulnerable in order to spoil her evening at the Government House ball.

Chapter 27

Golden Pagodas

"Do you know," asked Lin Yan, "that after death, the Chinese spirit takes on triple form, one going to the grave with the body, one to the underworld, and one into the tablet?"

Hellen blinked. This was not the Lin Yan she knew, the one who spoke with scorn about what she called her people's superstitutions, if indeed she mentioned them at all. There were ornate blocks of wood, which Hellen understood to be called tablets, on the mantelpiece in Mrs Chan's house. Did they contain an ancestor's spirit? On the mantelpiece? She kept a carefully grave face as Lin Yan continued with her unlikely treatise, wondering where it was leading.

"At the time of the Ching Ming Festival, for the welfare and peace of our ancestors, we must honour the relics of the departed," Lin Yan went on. "We go to our ancestors' graves and cut the vegetation away, repaint the tablets, transfer the bones to their Golden Pagodas, and make offerings of incense and food. You would like to accompany me?"

Hellen decided Lin Yan was teasing her. "Oh, yes," she said, laughing.

"I will bring a picnic lunch. You must tell your husband we may be late. The hillside where my ancestors lie buried is near to the China border. And there is much work to do."

George roared with laughter when Hellen told him. "Do you know what a golden pagoda is?"

She had seen many pagodas, those circular or octagonal buildings consisting of an odd number of storeys, originally raised over the relics of Buddha, or the bones of Buddhist saints. "Not a golden one."

"That's the catch," said George. "Chinese burials aren't permanent because land's too expensive. They hire a piece of ground for a six-year tenure. Then, at the Ching Ming festival, the family take a picnic out to the graveyard and spend the day exhuming the bones—"

"What!"

"What I said," repeated George, immensely enjoying the expression of horror on her face. "They clean and polish them, and pile them, feet first, skull on top, into a jar which they call a Golden Pagoda. Glazed brown pottery. We call them Grandfather's Bones jars. Mother had one made into a lamp. You've seen it. It stands by the book case in the drawing room. It's just the same as those you see banked on outlying hills in the New Territories. Every one of them contains the polished bones of someone's grandfather or grandmother. They're supposed to overlook a running stream, or the sea, because water guarantees protection from evil spirits."

"And your mother uses one of them as a lamp!"

"The Chinese are essentially practical people. The servants don't mind."

She didn't believe a word he said. He was trying to put her off going out in public with Lin Yan.

"Better wear riding breeches and a topee," advised George. "It'll be hot and messy out there." He crackled his newspaper into place. "This'll maybe teach you to hang round with Chows," he said disagreeably.

Even disbelieving George, it was with some apprehension that Hellen went to the railway station in Kowloon to meet her friend. Chinese were pouring into the station, all laden down with flowers and picnic baskets, hoes and spades, laughing and joking, But Lin Yan, to Hellen's immense relief, carried only a small picnic hamper, flowers, and a wad of paper slips.

"Spirit money," she said, flapping the paper slips. "To be placed on the lid of the Golden Pagoda to provide comfort for our ancestors in the other world." Hellen eyed her friend uncertainly. Then the train came, and along with the noisy rabble of Chinese, they climbed in and found a seat.

It was a lovely day with feathers of purest white cloud in a brilliant sky. As the train puffed up into the New Territories, Hellen put aside her doubts and enjoyed the views. They passed little villages huddled behind high stone walls, acres of paddy, fish ponds, lotus ponds, duck ponds so white with ducks there was no water visible. They wound in and out of leafy green hills, then emerged in open countryside. The hills here were taller, and more bare.

Lin Yan said, "Look out of the window, Hellen. There are the Golden Pagodas." There, indeed, were the replicas of Marcia's lamp. They stood in rows on the hillside, sombrely elegant, all crowned by hemispherical lids, and with the spirit money fluttering from beneath holding stones.

285

Hellen could contain her dismay no longer. "George said . . .' She swallowed. "Am I intended to scrape . . .'

Lin Yan asked gravely, "You do not want to scrape my grandfather's bones?"

Hellen flopped back against the hard seat, scarcely knowing whether to laugh or be angry. She closed her eyes. A cool breeze drifted in through the window. When she opened them again, Lin Yan said, "I have been teasing you." She looked very pleased with herself, and only partially contrite. "I have brought you to meet Oliver."

"Oliver!" Hellen jerked up in her seat.

"You must know I couldn't tell you, for you are so very bad at hiding your feelings where Oliver is concerned. George would be suspicious. Look at you now! If you could see your face!"

The train was slowing down. Hellen leaped to her feet, lurched to the side of the carriage and leant out of the window. There he was, standing on the tiny platform dressed in riding breeches and with that dear, familar lock of hair lifting in the breeze. She pulled back from the window and sat down with a thump. She could not speak. Lin Yan reached across and took her hand.

The train came to a halt. "What are you going to do?" Hellen asked, her voice trembling. "You are stranded until the next train comes."

"Not at all. I will take these flowers to my ancestors' Golden Pagodas. Spirits," Lin Yan said drolly, "must be looked after, for if they are neglected they become restless and roam the world inflicting hardships on the living. Most of the misfortunes of life are engineered by these underprivileged spirits, you know."

Hellen collapsed, laughing. "You are truly a very good friend."

The Asian girl looked pleased. "Oliver is bringing a pony for you."

Hellen thought how odd that it was that George had suggested she wear riding clothes. Lin Yan removed a package from the picnic basket for herself, then handed it to Hellen. "Here is your lunch. And there is one for Oliver, too. You may tie the basket by those straps to the saddle."

The train had stopped, the doors were being flung open, the Chinese were crushing excitedly through. Then suddenly Lin Yan was no longer there, and Hellen was stepping down on to the platform. Oliver came forward, holding out his arms.

They rode together far into the hills. At first they did not talk very much, only riding closely side-by-side, hand tightly held in hand. North of Lion Rock the terrain in parts reminded Hellen of Scotland. In other parts it was typically China, cut into small plots of varying sizes and shapes, descending in terraces from the lower slopes of bare hillside, yellow and acrid with crumbling river banks and tea coloured water. They passed a Chinese village lying snugly amongst a cluster of trees, smoke rising from its grey houses and the red "good joss" papers on lintels and door posts.

They passed rows of coolies working on the land, dresssed in traditional wrap-around trousers, loose jackets, and cone-shaped hats. "They somehow persuade the soil to yield three or four crops of rice and vegetables annually," Oliver told her. "Rainstorms in the typhoon seasons bring heavy erosion, but the Chinese bring the soil back and replant." He took her to see the little villages whose people's welfare were now his concern. He wanted her to know everything about his work. "I think about you all the time. You are never out of my thoughts."

"And you are never out of mine."

"I wish I could take you over the rest of the Territories, especially to the walled city of Kam Tin. The Beautiful Fields. There's a green with shady trees where the village worthies sit and watch the cattle browsing. And ponds full of green water with white ducks sailing on them, and carp underneath. The hedges are full of white dog-roses, and orange and pink lantana. The head of the village is called Tang. He can trace his Tang ancestry through twenty-six generations.

"When the British took the ninety-nine year lease on the Territories, the village resisted. Two thousand six hundred Chinese held out. Our troops drove them back. The Governor of the time took the city's iron gates to England. As a punishment, so he said. The village elders have never stopped asking for their return. It's going to be my first crusade when I acquire standing in the Service," vowed Oliver, "to bring those gates back, and have them reinstated.

Hellen noticed he said "when", not "if" and she was afraid, knowing her presence here with him was a threat to his future.

"The work is more satisfying than all that clap-trap in Hong Kong. If only you were with me." His arms and face were brown from the sun. He looked immensely fit. "Sometimes I'm wakened in the night by a barking deer, or a raucous crow-pheasant, and go out on to the verandah. If the moon's up I can see right across to the Sai Kung Peninsula. It's quite wonderful—or would be if you were here."

Neither of them asked, "What are we going to do?" They knew there was nothing they could do. There was no future, in the new Territories or anywhere else, except by an Act of God, and it seemed God had had plenty of time to make a decision.

They rode up to a tree-shaded hilltop and tethered the ponies while they ate the picnic food Lin Yan had brought. Little rice cakes, and

287

chicken, bean sprouts, and pigeons' eggs. Afterwards, they lay in the dappled shade. There was no passionate race to taste of the fruit that was forbidden to them by George, and by the sanctified act of that dreadful marriage made less in the eyes of God than in those of Charlie Marsh, the late Captain Boggis, and the second mate whose name she never knew. They talked and kissed and grew closer and closer until they merged, with the dappled sunlight, as part of nature.

"Last night," said Oliver, "I had a dream. That you and I were together on a hill—not here. Somewhere strange, and very, very green. Something quite frightful had happened." He repeated the words. "Quite frightful. Something so bad that neither of us could speak about it."

Hellen shivered.

"We were dressed in strange clothes," said Oliver. "And you were covered in dust."

"It was just a dream," she said. They were quiet then, looking down into the silent valley. Layer upon layer of silence. They listened to it, filled their hearts with it, and were at peace.

They rode on in the afternoon to the bungalow that was Oliver's lonely home. His Tin Lizzie, its black paintwork grey with dust, stood on the dry grass at the side. There were three bedrooms, starkly furnished, with pretty cotton curtains at the windows, a small sitting room with a desk were Oliver did his administrative work, and a kitchen containing the usual sparse collection of woks, chop sticks, a few bowls, some tin pans and the inevitable scrubbed wood table and chopper. Far over the fields, in the upper reaches of Tolo Harbour, sampans and junks rested at anchor on the blue and purple shaded water. Oliver pointed to a straggle of pines that ran down towards the Tolo inlet.

"One day I noticed birds circling and swooping on the edge of those trees, and some hawks directly above them. I went down to investigate and found two baskets hanging from a branch. There were ants crawling in hundreds up the trunk along the branch and down into the baskets. I cut the rope and brought the baskets down. There were two tiny babies in them, half clothed, with ants and flies clustering round their eyes and nostrils.

"Twins are a disaster to the ignorant coolie," Oliver explained. "Girl twins are a sign the spirits are angry. They're almost always put out to die."

"What did you do?" She was hungry for every detail of Oliver's life.

"They stank dreadfully, because they were encrusted with filth. I brought them up here and with the help of the boys, managed to soak their rags off. We gave them warmed buffalo milk, wrapped them in

288

towels and took them to the babies' home in Fanling. It's run by English missionaries. They're doing very well." He grinned, looking proud. "They're my babies. I christened them Po Chue and Oi Chue. That's Precious Pearl and Beloved Pearl. I visit them, and contribute to their keep. I'd love to introduce you to them, but I daren't take you there."

Hellen gripped his hand tightly. Out of his loneliness, some good had come. "Is it part of your job to stop this sort of thing?"

Oliver said ruefully, "If only I could. These superstitions are deeply rooted. There are evil old crones, usually going by the name of wise woman, in every village. They will torment a newly born girl baby with red-hot chopsticks to drive out evil spirits. They burn them by the ears, eyes or nostrils, which they consider to be outlets for the escape of the spirits. The screams and burning are supposed to frighten the spirits into flying off. How do you beat this kind of thing out of them? Missionaries have been trying for donkeys years."

They wandered round the garden. There were flower beds bearing witness to the endeavours of Mrs Sinclair, now overgrown with weeds as a result of Oliver's neglect. "Wherever an Englishwoman unpacks, there will be an English garden," said Oliver. "Somehow, I hadn't the heart to tend it."

Hellen looked down at the fruits of his despair, the weeds growing rankly among the brave little forget-me-nots, blowsy poppies, phlox and balsams, larkspur and enormous pink petunias, top heavy on their long stalks. "It would be nice for you to look at flowers," she said. "Why don't we clean it up together? We've never done anything—built anything—together. Let's make a 'Hellen and Oliver's garden'."

They searched out spades and trowels and hoes. They worked fast, watering the dry soil so that it more easily released the weeds, exposing stunted little carnations that had been shaded by the more virile pests. Afterwards, Hellen made tea because Oliver had sent his house boys off to their village for the day. They sat on the verandah looking with satisfaction on Hellen and Oliver's garden where pale-leafed marigolds, grown spindly as they reached towards the light, lifted their weak little heads, and the small, misty pink carnations proudly showed their many buds. They both had a defiant feeling of accomplishment, as though they had, on this day, the fourteenth of May 1921, promoted their cause by bringing flowers to life in a barren land.

Oliver reached out a hand and touched the piece of jade she wore on the gold chain round her neck. "It's bright," he said with satisfaction.

He smoothed the jade with his fingers. They lingered, entering the curve between her breasts, then curled round them, caressing them. She lifted her head sensuously, her eyes soft with love. They rose and went into Oliver's bedroom, with its big double bed. The bungalow, out here in the lonely New Territories, had been furnished for a married man.

They drove back to Kowloon. It was slow going and bone shaking. Oliver manoeuvred his car between the potholes on the little road that led towards the craggy ranges with Plover Cove and the Shatin estuary darkening as the sun went down. As they came up over the granite hills on a pass where the Amah Rock stood alone, a feeling of destiny overcame them both. Oliver reached out a hand. In that timeless moment, it was as though the world had stopped. In the hidden darkness of her mind, Hellen sensed an end.

At the northernmost point of Kowloon, where Nathan Road came in, they found a rickshaw coolie plying for business. "I daren't go any further," Oliver said, warily glancing this way and that. Too many people knew him, the Governor's nephew, by sight. He ran round to the passenger door, opened it, and Hellen slipped out. They had already paused in a safer place to say good-bye. Their hands locked. They did not speak.

As she sat back in the hooded seat of the rickshaw, looking down the long, straight road over the head of the half naked coolie who pulled her, Hellen felt the darkness come in again. It was as though threads, unimportant in themselves, were coming together. She did not feel afraid, but she had a sense of waiting, as though something beyond her control was about to begin.

The St George's Day ball, one of the big events in the social calendar, was held at the Hong Kong Hotel. Around the walls of the two ballrooms had been hung crests of English towns, as well as civic flags. The dais was decorated with the emblem of St George. A company of Beefeaters in full regalia formed a guard of honour for the official party. The stately procession made its way to the ballroom, Lettice looking lovely in gold lace with the newly fashionable flat-chested front, and her hem drooping prettily above her slim ankles; a Jenny Wren beside her peacock husband. She had not invited Hellen to tea again, nor ever would, Hellen thought. It was generally known that if you blotted your copy book in Vice Regal circles, you would not be offered another opportunity to err.

Hellen had waited in all day, half expecting a message from Lin Yan to say Oliver was coming, but there had been none. The Somersert Light Infantry band struck up "Roast Beef of Old England".

While everyone followed the official party with their eyes, Hellen's were hypnotically drawn to the door. With every bit of her strength, she willed Oliver to appear. All evening, whenever there was a disturbance, her eyes swept back to the door. When the fanfare rose to herald the arrival of the boar's head she came erect in her seat, willing him to march in behind that procession.

But he did not come.

Disappointment drained the life from her limbs and the sparkle went. Her eyes travelled broodingly over her fellow guests, resplendent in silks and jewels; over the florid, self-satisfied men, the pale, diffident men, all of one creed, one class, one insularity. Oh, what an English place this was, this tiny corner of China, she thought as the speeches extolling the motherland went on and on. Since her visit to Oliver in the New Territories she had been out of sorts with the Englishness. Even the cadets who spent years at the British Government's expense studying Cantonese, used it only expediently. They gave orders in pidgin to their servants, but to the populace, seemed not to talk at all. But Oliver was not like that. Oliver wanted to restore gates stolen from a Chinese village. Oliver, who would never be in a position to do so unless she moved out of his life.

Some pompous man was on the dais, quoting Wordsworth. "I travelled among unknown men, in lands beyond the sea. . ." She leaned her chin on a cupped hand, thinking her unhappy thoughts, only half listening. We are all equal in the sight of God except those with black faces, brown faces, yellow faces. She thought of the lovely Lin Yan who was unacceptable at bridge and cocktails and tennis and cricket and hockey. More than acceptable as a concubine. More fool her, George had said, that she failed to take up the offers. "What has she to lose?"

The last speech was droning to an end. ". . . This blessèd land, this earth, this realm, this England."

There was a movement beside her and Hellen looked up to see the taipan of Lonewood & Southby standing beside her.

"May I have the pleasure of the next dance, Mrs Curtain?"

"I'll be with you in Apple Blossom Time," sang the dancers. Keane said as they moved out on to the floor, "You've a very expressive face, Mrs Curtain."

She carefully composed it into a polite smile.

"Are you enjoying yourself?"

"Very much." She smiled in an attempt to conceal the fact that she was not enjoying herself at all.

Holding her away from him, Elliott Keane looked down into her face. And how is George's cricket going, Mrs Curtain? Did he run up some good scores last week?"

"Last week?" she repeated. Had George played cricket last week? She could not remember. She thought the mail had come in. After the arrival of a mail steamer there was always a spurt of business activity that kept George at the office until five o'clock. Then there would be a lull, during which time the men would drink a little at lunch time, and knock off around three o'clock for hockey or cricket. It was thought that if a young man wished to follow pursuits as healthy and gentlemanly as hockey or cricket, it was only right he should be given time off work in which to indulge them.

"George has been off early every afternoon this week," said his taipan.

She was aware of his curious eyes on her face.

"He's very keen on sport," she returned warily. When he intended to play, George would take to work a small portmanteau. And that evening she would have to ask Ah Wong to see that his sweat-soaked clothes were gathered up from the floor of his room. She had not seen him carrying the portmanteau for weeks. "He doesn't talk sports to me," she said. "You will have to ask him."

On the way home, on the Star ferry, she told George what his taipan had said.

George looked out into the darkness of the channel that separated Hong Kong island from the mainland. He fingered his moustache. In the pale light of the moon she thought he looked smug.

"Perhaps you would tell me what I should say at such times, to save myself embarrassment." She glanced away as she always did when the scar where George's ear had been severed, came accidentally into view.

"I don't suppose it will happen again."

"Do you mean you're not going to go about your own business in your firm's time again?"

"There's more to life than a job with Lonewood & Southby."

She was startled. "You're thinking of leaving?"

He seemed to consider his reply. "The reason I don't give a damn what Elliot Keane thinks," he said at last, "is because I have a cargo on its way that's going to set me up for life." He gave her a sidelong look, almost sly. "Maybe you'll like me better when I'm a millionaire."

Hellen caught her breath.

He leaned back against the rail. "You'll get more than a ruby ring," he said. "A trip round the world, perhaps? We could concoct a tale about you inheriting a fortune. They know I'm not getting any money from anywhere. But what about that rich grandfather of yours, heh? That industrialist, who pays for diamond necklaces and ruby rings? We could come back and have a house on The Peak, without any questions asked. How d'you like to be a leading hostess on The Peak, Hellen? With good joss," said George, "I might even be able to start my own hong. Or we could tootle off to America. How would you like that? A new start, eh? He leaned towards her, his excitement showing, and she could see this was not a sudden, reckless idea, but something that had lain in his mind for a long time.

"I will not go to America with you." She was shaking with shock and anger. "I will not go anywhere on your ill-gotten gains."

"What a prude you are," said George, the smile on his face suddenly replaced by a scowl. "As a matter of fact, if I go to America—and I may have to, if things go wrong—as my wife you will certainly go with me. You will have no choice."

"What do you mean 'if things go wrong'?" The shock had given way to splintery fear.

"You know what I mean."

"If you're caught?"

He gave her a queer, glassy look. "If I'm caught, I shall know where to lay the blame, because you're the only one who knows."

Then the ferry bumped up against the jetty and they were back in Kowloon.

Chapter 28

The Strike

Hellen was frightened. She toyed with the thought of going to Neil. George would never forgive her, but did that matter? She held back only because in her heart she knew that Neil had no influence over his son. And it would make him very unhappy. Marcia would be distraught. Nothing would be gained. She did not go riding, and neither did she seek out friends, for she was afraid to trust herself with a sympathetic ear. At night she lay awake worrying, and during the day wandered round the little shopping streets of Kowloon where she was unlikely to run into anyone she knew.

Then one morning, when Ah Wong had gone to market and Hellen was desultorily arranging some flowers in the hall, the doorbell rang, and there was Oliver, in a cotton shirt and white duck trousers, with his solar topee in one hand. "Is it all right to come in?"

Dazzled, her feet half way off the ground, she drew him into the hall.

"I had to come," he said. "I was worried about you. I've been worried ever since I dropped you that day. I had a premonition that something was going to happen."

She told him that George was going to leave the colony, taking her with him. Perhaps to America. And she told him how easily he had settled the Squeeze problem. "Ruth said the Triads are behind that."

Oliver said, "We have to run away." He spoke quite calmly, as though he had always known that was what it would come to.

She held his hands tightly while she told him what George had planned. "He will divorce me and name you, and that will be the end of your career," she said. "I can't let you give up everything for me."

He put his arms round her and held her very tightly. "I won't let you go." Then suddenly his head came up and he said in a soft little shout, "America! Why shouldn't you and I go to America? It's supposed to be the land of opportunity! Why shouldn't we make our fortune there?"

She felt dizzy with excitement. "What about your career?"

"Oh, stuff that," retorted Oliver.

And then she remembered another thing. "George said I'd better not try to run away. He said he had connections at the docks. He said he would know."

"Not if the cabin is booked in the name of Mr and Mrs Smith. And on a boat going to America. No one would expect you to be going there. We could take you aboard disguised as a sandwich or a bunch of flowers," said Oliver. "I'll get Denzil to fix it all up. Denzil's experienced. He's already done it."

Hellen lived through the following week in a state of emotional turmoil. Every morning, after George had left for work, she scanned the shipping news. There was a boat sailing for San Francisco on the tenth. She neither heard from nor saw Denzil.

Then one morning Major Tandy telephoned.

"How about a spot of tiffin with an old buffer?" he asked.

Hellen was delighted.

"Could you be at the Hong Kong Hotel by one?"

She came out of the front door wearing a pretty hat, saw it had begun to rain, and returned for a mackintosh, then hurried up the road and found a rickshaw. She felt sad at the thought of never seeing the Major again. The friendly bond that had been forged between them on *Narkunda* had strengthened over the time she had been in Hong Kong. She would never forget how he had given up his dance for Oliver that night at the Government House ball. There were so many people she would not see again. Ruth. Toby and Wanda Ayre. Kitty and Denzil. Lin Yan. She felt a lump come into her throat. Of all the friends she had made, Lin Yan was the one she most cherished.

In Central the rain was streaming down. A miniature flood swirled along the streets, carrying little stones and mud, hurling itself playfully up against the coolies' naked shins as they sloshed through. There was a rabble under the hotel's arches, dropping fares, plying for custom. People were shaking the rain from their shoulders and their umbrellas. Hellen paid the coolie and hurried through the doors into the lounge.

They sat down in the big comfortable chairs and Major Tandy ordered cocktails. A Manhattan. A Sidecar. Everyone was drinking cocktails now. They were the newest American import. People came by and they exchanged greetings. "You've made a lot of friends, my dear," said Tandy, looking pleased. "You've made your mark. I hope you're happy." She was reminded, as she looked into his eyes, of a basset hound they once had at Jolliffe's Farm. "Are you happy?" he asked kindly.

She wanted to tell him that soon she was going to be the happiest girl in the world. "I am happy, Major." She thought of Oliver, of running away with him, and the smile on her face went right through her. "Perhaps not in the way you're thinking, but yes, I am truly happy now."

"Y'know," he said, squeezing a tiny salted biscuit until it powdered between finger and thumb, "I have a feeling about you and young Oliver. P'raps not as wise as you might be, what." He brushed the biscuit from his fingers into an ashtray. "No reason why you should be, at your age. And people don't want you to be. There are plenty of bimbos out there love to see the Governor's nephew come a purler." He added hurriedly, "Not because they don't like him, mind you. For the sheer heck of it." He screwed his monocle into his left eye, leaned towards her and asked, "J'know about young Oliver's career, m'dear? Important not to foul it up, and all that."

There was a shift of feeling in her, as though something held back was trying to get through; should come through.

"Young people don't learn from example," he said. "I'm a dull old fat head, and there's no reason why you should listen to me. Thought I'd just tell you something, though. Care to listen?"

"What is it, Major?"

"Why I never married. Indelicate subject, you might think. Don't often mention it. Thought you might be interested, what."

She nodded, faintly surprised.

He cleared his throat, shifted his feet on the carpet, shifted them back again. "Y'know, I was engaged to the prettiest girl you'd find in a day's march, and a little squirt, nothing like my size, and with only a half pip to my one, took a shine to her. I knew he was a rotter. Couldn't convince her, though. Used to lie awake at night thinking how I could whale the tar out of him—I was a big chap even in those days—but in the end I didn't do anything. She married him."

Hellen asked concernedly, "Did he treat her badly?"

"Matter of fact, it was the greatest success. They had a splendid little family, he inherited a title, and rose to be a general."

She suddenly felt cold. "What are you trying to tell me, Major?"

"Oh, I don't know, my dear. Why should you listen to a gloomy old buster like me saying I had my little love affair? Just sometimes what you think is right, isn't. Not necessarily."

"You're saying I should give up Oliver?" she asked baldly.

"Hmn." He paused, scratched his ear. "I thought you gave him up when you married."

She was suddenly very angry. She leaned forward and said, in a sharp whisper, "I married George because he took me aboard

Bangkok Lady, drugged my drink, stole my luggage, and while I was unconscious, raped me." She sat back in her chair, two bright spots in her cheeks, her eyes stormy. "There!" she said. "I've been dying to say that to someone."

There had been no one to tell. Not without hurting George's parents. Not without rousing Oliver to furious retaliation. But dear Major Tandy with his old fashioned, decent values, he was the one safely to shock, and purge herself, because she needed to be purged of the unfair guilt she felt in the presence of Marcia, and Neil, and Oliver. "That's what happened," she said. "And now I've told you, I feel much better."

Major Tandy lifted his glass and sipped his drink. From his pocket he produced a silver snuff box and opened it, stared down at the brown snuff for a long time, then slowly put a pinch into each nostril. He pulled a handkerchief out of his pocket and wiped, in turn, the corner of each eye.

Feeling uncomfortable, Hellen looked away. "I'm sorry," she muttered. "I'd no right to tell you that."

One of the waiters came to say their table was ready. The Major rose clumsily and held out his arm to escort her into the tiffin room. "Come on, m'dear."

They were given a table for two near a window. Outside, the rain was still coming down. The waiter handed Hellen the menu. At sight of the Chinese list, the defiance in her broke through again. She ordered soup, and English steak that had travelled ten thousand miles on ice. A very English luxury. She felt very English, as though she had already left everything that was eastern and exotic behind. Choosing the steak was a kind of defiance.

Major Tandy toyed with his curry. He disconcerted her by wiping his eyes again. She was consumed with guilt. Glancing away, she saw a stream of grave-faced men, in business suits, coming into the room. Everyone looked up, watching them. They sat down at a long table. The Major asked rhetorically, "What's going on?" All over the dining room the buzz of chatter rose.

"Who are they?" Hellen asked.

"Shipping men. Heads of shipping firms. Must be something up, for so many of them to be meeting here."

Shipping men. His words touched a cord and she suddenly thought that some older person, someone less involved than Denzil, ought to know what had happened, when she and Oliver sailed away. She did not want people to chuckle and say elopements were catching, like measles, or jumping off the Forth Bridge. Perhaps, if she told Major Tandy, he might speak for her, now he knew what she had been through. She put down her knife and fork, pressed forward across the table and said softly, "Oliver and I are going to run away."

He did not look surprised. There was a fork full of curry half way to his mouth. He put it in, as though she had not just told him the most stupendous news. When he had finished, when his mouth was empty again, he asked, "Is this his idea, or yours, my dear?"

"He decided. I agreed."

"He's a good lad," said Tandy. He put down his knife and fork and stared ruminatively at the table cloth. "A very good lad. A right thinking lad. Chivalrous."

Hellen smiled gratefully.

Then he astounded her by adding, "But with a soft centre. When a man is like that, the woman has to be prepared to stand firm. Women are so much stronger than men."

As though she had not told him what George had done, as though he had not wept about it, he continued, "A man's career is his greatest asset. A man's career is him. Any man will give up anything for a woman if he wants her badly enough. Did you happen to know that Oliver will be the Earl of Stradlock one day, with many responsibilities? A vast estate, and a castle in Scotland?" He had put the monocle back into his eye, and was looking at her very hard.

Hellen caught her breath. "No," she said in a panicky rush. "No. His father is a younger son. The second son. He's not the heir."

"Not at the moment."

"What do you mean?"

"Hasn't he told you about his Uncle Cecil?"

"No."

"Cecil, Viscount Marathon, was very badly wounded in the war. He's not going to live."

"How do you know?"

"The old grapevine, what. Not personally acquainted with the family, but my sister knows Oliver's sister, Marigold Wolfe. Gossip, my dear. Gossip. But very authentic gossip, this lot."

She was preparing to run away to America with. . . . Her throat contracted. Lady Sylvia Ashton's words, only half comprehended at the time, and that on another level, came winging back over the months and miles. "It is possible, though not probable, that Oliver will inherit."

"There's absolutely no chance of Cecil's living to any sort of age," said the Major. "And he hasn't got a son. Oliver's father will inherit, then Oliver, in his turn. You would make quite a mess of things," said the Major tartly, "if you ran off with Oliver. Especially if George didn't divorce you. These old families are what makes England what

298

it is, y'know. How would you feel if you were the cause of the title slipping sideways, so to speak, and Oliver and his descendants losing their heritage? Come to think of it, he wouldn't have any descendants, unless they were—er—don't like to say it, what. Wrong side of the blanket. Know what I mean? A pretty kettle of fish."

There was a cold feeling in the pit of her stomach. But George had said he would divorce her, naming Oliver. That would not matter, in the circumstances that they were going to disappear into America where nobody was likely to hear, or if they did, to care, about a scandal involving a young Englishman who had not begun to make his mark in the world. "George has said he would divorce me."

"D'you think the Marathons would welcome a divorcée?" the Major asked. "Just thinking about you, my'dear. Divorce is pretty strong stuff. Wouldn't've thought you were the kind of girl to do that kind of thing to a man you love. To a dynasty, really. It's taking something on, I'd say, to mess up an old family like that. What!"

She sat there thinking numbly this was, in a way, what George had said to her, but without the Major's kindly wish to save her pain. A black silence of despair spread around her as she recognized that the whole sordid mess was something she had to live with, and make the best of. From the beginnings with Calum Finn, to marriage to a man who took opium from the dead—for it had belonged to Captain Boggis—and sold it to men who would die. She looked out bleakly across the years, hearing herself saying to some young girl in a hotel dining room, somewhere, "I had my little love affair. The man has gone on to do very well."

She would go home. She would find a way to side-step George. Someone would help her. Denzil, who was so good at these things. Or even Major Tandy, though she could scarcely imagine him booking a cabin for her in the name of Mrs Smith.

The shipping men were filing out. One of them stopped at their table. "Hello, Tandy." He smiled at Hellen and she recognised him as one of Ruth's friends. "You're doing very well for yourself, old chap," he said, patting the Major on the shoulder. "How nice to see you, Mrs Curtain. I hope you're keeping Harry here in order."

The Major said, "Now, now, don't tease. Mrs Curtain and I are very old friends. What's going on, Price?"

"Twenty-three Chinese employers have signed an undertaking to guarantee a wage increase without reference to the European shipping companies. We've had a meeting this morning to discuss it."

"You're going to up the seamen's wages?"

"No. We're not. You'll read all about it in the papers tomorrow."

"Ah well," said the Major, "we all have our troubles."

It was in headlines the next morning. The day following, the union sent out a call to all Chinese on ocean-going and river steamers calling at Hong Kong to strike in sympathy. The seamen walked back to their homes in China, joined by printers, barbers, boiler-makers, electricians, fitters, tea-house waiters and private house servants. Even the Peak tram drivers went, leaving the no-longer-idle rich isolated in their mansions, without even the night soil coolies to empty their thunder boxes.

Government House, it was said, had two Haaka staff. The Governor's retinue, even the Governor himself, rolled up his sleeves and knuckled down to whatever had to be done. At the Repulse Bay Hotel the residents went to work in the kitchens. The English were showing their strength in adversity. They weren't just a bunch of idle hedonists. An accountant with one of the big hongs nearly severed his hand in the hotel's butchery department. It was the blind leading the blind. They had only their commonsense to guide them.

Parents discovered their children. The wife of the Secretary for Chinese Affairs organised a baby sitting service so mothers could go out and try to buy food. Bridge parties were suspended. Women donned frilly aprons and sought to find their way round their own kitchens. Hellen went out and bought utensils. It was not possible for her to cook a square meal with Ah Wong's dangerous chopper, and a pair of wooden chopsticks. She went to Central to shop, travelling on a Star ferry crewed by naval ratings. It seemed they found the cross-currents of the harbour harder to navigate than the high seas, for the ferry arrived at the pier with a terrible crash.

With *Mrs Beeton's Book of Household Management* in one hand, and the bowls and knives and whisks on the table, Hellen set to work. She offered to provide dinner for George's parents as well, because Marcia, going out to Shanghai as a bride of nineteen, had never cooked a meal in her life. She was lucky to have her cookery book already. The *S.S. Autolycus* sailed from London with a full assignment of *Mrs Beetons*, the Hong Kong bookshop having run out the day the servants left. With the wives doing the laundry, men went to work in shorts and shirt sleeves. They were easier to wash and iron than white duck suits.

Ruth rolled up her sleeves and began work at the Café Wiseman that was endeavouring to supply all the colony's bread. Everyone had to pay cash for everything. There was no one to deal with chits. Lin Yan and Hellen worked at the Dairy Farm at Pok Fu Lam, that supplied Hong Kong with frozen meat and milk. They were picked up at the Star ferry by an army transport and returned by the same

300

method. Hellen felt cynical about the fact that Lin Yan, who was not allowed into the Hong Kong Club, the Cricket Club, or any of the other holy English places, was nonetheless allowed to aid the English in adversity.

Work was a novel experience, after nearly a year of idleness. On a certain level, Hellen was enjoying being useful. At least it helped to keep her mind off what she must say to Oliver, as well as the desolate future. There were no sailings for runaways. Even if Denzil could obtain a booking, even if she decided to flaunt her own needs defiantly in the face of the establishment, there were no ships to carry her away with Oliver to the land of the free.

She had no idea what part Oliver was taking. The cadets were doing duty as special constables. The Governor, declaring martial law, had set up military and naval posts along the borders with China in an endeavour to stop the exodus of workers. It was possible Oliver would be helping there. Passenger traffic on the Kowloon–Canton rail had closed down to prevent strikers leaving for Canton where food was more readily available, so there was no question of going to talk to him. Many of the hongs released their younger men to help. George rode round the streets on a Mongolian pony, armed with a gun. In some corner of her mind Hellen knew it was better for Oliver to be in the New Territories.

It was a frightening time.

When the day Hellen was waiting for came—what was she waiting for? She could not have said—she recognised it in Kitty Armitage's face. She had gone into the office at the Dairy Farm, still wearing her big, useful apron, for she had been sorting out the depleted stocks of tinned food, and was looking through invoices. A small, blonde whirlwind with her hair fallen loose and her hat in her hand hurtled through the doorway. In a sharp whisper, she hissed, "Hellen, come outside."

A feeling of dread assailed her, like a crystallisation of the doubts and uncertainties that had hovered in her brain ever since George went into the back streets of Wanchai armed with a gun. Swiftly, she took off the big apron and hung it behind the door while Kitty went out into the road to wait. It was a cold day. What the Chinese called a three-coat day, when the coolies in the streets seemed to shrivel and age like autumn leaves. She took down her jacket, shrugged into it, and wound the long scarf loosely round her neck.

Kitty had moved a little way along the path, and was eyeing the door anxiously, waiting for her. She looked doubly flustered now. She was not wearing gloves. She had jammed her hat on her head right down to her eyebrows, and some of her coat buttons were

301

undone. She said in a hoarse whisper, though there was no one within earshot, "He's shot Denzil."

The careful calm went. Hellen stared at her, stupefied. After all, she had not been ready for this. The mind prepares on another level.

"The bullet went through Denzil's topee. He's up at the hospital now. It grazed the side of his head. Hellen, listen. Hellen, don't you understand?" She grasped Hellen's arm and shook it frantically, as though she could shake the facts into her. "George has shot Denzil. Up in Wanchai, where the English are trying to put down the street fighting."

Hellen burst out defensively, "How could anyone know it was George?" It could not be. She would not have it. Kitty had to be wrong.

"Hellen, the Chinese are not armed. They're throwing sticks and stones."

"George isn't a murderer," said Hellen, feeling as though she would choke at any moment, speaking through stiff lips, remembering how George had knocked her down on the deck of *Bangkok Lady*; reliving the quivering horror of the moment she realised he had not mentioned her existence to his parents, or to the newspaper reporters who had interviewed him on his arrival.

Kitty was shaking like a leaf. "I think he is," she whispered. "He's in with those dreadful Triads. They do worse than shoot at people. Hellen, you've got to talk to him. Don't you see? You've got to talk to him. Denzil won't accuse him. He won't tell the police. He can't, can he? I mean. . . ."Kitty broke down, sobbing.

Hellen put her arms round her, comforting her.

"It's so easy to shoot someone in a crowd," sobbed Kitty, "and say it was an accident. He's trying to destroy Denzil." She made a great effort to pull herself together. "He's upset the taipan should have taken Denzil back. He was hoping to step into Denzil's job. Did you know that? He wanted Denzil's job. He's been doing a lot of little things that get Denzil into trouble. Nothing much on their own, but adding up. He's trying to—" her voice broke again"—destroy Denzil."

Hellen never knew, these days, what time George would be home. The men came off duty when the streets quietened. She opened the front door with her key and crossed the hall, her footsteps silent on the carpet. The door to his study was open. He was seated in the leather chair. She went and stood in the doorway, a terrible anger flaring through her because he was so calm after having done such a terrible thing. "You shot Denzil!"

He looked up tiredly, his eyes quizzical. "Oh, Christ! That's the final straw. Bring me a drink, will you, you stupid bitch."

For a moment she could do no more than stand rooted to the spot, staring glassily at him. Then, with a feeling of unreality, she turned and went into the dining room, kicking her shoes off her sore feet as she went, throwing her hat on to the hall table. She went to the mahogany sideboard that was losing its bright polish now that Ah Wong had been gone for three weeks. She picked up a bottle of whisky, took one of the wedding present glasses meant for Oliver from the cabinet she had bought for George with opium money, and went back to the study. "There's no ice," she said.

"Of course there's no ice, you stupid cow." George spoke still in that tired tone, quite lacking in venom. "You didn't expect some yak to wander down on its own with a load, did you? Bring me some water."

She went back through the hall, across the dining room, out into the passage and along to the kitchen. She filled a jug with water at the sink and returned to the study, numbly armed against further insult. She put the jug down on the desk. George had poured out enough whisky to half fill a glass, and was sipping it neat.

He said, "So I shot Denzil! Is that what he's saying?"

"You hit him in the head."

"Someone certainly hit him in the head. We were shooting across the heads of the crowd. They were getting dangerous. Bloody Denzil Armitage," he said contemplatively. "It would be him. And out in the crowd where he'd no right to be." George took another sip of his whisky, put it down and poured in some water. He finished it at a gulp, then replaced the glass on the desk.

"So it's all over Hong Kong, is it, that George Curtain, under the shield of the coolie uprising, went with a gun after the chap who stole his girl? Oliver Marathon has been banished to the New Territories for playing around with George Curtain's wife. It's the final straw factor? Enough to make Curtain pick up a gun?"

Hellen stood in her stockinged feet on the expensive Chinese carpet she had bought for George, to furnish George's house, which she did not wish to share. She moved forward a step and rested a hand on his shoulder. As she did so she realised it was the first time she had ever made a spontaneous gesture of warmth towards him. Even on board ship, when he had been wooing her so assiduously, she had never reached out to him. She said, "I'm sorry. I was upset less about Denzil than about the fact that Oliver is also somewhere. If you shot Denzil, you could shoot him."

"Yes," said George, still in that slow, contemplative voice. "Yes. I could do that." He looked up at her, his face creased. "Anyone will do anything, when pushed far enough. You said yourself you would kill me, or run away, if I raped you again." He paused, then said, speaking as though to himself, "Kill . . . run. . . . It's much the same. Does it not occur to you what effect your doing a bunk would have on me? Two women running away. There has to be something very suspicious about a chap two women run away from."

There was a long, strained silence. Through the window came the violent eruption of a lone cicada. "Ch-rr-rr-rkk."

Hellen said, "I'm sorry, George. I truly am."

It seemed to her, at that moment, life had not dealt him a fair hand.

Chapter 29

Joe North

The strike worsened. The Seamen's Union was declared illegal. The offices of the Tung Tak Guild and the Chap Yin Transportation Workers' Union were raided and closed down. There were a hundred or more unmanned ships at the docks laden with perishable cargoes.

The Hong Kong Club set up a cafeteria service. People went there for tiffin, carrying their own trays. The general manager of the Hong Kong and Shanghai Hotels rolled up his sleeves and went to work in the kitchens. The Chinese New Year, normally a time for the pealing of bells, and crashing of cymbals, the firing of thundering guns from the warships in the harbour, came and went without celebration. Putting on a brave fce, the expatriates said they were spared the acrid odour of firecrackers that normally at this time permeated the entire colony.

A senior partner in a firm of stevedores was shot dead by a hired assassin. Two thousand coolies set out on an organised march to Canton. Because they did not have permits to leave the colony, troop reinforcements and police went up to Shatin to confront them. Hellen, who had been on shift work at the Dairy Farm, was at home the morning Wanda rang to say there had been a massacre at Shatin. She and Toby were wondering if Hellen had heard if Oliver was all right. "Apparently a whole lot of troops set out from here, but they never arrived. The buses broke down. So there were only a handful of English to face the mob. We thought," suggested Wanda diffidently, "being a friend of everybody at Government House, you could ring and get details. That is, if they have any."

"Yes," said Hellen numbly.

"You will ring them? I mean," said Wanda, "we can't very well, but you could. You will, won't you?"

"Yes," said Hellen. There was a tight band across her chest, restricting her breathing and interfering with her voice.

"Are you there?" asked Wanda.

The handpiece slipped from Hellen's fingers and swinging, bounced against the wall. She turned to walk away, then turned back, numbly staring at the instrument as it spun back and forth on its cord. She could hear Wanda's distant voice asking anxiously, "Are you there?" Then there was a brr-rr-rr as the line went dead. She lifted the handpiece and hung it on the hook.

A massacre! Only a handful of English to face the mob! Two thousand coolies!

She went to the front door, opened it and stood looking out towards The Peak. A veil of cloud had come down on the mountain, as it so often did. The air pressed suffocatingly close. She went back into the house, through the hall, then out of the side door into the garden, as though she could walk away from the present. Its foreboding followed her. Her footsteps quickened. She went down the path that led to the garden shed where her cabin trunks were kept, along with the blocks of firewood they so seldom needed. She glanced distractedly to right and left as she went, looking for help, seeing only the green bushes with their bright red and yellow flowers, the fan-leafed gingko tree. In spite of the heat, she felt desperately cold. She crossed her arms over her breast and hugged herself, trying to bring some life and warmth back into her body. Her blood must have stopped moving.

A massacre! Two thousand coolies and a handful of English! The reinforcements had not come! She stood looking at the padlock on the door of the shed. If she shut herself in, they would not be able to bring her the news she could not face. Was this how it had to end, then? Not with a romantic elopement, but after all that, with a massacre. Not with her breaking Oliver's heart by refusing to ruin his career and his life. After a massacre, there was no life.

The Chinese were the cruellest people in the world.

She could not think of Oliver as dead. Oliver of the sparkling blue eyes, the lively, swinging gait. A life like that surely could not be snuffed out. It would take more than two thousand coolies to snuff Oliver out. But, two thousand of the cruellest people in the world against a handful of English! How many people constituted a handful? She remembered the pirates wielding their choppers on the deck of *Bangkok Lady*, and her mind slumped down into a great chasm of seeping darkness.

She went back to the house, through to the hall, and stood looking at the telephone. She could ring Government House, as Wanda suggested, and ask to speak to Lady Marathon. Except that she did not want to know. If she kept away from the telephone, no one would be able to tell her. Until she was told, it was only a rumour. And rumours could be unfounded.

A massacre!

There was a sound of footsteps on the path. She looked out through the open door and saw with craven fear that Ruth, wearing a grave expression on her face, was coming. Hellen was still. Even her heart seemed to stop beating. She smelt death in her nostrils, saw it in Ruth's eyes as she came over the threshold. Hellen made no move to greet her. One did not go out to meet death.

Ruth said, "I've got some dreadfully bad news for you, dear. Lettice Marathon asked—"

Hellen swung round and walked swiftly back through the hall, across the drawing room, and out of the glass doors. Down through the garden she went, walking, walking, wanting to be hidden where Ruth could not get at her to tell her what she had come to say.

"Hellen!"

She began to run. She ran joltingly, the way women less fit than herself ran, as though she was wearing high heels, and there was a very little strength in her legs. If she could keep away from Ruth, Ruth could not tell her everyone—the handful of English—had died massacred by two thousand coolies with long knives. Where was the shed? She stood, distraught and dazed, among the bushes, the snowball tree, the bauhinia, the accacia, and the red-flowered kapok, looking blindly and distractedly for the shed. She heard Ruth's footsteps on the path and began again to run. There it was. A refuge. She reached out despairingly. With futile insistence, she dragged at the padlock with her fingers.

"Hellen, dear."

She was cornered. She turned, leaning on the door, waiting with despair for Ruth to put a dagger through her heart.

Ruth was talking, but she could not hear the words. She knew Ruth was talking because her lips were opening and closing. She looked very distressed. She tried to take Hellen in her arms, but Hellen moved sideways to the edge of the shed, then backwards. People who brought bad news had no right to affection. Ruth was an enemy now. A great passion of hate rose up in her for this woman who had brought the news nothing would induce her to accept.

Ruth said, "Come inside, dear." She took one of Hellen's cold hands. Without being aware of walking, she found herself in the drawing room. A glass of water was held under her nose. "I'm so sorry," Ruth said. "Drink this, dear."

Hellen stared at the glass.

"How did you hear?" Ruth looked puzzled.

Hellen found her voice. "Wanda. Wanda rang."

Ruth put the glass down on the table and sat beside her. Her face had crumpled into a frown. "How could Wanda know?" she asked, lifting Hellen's hand and smoothing it between her own. "Hellen, dear, do you know what I'm saying?"

No. No, she did not know what Ruth was saying. If she said it again, she would block her ears.

"Your father. . . ."

Something was stumbling round in Hellen's brain, a vague awareness that they were at cross purposes. Ruth again held the glass of water out to her. The awareness became more acute, and at the same time more muddled. She asked in a puzzled voice, "How does my father know?"

"Hellen, dear," said Ruth, looking desperately concerned, now, "I've come to tell you your father is dead."

There was a moment of total silence, as though the whole world, all the birds and insects and people, had gone still. Then Hellen burst out laughing. She laughed until the tears ran down her cheeks.

Ruth jumped up and hurried through to the dining room. There was a row of cut-glass decanters on the sideboard, each decorated with a silver collar and a plaque reading Brandy, Whisky, Sherry, Port. Swiftly, she took a goblet from the glass-fronted cabinet and poured a measure of brandy. Her hands shook and some of the liquid sloshed over the side. She took a lace handkerchief from her pocket and swiftly wiped the wood surface, then carrying the goblet, hurriedly returned to the drawing room.

Hellen's head was resting against the sofa back. Her face, paper white but calm, was raised, her eyes closed. She was trying to think of her father as dead, but her thoughts would not go to Jolliffe's Farm. They could not go, because there was business here that must be dealt with first.

She said, without opening her eyes, "There was a massacre at Shatin."

"They're calling it that," replied Ruth crossly, "but it wasn't. There were two thousand coolies, and they wouldn't stop. What could a little group of police and soldiers do but shoot?" She spoke defensively. "Superintendent King fired a warning shot, but the mob surged on. The poor man was obliged to give orders to fire. In fact, only two coolies were killed. They really cannot call it a massacre," said Ruth. "That would be ridiculous. Anyway, the stupid coolies should have stopped. They should know the English wouldn't stand for that kind of nonsense."

Hellen wiped the tears from her cheeks. She said, quite calmly,

"My father is dead." Half a world away, this had happened. She could not grasp it. "My father is dead." She said it again. And then the sadness, coming from a distance, washed quietly over her.

"I'm so sorry," said Ruth. "Here."

Hellen looked at the brandy and shook her head.

"Do. Please do. It will make you feel better."

After a little while she took a sip.

"Why did they not cable you?" Ruth asked. "Why send word to Government House?"

Hellen closed her eyes again, as though that would shut the question out.

"Dear," said Ruth, "I hardly like to ask you this, in the circumstances, but have you not told them about your marriage?"

Hellen was aware that somethng had to be said. But not the truth. Not the fact that her marriage to George was nothing more than a passing phase. Not that once her father knew, holding his head high in the village of Lake Willow, he would say that his daughter had fallen in love with someone else.

Joe North did not believe, had not believed—she must think of him in the past now he was dead—in hiding things. He would look forward—would have looked forward—without considering what kind of man George was, to meeting him; adopting him as a son. He would make the marriage—would have made the marriage—into a concrete fact, which it must not become. Marnie would have had to listen to Lady Sylvia crowing that Oliver had come to his senses. She did not wish Marnie to have to face up to Lady Sylvia telling her that.

She opened her eyes and said, "It's a mess, Ruth."

"I'm sorry to say it, in the circumstances," Ruth said tartly, "but it's a mess you had better think about clearing up."

The strike was over. The *Hong Kong Daily Press* said it was a deeply humiliating end for both the government and the foreign community. The shipping companies had to increase wages. The government was obliged to reinstate the Seamen's Union. Nobody said, this time, that the victims were "only coolies". It had been a chastening experience, demonstrating the strength of the Chinese worker. Other papers announced that it had been scarcely a strike at all. Rather more a withdrawal of labour for political purposes. But they all knew now that the coolie class had power when organised. A sense of foreboding lay over the colony.

The servants came trailing back. Hellen found Ah Wong in the kitchen scornfully contemplating the utensils she had bought. The makee learn was scrubbing the floor that had seen no more than a mop for fifty-two days.

The funeral was a big affair. The bells tolled for a death in the village of Lake Willow, a sweet peal, for the soft red brick soaked up the sound and let it out gently over the green. The sexton received a shilling for ringing the death-bell. Three times three for a man, and three times two for a woman. Then the bells tolled the years of the life that had passed. The villagers paused in their work, leaning on shovels and hoes, looking at each other in awed dismay when the bells stopped speaking at fifty-four. You couldn't say a man had a good innings when he died at fifty-four.

The entire village turned out, the women in deepest black, those of the family heavily veiled, the villagers awkward in their Sunday best suits, because it was a Tuesday and out of order for Sunday best. The limousines were large, black and shiny, the pall-bearers impressive in their shining black stove pipe hats and come-to-Jesus collars. Sir Samuel Porchard, heading the procession, immediately behind the hearse in his black Rolls-Royce, knew how to make an impression. The coffin was the best money could buy, made of panelled oak, black as the pall bearers' coats.

There were dozens of dog carts, buggies, and a trail of pedestrians reaching right out across the green. The silage workers left their rakes and their open pit and the damp green grass to dry on the ground. The funeral was at two o'clock in the afternoon so the milkers could get back to their cow bails and their fat-uddered cows by four. The farmhands had been up early today, spreading their swedes and kale for the lambs that must be fattened for sale to the butcher within a month. There were foresters and forge workers and farriers, the headmaster of the village school, ploughmen and farm workers, the blacksmith, and even Dickon Ahern the odd job man. Everyone who had worked for Joe, or known him.

Old Archie Davy the gravedigger, who had been digging the graves in the churchyard since he was twelve years old, dug the hole. He was a lonely man, and lonelier for the death of Joe North. He went to church every Sunday but spoke to no one. If you asked him he'd say no one ever spoke to him. Except Joe North, who wasn't too snobbish to talk to a grave digger. One of nature's gentlemen, Joe North. Once saw him right with a new shovel when the vicar wouldn't pay.

"I'll make 'im real comfa'ble," he assured Marnie. "Real comfa'ble as 'e deserves. And I'll gather up the dead flowers so you won't have to worry, which is more than I do for most, I can tell you. My job ends with the filling in. Official, that is. But I'll see your hubby right."

310

Sir Samuel's floral offering was enormous. An exotic cross made of freesias, that most expensive of spring flowers, with an ornate card in a black frame and gilt lettering. Anyone could see it came from a person of substance. Lord Tynan sent a discreet little ring of spring flowers from Knight's Place gardens, daffodils and jonquils, put together by the second gardener who was thought to be adequate for the job.

Lord Tynan and his land agent walked into the church immediately behind the bereaved family, which was right, and gave distinction to the departed. The vicar made a poor job of choosing the hymns. No doubt the widow, if she hadn't been so distraught, would have done it herself. They began referring to Marnie as the widow immediately they learned for whom the bells tolled, for she could no longer be called Joe North's wife, which was what they had called her for thirty years. Nobody had anything against her, and no one thought she was uppish. She just wasn't one of them.

The hymns!

"Think, O Lord in mercy . . ." All that carry-on about stress and conflict and toils that never cease! That wasn't right for Joe North, they all agreed in the pub afterwards.

"'We plough the fields and scatter' would be more like it," the barman suggested, and someone else added, "Sun o' my soul'."

They nodded their heads over their tankards. Everyone was in agreement about that. The vicar was a newcomer, having been in the village only ten years, yet the way he carried on about Joe, spouting the facts they all knew from the pulpit as though it was news, telling them, as had known Joe all his life! You'd think Vicar was the one who had been born in Lake Willow, and his father before him. The hops for Harvest Festival always came from Jolliffe's Farm, he said. Of course they always came from Jolliffe's Farm. Where else? An upright man, the vicar said, ploughing a straight furrow. A man of deep sincerity and profound simplicity. A good man, of whom one could say he left only friends behind.

Well, they were all his friends and didn't need to be told by an outsider.

Many of the villagers had made their own wreaths from spring flowers grown in their gardens, and backed them with moss found in the woods along with late primroses. The air was heavy with the sweet scent of lilac, for everyone grew that. And lavender, white and purple. Those who were awkward with their fingers had brought enormous bunches of blooms tied with ribbon. Some had gathered them in the fields: ragged robin, feathery on pink stems, and lady's smock from the marshy patch down by the waterworks, as well as yew. The majority of the cards were home-made.

Sir Clancy Ashton considered whether, in the circumstances that the girl might still marry Oliver, he ought to put in an appearance. Lady Sylvia had written to Oliver's father for news, as well as his uncle, and his grandmother in Scotland, disconcertingly receiving no reply. Even Marigold Wolfe, Oliver's sister, normally a co-operative young woman, had been unforthcoming. Said there was a buzz on the line, and she couldn't hear properly, though the line into Kemble Manor was perfectly clear.

It must be said, and Sir Clancy and Lady Sylvia said it more than once during the week following Farmer North's death, that in he event of that foolish boy actually marrying the gel, things would be a degree more comfortable without the father. The mother might pass. Indeed, if one did not know her circumstances, one might take her for a lady.

They lowered Joe into the neat hole dug by Archie Davy, with his feet to the east, so that when all christendom rose he would be facing the Lord, and then those who had to return to work disappeared to change into their working clothes. Those who did not feel they would be comfortable in the widow's presence made off, whilst the rest trooped down the High Street in a raggedly line to take tea at Jolliffe's Farm.

Marnie officiated in the drawing room with quiet dignity, accepting the condolences of those who had loved her husband but never felt comfortable in her presence. Those whose curiosity so far got the better of them to comment that it was a shame Hellen should be so far away, received the identical reply. It would indeed be upsetting for Hellen not to be here.

It was the opinion of more than one in the village that it was Hellen's going off like that after one of the gentry that killed her father. They whispered it darkly in the bar of the Cock. Died of the worry, they wouldn't be surprised.

Only Lord Tynan received a straight answer, and that from Sir Samuel Porchard. "I'm a plain speaking man, Your Lordship, and I don't mind telling you," he said, standing squarely before the fireplace, rock solid as the granite of his home county, a sandy quiff topping his forehead with the hair receding on either side, "the lass appears not to be able to make up her mind. But it's not good enough. I'm sending her mother out, or I may go myself.

"Hellen's got to make a decision, one way or the other. It's not fair on the lad." He rubbed one ruddy cheek thoughtfully with the back of his hand. "Seems a nice enough young fellow, from what I've heard. I'm sure you'll agree, he ought not to be treated this way." Sir Samuel looked Lord Tynan square in the eye as he spoke, the flint behind his own overlaid with a twinkle.

Nobody frightened Sir Samuel. He'd earned his brass, and he'd earned his handle, and he reckoned himself to by anybody's equal. He didn't care whether his granddaughter married into the aristocracy or not. Privately, he thought they were a weak-chinned lot who would be well served by the infusion a bit of strong common stock, and being no fool, as he was wont to say, he had looked into Oliver's background. What was more to the point, he had looked into Oliver's immediate circumstances, and discovered the heir to the earldom was terminally ill, which meant that Hellen's young man would eventually inherit. He was not a spiteful man, but he was fiercely loyal and protective of his family. In his darker moments he liked to think of Marnie being kow-towed to as mother of a countess.

Lord Tynan, a tactful and thoughtful man, sent a message to the Manor saying he could not, after all, accept Lady Ashton's pressing invitation to dinner. Lady Tynan was indisposed, and he had suddenly to go to London. He'd be at his club for a night or two.

They came to the discussion on Hellen after everyone had left. "You can't mean that I should go to Hong Kong?" asked Marnie, appalled.

"I do. You can take your Aunt Myrtle with you. She'd enjoy the trip. And it'll help you to get over this nasty business." He gestured vaguely round the room, encompassing the horror of Joe's sudden death. "I'll pay all the expenses." It went without saying that he would, but he said it anyway.

"But what can I do? We don't even know her address. We don't know the name of the people she's staying with."

"You'll find that out easy enough. They know at Government House where she is."

"It's so embarrassing. Going to visit my daughter without being able to tell anyone I talk to on the boat where she lives."

"Not a bit," retorted her father stoutly. "You'll be just two ladies having a cruise. You don't have to tell them anything." He eyed his daughter thoughtfully. "I'll tell you what—I'll send her a cable, and if I don't like the answer, I'll go with you myself. And if she's up to any monkey business, Marnie girl, we'll bring her straight home. Straight home, and no nonsense."

Elliot Keane's company had lost a great deal of money over the strike. Shipping was now beginning to move but the news from Observatory Hill this morning was that a typhoon was making its way up from Manila. If it had not blown itself out before striking Hong Kong, all the shipping down at the docks would have to put to sea for its own safety. That meant further delay, because they would have to come in again to re-load, and then the mail boats that had been waiting in Singapore and Bangkok for the strike to end, would be on top of them.

He paced up and down the office, venting his frustration by kicking at the carpet with his toes. Now what was he going to do about the Ethel Merriman business? He rang the bell for his secretary. "I'd like to see Armitage, and after him, Curtain."

"Mis-ter Curtain not here," replied Oi Mei.

"Where is he?"

"He go play cricket."

Keane's lips pursed. Right! He'd jolly well get to the bottom of the matter this time. "Send Armitage," he said curtly.

Denzil came in looking bright and pleased with life. Keane pointed to a chair and he sat down. "How's the wound?" He glanced with wry amusement at the side of Denzil's head on which the band of hair that had been shaved was beginning to grow again. He apologised for smiling.

"That's all right, sir," replied Denzil cheerily. "If you shoot in the air, over the heads of little yellow men on Shank's pony, you're liable to hit a tall Englishman on a horse."

Keane chuckled. "Quite so. Ragging you about it, are they?"

"There hasn't been much else to laugh at in the past month or so. Any word of our ships?"

"They'll be a day or two yet." He walked to the window and stood, hands in pockets, with his back to the light. "I had a visit from Ethel Merriman. Long time ago, actually. Before the strike. Had other matters on my mind, then. She claims you owe her money."

Denzil jerked upright in his chair. "What!"

Keane looked down at his feet, then up again. "Listen, old chap, what my employees do in their free time is none of my business, but I can't have Mrs Merriman coming here to collect debts. If you want to patronise her bordello, you pay your way. Have you got that clear?"

Denzil's face was scarlet. It was difficult to decide whether from anger or guilt. "For heavens' sake, Taipan, I've been married only a few months. Why would I be going off to Mrs Merriman's?"

"If you haven't, then why should she say you had?"

Denzil's despair was evident, but Keane was in a bullying mood. "I've given her the money," he said. "Perhaps you'd like to reimburse me? In your own time, of course. Meantime, I'm sure you've not forgotten you are back in your old job on probation." As Denzil left the office Keane took his hat down from the rack. Now for George Curtain. If he wasn't down at the cricket club, he'd find out where he was, if it took him all night.

314

Chapter 30

Suspicion

Hellen was writing to Oliver. It was her fifth attempt. Her head was aching. The sky was heavy, weighted with black clouds. Her dress was damp, clinging to her skin. There was a tap, tap, tap and she swung round in her chair.

"Missie, one man come your door."

She tore the paper into small strips and followed the servant downstairs. She had long ago ceased trying to persuade Ah Wong to announce a caller's name. He did not wish to ask people for their names. Surely anyone who came to her door would be made welcome, whoever they were? Besides, he had difficulty with the pronounciation of English names.

Elliott Keane was standing with feet apart, Panama hat in his hand, frowningly examining the expensive hall carpet. At the sound of her footsteps he looked up. "Sorry to come upon you unexpectedly," he said with strained geniality. "Happened to be passing through Kowloon. Thought your husband might be here."

Hellen opened her mouth to say George was at the office, then closed it again. "I'm not expecting him," she replied with polite surprise. "It's barely four o'clock." She felt his sharp eyes watchfully on her face and gave him back stare for stare.

"Oh well, it was just a chance. Whew, it's hot!" He ran a hand across his brow. "Thirsty weather."

"I could offer you a cup of tea," she said diffidently, when it became clear he had no intention of leaving.

"How very kind of you." He went with swift footsteps towards George's study.

"This way, Mr Keane."

But he was determined to see the study. He was very bad at hiding his intentions. Or else he did not care. Hellen was uncomfortably aware of the way he managed a quick glance through the open door, and round the room, taking in the blackwood desk, and the pictures on the walls, before allowing himself to be diverted towards the drawing room. As he strode forward his eyes rested on the mahogany tea table with its inlaid mother-of-pearl, then moved to the expensive cretonne covers on the Lane Crawford sofa and chairs. He looked down with narrowed eyes at the silky Chinese carpet.

Feeling frightened, trying to appear as though she had not noticed his rudeness, Hellen turned on the ceiling fans.

"Did you know there are two black inverted cones showing on Observatory Hill?" he asked conversationally, turning his attention to the pictures.

Hellen now knew about gales and typhoons. Two black inverted cones meant trouble was expected from the south-east. A gale had a wind velocity of forty statute miles an hour, with gusting up to sixty. It was not necessarily a typhoon signal, but small craft would look for shelter in recognised anchorages. "There's been a stand-by red cone up for twenty-four hours," said Keane, staring broodingly at the beautiful curtains. "We used to have a gun go off. Everyone heard that. Still, Mrs Curtain, you've seen a few storms since you've been here." He stood in the middle of the room, legs apart, adopting an avuncular air, now he had got what he wanted, entrance to George Curtain's house and a sighting of the beautiful furnishings he could not possibly have paid for out of his Lonewood & Southby salary. "You should be accustomed to typhoons by now."

"Yes, of course."

"We've got several ships loading, at last. I don't want them moving out to sea before the job's finished, but my Captains say the moment the black hour glass shows, they're off, load or no load. They've got to look after their ships. It's bad joss."

"Do sit down, Mr Keane."

He settled himself on the sofa, eyeing the cushions critically. "You have a beautiful home, Mrs Curtain." Hellen heard intense curiosity behind his words as a request to explain.

"Thank you. If you'll excuse me, I'll go and order tea."

When she came back he was standing before the glass-fronted cabinet gazing at the wedding presents. He turned abruptly.

"I'll just have a quick cuppa and go," he said. "I ought to get back to the office."

She felt, with foreboding, that he had seen as much as he needed to see of George Curtain's lavish home.

"So what did he come for?" George asked, standing in the hall pulling

316

off his tie and battling with his collar stud. He dropped his topee on the floor for Ah Wong to pick up.

"In the first place, to find out what you were up to. Where were you?" When George made no attempt to reply she added, "After seeing the house, I think he felt he knew what you were up to, so he left."

George carelessly tossed his collar and tie on to the hall table. "It's as hot as Hades out there. Are all the fans going? It's been murder in the office."

"You haven't been in the office, George."

Ignoring her remark, he wandered through to the drawing room and stood looking round with a half smile on his face. "Impressed, was he, by all that stuff of yours?"

She was bewildered by his refusal to take his taipan's visit seriously. "Can you not see that you're skating on thin ice?"

George laughed. "A rich wife is a good alibi. Friend of the Governor, takes tea with the First Lady, rides H.E.'s race horses—or did. What's happened to that?"

She said in a sharp, angry voice, "Rich wives do not buy their own engagement rings. I saw him looking very hard at the ruby."

George glanced down at her left hand. "What a tit you are. You're not wearing it."

"I never wear it except when I'm with you." In her distress, she hurled the admission at him. "He always stares at it. Everybody does. No one of my age has a ring like that. Have you got a death wish?"

"Far from it. I'm a survivor. You should know by now. I tell people, if you marry a rich girl, you have to let her pay for the kind of ring that goes with her expensive clothes. Can't put a miserable little bit of glass on a finger when there's a bloody great diamond necklace round the neck."

"I would prefer you didn't humiliate me."

He shrugged, then turned towards the stairs, tugging with finger and thumb at his shirt that was sticking wetly to his torso. "Look at this! Soaked!"

Ah Wong spoke from the doorway. "One man come kitchen door, Master."

"Kitchen?" echoed George in surprise.

"Luff man, Master. Little bit Chinese," the cook boy explained.

George went swiftly through to the kitchen passage. Hellen followed. Before he caught sight of her and swiftly receded, she recognised the short, square figure and dark Asian hair of Charlie Marsh. A rough man, indeed. George went through the outer door in his wake, and into the yard.

317

A wild wind had entered the garden. It whined round the eaves and rustled the trees. The French windows were knocking back and forth. Hellen pulled them close and latched them. The garden was all movement, though without violence. It was only half-past four, yet the light was fading. She went back into the hall. George was standing by the telephone looking distinctly worried. He glanced up as she approached.

"What's the matter?" Hellen asked, then sharply, when he made no move to reply, "What was Charlie Marsh doing here?"

"None of your business."

"If a man is in trouble, it's very much his wife's business," she replied.

He gave her an odd look, almost, she thought, as though he would welcome advice, but the next moment he was himself again. He went purposefully off upstairs without a word. She followed him, worrying, and stood leaning against the newell post. He had gone to a spare room at the end of the passage where clothes seldom worn and oddments not at present is use, were kept. She could hear him rummaging round. There was a crackle as of paper, the pulling out of a drawer, the thump of something heavy and then, quite distinctively, the rattle of oilskins. She went along the passage and stood looking in at the door. A pair of seaman's boots lay haphazardly, toes together, legs splayed, on the floor.

"Where are you going?"

He bent down to pick up one of the boots, then straightening said, "I told you about the consignment. The one that's going to set me up for life."

She recorded in her mind, quite unemotionally, his use of the word "me".

"According to Charlie, *Lotus*'s Captain had a tip-off that the police are on the look-out so he wasn't able to dump the booty offshore. The police are waiting for her to dock. So I've got to get the stuff off and dump it somewhere safe."

"You can't go out in a typhoon," she protested.

"It'll probably blow itself out, or veer off." He gave her that same odd look. "I thought you hated me."

"I don't hate you. But I do want to say this: if you're taking these risks in the hope that I'll stay with you, then. . . ."

He stepped over the oilskins on the floor and gripped her shoulders, looking down into her face. "If you knew just how much street value was in this cargo, I think you'd want to stay with me."

"You're so wrong," she cried distractedly. "I'm protesting merely because I don't wish to live with the knowledge that you lost you life

318

doing something you mistakenly thought would impress me."

He thrust her violently away. As she crossed the landing, a hot rush of air came from her bedroom. She ran in to investigate. The curtains were hurling themselves at the ceiling, swerving down, flattening against the wall. There were hair brushes, nail scissors, a handkerchief sachet, lying on the floor. She leaned out of the window, grasped the shutters, and dragged them shut. The wind tore at her hair, splaying it across her face, blinding her.

It was dark outside now. She hurried from room to room, fastening the shutters over each of the windows in turn. In the junk room George, already changed into an old pair of trousers and jumper, was examining buckles and straps on the oilskins. He did not look up, and she left. As she came down the stairs a great whoosh of air burst through the hall. Ah Wong, with Neil's help, was pushing the front door shut. Marcia, with her hat in her hand and her hair all over the place, looked up and saw her.

"We wouldn't have come had we known," she shrieked. "You've no idea what's going on out there. It was so quiet at the bungalow. But the telephone had gone so we came down to see if you were all right."

"You had better settle down and resign yourselves to keeping us company," returned Hellen, thinking with relief that Neil might be able to dissuade George from going out. "Go into the drawing room. I'll ask Ah Wong—" She broke off as the doorbell sounded.

It was Denzil Armitage who erupted over the step and turned to push the door shut against the wind. Denzil in oilskins, and wearing a sou'wester. "Where's George?"

Hellen could see the anger in his face. She said, "You'll find him in the room at the far end of the passage upstairs." Denzil dropped both coat and sou'wester in a heap on the floor and made for the stairs, taking them two at a time. Hellen went back into the drawing room, thinking with relief that one way or another, George was not going to sea tonight. Ah Wong, making a great rattle and show with glasses and bottles, was pouring Marcia and Neil a drink.

A moment later there was the sound of heavy footfalls and they all looked up. Then Denzil was in the doorway, his face flushed, his eyes angry. "There's no one upstairs. Where's George?"

"What's the matter?" demanded Marcia, lumbering to her feet. "Why are you looking like that, Hellen? Where is George?"

"He must have gone down the back stairs. He wanted to go out in a boat."

They gaped at her. "Out in a boat!"

Neil had slipped back against his cushions. His face was still. His eyes were closed. Hellen saw then that he knew. He opened his eyes. "Better not ask questions," he said in a quiet, somehow defeated voice.

Slowly, Marcia deflated. Denzil and Hellen exchanged glances, and she followed him into the hall, closing the door behind her.

"So they knew," he said.

"So you knew," she countered.

"Kitty told me."

"He sees himself as a do-gooder," said Hellen, forcing herself to put on a show of loyalty she did not feel. "He says the government sells opium at a high price so only the rich can have it, but he sells it cheaply to the poor. He says it puts a bit of—relief—into the coolies' lives."

"Balls," said Denzil crudely. "He sends it into China where it commands a very high price. I know all about it from Kitty. What with the Triads and the smuggling and the concubine—"

Hellen said stiffly, "I told him he should take a concubine."

"You may as well know, he's always had one. She was a sing-song girl," Denzil went on in a hard, angry voice. "She worked the Western restaurants—Kan Ling, President, and Kwangchou."

"I don't need to know details."

"Listen." Denzil's voice was harsh. "I'm going to tell you. George set her up in a little place behind Nagasaki Joe's."

"Denzil! I don't want to know."

He grasped her wrist. "I'm telling you this, Hellen, only because it's all over and I don't want you backing down. Oliver is on his way back to the New Territories now. He dropped me here—"

"He's here!"

"He's gone on his way. Don't look like that, Hellen. You know he couldn't come in. But he'll be back as soon as I send the signal. I've got the steamship tickets. Can you be ready to run?"

Run! Run with Oliver, upset his family, and ruin his life? She asked herself shakily, her head whirling, only knowing that she had to avoid the subject of running. "Why did you come after George tonight?"

"He's out to destroy me. He's got to be stopped. He sent Ethel Merriman in to Taipan to collect an alleged debt of mine."

Hellen looked blank. "Who's Ethel Merriman?"

"You saw her at Happy Valley races, talking to George when Ruth was introducing you to Kitty and me."

"I remember. A beautiful woman with wonderful clothes."

"That's her. She runs a bordello but she's got more panache than all the society ladies put together. If she was in Paris or London, she'd be a courtesan. I'm not going to tell you about her now, but chaps sign

320

the book—she makes everyone sign—with the Governor's name, or the Prince of Wales's, or Lloyd George's, instead of their own. Nobody minds that, so long as they pay. But George has signed my name, and not paid. It has to be him. No one else would do it. Madam Merriman doesn't hesitate to collect bad debts. She's famous for going direct to the chairman's office, if the chap's in business, or the Commanding Officer if he's in the army, and refusing to leave until the miscreant debtor is found and has paid. She's been to Taipan, and he paid her on my behalf. Now he wants me to pay him. And what's more, my job's in the balance."

There was a sound from the doorway and they both swung round. "I intend to go down to the docks to look for George," Neil said. "He may not have got away yet." He crossed the hall and took his coat down from the rack.

After a moment's hesitation, Denzil said, "I'll come with you. I'll not get home tonight." He picked up his oilskins from the carpet.

"I'll come too," said Hellen.

They both said in chorus, "No. You mustn't."

"Stay with Marcia," said Neil.

"I've been out in a typhoon before."

Neil took her by the arm and looked into her face. His own was very grave. "Stay with Marcia, there's a good girl."

Chapter 31

The Second Typhoon

Marcia was crying. Her lace handkerchief, so small and delicate for so large a woman, was now soaked. Hellen said, "I'll get you one of George's."

"If you had been a proper wife," burst out her mother-in-law, "he wouldn't be doing this sort of thing."

Hellen retorted in a carefully controlled voice, though smarting from the unfairness of Marcia's accusation, "He was doing 'this sort of thing' long before I met him. That was why Kitty ran away."

"You could have stopped him. You were married to him. Kitty wasn't."

"I'll get you a handkerchief," said Hellen.

Upstairs was noisy. Even with the shutters closed, as firmly as the old house allowed, she was aware of the violent gusting. She could hear the trees groaning, and the wind raging through the branches. The eye of the storm was moving nearer. She shivered, thinking that small craft would not survive in this. She took one of George's linen handkerchiefs from a drawer in his tallboy, and went back downstairs.

Marcia said pathetically, "We hoped it was your money."

"But I did tell you, the day I arrived, that my background is quite humble."

"Oh, yes," retorted Marcia sarcastically. "Tenant farming, I remember. And the next moment you're wearing a diamond necklace! Of course one would expect the daughter of a tenant farmer to wear a diamond necklace and take tea with Lady Marathon at Government House."

"It's all to do with horses." Hellen endeavoured to smile. It was not an evening for quarrelling.

"What on earth do you mean?"

"Horses can bridge gaps." She qualified her statement, "Some gaps. Sometimes."

Marcia wiped her eyes again. They sat in silence for a while. "Do you think they'll find George?"

If he was as slick at getting seaborne as he had been about leaving the house, Hellen knew they had no chance. She said tactfully, "I'm sure they'll do their very best."

"If he drowns . . ." gulped Marcia. "He's all we have."

Hellen wished she could say they still had her. She pulled a handkerchief out of her pocket and wiped her face. It was the heat; the dreadful airlessness. She was aware that Marcia was watching her, condemning her because there were no tears to wipe away. The drawn curtains puffed inwards as a miscreant wind found its way through the shutters and the glass doors. Marcia begain once more to cry.

"Would you like a brandy? Coffee? Tea?"

"Oh, you are so callous!" Marcia was unreasoning in her despair. "Our son could already be dead and all you can think of is making yourself comfortable."

"I'll ask Ah Wong to get beds made up." She could have rung the bell, but she though, at that moment, if she listened to Marcia any longer, she would scream.

Ah Wong was sitting at the kitchen table, contemplatively tapping on the scrubbed wooden surface with his chopper. At the other end of the table the wraith Ah Ping was balanced on a stool, half asleep, her head hanging forward between her narrow shoulders. Fah Wong, seated on the floor holding a pair of chopsticks, was shovelling rice from a bowl directly into his mouth. Ah Saw was mending a piece of linen.

Hellen spoke directly to Ah Wong. "Make up the double bed, and one of the singles," she said in Cantonese. "Number two master and missie staying the night. And friend."

"Number four sister come," offered Ah Ping gloomily in Cantonese. Hellen frowned over the rest of the sentence.

Ah Wong explained in pidgin, "Signal led, gleen, led. Velly bat."

Hellen froze. "Red, green, red! That's typhoon force!"

They gazed at her with blank tolerance for her hysterical, precise English. She went back into the drawing room thinking that if George was caught in a typhoon force wind in a small boat, he would not survive. She reached out for something to say that would cover the sick horror of guilt she would feel at being freed by his death. "The makee learn said the signal has changed to red, green, red. I'm going to ring the police. They must have rescue craft that are capable of going out in this."

Marcia jerked upright in her chair, her broad face ugly with shock

323

and anger. "That's what you've been dying to do, isn't it? Do you know what the penalty is for smuggling opium?"

Hellen stiffened.

"Twenty—may be thirty years in jail."

"I'm surprised you didn't warn George."

They glared at each other. "Would you rather he died than be charged with smuggling opium? That's what it amounts to."

Marcia went to the French windows and drew the curtain. Beyond the shutters the wind was moaning through the garden. Rain lashed against the wood. It had come through where the two shutters met, and was streaming down the glass. "Red, green, red. No," said Marcia, as though she could change things.

"I only know what my servant told me. Perhaps you would like to talk to her? Shall I ring for her to come in?"

Marcia said furiously, "You're dying to call the police, aren't you?"

"Yes," said Hellen. "I couldn't live with my conscience if I didn't do everything in my power to save him."

"For what?" Marcia asked bitterly.

"Obviously it would suit me better if he drowned," snapped Hellen, beside herself with fear, and anger at Marcia's unjust accusations. "Do you think I want to be tied to a man who's in jail for thirty years? Face facts, Marcia." It occurred to her that it was odd George's mother should have that precise fact on the tip of her tongue.

"You cheeky thing."

"I'm sorry. I'm upset." Hellen recognised, ludicrously, that Marcia was referring to the use of her christian name. "I apologise. For everything. But I'm going to ring the police."

Afterwards, she went into George's study and dropped into his big chair, remembering how he had sat there looking up at her the day she accused him of shooting Denzil. It seemed at that moment all her life was spread before her, divided into little boxes from which there was no escape.

The Old Forest Hunt box, in which she had stood alone; the shipboard box, as she travelled nervously to an uncertain welcome; suffocating within the false pregnancy box; and then the lifting of its lid with the grotesque marriage ceremony on *Bangkok Lady*. Afterwards, George and herself, boxed up together, with Oliver outside.

And now, she asked herself, was she really fighting for the right to lock herself into another box for thirty years, to emerge eventually still as George's wife? Did the law allow divorce from a convicted felon? Probably not, she conjectured. Women had so few rights.

Marcia had emerged from the drawing room and was wandering aimlessly up and down the hall. Hellen sat still as a mouse, hoping not to be found. Then her mother-in-law was standing in the doorway. "What did you say to them?" Her face was small now, shrivelled with venom.

"I said he had gone out in a small boat to *Lotus*."

"So that they could search the ship?" Marcia's face twisted with despair.

Hellen corrected her in a quiet, carefully controlled voice. If she allowed her feelings to master her now, she was afraid she would scream. "So that they would know where to start looking for him."

"You needn't have mentioned the name of the vessel. With all the small craft being blown all over the place, he could be anywhere. And so could *Lotus*, for that matter. You could have said he was out in a small boat. Fishing, or something."

"I had to give them a lead on where to start.

"I really believe you hate my son."

Hellen rose from her chair. "Your room is ready for you. I've put out a pair of George's pyjamas." She did not apologise for failing to offer one of her nightdresses, for that would have been tactlessly to draw attention to Marcia's bulk

It was two o'clock in the morning when the bell rang. Hellen was still in the study chair. There was less noise from the storm there, because the one small window faced away from the main blast of the wind. She leapt to her feet and ran through the hall to open the door. Three men in dripping oilskins hurtled through.

"Success!" she cried, with intense relief, and then the taller of the three hauled off his sou'wester, and she saw it was not George.

Oliver did not speak, and nor did she. They gazed at each other in breathless silence. Then a voice from the top of the stairs called, "Did you find him?" Marcia, lumbering down, buttoning her coat over George's pyjamas, saw Oliver and stopped. "You're a little early," she spat at him. "Her husband isn't dead yet."

Denzil broke the appalled silence. "We've been everywhere."

Marcia said, addressing Neil directly, "She's rung the police."

"We went to the police," said Neil tiredly, as though correcting her. "It's hell down there at the docks. Where's the boy? Get him to take these wet things to the kitchen. Hellen, what about something to drink?"

She swept up the wet oilskins in her arms and went flying joyously through the house with water dripping over her feet and soaking through the front of her dress. She dumped her load on the kitchen floor. "Fetchee whisky!" she cried "Faai-di Tso." Hurry up.

325

Ah Wong asked impassively, "Number one master, he come home?"

She said, "No." Just that. Then she turned and flew back down the passage.

They were still in the hall. The three men had removed their boots and were rolling their wet trousers up to their knees. Marcia was standing facing Oliver. He had taken both of her hands in his. "We had to go to the police." He spoke very gently, as to a hurt child. "Try not to worry, Mrs Curtain. He may not have been able to find a boat. They may all have run for shelter."

"He would come home," retorted Marcia with conviction, withdrawing her hands, though without haste.

"Not necessarily. Not if he had business to attend to." Oliver made George's smuggling sound ordinary, and respectable.

Hellen watched mutely as he led George's unexpectedly docile mother through to the drawing room, then she picked up two pairs of boots and socks. Denzil took the other pair and followed her in silence. The kitchen was full of the rattle of oilskins being shaken and wiped dry.

In the passage outside Denzil said, "He couldn't survive in this."

"No."

"The waves are thirty feet high. No small boat could survive."

"No." It was as though her feelings had been locked up and the key thrown away. At that moment George did not exist. Had never existed. There was no sadness. No guilt. Nothing. She went back to the drawing room. Oliver, his bare feet splayed out on the carpet, with his hair lying flat across his forehead, wet with rain or sweat, was sitting beside Marcia on the sofa, still holding one of her hands between both of his. Neil was hunched into a chair.

There was an uncanny lull. They started and looked at each other, wide-eyed, each one of them knowing the centre was passing over the colony. Then Oliver leaped to his feet, drew the curtains back from the French windows, released the catch and opened the shutters. Hellen went out into the garden and stood in the fitful moonlight, looking round in awe at broken branches, and swathes of leaves piled against the walls of the house.

Denzil said with awe, "It's gone."

Marcia, looking ridiculous in George's pyjamas and her overcoat, with her bare feet squelching in the soaked grass, with her rumpled hair streaming down her back, said nervously, "If George is all right, he will come home now."

Hellen went back inside and ran from room to room opening shutters and windows. Forgetting she had servants, she sped upstairs, flinging everything wide, all the windows and shutters and enveloping curtains. Hot, dry air surged in, spreading over and around her like a benison. She went swiftly back down the stairs, treading lightly, and with a spring in her step. Ah Wong had brought rice cakes and pork dumplings along with the whisky.

"I didn't know it was George," Oliver was saying to Marcia. "I was sitting in the car, trying to make up my mind whether it was safe, after all, to drive over the pass, when he came by. He was wearing oilskins. He might have been anyone."

Hellen had an odd memory of listening to Oliver's uncle telling her, quietly and reasonably, but in a tone that brooked no argument, that she might not again ride his horses.

Neil said to Marcia, "I think we should go to bed."

"Yes," she said, preparing to rise to her feet. She said pointedly, but without looking at Hellen, "And I think she should come with us."

Neil's face was carefully expressionless.

"Are you coming?" Marcia demanded.

"No," replied Hellen.

Neil said, "Come to bed, Marcia."

"And leave them together?"

"The three of them," Neil replied. "I dare say we're all too worried to sleep, anyway, but we can rest."

On the threshold of the room, Marcia swung round, "I'm ordering you to go up to your room, Hellen."

Neil, looking about to break down in tears, let go of his wife's arm and, hunch-shouldered, went ahead. Hellen said bleakly, "I think you should look after your husband. He's very upset." She glanced across to the clock on the mantelpiece. It was nearly three o'clock.

Denzil said, "We'll wake you if we get news of George." He crossed the room and closed the door firmly behind her, then turning to Hellen said, "What I would like is another whisky. Then, if you don't mind, I'll bunk down on the window seat in the dining room."

"I've had a bed made up for you."

"Thanks. But the window seat will do."

Hellen and Oliver went out into the garden. The clouds were clearing, just enough to allow the moon to appear intermittently. They walked hand-in-hand across the wet grass, stepping over small branches, walking round the larger ones. The bougainvillaea had been torn to shreds. Frangipani lay horizontal across their path. The snowball tree was standing, but the wind had blasted the foliage. The trunk stood aslant, its weeping leaf-stalks bare, a skeleton in the moonlight.

327

They went on to the bottom of the garden. The moon came out again to show them the corrugated iron roof that had been torn off the shed, lying in pieces haphazardly against the wall. Then the clouds scurried over the moon, and the soft darkness closed in. Oliver put his arms round her, holding her very tenderly. Neither of them wanted to talk. They were in limbo, waiting for the fates to decide their future. Neither of them remembered that Denzil had two steamer tickets in his pocket. That plan belonged now to another age.

After a while the sky in the east lightened, and slowly the sun came up over the Nine Dragon Hills. "It might be better for all concerned if I were to go back to the New Territories," Oliver said. "If George turns up, I shouldn't be here. If he doesn't, it will look very bad to your mother-in-law. Perhaps Denzil will come with me. He won't be able to get across to the island until the sea quietens." Sensing her unwillingness to face the day alone, he added, "It's something you've got to go through without me, but I won't be far away. If it wasn't for the complicaton over Kitty, Denzil could stay. Shall I send him back this afternoon in the Lizzie? By that time you'll know. One way or the other, I mean," said Oliver uncomfortably as they went inside.

There was a sound from the landing and they both looked up to see Marcia, greatly dishevelled, still in George's pyjamas, standing on the top step. "Oh-h-h!" she said, her face twisting.

Oliver said pleasantly, "We couldn't abandon Hellen. Now you're awake, Denzil and I will leave her in your good hands and be on our way."

"You've heard nothing?"

Hellen said, "I would have wakened you if there had been any news."

The servants unrolled themselves and rose from the floor to make tea and toast. Denzil agreed to go home with Oliver. "I'll come back by train," he said, declining the offer of Lizzie. Then, diffidently, "You may need her yourself."

They were all a little jumpy, knowing news must come with the daylight. Oliver and Denzil left in a hurry, without uttering the usual pleasantries. Nothing was going to go well today.

Hellen leaned on the gate as they drove away, desolate and afraid. Through the morning stillness came the rumble and crash of waves pounding the sea wall. She had an urgent desire to go down to the harbour side; to test the sea's malevolence, and its strength. It was all at once necessary to know if the waves had been big enough, cruel and pitiless enough, to dash George's little craft to pieces.

Neil and Marcia were standing, fully dressed, in the hall. "I think it's better we should go home," said Neil. "You'll let us know immediately there's news, won't you?"

"Of course."

"I shall never forgive you," said Marcia. "Never."

Hellen recognised that she had sinned greatly against Marcia; in marrying her son and not making him into a new and better person; in calling her by her christian name. She had sinned in loving Oliver too, but that was a sin committed against many people; Vice Regal Hong Kong and the entire Old Forest Hunt.

Hellen was sitting at the dining room table, sipping tea that had long ago gone cold. The bakery was a shambles, the cook boy reported, and there was no bread. He had made some dumplings, and there were rice cakes over from the night before, but Hellen could not eat. She was looking at her watch, yet again, noting it was now nine o'clock, when the doorbell went. She heard Ah Wong's shuffling footsteps, then, in the deathly silence, the opening of the door. And George's voice, in a cheery Cantonese morning greeting, "Tso-san. Tso-san. Everything all right, Ah Wong?"

Ah Wong, replying in kind, said, "Ho, ho."

Hellen stood up. She was standing when George came into the room. "Well!" he greeted her expansively. His hair was neatly combed. He wore the same jumper and trousers in which he had left the house the night before. They did not look as though they had come into contact with sea water. He noted her stillness and the cheeriness went. "What's up?"

"So you didn't go to sea?" said Hellen.

"In that gale? Good God, you should have seen the waves!"

"We were very worried. Your parents have been here all night. None of us have had any sleep. Did it not occur to you that we would worry?"

"My parents!" echoed George.

"I think you must have been aware they were here. You crept out—"

"Crept!" he ejaculated, straightening his shoulders. "I don't creep out of my own house. I had business to attend to. I presume you told them that."

"I told them you were trying to go out to *Lotus*. That was what you told me."

"You little shit," said George, his good nature evaporating, icy fury coming in. He advanced towards her, shoulders hunched, his eyes narrowed. "You told them that?"

Ever since Oliver left, Hellen had been preparing herself for this. Husbanding the strength she was going to need in her own defence. "Where were you all night?"

329

"I took shelter with a friend."

"A friend who lives behind Nagasaki Joe's?"

There was a frisson of surprise, then he recovered. "What do you expect? If a chap's wife screams rape every time he goes within ten feet of her, naturally he looks elsewhere."

"Naturally."

"So you've been spying on me?"

"No. I imagine it's fairly generally known. Don't think I'm angry, or only in that you lied to me. If you remember, I suggested you take a concubine. Please go and see your parents. They're worried out of their minds. They had given you up for dead."

"Whose fault is that?"

"Go and see them." She walked past him, out of the door, across the hall and up the stairs. She went into her bedroom, closed the door behind her, and lay down on the bed. If only she could lose consciousness, even for the length of time it would take George to walk to Nathan Road, hear the bad news and return, she would be better able to cope with what was to come. Exhaustion took over. There was a sensation of drifting.

The door opened, then closed again. "I've something to say to you," said George. "Don't pretend to be asleep. No one goes off that fast."

She fought to open her eyes, pulled herself into a sitting position, swung her legs to the floor, and disorientated by the brief, unconscious moment, staggered to her feet.

George said with deliberate malice, "I've spent a lot of time puzzling over why you married me. There had to be a reason. I've come up with something. You weren't pregnant, were you? Was that, by any chance, a miscarriage you were having, all the way up to Lantau on *Bangkok Lady*?"

She was too tired and dazed for shock. The ashes of that dreadful memory dry and cold in her heart.

"By God!" he said. "You'd have copped it. Nobody plays that kind of trick on me." He leaned closer, reading her fear and her guilt, angry and triumphant as he harnessed the power this new knowledge had brought. "You rotten little tart," he said. "You weren't game to arrive pregnant, so you thought you'd foist Marathon's bastard on to me. It wouldn't have done, would it? All the fanfare of a new bride at Government House, and then it gradually dawns on everyone there's a bun in the Vice Regal oven. What were you going to do in Singapore?" George demanded mercilessly. "Pretend you had cold feet, then dump the brat and come on? Je-sus!" He rolled his eyes.

"The reason you found me not to be a virgin was because I was raped," she said.

George laughed harshly. "Of course. That's what they all say." He mimicked her, "I was raped." He turned, saying dismissively, "You've got rape on the brain." At the door he turned back. "I suggest you go and see my parents. You're the one who upset them."

"I think they want to talk to you."

He came back and stood over her again, looking closely into her face. "About smuggling opium? Is that what they want to talk to me about? The fact that you've told them I've been smuggling opium? Daddy wants to chastise his little boy?" George asked sarcastically. "Go and talk to them yourself."

Afterwards, she thought that if she had not lost consciousness for those few moments she might not also have lost her acute sense of self-preservation. But she was so tired she was rudderless. She could only think that George must be warned. She said, "The police know you were missing last night."

"You told them!"

She saw his terrible fury in the harsh lines that ran down from his nose, cutting deeply into his cheeks; in the expanded black pupils within his narrowed eyes, sightless with rage. She felt, rather than saw, him lunge towards her. Then there came the blow on the side of her head. For a dizzy moment, before losing consciousness, she thought she was hitting the deck of *Bangkok Lady*.

George was kneeling on the floor beside her, pulling her upright. "Listen to me, whore," he said. "Listen!" He shook her roughly. "See this?" He was waving a piece of paper in front of her eyes.

"Get over to Central on the first ferry crossing and cash it. Do you hear me, Hellen! When you've cashed it, hide the money. Do you hear me, Hellen?" He shook her, hard, and a pain shot through her head. "Cash it and hide the money. I'll be in touch to tell you where I am. You can bring it to me." He shook her again. "Hel-len! Do you understand?"

She nodded and another pain shot through. He let her go and she fell back on the carpet. After a while she heard voices downstairs. She leaned dizzily up on one elbow, listening. The voices were cool and quiet. Then George was laughing, sounding amazed; sounding reasonable; sounding indignant. She caught the word "questioning". She hauled herself to her feet and staggered to the door. She leant against the frame. Someone was saying, "We'd like you to come with us now. Do you want to have a word with your wife first?"

She began, uncontrollably, to tremble.

Then George said, "She's not here. She went to my parents."

The door opened, then closed, and there was a sound of footsteps on the gravel. She went as near to the window as she dared, and looked out. Five tall men were going down the drive. One walked in front of George, and one behind. One on either side of him. She backed away. The cheque was on the dressing table. It was made out for six hundred thousand Hong Kong dollars.

She picked it up, tore it into small pieces, then threw them into the bamboo waste paper basket with the picture of the song bird on the side.

Chapter 32

The Babies

YOUR MOTHER AND AUNT MYRTLE PLANNING CRUISE TO VISIT YOU STOP COULD LEAVE SECOND OF NEXT MONTH STOP REQUEST REPLY BY RETURN STOP PORCHARD

Hellen stood looking down at the cable, thinking that rural Kent did not prepare one for such bizarre events as had befallen her in the China Seas. Her family would never understand. And, more pertinently, they would be upset beyond measure. Now, she had to make a decision.

It was Neil who suggested a compromise. He wrote out the reply himself.

REQUEST DELAY PLANS UNTIL LETTER ARRIVES STOP LOVE STOP HELLEN

Neil insisted on calling a doctor who pronounced she had mild concussion and should rest. She had her excuse to nurse her problems and her bruises in the privacy of the house and garden.

"What will you say to your family when you write?" Neil asked. "Shall we talk about that?"

"I don't want to tell them."

"My dear, how can you avoid it? You may be able to write an ambiguous letter, but when you see them it will be different." He assumed she would go home as soon as the trial was over. Everyone assumed that.

She shrugged. "I don't know." She couldn't think. She did not want to think.

"He'll be convicted," Neil had said, passing a hand wearily across his eyes. "I'm sorry, my dear." He kept saying he was sorry, as though, if he had not brought George into the world, this could not have happened to her.

Neil came often to keep her company, Marcia not at all. Kitty Armitage came, and Ruth, and Wanda Ayre, and Lin Yan. Nobody, not even Neil, believed she had fallen against her bedroom chair, though it was in essence true. The wooden leg, jutting out, had caught her below the eye as she fell.

Only Ruth commented, she who had seen with dismay Hellen's expression as she emerged from that bedroom at the Hong Kong Hotel on the day of her arrival from Macau. "How absolutely caddish!" she said in disgust. "I always thought he was a cad."

The others maintained a discreet silence.

Nobody mentioned Oliver. Hellen assumed Denzil would have cashed in the steamer tickets, and discretion precluded his mentioning the fact. There were times to run away and times to stay and see things through. She waited in a vacuum.

"Sometimes I say to myself," said Kitty, seated in her pretty hat and summer dress on the Lane Crawford sofa—Hellen still could not think of the furnishings in number 6 Minden Row as her own—"I'm guilty of bringing all this down on your poor head. If I hadn't been so silly as to get in a pet with Denzil and get engaged to George, he wouldn't have rushed after me, and met you."

Wilful little heiresses experiencing a brain storm were not two a penny, as George could have said. What she had done to him in his Far Eastern corner of the Empire, what Hellen had done in going to Lady Sylvia's dance, those were the two sparks of destiny that had set up the sequence of events to be worked through before matters could be set right. Hellen did not see herself as defeated, only in another trough, with another peak to climb. It was a waiting period.

She did not go to George's trial.

"What will people say?" asked Marcia indignantly.

"At the worst, they will say she didn't stand by him," Neil replied. "She is not standing by him. She makes no pretence of it."

"You say that as though she has a right." Marcia's large face puffed with indignation.

Hellen had the story from the papers. The Police produced evidence that the opium was to have been unloaded from *Lotus* and secured to a marker buoy somewhere among the myriads of small islands on the approaches to Hong Kong. It was a familiar method of bringing in contraband. To pick up the booty, smugglers used Thai fishing trawlers adapted for the coastal trade of China. The long, indented coastline of the mainland made it easy for a junk to land a consignment of opium undetected.

The police already knew *Lotus* was making a drop, but that evening, because of the wild seas, she was unable to tie up to the buoy. Charlie Marsh panicked when he saw the ship heading straight in and came to see George who decided to cast caution to the winds and make an attempt to meet her. Anything to stop her arriving at the dockside with his incriminating goods. In the event, no boatman was willing to take him out.

George gave the names of his Triad confederates and three more men were arrested. Perhaps he was not bothered about retribution. In twenty or thirty years people can die, or forget.

"Is it true the government sells opium?" Hellen asked Neil.

"In essence, what George told you is true. It has been going on since the eighteenth century. An Emperor of the Manchu dynasty, possibly Ch'ien Lung, was only too happy for traders to buy in China, but he would take nothing but silver in payment. When the western governments were forced to halt the exodus of silver, traders looked round and discovered the answer in the poppy fields of Bengal.

"The East India Company didn't want their labour force debilitated by drugs. The health of the Chinese coolie was no concern of theirs. It's true the great hongs grew bloated on opium profits." Neil looked resigned. "If Ch'ien Lung had opened China's ports to a wider range of goods, it might not have happened. Who knows?"

George's problems were, as usual, someone else's fault.

When Neil came to tell her of George's conviction, Hellen took the ruby ring out of its hole in the mattress and handed it to him along with the pearl necklace George had bought for her. "Give them to his mother," she said. Marcia would look upon the jewellery, not as dead coolies, but as keepsakes.

The next morning, dressed in a loose gown of thin cotton, her feet in flat-heeled walking shoes, a solar topee on her head and her painted sunshade in her hand, Hellen set out for the railway station in Kowloon to board the Canton-bound train. It had been raining heavily during the night but now the sun was out. It was going to be a scorching day. Already steam rose from the wet road.

The train puffed its way through the tunnel under Lion rock, the edifice that divided the Kowloon peninsula between Kai Tak and the Shatin valley, through the level stretches of golden paddy, breast high and looking like wheat. Steam rose from the hot, surface damp of the earth that was too hard and dry to absorb the rain.

They passed the little walled villages, the fishponds and the duck ponds with their snowy quilts of ducks. They wound through the pine-clad hillsides lined with Golden Pagodas where she had begun that last wonderful day with Oliver. Coolies in umbrella hats embarked and disembarked at the little stations of Sha Tin and Tai Po.

None of it touched her consciousness.

At last the train pulled in to Fanling. It was not far to walk to Oliver's house, as she remembered, forgetting she had ridden there and returned by car. She walked with the sunlight dazzling up from the rutted, dusty road. A pall of silence lay over the land. The rain had not fallen here. Where clumps of bamboo, tall as a house and with canes as thick as a man's wrist, drooped over the road, she paused to shelter for a few moments from the savage sun. Her mouth was dry as the dust that rose round her ankles with every step.

A Chinese field worker offered her a ride in a buffalo cart and she accepted gladly, dangling her feet over the back like any coolie woman. It was a painful journey, ferociously bone-jolting. The hard wheels sank into ruts and lurched over inclines, the axle shrieking from its unoiled base. She nervously endured the driver circling his leather-thonged whip as though attempting to lassoo her hat.

The first thing she noticed when the bungalow came in sight was that Lizzie was missing, and then the closed and shuttered windows. She went up the path to the front door, trying not to look at the garden—Hellen and Oliver's garden—returned to weeds and cracked, dry soil. She tried the handle of the door, jerking at it in a frenzy, as though her entrance would somehow produce Oliver. Then she sat down on the verandah with her knees pulled up under her chin, looking at the sky where a vulture soared on the air currents. She did not cry, though some more vulnerable, less scarred and tortured person within her, wanted to. She felt no shock. All the way up from Kowloon she had known this was what she would find, but she had had to come.

Now, perhaps, she could go home; now she had seen for herself what Sir Rowan Marathon, omnipotent Governor and mandrake of Oliver's destiny, could do with human beings. Was this the last lesson in Lady Sylvia Ashton's book? That you can't beat the system?

She trudged back to the railway station, through the furnace heat of the day, feeling grim and empty and lonelier than she had ever felt in her life before. There was no one from whom to hitch a ride. The carts, churning up the choking dust, were going in the opposite direction.

There were two hours to wait for the next train from Canton. She spoke to the clerk in halting Cantonese, asking him if he knew the whereabouts of the babies' home. Oliver would surely have told the missionaries where he was going when he came to say goodbye to his two little wards. Brows raised questioningly, the clerk, no doubt confused by her faulty tones, rocked an imaginary child in his arms.

Hellen nodded.

He issued directions. Turn left at the crossroads, then right. An outcrop of tall something. The word defeated her. But the home, it seemed, was not far away. Her feet were too hot and swollen to

336

hurry. The tracks here—it could scarcely be called a road—ran between dusty bamboo thickets. Ahead she saw a hedge of cactus, six feet high and grey with dust. Cactus! that was the word that had escaped her. She came upon wrought-iron gates flanked by ancient cypresses that were full of chattering magpies.

As she stood looking through the bars a servant emerged from the lodge and let her in. She went up a path between Kapok trees, the feather tamarind and fan-leafed ginkgo, and came upon a house with a triple tier of porcelain tiled roofs. Miniature metal animals snarled from the ridgepole and upturned eaves, keeping evil spirits at bay. She climbed the steps to a pillared verandah.

A white woman wearing an over-long, shapeless skirt and loose blouse, her hair drawn casually back, emerged from the hall. She greeted Hellen with surprise and concerned goodwill. "Do come in. Have you walked? Where from? You look done in!"

"I won't take your time. I have to catch the next train," Hellen said. "I came to enquire about Oliver Marathon who brought two little girls here."

The woman's face lit up. It was one of those faces that lit easily. A face made for prayer, and hope. "Indeed he did. Po Chue and Oi Chue. Have you come for him? I mean, on his behalf? He used to appear every few days. He used to bring money—not that he needed to, but it was a help. Then he stopped coming. Has something happened to him?" Her smooth face composed itself for the receipt of bad news.

Hellen gazed at her with the same kind of despair that had led her to tug frenziedly at the knob on Oliver's door. Without waiting for her to find her tongue, the woman said kindly, "I'm Sadie Horne. I'm in charge here. You look quite exhausted. At least let me give you some tea."

"I'm Hellen North." She spoke as though she had never stopped being Hellen North; never become Mrs George Curtain. "Thank you. But. . . ." She showed her palms, grimy with dust and sweat.

"I'll take you to the washroom first."

In the looking glass Hellen saw a face she scarcely recognised as her own, so marked it was with sweat and dust; so ravaged with despair. Tears came to her eyes and ran down her cheeks. It was some time before she could bring herself to emerge. The tears would not be stemmed. They squeezed through even when she closed her eyes tightly, as though in the depths of her some sea had broken its banks.

There was a gentle tap at the door. "Are you all right?"

She had to emerge, still crying. Not really crying, but streaming from the wound of Oliver's disappearance.

In the hall a table had been set up and there was a tea basket with cups and little cakes. Sadie Horne had seated herself on a low chair. Beside her was a double portable cot cleverly constructed from thin bamboo canes. Two black-haired, slant-eyed mites with tiny, exquisite mouths gazed solemnly up at her. "This little one is Po Chue, and this Oi Chue." Then she gave her attention to the tea.

"Hello, little ones," Hellen said softly, smiling through her tears. She extended a forefinger from each hand and the babies grasped them. "How strong they are." The tears, miraculously, stemmed. The high-pitched, twittering voices of children, like a flock of jungle birds, filtered in from the garden.

"They're going to grow into wonderful girls. We're very grateful to Mr Marathon."

"What will happen to them?"

"Who knows? Perhaps someone will give them a home."

In Mrs Horn's smile Hellen read a spark of hope. She thought of Lin Yan, who had a home and money and goodwill, and a family of aunts and cousins, but no one directly of her own. Perhaps two full-blooded Chinese children might help to bring her to terms with her Chinese heritage?

"Sit down, my dear," said Sadie Horne. "When it's time to go my gate-keeper, who is also my rickshaw man, will take you to your train."

"I thought you would know where Oliver is."

Sadie Horn made no comment. She was accustomed to broken dreams and tragedies. Miracles to her were babies saved from ignorant parents, and the birds. Hellen drank cup after cup of tea as though there was a desert inside her, shrivelled by the sun, laid waste by the torrents of tears. She nursed Po Chue and Oi Chue. Some of the little orphans came running in from the garden.

"If you'd like to stay and help we'd be glad to have you," said the missionary.

"I'm leaving Hong Kong soon." She emptied her purse. "This is all the money I have with me. I'll send you more."

Her hostess smilingly accepted it. "We're always grateful for help."

Hellen said good-bye to the children. Sadie Horne accompanied her to the gate with a baby on each arm. "Don't forget my offer," she said as they parted. "Come any time."

As the train gathered speed Hellen looked out with darkness in her heart at what she had once seen as beautiful: at the livestock closely fenced for protection from cruel hawks; at the clumps of yellow bamboo cane on the edge of the swampy marshes that were favourite breeding places for malaria-carrying mosquitos; at the decaying vegetation; at tree logs lying bleeding where workmen had vandalised with axes and saws. The dusty-walled villages washed with the pale light of the setting sun were prisons, now.

She thought about what she would say to her family when she arrived home. Neil had said she owed them the truth, "I was drugged, then raped, then I married the man. We were captured by pirates. Some of the crew had their heads chopped off. Then he, my husband, went to jail for twenty years. So I came home."

No. What had happened was that she had found Oliver, then lost him again.

That evening she telephoned Denzil. "Where is Oliver?"

'We don't know." He sounded distressed. "Surely you realised, we don't know. We'd have told you, if we did."

"Yes."

"They could have put him on the Trans-Siberian railway," said Denzil diffidently. "In which case, he'd be in England now, and able to send a message. A lot of shipping was on the move. But surely he'd have sent a message from a ship."

Hellen had an immediate picture of Oliver handing a cable in at the Purser's office, of it going to the Captain, and thence, obeying orders from the Governor of Hong Kong, into the Captain's waste paper basket.

She went out to the garden. Fah Wong had propped up bushes damaged by the typhoon. There were cicadas in the trees. Their shrill music, like the metallic pinging of a guitar string, shredded her nerves. When they stopped, their silence was unnerving, too. There was a small sound and she looked up. Neil was emerging from the French windows. He came and sat down in the cane chair opposite her. She fingered the piece of jade that hung always on a chain round her neck. She wore it openly now.

"That's a nice piece," he said.

"It's supposed to bring luck. The clasp is stamped with the figure nine. The Chinese lucky number."

Neil's face twisted. "George was convicted on the ninth of the month." He added, as though hammering the truth into his head, "On the ninth of July 1921, the Year of the Dragon, our son was sent to jail for twenty years. Did you know it was the Year of the Dragon? It worries me that he ratted on those Triad chaps."

Hellen said comfortingly, "He ought to be safe in jail."

"They're in jail, too." After a while he went on, "Marcia and I are going to Canton for a couple of weeks. A friend has offered his house on Shameen, the foreign concession."

"What?"

339

"It's a protected island. A sort of 'safe house' for foreigners. A little bit of Europe. Most of the consulates and foreign firms are located there. Our friend is a banker. He's going home on leave. He's offered us the use of his house. Will you come with us? We want to get out of Hong Kong for a while."

"Your wife wouldn't like it."

"You and she must get together. If you let too much time pass, you never will. Say you'll come. One can hire ponies there, or buy one for fifteen shillings. We could ride out to Swallow Cliff. It's dramatic, and beautiful. Stone cutters in the Ming Dynasty left it in the shape of a lotus flower. Swallows make their nests there. And there's a ride to White Cloud mountain. You pass a monastery where you can hob nob with the monks."

She could see he was thinking of her as the daughter he never had. Someone he loved; who could, if only she would, fill a gap in their lives.

"There's a pagoda, too, some distance out of town. Six hundred years old and eight storey's high. Not a religious edifice. It's for luck. September the ninth is the day for people to climb to the top, and for those who reach it, there's good fortune."

The ninth. "I'll think about it." She was echoing what she had said to Sadie Horn about working in the babies' home. There were so many different ways in which she might expunge her guilt, if indeed her guilt existed. They were dropping into her lap like autumn leaves.

"Give me the address and phone number. I want time to think, and make decisions.

"You won't disappear? You won't go without saying good-bye?"

Her eyes brimmed with affection, not very short of love. "I won't do that."

340

Chapter 33

Canton

"Ah Wong, catchee trunks. Putee topside." Hellen no longer wanted to battle with Cantonese. It was all over, now.

The servants brought in the trunk and the big box from the garden shed. She began to get her things together. She was going, but where she did not know.

Then one morning Charlie Marsh appeared at the front door. He pushed past Ah Wong and walked straight into the hall. "Get the missus," he demanded.

Hellen was in the dining room, packing china and glass. She heard the coarse, familiar voice and came swiftly out into the hall, glaring at him. "My husband isn't here, Mr Marsh, as I am sure you're aware."

He came slowly towards her, a squat, formidable figure, his enormous black eyebrows low over the faintly Chinese eyes. He grinned, exposing broken teeth. She caught her breath, remembering that his teeth had been even before the pirates attacked. "There ain't nobody in Hong Kong ain't aware where George is," he said sarcastically. "I 'ave to talk to you."

"I have nothing to say to you," she retorted, speaking quickly and nervously. "My servant will show you out."

Before Ah Wong could do more than move tentatively forward, Charlie Marsh limped fast across the hall, grasped her by the upper arms, and pushed her unceremoniously into the dining room, kicking the door shut behind him. "I've come for the money," he said.

She backed clumsily round the table, trying not to show her fear. "I don't owe you money."

"George give you a cheque before he wus arrested."

"I haven't got it." His eyes slitted until only the dark pupil showed. Fear, real fear, lanced through her. She added, the words spilling one over the other in a shaky rush that robbed them of authority, "Now will you please leave my house?" She stopped herself just in time

341

from adding, "Before my servant throws you out." The frail cook boy would be matchwood in the hands of this powerful seaman.

"Get it, girl," he said, his broken teeth clenched. "Get it, fast."

Her fear held her paralysed. He lowered his black head. He had the look of a bull about to charge. "I tore the cheque up." She spoke in a trembling rush. "Please believe me. I tore it up."

"You—" He gulped. Then, "Nobody tears up a cheque for six hundred thousand dollars."

"George gave the cheque to me when he hoped to be able to get away. But he was arrested here, at the house." She tried to speak coldly but the words came out fluttery with fear, "Six hundred thousand dollars is not much use to a man in custody. Naturally, I tore it up."

Charlie Marsh seemed momentarily at a loss for words. Then a cunning look came into those eastern eyes. "With George locked away for twenty years, you could use that money. Only you're not goin' to get the chance, because 'e's not goin' t'be in jail much longer."

She put a hand over her mouth to stop a shriek. "What do you mean?" She was no longer aware of the trembling of her voice, nor of the menace of Charlie Marsh. There was a greater fear now.

"He's goin' to be sprung. What's the use of 'avin' friends if they can't get you out of jail? Now bring out the money, girl, because 'alf of it's mine, and 'e needs the other 'alf to get away."

She put both hands to her face as though she could stem the frenzy of fear and despair.

"Are you goin' ter get it or not?"

"I can't. Please believe me, I can't. I haven't got it. I tore it up," she repeated.

Charlie Marsh made a gruff, grating noise in his throat. He looked round as though expecting to see a spitoon. For a horrified moment she thought he was going to spit anyway.

"Who's helping him to escape?" she asked.

" 'is friends."

"Triads?"

Charlie Marsh moved sideways round the table, coming nearer. "There's Triads and Triads, ain't there? There's gangs. Some is friends, and some isn't. What about the ones George welshed on?" He thrust out his dark, whiskered chin, "What about them?"

I don't know what you mean."

"They're not friends, are they? Not the ones 'e welshed on. They'll 'ave George's guts for garters when 'e gets out, if 'e don't get away fast. 'E needs the money to get away." Charlie Marsh came nearer, creeping, limping. He was approaching the end of the table. She could now smell the foul, rank tobacco on his breath.

Why didn't Ah Wong come in? She was afraid to scream; afraid to do anything that might provoke. Charlie Marsh was now at the end of the table. She moved further to the right. She said, "Even if I had the cash, George didn't give me authority to. . . ." She saw the quiet settle over him, and was afraid to go on.

"You didn't know 'alf that money wus mine?"

"No."

"Swear?"

"What do you mean? George didn't explain anything. He merely asked me to take the cheque to the bank and said he would be in touch to let me know where he was."

"'E didn't say give 'alf of it t'me, if I came?"

With fear, she heard the ominous change in his voice. "Why should you entrust all that money to George? Why didn't you have your portion in your own name?"

"I got me reasons."

"If you want me to believe you, you had better tell me what they are."

He hesitated, then explained with apparent reluctance, "I got a criminal record and I don't want no questions asked. I'm the one what brings the stuff in, aren't I?"

"Are you? I don't know."

"Most often, I am. If I get caught they can look in my bank account. Get it?"

"Yes," she said."

"So, 'e was goin' to run away with our money!"

She was very frightened. She took a step backwards and reached out towards the bell on the sideboard. At that moment the door opened and Ah Wong came in, silent in his black cloth slippers. In his right hand he held his terrifying chopper. He looked down at it thoughtfully, testing the edge with his thumb, then he looked up at Charlie Marsh.

There was a deathly silence. Charlie Marsh pulled a knife out of his belt. The blade was about seven inches long. He, also, ran his thumb along the cutting edge, then with a brief but telling glance at Ah Wong, put the knife back in its sheath and limped to the door. Ah Wong followed him. Hellen heard the front door open, then close.

Ah Wong returned to stand impassively in the doorway. "Missie all light?"

She nodded. "Thank you, Ah Wong."

When he had gone placidly back to the kitchen with his terrible weapon, Hellen sank shakily into one of the ladder-back chairs and leaned forward with her head in her hands.

If only Neil and Marcia had not gone to Canton.

If only she had not torn up the cheque. She considered going to Ruth for advice, but she would feel obliged to inform the authorities. Should she go to the authorities herself? Should she "welsh" as Charlie Marsh said, on George?

The telephone rang. She leaped up and ran into the hall. As she took the receiver down from its hook she said aloud, speaking to whoever it was that granted wishes and miracles, "Please, please, let this be Neil."

It was not Neil. It was Lin Yan.

It occurred to Hellen that perhaps the granter of miracles had not entirely let her down. Lin Yan, that most precious and trusted of friends, unconnected and unconcerned with George, was the one to go to for help.

With delicate fingers, Lin Yan removed the egg-shell lid of her porcelain tea cup. They were in the drawing room of her house, half way up The Peak.

"He has done enough harm to you," she said. "His parents must deal with this matter."

"You don't think I should go to the police?" It was disturbing, this unsteady pitch of the mind between right and wrong. Between not wanting George out of jail, and not wanting to live with the fact that she had been instrumental in keeping him there. It was the night of the typhoon all over again.

"You will go and see his parents," said Lin Yan firmly. "The train takes only four hours, but there will be sad memories if you go through the New Territories. Why not take the steamer?"

"I'm too frightened to go anywhere. I was scared coming here. I'm not certain this man believes I tore the cheque up. I've brought my overnight things. The bag's in the hall. I was hoping you might let me stay the night. I'm really too frightened to be by myself in Tsim Sha Tsui."

"Then I shall go with you," volunteered Lin Yan, with a sweet smile. Hellen wanted to say, "How kind you are." She remembered afterwards that she had not.

"Now, let's talk about what you would like for lunch tomorrow," said Lin Yan with an air of having taken over. "I will instruct my cook boy to pack a hamper for us. And then we will telephone the Curtains."

In the event, there was interference on the line. Neil's voice came

344

only faintly through the static. Hellen eventually gave up and replaced the receiver. "Does it matter?"

Lin Yan replied consolingly, "No."

"Let's give ourselves plenty of time," Hellen said in the morning. "I'd like to take the wedding dress back to Minden Row."

Lin Yan demurred. Yet it would have been safe at Minden Row. If only one could know what lurks round each corner, waiting to happen. But then, had they known, Hellen would not have gone to Canton at all.

She went to the bank in Central to draw out some money. Lin Yan's servant, Ah Seng, indistinguishable in the bustling crowd in his shapeless black trousers, coolie tunic and umbrella-shaped hat, waited outside, the girls' over-night bags strung from a pole across his shoulders.

They crossed in the Star ferry. Hellen took a rickshaw, leaving Lin Yan waiting picturesquely at the terminus, her painted sunshade held negligently over her shoulder, and her servant hovering nearby.

Ah Ping let her into the house. Ah Wong, she said, had gone to market. "I two three days go Canton," Hellen told the makee learn. The tiny servant nodded impassively.

She ran upstairs and collected her riding clothes, a change of underclothes and some comfortable shoes. As she ran downstairs there came the high-pitched rattle of Ah Ping's voice raised in protest, and then Charlie Marsh erupted into the hall.

"Gimme the money," he said, limping swiftly to the foot of the stairs and blocking her way.

"I told you, I haven't got it." Hellen's terror was tightly reined.

"Maybe you didn't have it yesterday, but you've got it today." He added with a sneer, "Think I don't keep me eyes skinned?"

So he had followed them and seen her go to the bank! Hellen reached into her handbag, drew out her purse and showed him a small wad of notes. "These are from my own account. It's all I have."

He snatched her bag, scrabbled around in it, then handed it back. "What's in there?" He nodded towards the suitcase in her hand.

"My own clothes. There's no money in there, and you have no right to search my bag."

"Gimmee."

She threw the suitcase at him. She might have thrown a cushion for all the impact it made. He caught it in his arms, lifted one foot to a stair tread, and opened the case on his knee. He ran his hands through her clothes, shut the case, and dropped it on the floor, then swinging round, limped swiftly through the open door into George's study. She remained where she was, knowing she was powerless to stop him. He had already pulled out a drawer in the desk. Triumphantly, he waved a cheque book in the air.

"You're welcome to it," she said.

He grinned and limped across the hall leaving an unpleasant odour of unwashed clothes, garlic, and the smells of the street. At the door he turned. "I s'pose you was lyin' when you said George didn't mention this money was only 'alf 'is?"

Had she said that? She could not remember. "If you come here again I will call the police," she said. Perhaps George did owe him half of the ill-gotten gains. She felt it was no concern of hers.

The two girls, with the first class deck virtually to themselves, sat side-by-side under an awning as the river steamer went north then turned into the estuary of the Pearl River, so broad here it seemed still to be a part of the China Sea. Mandarins and their well-dressed wives played mah-jong at a table in the saloon and there were coolies jammed like hens in a hen coop on the lower deck.

Hellen picked nervously at a pulled thread on her skirt. "Charlie Marsh knew I had gone to the bank this morning. There's nothing the Triads can't find out. Can't do. They're in the police. They will be there among the prison warders, you may be sure. A warder could help George escape."

Lin Yan said enigmatically, "We will see."

"I've worked out the money. Six hundred thousand Hong Kong dollars is eighty thousand pounds sterling." Hellen was thinking about the ruby ring; the expensive carpets and furniture at Minden Row. George had made himself forty thousand pounds with his opium smuggling. Enough to buy a house on The Peak and set himself up in business. Enough to run away with, and buy a splendid mansion in London, if he wished to set up there. "Eighty thousand pounds," she said with awe, " all for him, if he doesn't give Charlie Marsh his share."

"Try to enjoy the scenery," suggested Lin Yan. They passed sampans and set them bouncing in their wash. As the river narrowed perky little green islands reared up, crowned with trees, and alongside, bare brown humps of rock. The banks drew in. Field workers appeared, and there were fishermen plying their trade from sampans bobbing in the steamer's wake. They ate their lunch, sliced pork spread delicately with coriander sauce and wrapped in tissue-thin wheaten pancakes; fresh water shrimps; pieces of duck, crisp and brown. Lin Yan's cook boy had done them proud.

As they approached Whampoa, the port of Canton, there were container ships, rusty scows, and busy little junks like water-borne snails with their houses on their backs. The Eurasian girl attempted to divert Hellen by telling her about Canton, the flower city where the streets, she said, were full of blossom trees. "People decorate their houses with flowers at the Chinese New Year. The red kapok is Canton's emblem."

"How lovely," said Hellen, not knowing then that she would never again willingly look upon a kapok blossom, that reminded her ever afterwards of blood.

In the late afternoon, on the approaches to the city, the big steamer became like a mother duck followed and surrounded by her brood of sampans wending their way home from their day's fishing, or bringing the toilers from the fields. Hellen felt China, that truly alien country as Hong Kong was not, closing in. She jumped up and stood tensely at the rail as the vessel crept towards the landing stage.

She saw Neil immediately, standing tall and calm in the midst of a noisy crowd of coolies, waving and shouting greetings to friends on the lower deck. He writhed through to meet her as the gang plank was pushed aboard. Laughing, yet anxious, he clasped her hand and drew her towards him.

"I hoped you were coming. I couldn't make out what you were saying. I've met the trains. I am so glad to see you." He kissed her robustly. It was the first time he had kissed her. She drew her companion forward. "I've brought my friend, Lin Yan." She introduced them. Neil tried, without success, to hide his surprise.

Hellen reacted with indignation, immediately stifled. She made a swift and inevitably ill-considered decision to shock Neil in this public place, rather than risk insult to her friend.

"Lin Yan had to escort me," she said, drawing a protective cloak round the Eurasian with a statement that hit Neil directly between the eyes. "I was frightened to come alone. It's to do with George—and some unsavoury friends of his."

She was sorry, immediately the words left her lips. Momentarily, she thought Neil was going to faint. His face turned as white as his solar topee.

"Where are your bags?" he asked, his voice quiet now.

"With Lin Yan's servant, over there." Hellen nodded to where the small coolie stood, timelessly patient and picturesque, with the two suitcases strung from his pole.

Neil found rickshaws and they set out, with Ah Seng trotting along behind. Neil sat hunched in his seat. He had lost weight, Hellen now noticed, and his face in repose was drawn. She tried to block out her thoughts by concentrating on the life around them. There were baskets of live ducks being carried from some market on the back of bicycles; baskets of vegetables; families squatting on dirty pavements round a fire, watching their food cooking in iron pots. There were coolies eating, and others curled up on the ground, sleeping. There were wayside stalls, and a man bearing a squealing pig tied by its feet to a pole. She saw it all as though on a screen.

They came to the protected island of Shameen and rode through the tall gates guarding the bridge. Here, on this quasi-European mudbank in a foreign land, was a wide boulevard and big, elegant houses, tall trees, a square of park full of well-tended flowering shrubs and blossoms. Neil's rickshaw pulled ahead. As they approached the southern tip they again saw the Pearl River with its tiny sampans scudding for home. The rickshaw coolies pulled up before an elegant Edwardian house with large windows and wide verandahs. Neil led the way up the steps to the front door. A servant must have seen them coming for it was immediately opened by a "boy" in an immaculate white jacket and wearing oiled silk trousers at half mast.

"Make yourselves comfortable," said Neil, leading them into a small sitting room. "I'll have to find Marcia. I may be a little while."

Lin Yan's eyes met Hellen's across the room and she glanced uncomfortably away. They both knew that Marcia would have to be reconciled to her Eurasian house guest. They sat in silence. In spite of the diligence of the fans whirring in the tall, plasterwork ceiling the air in the room seemed not to move. Hellen lifted her hands to her hat, then after all left it on her head. She removed her gloves. "I wish someone would bring tea." Lin Yan smiled an enigmatic smile.

It was quite ten minutes before Marcia came, and even then, with time to compose herself, she still bore traces of indignation. It was in the over-brightness of her eyes, her pursed lips. She came bustling in, nodding cursorily to both girls, then, without waiting to be introduced to Lin Yan, spoke directly to Hellen.

"Neil tells me you bring some sort of news of George. What is it?" She, too, had lost weight. Her loose brown dress hung untidily on her big frame. There were wisps of hair floating loose on either side of her head, and the coil at the back hung askew, as though she had torn at it in anguish, and it had shed some of its pins.

"Yesterday afternoon. . . ." Hellen began with Charlie Marsh's visit. They heard her out in silence.

Neil sat back in his chair. His eyes were dark and full of distress. "It simply isn't possible for George to escape—to be 'sprung' as you say. He would be very heavily guarded. I think this chap—what's his name? Marsh—is trying it on in order to get money out of you. I'm sure that's all it is, Hellen. You'd better stay. You'll be perfectly safe

348

here. The gates are guarded all the time, and closed at sunset."

"I'm sorry you had to be bothered," said Marcia ungraciously, nodding towards Lin Yan. "It does seem to be a storm in a teacup."

Lin Yan said, sitting very straight with her small hands folded in the lap of her cheongsam and her head held elegantly high, "The man Charlie Marsh came with us in the steamer."

Hellen's mouth dropped open.

Lin Yan said, in her sweet, gentle voice, "I knew he couldn't do anything to you. Not on the steamer. Anyway, he was down below in third class. I'm certain he only wanted to know where you were going. I looked round as we started out and saw him stepping into a rickshaw. I'm sure he saw me watching, and didn't care. He only wanted to know where you were going," she repeated.

Hellen jerked upright in her chair. "He took the cheque book. If he's going to see George, George can write him a cheque." Her voice rose to a small shriek. "Why would he follow me?"

Nobody felt they could answer that.

She said with raw fear, "George wants to contact me. Why else would Charlie Marsh want to know my whereabouts?"

Neil said gravely, "Please believe me, Hellen, it's not possible for George to break out of jail."

"No? Did you know he's mixed up with the Triads?"

Neil's eyes dilated. Marcia gasped, then recovering herself, said angrily, "How dare you! Do you know what the Triads are?" She rose to her feet, clumsy in her anguish.

"They control all the gambling rackets, and extortion rackets, and drugs, and prostitution." Hellen bravely looked her in the eyes.

Marcia put a hand to her mouth, as though it was she who had spoken the unspeakable.

Unnerved by Neil's refusal to believe George could break out of jail, frightened out of her wits, Hellen momentarily lost all sense of propriety. "If one is married to a man who goes with prostitutes, one is liable to be au fait with these matters."

Marcia stared at her, aghast, then turned and stalked out of the room. Neil rose and followed her. Hellen turned to Lin Yan. "It was my fault," she said, sweetly contrite. "I didn't want you to know, but in the end I had to say it, so that Mr Curtain would take your story seriously."

Hellen said miserably, "Why don't we go home? By train. Tonight. I could go to the Hong Kong Hotel until there's an available berth on a ship. George wouldn't dare turn up there."

Neil came back into the room. "You've upset Marcia dreadfully. It was really very unseemly of you to mention . . . er. . . ."

Hellen thought she saw a twinkle in his eyes. "I will apologise," she said. "And I apologise to you. If there's a train back to Hong Kong tonight, we would like to go."

Neil took her hand. "There is no train. And if there was, I wouldn't want you to go. Please believe me, my dear, when I say it simply isn't possible for George to escape, and it certainly isn't possible for that man to get past the gate keeper on Shameen. You really are perfectly safe here. Stay a while and make friends with Marcia." He turned to Lin Yan, saying with distant courtesy, "We would like you to stay, too."

Hellen felt a tear on her cheek and wiped her eyes. "I dare say I'll feel better when I've had a bath."

He smiled. "I dare say you will. We'll see you on the upstairs verandah when you're ready."

Two amahs showed them to their rooms. On the upper landing they separated. Hellen hesitated, looking uncertainly after Lin Yan as she was led up a further flight. Then the amah signed to her to follow. She went along a wide passage and entered a large room comfortably furnished with a big double bed, mahogany chests, and a dressing table inset with mother-of-pearl. There were doors opening on to the verandah.

She bathed and changed, then opened her glass doors and went outside. Marcia and Neil were already settled into rattan chairs. Lin Yan came hesitantly to join them. Hellen gave her a questioning smile and she smiled ruefully back. The number one boy served their drinks from a wheeled trolley. A wonderful breeze came off the water. To the south, the busy little ferry boats plied to and fro, bridging the two parts of the city. They watched the evening craft nosing in to their moorings, juggling for position, tying up outside and alongside and outside again, until all that floating life was entwined like the straw of a hat.

"There won't be one of them left there in the morning," Neil said. "Whatever the weather, they're off to sea at four o'clock. These are the fisher and cargo boats. The rover craft. Permanent moorings are further north. That's the pleasure district," said Neil, looking mischievously at Hellen. He rose and went to look for his pipe. As he disappeared inside the house Marcia said bitterly, "Once you lower the tone, a man will feel free to say anything to you. It's up to the ladies to maintain standards."

The evening passed surprisingly pleasantly. After dinner they played mah-jong. It was as though a truce had been drawn up between Marcia and Hellen. Later, in her night clothes, Hellen went back on to the verandah, and stood leaning on the rail looking out in the moonlight at the river craft. There was a movement in the darkness of the doorway and she jumped nervously.

"It is I." Lin Yan emerged to join her in the gloom. They stood together at the rail.

"Is your room all right?"

"Very suitable." Lin Yan's reply was laconic.

Hellen sighed sharply, remembering that Ruth had said she might not like what she saw, but she was not going to change things. "Anyone could land on Shameen from the Pearl River," she said, "and presumably from the creeks on the other three sides. The gates on the bridge are a sham."

Lin Yan moved closer, putting a comforting hand on Hellen's arm. "Why would George want to come here?"

There were a dozen answers from which to choose. Perhaps he needed her as a shield. Perhaps, in his own way, he was in love with her. It could be lonely, going out into the world to hide. Or perhaps he felt there was some sort of kudos in having the girl who had been going to marry Oliver Marathon. She shivered. "I can only think— because he wants me to run away with him."

She lay in bed that night listening to the shrieky music on the water and the clamour of the boatmen coming down with the tide; and she was very frightened.

Chapter 34

The Real China

It was clear in the morning that they were not going to be able to leave Canton without grievously upsetting Neil.

"Just one day," he begged. They might never see each other again. Or not for twenty years. "I'd like to show you the city," he said. "There are wonderful silk shops, ivory shops, shops selling silverware and jade. You must see Silk Street.

"And this afternoon," he hurried on, "I'd like to take you on the river. The river life's fascinating, too. Please stay, I'll put you on the train tomorrow, if you're still determined to go." He read Hellen's wary look and added, "Please."

She wished she could say it was not Charlie Marsh of whom she was afraid, but George. She wished she could believe Neil when he said his son could not break out of jail. She did not want to mention the Triads again, in front of Marcia. She looked wanly at Lin Yan who said, "It would be nice for you to see Canton."

Not surprisingly, Marcia did not wish to accompany them. They hired three rickshaws. The coolies ran lithely over the granite blocks, recklessly diving in and out of hurrying pedestrians as though there was no time to lose. The cries of the traders and the street hawkers followed them, the tinny rattle of coolies' chatter, the rumbling and creaking of buffalo carts. At every street corner Hellen glanced round swiftly, though knowing if there was a squat Eurasian seaman following his face would be hidden by a wide straw hat, making him indistinguishable from the mob spilling through the arcaded sidewalks and the streets.

Neil took them to a strange garden where orange trees, though standing twelve inches high, bore fruit. Where forest trees were dwarfed to the size of rose bushes. Hellen was scratchy. "That tree was meant to be twenty, or thirty, or forty feet high." She looked with distaste on its trunk and branches that were twisted like a snake.

"How can they enjoy deforming living things?" She wanted to leave the garden. It reminded her of the way the pirates had so easily, so casually, deformed George.

They climbed back into their rickshaws and swung off to visit Pagoda Street where stood the residence of the Military Governor of Manchu days. Neil took them up the narrow, steep stairs inside a pagoda. Hellen found it sinister and unnerving. She breathed freely only when they were on their way again.

In Silk Street, a cavern of wonder with gold-lettered signs and bolts of richly coloured brocades carelessly displayed, Neil insisted on buying both girls a length of silk. Lin Yan chose a delicate egg-shell blue. Hellen held the silk across her friend's front, hoping she would see in the mirror that the pale colour had taken the glow from her skin and eyes. Lin Yan looked wonderful in bold peacock blues, rich reds, and glittering gold.

Lin Yan smiled. "This is what I want."

Neil and Hellen stood in the colourful street while Lin Yan waited for her package to be wrapped. "It's odd," he said, "but Chinese girls, if they're in love with an Englishman, or if they've got mixed blood, yearn to cut off their hair and wear western clothes. They do themselves a great disservice. They do far better to make the most of their unique Chinese beauty."

"Lin Yan has a quarter English blood."

"You'd never know," he said.

"And she's in love with an Englishman."

"Is she going to marry him?"

"Who knows?" Hellen turned away and climbed into her rickshaw. "I can't."

Neil's face was a study. "There's a rum go," he said at last, and then Lin Yan joined them, all smiles.

After lunch they hired a tourist boat. There was peace on the quiet water with only the three of them and the boatman, and much to see. They passed the floating bordelloes, enjoying intriguing glimpses of interiors with rich curtains and painted panellings. They saw a painted lady sitting in a bow, still as a grown-up doll, waiting for custom. They saw a woman rowing a sampan and singing Chinese songs to round-faced children, solemn as baby dolls.

Neil was inexhaustible in his endeavours to entertain and inform them. They saw a mother pulling a child in by means of a wooden float chained to its waist. "That float will double for its pillow tonight," said Neil. "Chinamen are frugal to a fault."

Hellen stole a glance at Lin Yan, serene beneath her sunshade, but she only smiled. Hellen had found a feather pillow on her bed the night she stayed in her house. She wondered if Lin Yan re-arranged her elaborate hair style every day, or if she too slept on a wooden pillow.

They went through the busy part of the river, where canoe-paddling hawkers plied among the flower boats for custom, offering bean curd and shamshoo. They went far up the river, out into the country where the sugar cane, bananas and pineapples grew, then on into a serene landscape, reminiscent of eighteenth and nineteenth-century engravings of Oriental scenes. As the sun went down coolies came trudging towards the river bringing their tools and farm implements, to stow them away for the night in shacks constructed of banana leaves.

"I am glad I stayed," Hellen said warmly. "It's been a wonderful day. Thank you, Neil." She was thinking that if she never saw him again, there would be these tranquil hours to remember, his warmth and kindness.

On the way back down stream, where a tributary ran off, Neil issued an order to the boatman in Cantonese. "I want to show you a duck boat," he said to Hellen. "It's only a short distance up here."

Hellen demurred. "It's getting late." She was afraid of being caught by darkness outside the safe-unsafe island of Shameen.

"This won't take long," he assured her, "and it's a sight you'll never see again."

The boatman swung the bow to starboard. They came upon the duck boat moored to a bank adjacent to a rice field. "They come here in the morning," said Neil. "The ducks march down the gangplank and scatter over the fields to spend the day feeding on bugs, worms and insects. They're the farmer's best friends."

Hellen sat stiffly in the stern, chafing, nervously aware that the sun was going down.

Presently there was a long drawn out call from the duck shepherd, and thousands of birds, quacking noisily, came running from every direction, fleeing like startled sheep across the gangplank and into the ship. The onlookers went into paroxyms of laughter. Then the duck shepherd, standing on the bank, unfurled a long whip. The late stragglers scrambled and screamed in a frenzy to get aboard. Hellen turned away, hearing the crack of the whip and wincing at the intensified shrieks of those ducks who had to pay the price for being the last aboard.

"How I hate them!" she burst out. "Do they have to be so cruel?"

Neil cast an anxious look at Lin Yan, impassively watching. "We're on our way now," he said soothingly.

But the boatman seemed disinclined to move. Neil spoke to him sharply. The two men argued.

"What's going on, Lin Yan?" Hellen could pick out only a word here and there.

"He says he lives near here. He doesn't want to take us all the way back. Mr Curtain is threatening that the Consul General will have him shot. And he has offered cumshaw."

Cumshaw. A bribe. A gift.

Neil put his hand in his pocket and drew out some notes. Another argument ensued. He turned to the girls. "I'm frightfully sorry. I've persuaded the wretch to take us to the nearest place where we can get rickshaws. It's the best I can do. He says the detour to the duck boat wasn't agreed."

Hellen looked again at the sky. The sun was sinking over the horizon. The tree shadows were long on the banks. She shivered, feeling afraid.

The boatman turned his craft round and ferried them back downstream. "He says we'll get transport here," said Neil. "I hope he speaks the truth."

They disembarked and went up a narrow dirt road that led to a main thoroughfare full of rattling bullock carts. There were no rickshaws in sight. "Look on it as an adventure," said Neil comfortingly. Hellen gave him a tight smile.

They walked past row upon row of dirty shacks, past stagnant ponds where hens and ducks scratched for their food in the dusty earth; past roadside warehouses thatched with palm where huge bales of rattan lay waiting for collection; past market stalls, and humble homes perfunctorily decorated with dusty flowers growing out of kerosene tins.

As twilight was settling in they came to an intersection where there were half a dozen rickshaws plying for trade. Neil cried triumphantly, "Here we are. What did I say? It wasn't so bad, was it?"

They climbed thankfully aboard. The coolies gave them a rough ride, swinging round corners and jolting over stones. Hellen grew increasingly uneasy as they swept through narrow alleys where strange shadows lurked in dark places. They came to a square edged by tall buildings and mean-looking booths. In the midst of an eager, noisy crowd, the coolies halted, lowering their shafts. One of them turned with a happy grin. "Liver pilot. Chopee off head," he said. "Surplise for you."

Neil ordered them angrily to continue on their journey, but the bearers only grinned and stood their ground.

"What's a liver pilate?" Even as she spoke, Hellen remembered the Chinese substituted an l for an r.

"He says we must stay and see the execution," said Lin Yan imperturbably.

355

Neil shouted at the coolies, demanding that they continue their journey. The crowd parted and two coolies appeared carrying a pole from which a basket was suspended. Trussed up in the basket was a small Chinaman with a placard covered in bold Chinese ideographs, hanging round his neck. From her small knowledge of Cantonese, stumbling and guessing, Hellen read what appeared to be a list of the man's crimes. Grasping Lin Yan by the hand, she took to her heels. The coolies came after them, carting their empty rickshaws, screeching like tomcats, stretching out their free hands, demanding their fares. Neil shouted after them, threatening them. In the ensuing clamour the girls reached the street beyond the square. Neil came hurrying and there was another altercation. With bad grace, the coolies allowed them all aboard.

They jog-trotted in silence through the gathering darkness. The gates of Shameen were closed but Neil was able to find the gate keeper and have them unlocked. It was with a feeling of thankfulness that they crossed the bridge and entered the tranquil community.

Marcia was distraught.

"A small brush with the natives," Neil explained. "We've seen worse than that in Shanghai. One becomes hardened, in a lifetime of China. I'm sorry it had to happen to you, though, dear," he said to Hellen, taking in her obvious distress. "Not good form at all, but what can you do? We were on foreign soil, and that's how the natives are."

Hellen glanced at Lin Yan and saw in her classical Chinese calm that she was a part of all that happened here, and wondered if, left to her own devices, she would have stayed to witness the execution.

It seemed, afterwards, those few hours had been an acclimatization, as though fate had briefly lifted the curtain on China to prepare them for what was to come. Lin Yan had tactfully retired early and Hellen followed, wanting tomorrow to arrive quickly. She did not wake immediately the noise started. It began as a faint but insistent knocking. She was dreaming, comfortingly, about Oliver, as she so often did. The knocking came in, closer and closer, until it drove the dream away. She sat up in bed, rubbing her eyes, but the sounds had ceased. She lay down again and prepared to go to sleep.

The next moment there was a sound of voices and hurrying footsteps in the passage outside her door. She jerked upright, leaped out of bed and, pattering to the window, drew back the curtain. It was just pre-dawn, that time when the darkess begins to lift, yet with no trace of the sun in the east. She slipped into her thin silk dressing gown and opened the door leading to the passage. The lights were on. She could hear a commotion in the hall. Marcia's voice, then Neil's. Then a flurry of footsteps and Lin Yan, in a bright pink gown with frogged fastenings, her black hair streaming down her back, came flying down from the upper floor.

"Come with me," she whispered urgently. "There's a back staircase from my room. George is here, with Charlie Marsh."

Hellen stood frozen, with a feeling of inevitable doom, knowing that all the hiding places in the world could not conceal her, nor prevent what was to come. Then there was a leaping of footsteps on the stairs and George emerged on the landing.

"So where's the money?" he demanded.

Hellen opened her mouth but there was no sound. He was coming towards her. His moustance had gone, as had his hair, leaving a dark shadow where it had been. He did not look like the George she knew, except that his eyes had the same angry darkness. Outside her astonishment at his appearance, Hellen was thinking with fear that he must not hit her again. As he came close she moved swiftly, and taking him by surprise, ducked. Grasping the skirt of her nightdress with both hands, she pelted down the stairs.

They were there in the hall, Neil and Marcia in their night clothes, Marcia's hair untidily round her shoulders, Neil looking rumpled, distressed and angry. Hellen rushed to the shelter of Neil's arms. "Tell him I haven't got the money," she cried.

Neil spoke with authority. "She tore it up, George."

He turned angrily to Charlie Marsh. "Now what do we do?"

"Write another," Hellen said. "Mr Marsh has your cheque book. He can cash it tomorrow, here, on Shameen."

George came and stood directly in front of her, looking threateningly down into her face. "Swear to me you tore it up up."

"I swear."

"You bloody fool," said George viciously. "You've been nothing but trouble."

Marcia was looking at her son as though she had never seen him before.

"Write another," said Charlie Marsh. "It's gunner be light soon. Hole up here, and I'll be back tonight."

George took the cheque book out of his pocket. "Pen." He looked impatiently round, as though expecting someone to produce it from their night clothes.

Neil indicated a small desk standing beneath the telephone. "In the drawer," he said.

Marcia began quietly to cry. Without moving, Hellen, out of the corner of her eye, saw Lin Yan standing very erect at the foot of the stairs. There was silence in the hall except for the tap of the pen on the ink well, and the scratch of the nib as George filled in the cheque.

357

Charlie Marsh examined it intently, folded it and pushed it deep down into his pocket. "So long," he said and, turning, opened the door and disappeared.

They must have been on the doorstep, waiting. Suddenly the hall was full of small Chinamen wielding knives, and unbelievably Charlie Marsh stood behind them, gun cocked. "You better come quietly," he said.

George recovered first. He lunged towards Lin Yan, and holding her in front of him, backed towards the door that led into the dining room. Charlie Marsh's finger curled round the trigger, but before he could pull it one of the little men sprang forward with lifted knife and jabbed it into Lin Yan's breast. She fell like a stone, and then they were trampling over her, leaping on George, babbling and shrieking in voices that went up and up to a high-pitched crescendo that tore at the ears and made the blood run cold.

George was on the ground, bellowing and screaming and writhing. There were only five Chinese, but at the time Hellen seemed to be fighting her way through a crowd. Somehow, she managed to pull Lin Yan free and drag her across the floor. Blood pumped out of her in a ghastly red tide. Hellen knelt, holding her in her arms. Lin Yan opened her eyes. The noise drowned what she had to say. Hellen heard only "happy" and "ancestors".

"Please don't die," she sobbed. "Please, please don't die." With fear and despair she felt the warm wetness of Lin Yan's blood soaking through her sleeve and running down over her knees. "Get the doctor," she shrieked, looking round frantically for Neil. Marcia's face was buried in his shoulder and his arms were around her. He, too, looked about to collapse.

One of the little men went outside and returned with a rope and a stalwart pole about eight feet long. Neil let Marcia go and started forward.

"These chaps are quick with the dagger," said Charlie Marsh threateningly. "If I wuz you, I'd stay where y'are."

"What are they going to do with him?" cried Neil, distraught.

"What's the punishment for welshing on yer friends?" asked Charlie Marsh nastily. "Not to mention getting off with other people's money. Ling Ch'ih."

Hellen felt her blood run cold. Ling Ch'ih was an ignominious slashing, or lingering, death.

Neil leaped for the telephone.

Charlie Marsh gestured laconically with his gun. "Wire's cut."

"Look here—"

"Shut up. Nobody does the dirty on Charlie Marsh and gets away with it."

Neil dazedly lifted the receiver, listened, then despairingly allowed it to drop. It swung back and forth like the pendulum of a clock.

Hellen, in an agony of grief and guilt, held the Eurasian girl to her heart. Lin Yan's blood poured over her hands and down her front, not pumping now, just pouring. Silently, she wept.

They trussed George up like a turkey and tied his hands and feet to the pole, like the pig Hellen had seen being carried along the street yesterday when they were coming from the steamer. Then four of the little men lifted the pole on to their shoulders, two in front and two behind, and went swiftly out of the house. Neil started forward, but Charlie Marsh threatened him with his gun, and he fell back.

"So long," said the seaman, adding as an afterthought, "You won't get the bits back right away. You know the Chinaman's way of looking at things? They're not dead 'til all the bits is cold. S'long."

He slammed the door.

Chapter 35
The Return

George's funeral was brief and painful. Neil, Marcia and Hellen were the only mourners. His mutilated body was returned, as Charlie Marsh had said, as soon as it was cold. The police had been powerless to discover its hiding place until the Triads were ready to hand it over. Hellen felt no grief, only a sense of the inevitability of things.

Afterwards, while Marcia rested and grieved, she and Neil talked. They had grown closer over the bad days. He supported her through Lin Yan's funeral, which had been held the following day. In death Lin Yan was not to be spared the Chinese junketting. Over the gateway of the ancient temple, set in stones, was the pearl of wisdom, the dragon of strength, and a fish for liberty. A framed photograph of the deceased, decorated with flowers, had been hung on the wall of one of the open-fronted cubicles set aside for those recently dead. There were tiny dishes of her favourite food to sustain her on her journey to the next world, and two big lanterns marked with blue to light her way. Had she reached eighty years the lettering on the lanterns would have been red. Red was for happiness. Lin Yan had not been accorded the happiness of a long life.

Somebody had contributed a paper boat and solemnly burned it in the sandalwood incense burner, so that she would have transport to heaven. And paper shoes for the walking part of the journey. Paper money was burned for her use in the next world, and a paper house in which her spirit would dwell. There was paper furniture, and a cut-out of a house boy to wait on her, so that she could continue the elegant existence she had been granted on earth.

Hellen noticed with distaste that there were flies round the food, but Mrs Chan told her relatives would bring fresh victuals every day for the duration of the show, which was to be forty-nine days. Every seventh day a service would be held. She hoped Hellen would attend.

360

But there was a P&O ship coming in, and Denzil Armitage said he would move heaven and earth to ensure she sailed on it.

Hellen walked with Mrs Chan in a courtyard behind the temple, the Chinese woman tottering on her tortured little feet. There were young people praying at the loyalty tree: girls asking for a good husband who would not take another wife; young men praying they might find a girl who would work hard for them.

"Better Lin Yan go to ancestors than bring disgrace on family by marrying Englishman," said Mrs Chan, her black eyes like round dots in her sad, wrinkled face.

"She wasn't going to marry anyone, Mrs Chan."

The Chinese woman said fiercely, "I find English wedding dress in her house."

Hellen opened her mouth to explain but Mrs Chan continued implacably, "It have been burned."

"Let's go," said Neil when she came numbly back to him. "You look done in. Don't grieve too much." He took her arm and led her towards the street. "What's that parcel? Can I carry it for you?"

"Mrs Chan found it among Lin Yan's things. My name was on it. She said, quite without rancour, 'Your husband killed her, and she left you a present.'"

"That's the Chinese all over. Fatalistic."

"It's the silk you bought. She must have chosen it for me." Hellen slit the paper with her fingernail and looked down at the pale pattern that she realised now Lin Yan would never have worn. "She wouldn't accept it from you."

Neil said uncomfortably, "It was a shock, her turning up like that. One doesn't, you know, entertain Eurasians in one's home."

"Did you know she was put to sleep in a servant's room?" Hellen said bitterly, "Lin Yan was acceptable at Government House. I should have though she warranted a guest room with you."

"The First Lady can afford to make grand gestures."

Now, sitting on the verandah of the bungalow on Nathan Road, Neil said, "We're here to learn. Sadly, one learns nothing from a bed of roses. Life's short, my dear. It may help you to know, when things seem exceptionally bad, that taking an overall view, life's little more than a passing breath. We're born, we learn a thing or two, we die. In terms of the infinite, it's just a phase."

She wiped a tear away. "It's more than a breath, though it doesn't have to be a typhoon. It's said to be a gift. I've learned a great deal since I left England." When Hellen thought about the girl she had been, resolutely riding to hounds in Kent, not fitting in, she scarcely recognised her.

"Why did you marry George?"

"It's better not to ask. It doesn't do either of us credit. There's one thing I would like to say: George would be dead now even if he had not married me. If you deal in death, that is what you get. Death."

"I know, my dear. I know. What will you do now? You've lost them both."

"I haven't lost Oliver," she said softly. "I cannot lose Oliver. When someone has all your love, he can't stay away. He is obliged to find you and make you into a whole person again." She said softly, "My heart knows where he is."

They sat in silence for a while. "Will we see you again?"

"Who knows?" The East, with its barbarity and its beauty had bitten deeply, but in the wounds tentative roots, like small rice seedlings, had taken hold. She rose from her chair. "Thank you for seeing me through Lin Yan's funeral. Tell Mrs Curtain I don't expect forgiveness for not being able to love George. If he had, as he led me to believe, loved me, I would have tried."

Neil went to answer the telephone. Hellen stood gazing out into the banyan trees. He was back quickly. "It's Government House," he said. "There's a cable for you."

It was Roger Cadman.

"A cable from Oliver!" cried Hellen.

"I don't know who it's from," he replied. "Shall I have it sent over to you? Or would you like me to read it out?"

"Read it, please." While he tore the envelope open she thought she would go mad with suspense.

Roger said heavily, "YOUR MOTHER AND I ARRIVE HONG KONG 28th STOP PORCHARD."

Hellen collapsed into the telephone chair and burst into tears.

Perspiring coolies laden with baskets of flowers and fruit pushed their way up the gangplank. Ladies dressed to kill, laden with chocolates, gifts of lavender water, books, poured aboard. The professional See-ers-off Club were there in force, armed with bottles, aggressively determined to cheer up anyone sailing alone.

A sailing was always an excuse for a party, but this one offered a little more than most. Everyone in Hong Kong knew that poor Hellen Curtain was going home. All her friends had come, and some who were not her friends, to glimpse in the flesh the girl who had featured so startlingly in the papers over the past weeks.

Neil, as father of the notorious George Curtain, stayed away, unwilling to expose himself to whisperings, and nudgings, and stares.

362

Marcia did not come because she believed, implacably, that Hellen had been the cause of her son's ruin and death.

In Hellen's cabin there were bouquets of flowers from people she scarcely knew. From Mrs Elliott Keane, wife of George's taipan. Her husband had visited, expressing sympathy tinged with embarrassment. She did not see him as guilty in talking to the police, merely as a link in the chain reaction set off by George's behaviour. There was a bouquet from Kitty's parents. A sign of their gratitude that Kitty had been spared her ordeal? From Lettice Marathon there was a bouquet of roses borne to the ship by the two aides who were Oliver's friends. Shamefacedly, they laughed off their friends' jibes.

"Carrying flowers! What next?"

"Her Ladyship won a late battle," said Jack Lovell, dryly explaining the personal touch.

A brass band on the quay did its best to drown the chatter. Shroffs' agents rushed round the decks endeavouring to secure payment for signed chits. Credit was automatic for the English, but once the propeller turned, all debts were automatically cancelled. The agent had to be quick.

"Keep in touch," friends said. "Let us know. . . ."

Hellen nodded, and smiled.

Ruth, lovely in a hat trimmed with violets, and with violets at her bosom, fingered her frilly parasol. "About your mother and grandfather, dear?"

"I'm getting off at Singapore to meet them."

"How can you bear to go back, after what happened?"

"I've no choice. Besides, it might serve to lay some ghosts. You'll go and see the babies, won't you? And send me a photograph now and again?"

Ruth said, "They'll go back to their peasant families when they're older. They'll be all right." Helping coolies was like spitting into the Yellow River and expecting it to rise. "I shall miss you, dear," she said indulgently.

"All ashore that's going ashore". Hellen hugged her friend. "Thank you for all you've done."

"Looking back," said Ruth wryly, "I seem to have made a mistake or two."

The ship moved away from the quay and the tangled web of coloured streamers broke, drifting down into the water. The friends Hellen had made during the past year grew smaller and smaller until they merged into the wharves and Kowloon.

Jessica had the good looks of the Marathon wives, for they were discerning men. Her long chestnut brown hair lifted prettily away from

363

her head and allowed itself to be wound into a variety of styles. Even in the rainy season, when all the other Colonial wives looked drab because the damp wilted their hair, hers managed to look well.

Her complexion had suffered from twenty-five years in the tropics, but so had the complexions of all the other women. Anglo-Saxon skins did not stand up to the fierce sun of Malaya. In spite of the big hats and veils, the sunshades, the shady verandahs, the care, they ended up wrinkled as last season's apples. What people did notice about the British Resident's wife was her bright, smiling eyes, and her air of serene goodwill.

She was happy to be returning to Scotland. She thought her husband's talents lay closer to country squiredom than colonial administration. The Honourable Bernard Marathon was not a strong man like his brother, and neither did he have Rowan's ambition. Lady Sylvia Ashton had been exaggerating when she told Hellen he was in line for a governorship.

It was Jessica's strength that Oliver had inherited. Bernard said his heart ruled his head, but his wife did not think so. The combination Oliver had of hidden power, a certain vulnerability and a love of human beings, was one that made for greatness, once maturity set in. He also had the wily streak with which some of the Marathons were blessed.

She glanced down at her sister-in-law's cable—the longest cable in the world, as she had commented to her husband, running to five sheets. Well, she conceded, Lettice had been Oliver's mother, to the extent that he had a mother at all, for the past half dozen years. No doubt she knew him better than they did.

As she watched her husband strolling across the lounge of Raffles' Hotel she folded the sheets and tucked them under an old copy of *The Field*. All magazines in the East were at least two months out of date, and more often than not, six, but the women lapped them up, for they were the visual contact with home.

He came and stood looking down at her in the big armchair. "*Devanha*'s due to dock at eleven." He fingered the gold chain draped across his chest. "I don't mind telling you, I'm not looking forward to this."

"I'm sure she's charming, darling."

"That's not the point, is it? After all the effort Rowan has put into breaking this affair up . . . I'm surprised at Lettice."

"There are some things you can't break up, darling."

"I can have a damn' good try! I don't care to think of my only son married to the widow of a murdered jail bird."

She winced. "I only want Oliver to be happy."

"Pshaw! I'll give her lunch. That's as far as I'm prepared to go." He pointed at the corner of the cablegram sticking out from the pages of his wife's magazine. "Lettice must have taken leave of her senses."

Under the shady flame trees the jinrickshas sipped some doubtful syrup provided by a Bengali hawker. The British Resident climbed in and the native set out at a run for Johnston's Pier. As they wended their way through the carriages, hackney gharries, and bullock carts, he looked out broodingly at the Malay coastal vessels with their dart-like sails, and the lighters anchored along the river edge, thinking it had been a bad year, what with the worrying reports of his brother Cecil's continuing decline; Rowan's despatches from Hong Kong about Oliver's insubordinance; and now his father's death. Still, he didn't really mind going home. He'd been abroad since the age of twenty when he was appointed third aide to the Governor of Burma. It would be nice for Jessica to see more of Marigold and the grandchildren. Scotland would be cold, but there would be compensations. And if Cecil was really going to die, one of the brothers ought to be there. He thought of the Earldom that would inevitably come Oliver's way, and his jaw hardened.

Hellen spoke to the Purser, "Is there a message for me?"

"No, Miss North."

The tall man standing with his back to her turned round sharply, and stared.

She looked up at his face and recognised the eyes, those blue Marathon eyes.

"Mrs—er—Curtain?" he asked.

"You must be Oliver's father." She went on gazing at him, looking for Oliver, seeing only the eyes. Nothing of Sir Rowan, either, except for the eyes.

He said courteously, but without warmth, "My wife and I hoped you would be free to lunch with us."

She knew, then, that Oliver was not with him. "Thank you."

He turned to face the gangplank, gesturing to her to accompany him.

"I need a porter," she said.

One of the coolies pounced. "Raffles Hotel?"

She nodded and led him to where her cabin luggage lay.

Bernard Marathon said sternly, "You're not staying?"

"I am meeting my family here."

"Oh." He touched his generously proportioned moustache. She sensed he was not happy about her staying. Sir Rowan would have done a better job of covering up.

"Is Oliver here?" she asked, looking directly into his eyes.

"Here? In Singapore, you mean? Why, no."

She knew by his hesitancy, and the touch of bluster, that he was lying.

"If that's why you're disembarking, you may as well—er—continue. Stay on board, I mean."

Hellen said distinctly, "I am to meet my family here. My mother and grandfather." Even if they were not coming, she would have had to disembark today; even if the booking had been made right through to England, which it had not. All the way down through the South China Sea—no, before that, before buying her ticket—she had known that Singapore was her destination.

Oliver's father was quiet as they rolled back through the wide, leaf-lined streets in the gharry. She needed the quiet. They came into Raffles Place, then to the heart of it, the pillared and arched façade of Raffles Hotel. The ghosts she had come to lay were all around her now, for this was where it had begun, the great detour organised by George out of the mess created by Lady Sylvia Ashton and Calum Finn. Poor George, she found herself thinking, if he hadn't. . . .

But he had.

"Aren't you getting down?"

Oliver's father was standing impatiently on the pavement, holding out a hand to assist her to descend. "Didn't you visit Raffles on the way out? I thought everybody did."

"Yes."

"I thought you looked as though—I thought you looked surprised."

"I came here to lunch."

Jessica sat up straight in her chair. Was this the girl who had caused all the trouble? This slender, elegant creature in the understated silk dress and the large, shady hat?

Without waiting to be introduced, Hellen stepped forward, holding out her hand.

Oliver's mother had the look of Lady Marathon. She had the sweetness, but with something sharp as well. An extra intelligence. And there was a twinkle in those bright eyes. Hellen liked her immediately. She had a feeling Oliver's mother would not have lied to her. They sat down and she took the bull by the horns. "Your husband tells me Oliver is not in Singapore."

"Not in the city."

"Where is he?"

"He's up-country. Working on a rubber plantation."

"How would I get there?"

Jessica glanced at her husband. Momentarily, he looked non-plussed. Then annoyed. He said, "Let's have a drink, shall we? What would you like, Mrs Curtain?"

"Do call me Hellen," she said, falsely calm. "I'd like fruit juice." Then she remembered the fruit juice that had been prepared for her on *Bangkok Lady* and, unnerved, she gasped. "No. Gin."

"Gin!"

Oliver's mother said, with an air of spreading oil on troubled waters, "There's a very nice drink here that they call a gimlet. Gin with lime, on ice. Rather good at mid-day. Perhaps you'd like to try it?"

Hellen nodded. "Thank you." The waiter took their orders. Somehow, she composed herself. "How would I get to this plantation where Oliver is?"

Jessica looked down at her hands. Bernard pulled a gold cigarette case out of his pocket, carefully selected a cigarette, lit it, then replaced both the lighter and the case in his pocket. "Mmn," he said, using exactly the same tone his brother had used at the Government House ball when chastising her for riding his horses. He looked up at the fan directly above them in the ceiling and said, "I suppose we could call him down. It might be inconvenient, but I suppose we could, at a pinch, if you really want to see him."

"Don't call him," said Hellen, "just give me the address."

"Some of these plantations are four hundred miles to the north."

"The one Oliver's on? Is it four hundred miles to the north?"

He said quite firmly, "I will see what I can do."

When she had gone to her room to tidy herself for lunch, walking very straight with her head held high, Jessica looked quizzically at her husband.

"Demned girl was only booked to here." He told her Hellen's family were coming. "What the devil do you make of that?" He took the cable from his wife's hand. "According to Lettice, she's on her way to England." He read out the relevant phrase: "MEET THE SHIP AND TAKE HER OFF."

His wife smiled. Sometimes she wondered if Bernard had forgotten what it was like to be young and in love. "She's beautiful, isn't she?"

He flung her an angry glance. "That's not the point. Gin!" he ejaculated in disgust.

Chapter 36
Oliver

There were a dozen exits from Raffles Place. Hellen started along Change Alley, looking at the junk stalls, the shoes, watches, torches and cutlery laid out on display. At the harbour edge she stood watching the Chinese in faded blue jackets, shin-length trousers and straw hats propelling their sampans on the sunlit water.

She halted again in the hustle and bustle of Battery Road, gazing up at the magnificent edifice of the Hong Kong and Shanghai Bank, and found herself wondering dispassionately if Charlie Marsh had succeeded in cashing George's cheque.

She went down Orchard Road, beneath the shade of nutmeg and pepper trees, where street barbers plied their trade; she watched the men in the market squatting by hawker baskets while amahs haggled over the price of fresh fish; she watched children playing.

Amidst the frenetic bustle of Chinatown where tiny shops sold lacquered ducks, flat as pancakes, birds' nests and sharks' fins, she turned a corner to find paving stones stained red with betel juice, and languid Indian women in vivid saris walking with their men, shirt tails hanging outside their trousers.

She walked past spacious bungalows set in compounds, full of elegant palms and feathery sago hedges; stood beneath casuarina trees listening to the hot breeze whispering. She found the botanical gardens and wandered among orchids, tropical ferns, emerald strips of primeval jungle, and ponds where her own reflection looked back at her. As she walked she grew more tranquil. There were no other white women to meet. They were all, no doubt, like Oliver's parents at Government House, enjoying an afternoon nap under the fans.

She returned to the hotel weary and with her dress sticking damply to her skin, but with a feeling of having faced up to Singapore with its drugged fruit juices, its lies, its fear and despair. Now, she was ready to look for Oliver.

There was a note on her dressing table addressed to Miss Hellen North. Feverishly, she pushed her thumb under the flap.

Her eyes went straight to the signature. Lance Moore. It was written on P & O office stationery.

"Mr Marathon tells me you're at a loose end. May I take you out to dinner? I'll come to Raffles at eight. If you've got something better to do, leave a note at the office."

There was a tear on her cheek as she folded the note and put it back in the envelope. She could only think that this man might know where Oliver was. Or could perhaps find out.

Lance Moore took out his watch as he came into the hotel lounge. Five minutes late. But she was in no position to complain, this girl who would be fat, dull, and looking for a husband. Unfortunately, getting on in white Singapore was a matter of being a good puppet when those on high pulled the strings.

Hellen saw him come in and knew immediately that this six feet tall, devastatingly handsome man was the one Oliver's father had chosen to tempt her. She stifled a sigh as she rose from her chair.

Lance stood looking across the room. Not her! Not that girl with the beads round her forehead and the soft dress spattered with roses! He glanced anxiously behind, but there was no one there. She had to be smiling at him! He came forward eagerly, holding out his hand.

"I have to apologise," said Hellen wryly. "Mr Marathon didn't warn me he was going to force some poor innocent man into taking me out. You don't have to, you know. I'm perfectly happy dining here on my own."

"But I'm delighted. Honestly. What would you like to do? We could go to a restaurant first, then on to the Tanglin Club to dance."

"You're really awfully kind, as well as obedient," she said wryly.

He took her arm. "Enough of that. Come on."

The restaurant was by the beach where they could look out on the moonlit water. Lance Moore was amusing company. "The Honourable Bernard? No, I don't know him," he replied in answer to Hellen's question. "He doesn't live in Singapore. He's here to say goodbye to the Governor, I gather. And see his son, I suppose."

She had jumped when he said "his son".

Over coffee Lance asked, "Why are you being so cagey? Why don't you want to tell me why you're here?"

"What do you know about Mr Marathon's son?" she countered, fingering the jade pendant at her throat.

"Not much. He's supposed to be working in the offices of the Chinese Protectorate, but—there's some problem, I think. Rumour has it that he wants to resign from the Colonial Service. He's been

369

allowed to go up-country and work off steam at Paya Besar. That's not a rumour. I do happen to know he's at Paya Besar. Why do you want to know all this?"

"Paya Besar?" She by-passed his question.

"That's the name of a rubber plantation. It's Malay for large swamp." He reached across the table for her hands. "Why are we talking boring gossip about other people when we could be talking about ourselves?"

"We're talking about me," said Hellen. "I'm the problem."

Lance Moore groaned and released her hands. "Just my luck."

She laughed softly. "Oh, come. With your looks! Admit it, you were chosen today for your looks."

Lance looked sheepish.

"How far is it to Paya Besar, and how does one get there?"

"Maybe seventy miles. Eighty. You go by car or train."

"When do the trains run?"

"There'll be one in the morning." Lance frowned. "Are you going to marry Oliver?"

"His father's hoping I won't. I expect he's hoping I'll fall for you."

"Why not?" he asked engagingly.

"You can come to the wedding. Or the elopement. I expect it will come to that."

Lance Moore eyed his glass while the waiter filled it, then looked up with a mischievous grin. "I've got a new car. I've only had it a month. It hasn't had a recent run."

Hellen caught her breath. "Do you know the way?"

"Sure. My parents live up there." He pulled his watch out of his waistcoat pocket. "There's just about time to get to Paya Besar and back to work in the morning."

Hellen was already half way out of her chair.

"I must warn you," said her escort, "it's a mighty rough road. You'll be covered in bruises and dust."

She pointed excitedly out of the window towards the harbour. "Look at the light. It's bright as day."

"A spiffing night for a drive." He filled up her glass and raised his own. "Here's mud in the eye to the Honourable Bernard." He shouted across the restaurant, "Boy, the chit."

"Coming, Tuan."

The car was outside the bungalow he shared with friends. They ran all the way there. It was a two-seater Sunbeam tourer, with the hood folded down. "This is a jump in at the deep end for the poor old girl, but she's going to enjoy it," he said, giving the car a hearty whack on the rear mudguard. "Keep your fingers crossed that we don't break

370

down, or get trampled by elephants, or eaten by a tiger, or run out of gasoline. I say," he looked with dismay at her pretty dress, "oughtn't you to go back to the hotel and change?"

"No." She was beside herself with excitement. There was something wonderfully bizarre about dashing through the moonlight and the jungle in a flimsy evening dress wearing champagne-coloured silk stockings and delicate shoes, with a beaded band round her hair; fleeing to Oliver with stars all over the sky and the moon shining down on the water; hurling the past far into the jungle as they raced through, leaving it there to die.

"Hop in, then." He took the crank handle from under the seat and fitted it into the bonnet. The engine roared to life. He leaped up on the mudguard, then into his high seat. They went over a bridge at a rattling pace and into the heart of the island, through forest and jungle and so to the causeway that would lead them into the state of Johore. The Straits were a sheet of silver, dotted with little boats and sampans, and one big steamer making its way west.

"This is the time to go," Lance shouted over the roar of the engine and the rush of the wind, "when wild drivers and meandering buffaloes are safely asleep." They had the road to themselves. They scarcely needed the headlights, so bright was the moonlight. They swept past inlets where the high thatched houses of sea gypsies reared up on stilts in the water, swung round terrifying hairpin bends past derelict vehicles reposing in ditches, a reminder that it was not really safe to drive at such speed.

They laboured up a steep, tree-clad hill. The radiator belched great jets of steam. They swept down the other side and across a solid little bridge built over a swiftly flowing brook. Lance braked, took a tin out of the dickey seat and climbed down to the water. The metal cap of the radiator was so hot he had to use the wind-screen rag to protect his hands. He cranked the engine and they were off again, dashing through mile after mile of agricultural land, green from the rain that kept the country moist all the year round. Now there were bungalows set on stilts among the tall coconut palms. Here was a herd of elephants dozing in a clearing.

"There's your elephant," shouted the driver, leaning forward over the wheel, gritting his teeth, flashing glances this way and that. "Now for the tiger!"

Hellen rocked with excited laughter.

"Watch out for buffaloes. Are you really going to marry Oliver? It seems such a waste, when you could marry me. I'd get on well with an adventurous girl like you, rushing round the jungle in beads and bare feet." Hellen had removed her shoes and was resting her feet on the dash.

371

"Yes. I really am."

"It does seem a pity."

They came to Paya Basar quite suddenly. There was a sign by the roadside, easily readable in the moonlight. "That's it. That's the end of your journey." Lance turned off the engine, took a gasolene can from the dickey and proceeded to fill up the tank.

On the right hand side of the road a big bungalow sat among tall coconut trees. There was no sign of life. On the left were long lines of para rubber plants, three or four feet high, planted out among the burnt and rotting timbers of the primeval forest.

"Well, ma'am," said Lance as he replaced the empty can in the car, "I've got to get back, or I won't make it to work in time and my boss will get on to Government House and tell that old beggar that I've run off with you. Let's go and knock up somebody."

"No, really. Please just leave me. I'll be perfectly all right. It will be light soon." She needed to be alone now. He opened the door and climbed down. "How can I ever thank you?"

"By asking me to the elopement. That'll do. I say," he exclaimed in dismay, "you are covered in dust."

She looked down ruefully at her crumpled skirt.

"Now, I can't leave you here, outside a shut up bungalow."

"You can, actually."

"You are an independent miss!" But he smiled. "A kiss for the chauffeur then, if you don't mind."

She kissed him warmly on the cheek. "I'll be in touch." She waited until he had gone bouncing off down the rough road, driving with one hand on the wheel, waving a farewell with his left arm in the air, then she turned. There was time to fill in.She went in among the shadowy rubber trees and stood looking at a pattern of cuts running down one of the trunks where a slice had been shaved off the bark. The white latex rivulet ran down to a half coconut shell attached to the bark. An early morning pheasant called, "Ku-au, ku-au."

The ground rose here. She began to make her way towards the hilltop. She could not have said why she was going there instead of to the bungalow, except that was where she was being drawn. It was lighter here. She climbed up a rocky path, bordered only by scrub and grass. It was cool now, and silent, except for the early sounds of the waking birds. The moon was fading, and over on the horizon a sliver of white showed. She walked right up to the top of the peak and stood looking out on a vast panorama of forest.

The white in the sky changed to gold, then pink. The pink spread, darkening to rose, then crimson, until the sky was a great tapestry of brilliant light with the rim of a fireball creeping up over the dark horizon. She was awed by the sky's savage beauty, by the immense loneliness, and the silence. She sat down on the grass with her knees pulled up, the palms of her hands behind her, and her face lifted to the light. She felt she was part of this great empty world. She felt exhalted. Almost holy. Practically divine.

There was a sound in her ears, a soft crunching as of footsteps on grass and earth. She did not open her eyes because she was afraid of frightening away the sound that was the music in the silence. Then she felt a closeness, and a gentle, velvet-soft touch on her cheek. Oliver's voice said, "Are you real?"

Her lids lifted and there were Oliver's eyes, looking into hers. She held out her arms and he took her hands, kissing the backs of them as he had on that very first day under the oak tree on a Kentish hillside. Then, very gently, he turned her to face the wooded hills.

"Remember that dream I told you about, when we were in the New Territories together? I said I dreamt we were on top of a hill, looking out on trees, and wearing strange clothes?" He indicated her dusty evening dress, then his own crisp tropical gear. "And that's the view," he said.

They retreated beneath the shade of a flame tree and leaned up against the trunk with their legs stretched out before them. "Remember this?" asked Oliver, looking up into the branches. "Remember when we met, when I knocked you off your horse and we ended up sitting under a tree, talking, just like this. We seem to have come full circle. Whew! What a circle!"

They were silent, over-awed at the magnitude of the hurdles they had survived. He fingered the jade pendant at her neck. "You've still got this."

"It kept me safe."

He kissed her again. Again, he kissed her. And again. Already, he had kissed her breathless. She never wanted him to stop. "I must tell you why I went without saying good-bye. The day George was arrested, I was escorted on board *Karmala*, which happened to be in. I could have sent a radiogram to you, but it seemed to me that if I were to beat my uncle at his own game, I had to ensure that no rumour of any sort of insubordination reached him. If he didn't know what was going on, he couldn't take evasive action.

"I knew you'd go home, and you would have to pass through Singapore. I was going to jump aboard your ship and go with you. Then I heard George was dead. The powers that be, no doubt obeying my father's orders, sent me up here, out of the way. Yesterday morning I was awake very early. Jumpy as a cat. Something told me I ought to be in Singapore. I got out of bed when it was still dark, or would have been but for the moon, and went for a walk. I landed up here, watching the sun rise. It was then I recognised the view, and knew this was where we were going to meet.

"My father couldn't stop it happening," he said. "No power on earth could stop it." He put a finger beneath her chin and lifted her face. "You could say you routed him, but the means to rout him was put into your hands.

"Lance Moore!" he said. "I've heard of him. Whoever's up there arranging things," he pointed towards the sky, "has a sense of humour, choosing that famous ladies' man, to help." They laughed together. "So, we won't be getting married at Government House, Hong Kong, but Singapore will do."

"We won't have to elope?" Hellen asked.

"A Marathon invented the elegant about-turn," said Oliver. "They won't want some sinful newspaperman in twenty years' time digging into the past and coming up with a skeleton. Immediately they recognise they're beaten, they'll rally round."

She told him about Mrs Chan's destruction of the wedding dress.

Oliver groaned. "Still, the Chinese are quick and expert dressmakers. We'll get you another." They were silent again, thinking of Lin Yan.

"Were you in love with her?"

"I suppose so. All the chaps were."

"She gave me a piece of silk. I'd like to have something of her to wear on the day."

The silence was broken by a group of chattering mynah birds in the branches.

Sir Samuel Porchard and his daughter stood at the rail of the *Khyber* looking out on the gently rolling sea. He was reading, for the umpteenth time, the radiogram that had been brought to his cabin this morning.

DISEMBARK SINGAPORE STOP WEDDING ARRANGED FOR 24th AT ST ANDREW'S CATHEDRAL STOP SEND YOUR LUGGAGE TO GOVERNMENT HOUSE STOP LOOK FORWARD TO MEETING YOU STOP BERNARD MARATHON.

Marnie was smiling sadly, thinking how nice it would have been if Joe could have shared all this.

"Well, Marnie love," Sam said, "this is the sort of thing I brought you up for. Not that you've been wasted so far. You made Joe a splendid little wife, but you've never had a chance to use the finishing school stuff that cost me so much brass. You'll feel comfortable in Vice Regal circles, with the education I gave you." He puffed out his very considerable chest and blew cigar ash into the wind that swept across the Malacca Straits. A man like him, who had made such a success of life, with scarcely any education at all, could hold his own anywhere. "The minx has given us a headache or two but she's done us proud, in the long run."

Marnie said, "I'm so glad she's not, after all, to be alone at her wedding. I'm so glad we came."

"Y'know," he growled, "Governor or no Governor, if there'd been any funny business, I wouldn't have hesitated to take her by the scruff of the neck and pack her off home. But there you are," he patted his daughter's hand affectionately, "it's all over now, bar the champagne."